THE AUTHOR

ADELE WISEMAN was born in Winnipeg, Manitoba, in 1928. She graduated from the University of Manitoba in 1949 and then, to support her commitment to writing, found employment as a social worker in England, a school teacher in Italy, and executive secretary to the Royal Winnipeg Ballet.

In her first novel, *The Sacrifice* (1957), which won the Governor General's Award, Wiseman recreates, through the lives of Jewish immigrants in a central Canadian city, the biblical story of Abraham and Isaac. In *Crackpot* (1974), she tells the poignant tale of the irrepressible Hoda. All her writings bring into Canadian literature the culture and the tradition of her Jewish heritage.

In *Old Woman at Play* (1978), an illustrated account of her mother's doll-making, Wiseman explores and meditates on artistic creativity.

Adele Wiseman died in Toronto, Ontario, in 1992.

CRACKPOT

ADELE WISEMAN

AFTERWORD BY

MARGARET LAURENCE

First New Canadian Library edition 1978.
This New Canadian Library edition 2008.

This book was first published in 1974 by McClelland and Stewart.

Library and Archives Canada Cataloguing in Publication

Wiseman, Adele, 1928–1992
    Crackpot / Adele Wiseman ; with an afterword by Margaret Laurence.

(New Canadian library)
First published: 1974.
ISBN 978-0-7710-8886-5

    I. Title. II. Series.
PS8545.I85C7 2008   C813'.54   C2007-906233-4

We acknowledge the financial support of the Government of Canada through the Book Publishing Industry Development Program and that of the Government of Ontario through the Ontario Media Development Corporation's Ontario Book Initiative. We further acknowledge the support of the Canada Council for the Arts and the Ontario Arts Council for our publishing program.

Typeset in Garamond by M&S, Toronto
Printed and bound in the United States of America

McClelland & Stewart Ltd.
75 Sherbourne Street
Toronto, Ontario
M5A 2P9
www.mcclelland.com/NCL

    4   5   6   7   15   14   13

*A
Kaddish
for
Esther*

He stored the Divine Light in a Vessel but the Vessel, unable to contain the Holy Radiance, burst, and its shards, permeated with sparks of the Divine, scattered through the Universe.

ARI: *Kabbalistic legends of creation.*

ONE

Out of Shew. Bed and Golda came Rahel. Out of Malka and Benyamin came Danile. Out of Danile and Rahel came Hoda. Out of Hoda, Pipick came, Pipick born in secrecy and mystery and terror, for what did Hoda know?

In the daytime her frail and ever-so-slightly humpbacked mother, or so they described her to blind Danile before they rushed them off to be married, used to take Hoda along with her to the houses where she cleaned. And partly to keep her quiet, and partly because of an ever-present fear, for she felt that she would never have another child, Rahel carried always with her, in a large, cotton kerchief, tied into a peasant-style sack, a magically endless supply of food. All day long, at the least sign of disquiet, she fed the child, for Hoda even then was big-voiced and forward, and sometimes said naughty things to people. Rather than risk having an employer forbid her the privilege of bringing the little girl to work, Rahel forestalled trouble. Things can't go in and out of the same little mouth simultaneously.

Hoda for her part enjoyed eating. She was on the whole

1

a good-natured child. Even in the moments when her jaws were unwillingly at rest she was content to let her flecked ash-grey eyes linger contemplatively on the yellow and white dotted kerchief sack for what she felt were long periods of time while she restrained herself from disturbing her mother at her work. When at last she could refrain no longer, for she was only a child after all, Hoda would give vent to a surprisingly chesty contralto. "Ma-a-a," she would rumble, "Maa-a-a-a-ah!"

Rahel would rise quickly from her knees, wipe her hands, untie the kerchief, and give her daughter another little something to chew on. It amused some of her employers to see this continuous process, and they entertained themselves by feeding the child too, just to be able to comment, in what Rahel mistook for admiration, on how much she could put away. Hoda herself never refused these gifts of food, though there was something of aloofness, even of condescension, in her acceptance, as there is with some zoo animals that people feed for their own amusement. It was as though in allowing them to play their game she was not necessarily accepting their terms of reference. Occasionally a woman with kindly intentions would scold Rahel for letting her little girl get so fat. Rahel misinterpreted the kindly intentions and resented these critics who wanted her to deny her child. She saw in it simply another sign that it is the way of the rich to deny the poor, and continued to make sure that her child was bigger and more beautiful every day. Why else does a mother crawl on her knees in the houses of strangers?

Still others of the women whose homes she cleaned took advantage of the presence of the sack and allowed themselves to assume that since she had brought her own food they didn't have to provide any lunch for Rahel. Such days were hard for her, for she was too embarrassed to remind her employer that lunch had been agreed on between them when they discussed terms. At the same time she would rather starve than take food from her daughter's mouth, of which she considered the yellow sack to be a simple extension, as her own breasts had been once. So she worked through the long day of cramping hunger pains, tasting only her distaste, but still feeding Hoda all the while, automatically and without resentment.

Work was not easy to find, for she did not look very strong, and besides people did not like the idea of a Jewish woman hiring herself out to do what they considered to be demeaning tasks. On the other hand people felt sorry for her, hump-backed, with a blind husband sitting at home and a fat child to lug about. And they knew, for such things *get* around, though Danile and Rahel never spoke of it in public, how badly Danile's wealthy uncle had treated them when he had discovered that he had been tricked into sponsoring the immigration to the new world of the skeletons in the family closet. "Whaddaya want from me?" he told his wife, as they argued the matter night after night in bed. "Nobody told me they were cripples. Duds!" And he cursed his opposite number, Rahel's rich uncle in the old country, who had negotiated the affair with him so handsomely, and had, it turned out, at small expense rid himself of a chronic burden. "No wonder he's rich," raged the uncle of Danile, with a fine mixture of chagrin and admiration.

In effect, Uncle Nate had thrown them out, though he hadn't actually had to go that far, for Rahel, gentle always in her actions, though not necessarily in her judgments, had not waited for him to behave as badly as he gave indication that he was capable of doing. Gauging very quickly the temper of the uncle's household she had gone out, found and rented the shack, and moved her family into it. Then, since she had no other skill, she went among the neighbours and offered herself as a charwoman. In this at least she had plenty of experience. At home in the old country, before her unexpected marriage, she had been the one who had cleaned house and looked after the long line of little sisters her mother had conceived of her soldier father when he sent word he was in the vicinity and she made her periodic visits to the woods and fields near the camps where he was stationed.

At first, only the enemies of Uncle Nate took her in to clean for them, as a way of embarrassing the big man. But these people wanted at one and the same time to show that they were made of finer stuff than Nate and to make sure that Rahel did not expect special treatment, just because she was a Jew and related to wealth. Consequently they were the hardest to please, and Rahel ended up by doing most of her cleaning for people who were not much richer than herself and who would occasionally hire her, perhaps once or twice a year, when they needed a thorough turning out of their homes.

Sometimes, for all that her mother tried to prevent it, Hoda would get into trouble. There was one woman, for instance, who made fun of the child's chesty call of "Maaa-a-a!" by counterpointing it with a nasal "Baaa-aaa!" like that of a catarrhal sheep. She repeated the game several times during the day. Each time the child turned unblinking eyes on her, with a solemnity that made her laugh, and continued to contemplate her ruminatively over her snack. Finally, the tease made the mistake of coming too close, and making her noise right in the little girl's face. With a lunge surprisingly swift in one who was almost wider than she was tall, Hoda clamped her teeth on her tormentor's nose, producing immediately a sharp improvement, if not in the pitch, at least in the sincerity of her utterance, an improvement which the child acknowledged at once with a hearty, wicked chuckle.

That was bad enough, but what was worse as far as Rahel was concerned was that she couldn't extract an apology from her normally tractable daughter. Hoda watched silently, growling in her throat behind her crust, her grey eyes smouldering, while her mother apologized and placated. She submitted passively while her mother spanked her to assuage the wounded nose of her employer, and even let out a theatrical bellow during the process, though all concerned knew that Rahel's hand landed very lightly, and the employer's humour had anyway taken a magnanimous turn by now and she was just as theatrically begging her cleaning woman not to beat the child on her account. She even brought a cookie as a peace offering, in token of forgiveness, and Hoda was pragmatic enough to accept the offer, with an ambiguous grunt which might have been taken to indicate forgiveness too.

When night came and Hoda was put to bed her blind father told her the good stories. These were real life, not yes and no and hush and shame shame say sorry. Daddy told her who she was and where she came from and what had happened. Real things.

"No," said Danile, "you wouldn't believe our luck, for on the surface aren't we the unluckiest people in the world? But study things, study and you'll see. God only seems to punish."

Listening from the kitchen, where she was cleaning up the supper dishes, Rahel argued in her mind as she would never do out loud.

God only seems to punish but your suffering is real, Danile.

"By the time I was seven years old," continued Danile, in that voice of his that was filled with awe, so that one thought he was about to reveal some wondrous accomplishment, "yes, when I was not much older than you are now my little Hodaleh, I was already going blind."

Hoda snuggled closer. Danile rejoiced, holding her, his child, a big, soft, tangible circumference, all warmth and movement.

"I would stumble over things; the world shrank; there was fog everywhere. My mother said, 'Danile, what's the matter with you child, can't you see where you're going?' And I said, 'No, Mamma.'"

Hoda shuddered. Her father's voice always sounded strange when he said that part. "No, Mamma," not like a daddy voice at all.

"Danile, what's the matter with you?"

"I don't know, Mamma."

Why do you talk about it so much? thought Rahel. *Why does she have to know such things? She's strong and healthy. Nothing will happen to her, while I live.* But Rahel shuddered, too, sensing her own fragility.

"When my mother understood that I really couldn't see, she was furious, not so much with me as with herself. She said it was her own fault for not having watched over me carefully enough. She cursed the negligent moment when she must have left me long enough for me to turn my innocent eyes upward and look too boldly at the sun. Only a child or a fool will be bold enough to try to see into the sun, and for this the sun with his pitiless stare must have punished me. 'Why did you have to stare at the sun?' she used to ask, after all the journeys and medicines and incantations had failed to help me. 'What did you think you would find there? Foolish boy.'

"And I used to ask myself the same thing. I didn't know why I had stared at the sun, or when, even, though I knew I must have done as my mother said. Why then had I wanted to see into the sun? And what did I see? And why am I punished for it? Even now I sometimes think that if I

6

knew what I had seen I wouldn't mind the punishment so much, though of course I know it's a nonsensical thought. God blinded me for reasons of His own, and the loss is nothing to the gain. For if I had not been blind and your mother had not been a little crooked many wonderful things would not have happened and you would probably never have been born. Shouldn't I call that luck?"

Hoda chuckled a happy assent.

Rahel had carefully placed another split log in the stove. Now she slammed the full kettle noisily on the hottest part so that it splashed and hissed. *Only a child or a fool . . .* All her life, all her childhood and all her girlhood she had prayed, at times with an almost demented intensity, for that deformity to disappear. For years she had gone nightly to bed, forcing herself every night to picture and to believe in the picture of herself arising the next morning and simply, luxuriously, stretching herself straight as everyone else did. That skew of her body wasn't really hers; she wasn't really that way. If they hadn't done that to her when they were in such a hurry to drag her into the world she would have been just like anyone else. Then suddenly, unexpectedly, perversely, her prayers had been granted. But instead of the miraculous disappearance of her deformity the humiliating miracle of her marriage had taken place, marriage to a man who would never be able to see her twisted body. Why then did he insist on crying it forth as a source of pride, as her particular, lucky charm? This was what exasperated Rahel, this and the fact that he wasn't even accurate about it. To listen to him you'd think she had God knows what between her shoulders, with his little crookedness and his humps and his lumps. And then there was also the high-handed way he had of dismissing it sometimes. There is a difference between having your deformity minimized and having

7

it belittled. Rationally, she knew Danile was trying to do neither, knew and reproached herself because her objections were in themselves often contradictory. Still, it wasn't a hump on her back; it wasn't, properly speaking, really on her back at all. It was her right shoulder that was hiked up, but it didn't hunch her over. It just threw her somewhat out of kilter. Actually, it wasn't a hump at all. If she hadn't happened to be so small in build it might not even have been so noticeable, or so her mother had often said. A tall woman can carry these things off. But it was no use trying to point all this out to Danile. He wasn't interested in the anatomical fact. And in a way, if you followed his way of thinking, exclusive of all the other ways which the world knew and accepted, he was right. You can't hedge a miracle.

Once only Rahel had tried to argue with her husband over his interpretation of their fate. And he had explained to her, as though it were the key to all enigmas, that it stands to reason that God's open hand can be as terrible as his fist. Unconvinced, she had nevertheless felt petty and ashamed of the peevishness of her nature as compared with the generous innocence of his own.

"My father," he was saying now, "though he was only a tailor by trade, was a wise man. He used to say, 'It's God's will. You have a fine memory. Not many could have picked up so much by ear as you. And if you can't see the Holy Work you can hold it at least, feel it, keep it close to you, live with it. Even so you can be blessed.'

"I often ask myself, *How did he know?* For didn't the Book lead us past the barriers into the new world? Have I ever told you that story?"

"No," lied Hoda promptly.

"Danile," called Rahel. "Enough already. Put her to bed."

"No, Ma!" bawled Hoda.

"Just a minute more," said Danile. "I'm in the middle of a story. You and your mother were really the heroines of that one," he continued to the child, but speaking with transparent cunning, loudly enough to make Rahel smile in spite of herself.

"We had come all that long way, right to the edge of the big ocean I was telling you about, and one day your mother was talking to some woman, another immigrant, and this woman says to her, 'You don't think they're going to let you into the new world, you and your husband? They want only whole people in America.' An ordinary man, you understand, travelling with a child and a woman with a slight hump, well maybe. But a blind man too? No. You see my child, the new world is almost like heaven. They want you to be perfect before you get there, at least on the outside. In heaven of course they are more interested in what you are inside.

"Anyway, what did your mother do? From the day of our marriage, when they brought us home from the graveyard and we talked together for the first time, she had insisted that I was to go about like a modern Jew, beardless. Every day she shaved me herself. Now she comes running to the hut where we men slept, and she says to me, 'Danile, you must grow a beard. When our turn comes for the immigration examinations you must look like a serious scholar.'

"*What's this about a beard?* I ask myself. *Why all of a sudden a beard? A beard she wants? All right, I'll grow her a beard.* So I grew my beard. And while we waited for our summons she lectured me, over and over.

"'Remember, Danile,'" he imitated his wife's voice, to the delight of the child. "'Remember, Danile, the child on one arm, the Book in the other hand, and held up to your face,

9

as if you can't be pulled away from it for such trifling things as examinations and interrogations.'

"And when the time came at last I did exactly what she said, because when your mother says, she says. But I was so nervous I kept asking her, 'Is it all right, Rahel? Does it look all right?'

"And she would whisper back, 'It's fine, it's fine, only turn the page sometimes.'

"Well, that's all very easy when you're sitting down. But after awhile we had to get up and move with the line, from one crowded room to another, each one more crowded and hotter than the last, and in each one my little daughter was growing bigger and heavier. Would you believe it, I could actually feel you grow? I knew my little girl was going to grow up but I didn't expect I would actually catch her in a growing moment. Let me tell you my juicy one it wasn't so easy to hold you that way, nonchalantly in one arm, growing as you were right there and then into such a sturdy little vessel. We had to wait a long time. My arm began to ache. I began to ache all the way down one side. I had to shift and heave you every time your mother reminded me to turn the page. Finally, I couldn't hang on to you with one arm any longer. You had simply grown too heavy. So I tried to slide you over so both arms would take some of the weight. Just then they called our names.

"Your mother grabs me under the arm to guide me, but pretending it's because she's frightened to leave my side, and also a little bit, probably, from the way she's pressing against me, to try to hide her shape. So she's dragging my tired arm one way, you're sliding the other way, and the book I'm supposed to hold in front of my face is sitting on my hand under your little behind. When I finally struggle it out and poke it up on the other side of you I hear your mother's voice whispering, 'It's upside down, Danile!'

"By this time I'm in such a sweat I don't know if she means the book is upside down or my daughter. So I begin to feel you around surreptitiously, and that's when you decide to let us all know which side is up. I must have wakened you with all that shifting and sliding, because suddenly you begin to roar out, blood-curdling bellows, like it seems to me I've never heard you cry before. That doctor couldn't believe it. 'Only nine months old?' he says. 'She's going to be a healthy citizen.' My heart jumps when I hear this. We're already citizens together. And while I'm soothing you and bouncing you with new strength and you, thank goodness, won't stop yelling, your mother deals with the officials. On their part they are in such a hurry to get rid of us they become even blinder than I am.

"'Yes that's fine, that's all. You can go.' When I heard those words I felt such a surge of friendship, I wanted to stop and thank them, but your mother wouldn't let me; she dragged me right out of there. When she got me out on the street she began to cry; 'What for? Now is no time for tears.'

"'Oi, Danile, Oi Danile, the Book is still upside down!'

"But upside down though it was, and held by a blind man, it led us safely into this land. You see how right my father was? The Book is holy; knowledge is a wonderful thing if you know how to use it, even ignorant people, like your mother and myself. Sometimes I sit with the Book in my hand and think how close the Almighty has let me come to wisdom while I must remain so far. And yet, He lets His words come to our aid in His own way."

"All right, Danile," called Rahel, "enough now. Let the child get to sleep."

"No ma!" bawled Hoda.

"Not that I'm completely ignorant," Danile continued, as though trying to correct a false impression. "While he lived my father would take me every day to the synagogue and I would learn with my ears, just as your mother and you take me now on the way to work. My ears are quicker than many another student's eyes. Often I heard far more than they could see. 'That's Reb Simcha coming in the door, scraping his feet so: chuff chuff chuff.' Or I'd call out, 'Shahmus, bang on the rail there, and shout for the women to keep quiet upstairs. Maya the herring is having an argument with Petya long finger's wife.' And sometimes the Rov himself, not just the Shahmus, would shout up to them on my say-so: 'Women up there, Maya and Gitl! Be quiet! Aren't you ashamed to be arguing in the House of God?' And they would be silent in shame and in wonder that he had recognized and called them by name."

Hoda liked the funny parts. The quickness of her father's ears, though she had never seen them move, was a source of great pleasure. When she came home with her mother from work, while they were still blocks away from the house, she would try to coax her mother up on her toes, so that they should approach the house without him hearing. And when he called out, invariably, "Who's there?" as the door creaked open, she would rush forward with mingled disappointment and delight.

"You heard me! You heard me!"

And Danile would reply, "Oh no, I didn't hear you; I heard a tiny little mouse go 'squeak squeak squeak!' When did you come in?"

Rahel waited for them to finish laughing to call Danile finally away before he could begin to speak again. Left alone he would go on as long as the child demanded. Such was his nature. She could still remember those first few bewildering days of her marriage, which had been also the last few days of her mother-in-law's life. When Malka, known perversely in the town as Benyamin the tailor's needle, because she was so stout, had raved in her sickness, it had been Danile she had raved about, and his blindness, and the brightness he had stolen from the sun on the day of their contest, that brightness which she swore he had stored in him forever, for he had a nature of extraordinary sweetness. Of course that was a mother's view. That same sweetness made some people feel that there was something unnatural about him, as though he were a little feeble-minded and incapable of truly understanding the gravity of his own plight. And incapable too, perhaps, thought Rahel, not for the first time, of feeling the insult of being married off to one they called a hunchback, a man as handsome as he, and under such circumstances too. And yet, he too had some cause to consider himself lucky, even to her way of thinking. If the plague hadn't carried her off so soon he might have found himself married to Selma the idiot, who slept in the fields and covered her head with her skirts when she heard a man approaching. Who would be looking after him now?

What more do you want from life, Rahel? she often asked herself as she went about her work, her mind not foreign to a certain private irony. *You have been nurtured by the open hand of God Himself. Who would have believed that even plagues can be good for somebody?*

As Danile told it, "What's a plague? A sickness. A cholera. In a plague everyone is blind together. It runs about of its own accord, invisibly, attacking without respect, rich and poor, high and low, good and bad. Plague has no favourites, except, so they say, it has a little bit more respect for Jews than for other people. It's true, it kills fewer Jews, and that's a fact. The others say to themselves, 'Look at that, the Jews are only lightly brushed by the plague; so few of them fall, while we are being carted off in wagon-loads. It must be true they have a God!'

"But their priests and their leaders don't like that. So they say to them, 'Beware the Jews. They make evil magic that sends the plague your way. To get rid of the plague you must get rid of the Jews.' That's when these people become a plague in themselves, through their ignorance. When I stop to think of it, in actual fact your mother and I, with God's help, really saved the town from a double plague. Because of course it's all a lot of nonsense. They could see for themselves the only magic we made was the same magic they were making. We drew the same circles around our houses with charcoal to keep out the sickness. We too hung cloves of garlic and lumps of camphor in sachets, around our necks for they have great strength in them to ward off plagues. You can smell their power. The only difference was that we had our God and no magic works without Him, and they want everything to come easily and if it doesn't come they go berserk.

"Well, that was in the old town, in the old country, where your grandmother lives still, and all your aunts, and maybe even your grandfather by now, though when last we heard he was still serving the Czar, poor man. If things hadn't gone so badly for him, and the Czar hadn't got such a murderously tight hold, how much easier life might have been for your mother's family. The trouble is there are so many things to look out for in life, and your grandfather, Shem Berl, is a simple, trusting soul. They put a paper in front of him and tell him to sign his release from the army, after ten long years, so he signs. Can he help it if he can't read Russian? So they toast him tovarich, and he finds he's signed on for another five years. So he serves his time honourably, as fine a tinker as you could meet in any army in the whole world, and when it comes time

14

for his discharge they say to him, 'All right, Shem has served his time. Now what about Berl?'

"So he says, 'I'm Shem Berl.'

"But the Czar's tail won't hear of it. 'Two names, two soldiers for the Czar from your family! Shem has served and Berl must serve!' So Shem Berl called on both his dead grandfathers, after whom he was named, for double strength, and he served again.

"When the time came for him to be discharged a third time, he swore up and down he would sign no more papers. No one could hold him now. He was going home. And home he came, at last, to his wife, to his family, to his responsibilities. When he arrived he found the whole family in a turmoil, his wife biting her lips, his sisters wailing, his mother in hysterics. They had come, those brutes, to demand that his baby brother, who had grown up in his absence, should now serve his time. His mother was convinced the Czar had cast his evil eye all the way from Petersburg especially on her boys. She knew once her little Mendl was dragged off to the army he would never return, for if Shem Berl was desirable to the Czar, Mendl must be half again as desirable, for he was the joy of her old age.

"What was Shem Berl to do? His wife begged him; his daughters pleaded with him; his brother-in-law, your rich uncle Laib who sent us here, threatened him, but your grandfather shouldered his pack once again and gave himself as a substitute for his brother.

"That's how it came about that in the time of the plague, luckily for us all, he was far away, for had he been home he might not, poor man though he was, have allowed them to take his daughter, even for the sake of the dowry. He had too much pride. But now was not the time for pride. Now was a dreadful time. Even sitting at home, for my mother would not allow me out of the house, and hearing the stories of what was happening, and the cries and the groans of the sick and the bereaved in the streets, and without ever imagining the part I was to play, I knew that such frightful events were meant to show something, if only a man had the wisdom to understand. People fell to their beds like wheat in the fields, tossing and turning and flinging themselves about senselessly like grain being winnowed in God's private machine. Many flew straight into the afterlife, where the Almighty must have made a very fine loaf of his harvest, for some of the town's best never stood upright in this world again.

"They tried everything to fight it. Soon there was not a clove of garlic to be bought anywhere in our district at any price. Nothing helped. The sickness held its breath and fell upon people and turned them inside out before the strength of the medicine could take hold. It leaped over the black rings of safety and raged within the barriers as fiercely as without. Once it had forced its way into a person it burned, it flamed, it tore out everything he had inside of him and sent it blazing out both ends.

"I know. I heard it. I think I actually heard it enter our house. I know I heard it edging into my mother's voice. I could hear it in her breath. I heard it wrestling with her. I heard her pleading with it. I heard its cry of triumph when she fell writhing on the bed. At first she tried to help herself. Then she couldn't. She could only struggle. That wretched smell grew stronger. Her cries went on and on. I wanted to help her, but she kept screaming, 'Don't come near me, Danile! Stay away! Don't you come near me!' in such a voice, as though I were another enemy. I didn't know what to do. I wanted to

16

fetch help, but she screamed at me not to leave the house. The plague was all over, out there, waiting for me.

"Not to come, not to go, not to be able to see, not to know what to do. I went to the door. I shouted out, 'People, help! People, have mercy! People, save my mother! Help us! Help us!' No one listened. No one came. I wept. I asked my God why he had made me less than a man. Then I took my Book, and I held it in my hands, and I sang. To drown out her suffering I sang, not to hear her cries so nakedly and so that she should not hear me weeping I sang all the holy words that I knew, ignoramus that I am, over and over again, in the strongest voice I have so that perhaps, if nothing else, the power of the words and the strength of my voice alone would sustain her with the help of God.

"And she was still alive when they came. At first, when they burst into the house, and they cried out joyously, 'She's still alive!' I thought that they had come to try to save her. But that was not to be. They were glad for another reason.

"You see my child, these plagues do not concern simply individual persons. They are not simply a matter of this one collapsing and that one dying and of one blind boy's sorrow. Things had by this time reached a point where the whole community was threatened, not only by the epidemic itself but by the madness of the surrounding peasants. They were jealous because the Jews were not dying off as quickly as they, and word had come that unless by some miracle the sickness could be banished they would fall on us and destroy what the disease had not dared to touch.

"It was a time for desperate measures. The beautiful ones of the town came together to confer, those who were not too frightened or too afflicted, the wise and the holy and even one or two of the rich. Among them was your mother's uncle.

17

"When all else fails there is an action which can be taken, a gesture which, made properly and with God's blessing, can restore the forces of life where only the forces of death reigned before. The beautiful ones knew that the time had come to make this gesture.

"Now the thing to do is to take the two . . ."

Rahel noticed that Danile always hesitated slightly at this point, as though even he were flinching at what he was about to say. But the hesitation was so slight it was perhaps perceptible only to her, or perhaps she only imagined that he was flinching too.

". . . they take the two poorest, most unfortunate, witless creatures, man and woman, who exist under the tables of the community; they dig them up, he out of his burrow in the woods, she from the heap of rags in which she crouches, and they bring them together to the field of death. It is the tradition to take the craziest and the most helpless you can find. Who else would go? But after all the community is trying to do them a favour too. The town provides the bride with a dowry, furnishes, if they are homeless, a little mud hut for them, and undertakes to look after them. Everything is done just as for a proper wedding, which they would never have been able to afford for themselves. Indeed, usually they did not have the wit to know what it was all about anyway, and wandered off to their own separate burrows afterwards.

"So the beautiful ones decided that now was the time to marry off such a pair and lift the curse of the plague and the threat of the pogrom from our heads. But whom to choose? There was a shortage of idiots in our community that year. The man the children called Golgol had been killed in a pogrom the year before. When everyone else was barricaded behind doors and the bandits were approaching he suddenly ran out from somewhere, beckoning to them and shouting in the friendliest fashion, 'Kill Jews! Kill Jews!' Strong as an ox he was. He was still running and they were still shooting bullets into him long minutes later. And the unfortunate Selma, a true grotesque; I remember her from when I could still see; she too had been taken off by the plague.

"So your mother's uncle spoke up. He reminded the others of his eldest niece, far from an idiot, of course, a very intelligent girl, and not even homely; and furthermore, he dared say, and who would dare deny? from a decent family; indeed she was herself a hard-working, good-natured girl, as who should know better than he, the child of his own sister? Hers was merely the slightest deformity; nevertheless if the town were to offer a reasonable dowry, he himself would contribute to the cost of a marriage not dishonourable. He was in a position to influence his sister; she would see the sense in it, and the community would, naturally, in gratitude, keep their pact with the Almighty and continue to take care of the couple, if, that is, a suitable mate could be found. He's a clever man our uncle. And we can't blame him entirely. He had daughters of his own to provide with dowries.

"Then someone else remembered that I had been seen at the door of our hut, weeping and pleading with the world to come to the aid of my mother. My father was dead, my mother dying, my prospects poor. If by chance my mother was still alive I would be a logical groom. If my mother was gone already it would be too late. The situation was too desperate for them to be able to wait over a period of mourning.

"That was when they came running to our house. At the same time the uncle hastened to speak to your poor grandmother. What could she do? If it was anything like the way it happened to me she did not get much time to think about it. Nor did your mother. They carried her off for the examination, saw that she was whole, that is healthy, and took her to the ritual bath."

Rahel squirmed but dared not interrupt. If the child asked for an explanation here, then she would really put her foot down, she promised herself. Why he had to go through every little detail she didn't know, she really didn't. But Hoda was too engrossed at this point to ask questions.

"As for me," Danile was saying, "before I knew it I was being led – no, dragged – no, carried from the house. It was a hot day, clammy. I struggled like a wild thing, slithering about in their hands and my sweat. They had a hard time holding me. They tried to explain what we were about to do but all I knew was that I should not be leaving my mother now, without a voice to cry out for her. 'Have mercy on her,' I pleaded with them, over and over again.

"'Yes, yes,' they made me hear them finally. 'Don't worry. She will be taken care of. The plague will disappear if you come with us now. God will aid us, if you will come.'

"Their words forced me to begin to realize what it was all about. I had been begging for God's help. Dared I refuse to play my part? Perhaps it was fated. If this was so I must be calm. My heart must cease flinging itself about. I must no longer weep like a child. I must make no sound. I must pay attention, yes, perhaps for the first time in my life. There was a question being asked and soon, soon, perhaps even now, I and only I would be called on to reply. But how reply? Who was I? What was my attention worth? Strain though I might, I would never suffice. All I could know was my immeasurable ignorance. *Very well,* I thought, *if that is all I can know let me know that at least.* And even as I was floundering thus, words fell away. I became one living alertness. Nothing could pass me by. Everything that existed had to pass through me, even the breeze that sprang up and whispered in my face as we approached the home of the dead. They led me carefully here, for there were many newly dug graves. I trod on damp clumps of newly turned sod that seemed to move beneath my feet like living things. That was so; there was no stillness anywhere. There was only movement, anticipation, the breath of the universe. And I was no longer a blind boy being led beneath the canopy to meet his unknown bride in the village of the dead. Do trees have eyes? What can the stars see? I saw what they saw and I knew what they knew then. Don't ask me what it was, I couldn't grasp the wholeness of it for long, but for one moment I knew, I acquiesced, and I was known.

"Since that moment I have never been truly afraid, not in the holy way, with the fear a man might wish for. Ordinary fear I knew again, and soon. Who marries without tasting that? That returned when I felt Rahel at my side and knew she was trembling too. Who was I to have a bride trembling beside me? I was so frightened I don't even remember how it went, what they said, how I replied. I fumbled for a long time with a ring and a soft little hand that kept disappearing. It was not so much that I couldn't see, but all of them, the ring, my hands, her hands, wouldn't stop moving, all in different directions. Finally, a gentle little voice took pity on me, as she has taken pity on me ever since. 'Let me,' she whispered, and all was well."

Danile knew that Rahel did not entirely approve of his habit of giving the child a detailed version of these events. But once he had begun to speak it was hard for him to leave off trying to describe the way it had felt and what it had meant. If he told too much, well, those things the child wouldn't understand anyway. They would pass her by. But because he felt a little guilty about it, he always tried, when he suspected he might have talked too much, to round off his tale with a compliment to Rahel, to smooth the edge of her disapproval. It was by way of a little gift, and as he spoke he meant it, discovering as he went along the truth in every word he said; but it was often so awkwardly dragged in, or else so triumphantly emphasized, that it managed, by its very incongruity, to make her laugh when she would have liked to scold.

Hoda herself would accept no abridgements or truncations. If he varied his description she would backtrack with him, collating the versions. Sometimes Danile had a hard time remembering what he had said last time. But the child did not forget.

"What did the sun say?" demanded Hoda.

"The sun? What did the sun say? Well now, oh yes, the sun peeked in under the canopy while the ceremony was going on and he said, 'Look at that. He's found himself the prettiest pair of eyes in the whole village.'"

Hoda laughed her satisfaction. "And what happened when you came home?"

"I said to your mother, 'I'm sorry, my mother is sick.'"

"And she replied, 'Yes, I've heard.'And straightaway she set to work looking after us both, as though it were meant to be and it had always been."

"But did Bobba really die?" asked Hoda, who fought and strained through her grandmother's illness, every time her father described it, trying to keep her alive.

"Yes. She lived long enough to make it possible for us to save the community, but when the turning point came in our fortunes she did not have the strength to climb back to life. Who would have imagined that would be possible? My beautiful mother. She was the sturdiest woman in the village. Why, even when I was fully grown, and they say I am quite a tall man, I couldn't get both my arms all the way around her. You take after her. I can tell by the feel of you."

"I wouldn't die," said Hoda.

"Of course not," said Danile hastily. "Only in build, not in fate, please God."

"You see what you get?" muttered Rahel.

"And the plague went away?" asked Hoda, checking off the familiar items to make sure.

"Yes, of course," said Danile. "That was the wonder of it. Almost immediately, the plague began to disappear. Some people even got well again, and that's a sure sign of the power of our wedding."

"And the pogrom went away?"

"There was no pogrom. The plague left them too."

"What happened then?" Hoda was persistent.

"Well, then we settled down. Everybody was very grateful to us, at first, anyway. They saw to it that we had food to eat. And then of course your mother is such a good housekeeper that she stretched out what we had."

"And then?"

"And then time passed. Well, you can't blame people entirely. While the danger is there they will do anything, be grateful to anybody. When the crisis is past they begin to forget how it felt; they have other problems and the obligation begins to seem as much of an imposition as the original danger. I don't know; it's hard to figure it all out. There seems to be something not quite altogether between time and place and feelings and events. The pieces don't match up; they won't hold still, the right time, the right place in life, the right feeling, the right length and strength for each. It never lasts long enough or it comes too late, or it doesn't matter anymore to one and it matters too much to another; there are just too many pieces, each reaching for the others, and each being swept along in a different direction. You can't blame people. They don't know enough to be able to piece it all together. They can't even hold still themselves. That's why I want you to go to school and study. When your moment comes, I want you to be prepared to know what it means."

"So what did you do?" asked Hoda, in a voice which, to her mother, sometimes seemed to have a kind of inexorable sternness, as though the child already knew enough to disagree, or at least to keep her own counsel.

"Do? Nothing really. We kept alive." Danile too was sometimes made vaguely uneasy by the intensity with which the child kept after the story, though he could not resist her interest for long.

"What about my sister?" asked Hoda.

"What about her?" said Danile, stalling, for he could feel Rahel's disapproval in the air. Why shouldn't the child know that she had had a sister? Why shouldn't the poor little thing have her brief existence acknowledged?

"Malka," Hoda prompted.

"A name for my mother," said Danile tenderly. "Who could foresee such luck? And she was perfect, absolutely perfect. I ought to know. Didn't I hold her in my two hands with your mother buzzing at me to be careful, please be careful, as though I had to be told? Even the midwife said she was perfect. Whatever they said afterwards and for whatever reason the Almighty snatched her away again so soon, she was not a crippled child."

Of course she wasn't! A familiar resentment boiled up in Rahel, smarting in her eyes. *Perfect, perfect.*

"She was delicate, yes," Danile went on; "too small, too thin, too exhausted with the effort of being born too soon to be able to continue to pump her own life for long. That's what the midwife said, or something like that. When she stopped breathing, your mother and I said nothing to each other, but I knew that we both had the same thought. Perhaps it simply wasn't meant for people like us to bring children into the world. That thought was black enough, but when our uncle came to offer his condolences, we found out that it was not such a new idea. Many people had been thinking the same thing all along."

Rahel could not contain herself. "You wouldn't have thought they would take such an interest," she burst out, "from the way they had been forgetting all their fine promises to us. For all they cared we could have starved a dozen times over. Whenever someone felt in extra need of a good deed to be recorded with the One Above to offset something he felt guilty about below, he'd throw a coin our way, or send some food from the bottom of his table. For this we were dragged through the streets to stand miserable among the dead."

Hoda stirred as her mother spoke. Her mother seldom joined in the stories, but when she did something happened to them; new feelings came into them that made her uneasy. For some reason that she could not fathom, because her mother was the softest, safest person in the world, the stories hurt more when her mother helped to tell them.

"It's true," said Danile gravely. "If it were not for your mother running to the baker's and sitting up with the dough all night while it was rising, to prevent it from spilling all over the ovens, weeks would have gone by without us tasting either a piece of bread or the bite of herring she earned in the marketplace by day."

"And now," Rahel continued as though to herself, so that the child had to crane to hear, "my fine uncle comes and in so many words he congratulates us for having the good sense to lose our child. In spite of hard times, he tells us, the town is willing to continue to support us. But there are some people who are grumbling that we are taking advantage of them. There are some who say that wards of the town have no right to raise a family at the town's expense. And there are some who say that it is not fair to bring more crippled children into the world for others to take care of. Crippled! Oh of course, says uncle, he personally is not one of these people, but he can see their point. And we can see his point well enough. If the town should decide that we have forfeited the right to even the pretence that they are helping us, the burden would be his."

"Well, we can't entirely blame . . ." said Danile.

"No wonder she did not have the strength to go on breathing," continued Rahel in a whisper, "with the weight of the disapproval of all those beautiful people lying down on her. No wonder she couldn't breathe."

"So I said to him," said Danile quickly, to distract the child from the fact that her mother was weeping. "I said, 'We are not wards of the town. We are wards of the One Above, entrusted to the town.'

"And he said, 'Since when are you such a big philosopher? You sit and talk to the Book all day with nothing to worry about. Everything is brought to you. Has the Book begun to answer you already, that you're splitting hairs with me?'

"Not that I can blame him entirely; what he said was true. But it was no answer. And I wanted to tell him so. I wanted to tell him that we did not need the town's help if they chose to go so against the spirit of our covenant. But I was afraid that he would reply as he had the right to, that it was all very well for me to sit and play at being proud, for I had a frail and delicate creature, his own niece, working day and night to support me. A man like me is in no position to tell a man like Uncle anything at all. So I kept silent, and since he is not really such a harsh man through and through, he likes simply to have his own way, but wants no hard feelings if he can help it, when he left, to show that all was well between us, Uncle gave us a very generous tip."

"We couldn't afford to throw it in his face," sighed Rahel.

"I'm surprised you didn't," said Danile. "Do you know that same rich uncle never dared say a word to your mother against her father? With your grandmother he would curse and rave, but when your quiet little mother was around, not a word about Shem Berl the soldier. Well, we too can be charitable. So we kept the money. Why should we deprive him of a generous gesture to his credit Above? Poor Uncle. If only he could have foreseen the result of his visit he might not have ended it with such an expensive flourish. He would have kept his hand in his pocket and saved the money for our travel fare. It's a fact, if he had not come and upset us that day, you might never have been born. But that very night you began to knock on the door of life, saucy little one that you are. Had we not been so disturbed and unable to sleep we would probably never have heard you. Instead, while your mother and I lay weeping, you called out to us, and we heard you say, 'Where is it written that the townspeople, even the most beautiful ones, can give orders to the source of life? What is meant to be will be!' And though we were afraid to take the risk of so much disappointment again, in the end we could not resist your voice."

"And you opened the door?" asked Hoda, beaming expectantly.

"Yes!"

"And I came?"

"And you came."

"And Uncle was mad?"

"Mad? Mad enough to cudgel that clever head of his and do us a real favour at last. Who ever thought that blind Danile too would live to see the new world?"

"And I didn't even die!" Hoda laughed triumphantly, her voice trumpeting out, as though her arrival and survival were a signal victory for the forces of virtue. Danile could not resist her laughter and laughed with her, with something of the same triumphant innocence in his voice. Rahel, who could not laugh so easily, was nevertheless strangely touched. Her impulse, always, was to protect these two, but at times she had the not entirely comfortable feeling that they could, in some ways, take care of themselves far better than she knew. But that was something else, something apart from the twenty-four real hours a day during which they needed her, the real life, feet-on-the-ground, world-on-your-shoulders, hours. Perhaps that was what her hump was for, to balance the world on. Rahel found herself laughing too. *If that's what it's for I'm not complaining. Just let me lug my load around a little longer.*

Twenty-four real hours, a hundred little things an hour. If she hadn't been attentive to what was happening in the real world, and quick to react, she might still be going from one grocery store to another, trying to find a nugget of camphor like the one that she was even now sewing a little bag for, to hang around Hoda's neck. The minute she had heard talk of the danger of an epidemic of infantile paralysis in the city she had known what to do. Straight to the grocer! She had paid a whole dollar! And even so the grocer had told her she was lucky that he still had a few cubes left. There had been a rush on camphor in drug and grocery stores all over the city. Well, thank goodness; far-flung and strange in its ways though it was, the new world was not so entirely barbaric as to be without some acquaintance with the life-preserving medicaments.

TWO

T he house was small, grey shingle with a tumbledown
porch, the only house on the avenue that was set well
back from the street. Spooky, the stranger kids from
further down the block used to call it, when they ventured this
far from their own territory and hurried by hopeful and yet
fearful of catching a glimpse of the hunchbacked witch and her
husband the scary blind man. They were afraid, too, of the fat
kid, only not so much afraid because, though she chased you
down the street and swore at you when you called her names,
she couldn't run very fast, and if you doubled back and forth
very quickly you could get her charging and hollering without
having to do much running yourself at all. But the danger was
that she might call her parents out of the haunted house, and
you couldn't escape if they caught you in their spells.

Even before they had moved in, the house, often vacant
for long periods of time, had been considered a pretty creepy
place by the children of the neighbourhood, so much so that
even in the daytime only the nerviest would venture far into
the yard in spite of the temptation of big old trees to be
climbed. They were not surprised, therefore, that really spooky

people had come to haunt it openly. The grown-ups of the district made a more mundane mystery of the uneasiness they felt in the presence of gratuitous misfortune. "I don't know what they live on. How can they get by on what she earns? They must get something from that rich uncle. You never see him come around though. Well, the child doesn't starve."

But there are subtle shades of well-being that perhaps only the truly misfortunate can experience. To Rahel and Danile the very decrepit condition of the house was a positive virtue. Rent was cheap for a place where the tree roots had grown under the verandah and were year by year heaving it more eccentrically askew. The whole verandah was like a wooden wave, in the process of a long, slow-motion undulation. Danile, who was inordinately proud of his cat-footedness in his perpetual dark, actually claimed he could feel the verandah heaving ever so slowly beneath his feet, and always tapped his way across it with his legs somewhat astraddle, as though he were on the deck of a ship. "You understand, Hodaleh," he told his daughter, "how living things must stand before secondary creation. A porch is a very fine thing, but can it gainsay a tree?"

Hoda was rather proud of her tumble up and down porch and the tree that was giving it a ride. She too could feel it, if she stood very still beside her father while he was talking, with one foot on a lower plank and another on a higher. She showed it off to her friends, too, the kids from next door and across the street, but sourpuss Gertie, who didn't know anything anyway, said that her daddy had told her ma that this whole house was falling apart and it ought to be condemned by the city, and anyway she lived in a newer house with green paint on it. Well so what! And that dumb Thelma didn't have to laugh that way at what Gertie said, as if they had other secrets about you too. First she was your friend and then she went over to Gertie's side. But they weren't so mean when they wanted to come in the yard to play, the boys especially. You could have a lot of fun in Hoda's yard. It was rank and weed-grown and full of trees you could hide behind and climb and jump from.

Sometimes Hoda's friends came into the house too, but they didn't like that much because they didn't know how to answer Hoda's father who talked to them in Yiddish and told them to study, study all the time, when he couldn't even see them – or could he? *Suppose he was really watching you very carefully from inside his eyes all the time?*

But nobody else had a shed like Hoda's, made of boards and old tin plate advertisements for soft drinks and a partly collapsed corrugated tin roof. Once a stable for somebody's horse, and now piled with rusty and interesting junk and smelling damply, enticingly foul of mouldy old things you could poke about in and pretend with, the children would play and explore here for hours, with Hoda as the bossy hostess of their revels.

There are things you can do and things you shouldn't do and things you mustn't get caught doing. If you got caught they were likely to become things you absolutely shouldn't do. A lot of things you liked got spoiled that way. Not that Hoda wanted to keep secrets from her parents. She didn't, as a matter of fact, because that weighed on her stomach and made her feel bad. She usually ended up by half-confessing what she was afraid her parents might not approve, and she was usually right, they didn't. But occasionally she was relieved when it turned out they didn't object to a game she really liked, that some of the kids thought was bad, like Doctors and Nurses.

"What were you doing in the shed all that time?" Rahel asked over supper.

"We were playing a game," said Hoda. "It's called Doctors and Nurses. I like it."

"Doctors and Nurses?" Danile was delighted. "You want to be a doctor or a nurse when you grow up?"

"Or a patient," said Hoda.

Rahel shuddered, "Heaven forbid!" Children are funny. "You eat up your supper and drink your milk and you'll never have to be a patient, please God."

Parents are funny. Hoda liked being a patient. She liked taking her clothes off and letting the other children examine her. She liked being touched, she enjoyed fumbling in the shed. "Sometimes I'm a doctor," she said obligingly.

"To be a doctor is a great honour," said Danile, "and a great responsibility. You must study, study, study. You must spend your whole life helping people."

"I'll help you," said Hoda positively.

Rahel heard the promise with a pang of fear. Nowadays at a word, her flesh and bones could turn to fear inside of her, an ooze of sick fear that sank to her belly and solidified, adding layer on layer of cold, hard fear to whatever was growing there.

"The doctor was at our house again," Hoda told her friends Gertie and Thelma, importantly. "My mother has something in her stomach that's as big as a cantaloup."

The others were impressed. "Right in her stomach?" asked Thelma.

"Yes. Right here." Hoda laid a hand on her own rotundity, which might well have contained something of almost equivalent size.

"That's nothing," said Gertie, in whom the competitive

instinct was strong. "My father has something that's as big as a banana."

"Well, my mother's is as big as a watermelon," challenged Hoda. "The doctor said so."

"I saw it myself," Gertie held her own.

"They want to take my mother to the hospital to cut it out," said Hoda.

"My father too," said Gertie, but from the way her voice wavered it was clear that she was not so certain.

"My mother cried." Hoda pressed her advantage. "She doesn't want to go. I promised I'd look after my daddy when she's gone. I can do it easily."

But Rahel was not yet ready to submit to the knife. Neither nature nor experience had predisposed her to optimism, and she could not accept, with Danile's ready faith, the doctor's assurance that all would be well. *The knife will have to wait for its victim,* she told herself grimly. There were arrangements to be made; she didn't know what these arrangements were to be, but something had to be done. Something, something, but what? How to protect them? How to safeguard? There were a million dangers that neither of them knew about, that they couldn't be warned against except at the right time, and by someone who understood them and could make herself understood. You couldn't arm a child for life as you would send her to the grocery, with a shopping list and a change-purse in her pocket, and a warning to look both ways before she crossed the street. As it was, Hoda was apt to lose herself in a half hour's contemplation of the candy counter, from which she would eventually return with a rope of liquorice dangling black from her mouth, bought on credit, the child having forgotten about both the list and the change-purse. And worse still, who knew whether she had looked both ways?

The more anxious Rahel grew the more she accepted as inevitable the fact that she would not survive an operation. She grew therefore the more determined not to enter the slaughterhouse. If she had not become worried over her symptoms in the first place, she reasoned, she would not be in this turmoil now. Very well, she would ignore the symptoms and pretend she had never had the doctor in to frighten her. But the only reason she had seen the doctor, she was reminded when she tried to follow the new regime of ignoring the symptoms, was that it had become an agony to work.

Whichever way she turned the trap was already sprung. She was caught. All that she could do now was beg for mercy. But whose mercy? Danile's uncle? Rahel had no illusions about the likely outcome of throwing her dear ones on the mercy of uncle for anything more than the briefest moment of sentiment. The mercy of God, then? Faced with the question Rahel had to admit how little it meant in practical terms. If God were disposed to be merciful, all well and good; no one would be more thankful than she. But you can't rely on what you can't control. There had to be something that she could do, but what?

"What about a corset, doctor?" she had asked him, timidly. "They say a corselet will hold me in so it won't hurt so much when I'm working. Do you think so, doctor?" All she wanted was a word from him that would justify the expense of a corselet.

But he had answered her explosively. "I'm trying to tell you the only thing that will help you, and you talk to me about a corset!"

"I know, I understand, doctor," she placated. They liked to cut into you; everybody knew that. "But meanwhile," she persisted, "till then, doctor, wouldn't a corselet help?

Meanwhile, until the operation I mean . . . doctor?"

"Meanwhile, doctor!" the doctor mimicked her bitterly. But she didn't mind his rudeness. She had been warned he was not a polite man. That was his way. You had to be careful what you said to doctors. "Meanwhile you women have a way of putting things off and putting them off and afterwards your families blame us . . ."

"Are you trying to frighten me, doctor?" she had said, facing up to him bravely, though her voice trembled a little on the last word. Try as she might to leave off his title, to address him as person to person, she couldn't. With every phrase his magic name slipped out, tremulously, like an incantation.

"No," he had replied, relenting. "No, I don't want to frighten you. But it's no child's play, I want you to understand. It's just not healthy to carry things like that around."

"I understand, doctor," said Rahel humbly, fearing that she understood too well. Nevertheless she culled from the consultation some small, scarcely justifiable relief. He had not outright said that she needed the operation immediately. It was not yet an emergency. She might be permitted to carry on a while longer, if she packed her pain tightly into a corset. And maybe meanwhile she would think of something. She was grateful to the doctor for this, in spite of the fact that when she thanked him on taking her leave he muttered gloomily, "Don't thank me, listen to me." It made her feel a little sorry for him. Even doctors have their troubles. But at the same time even doctors can't have things all their own way, cutting you open whenever they feel like it. Maybe the time would come when he would really have to some day. All right; what must come must come. But meanwhile? She had lived with a hump on her back all her life. No doubt she could also support a lump in her stomach. It was not as though she were an ordinary woman, unused to special pain. Perhaps, it occurred to Rahel now for the first time, perhaps pain and deformity are given to special people who have the strength to bear them. Normally, she would have rejected the idea outright, for she saw no special virtue in suffering, and the idea of God's favour being the result of a kind of competition in which the winner received the privilege of extraordinary suffering was repellent to her, since she was not one of those genuinely talented unfortunates who enjoy their misery. But now she took a certain grim satisfaction in the thought, for it enabled her to shift her mind somewhat from the doctor's terrifying simplification, and to repeat to herself with something of the savour of righteousness, that she could be equal to her pain, and bear it a while longer. After all, there were more important things; the child, for instance.

Hoda was growing up. Hoda went to two schools. One was the poor people's Yiddish school. After four o'clock, when English school was over, she went to the Worker's school to learn to read and write Yiddish, so that she would be able to read to her father when her mother was too tired. And she learned the things a Jewish child should know, all about the history of the Jews, and Judaism, and socialism, which was the next best thing. Then on Sunday mornings there were gym and tumbling and ballet and art classes. Hoda lined up for a couple of Sundays, together with a whole row of other little girls who, with their hands clutching the backs of folding chairs, tried to hoist their legs gracefully into unnatural positions, in imitation of the tightly muscled little woman who was the teacher and who called out interminable instructions from the head of the line in a sharp, crackly voice. But the titters from the other children, particularly the boy spectators who were waiting for the hall so they could get on with their tumbling class, and the outright hilarity when her folding chair collapsed, combined with something deep inside herself which told Hoda that she could be if she really wanted to, but she just didn't want to be a ballerina anyway. She turned then, from ballet to the art class, where she found, as she told her father happily when she brought her drawings home to describe to him, that even though the teacher hadn't actually said so, she was maybe even the best in the class.

On the whole Hoda didn't mind Yiddish school so much because it wasn't hard and you could be pretty bad and make noise and you weren't afraid of the teacher. He was just a human Jew like everybody else. Every day he would come in and wait till the class got quiet by itself because he said children should want to study. And then, when they had wasted as much time as they could and were finally made uncomfortable by the rapid blinking of his eyes behind his spectacles while he pretended to wait indifferently – *what would he do if they never stopped?* – they would quieten down and he would begin to speak. He always began very quietly, with a soft and lovely voice, and talked to you just as if you were grown-up and would understand everything he said and would naturally agree with him. And his hands would throw you out and draw you in like a yo-yo he was doing tricks with. And gradually his voice would get louder and more and more excited and he would talk faster and faster, all about workers and suffering and heritage and responsibility, and the tricks with his hands would get more and more complicated, and he would do about ten perfect "round the worlds" with both hands, and he would run around a little, to and fro, and sometimes even standing in one spot. And finally, when there was a great roaring and yelling and declaiming and waving going on and filling up the whole room ready to burst, he would stop suddenly, and silence would rush in and stun the class, and he would grab his books from the desk and turn and rush out without another word.

Once a month, when he came to collect payment for the school, he would sit and drink his glass of tea and tell her parents that Hoda was getting along very well; but there was something shy and miserable about him then, and he never showed her parents what he could really do. Hoda felt a little sorry for him inside of herself, particularly when she remembered the time he had rushed from class, and big, hairy Ralph the orangutan had run up to the desk and climbed right on top of it and started to yell and rave and wave his arms about and jump up and down, and in the middle of it all the teacher had come rushing back in to pick up his notebook, and he had stopped and looked around him, blinking in such a funny way at all of their frozen laughing faces, as though they were all his enemies, and his wire-rimmed glasses had got all clouded up and he had closed up his face and grabbed his book and rushed out again without even punishing Ralph or saying anything at all, and Hoda always remembered that she had been laughing, and was always afraid that he remembered too.

English school was quite different. Here you daren't talk, and the teachers had droughty faces and crisp, unloving voices that told proudly how westerners had beaten down the wild Indians and crushed the treacherous half-breeds and made the great new continent a place fit to live in. Now our boys had to go back to clean up Europe. They would beat down the Kaiser and crush the Germans and make the old countries fit to live in too, and it was about time, after all the noble little island had suffered.

Hoda always told her father what she was learning at school.

"Yes, yes," said Danile. "England. I've heard of England, and Scotland too. In fact I think we passed it on our way here. You probably saw it yourself only you were a baby then and didn't know it."

And Hoda, proud to be maybe the only one in the whole class who had actually seen the ruler of the waves, came to school and told her teacher about it. Teacher smiled and said "Yes?" But she didn't tell the class as Hoda had hoped she would, so Hoda had to tell them herself, at recess.

It was all a heroic struggle and we were all in it together and we were going to win because destiny was on our side. Hoda was not surprised to be on the right side of destiny. She knew that one day soon everything was going to be good all over. Still, even though they were all supposed to be on the same side something always spoiled it. In the service of destiny Hoda was given two knitting needles and a blob of tightly wound wool that had been unravelled from somebody's old sweater. She discovered that somehow she could not work the same modest miracles with the needles that she could with a pencil and a sheet of paper. With fat, fumbling fingers she painstakingly knitted, nevertheless, in proof of her patriotism and to gain competition points for the row in which she sat in class, some hopelessly crooked squares that were to be sewn together as afghans and sent, with affectionate little notes from the girls in grades three to nine, to keep the boys warm in their trenches and show them that the children back home were thinking of them.

Hoda took a long time at her knitting, and sat shame-facedly through many a tart reminder to slowpokes, reminders directed, she was convinced, solely at herself. She dreaded the moment when the strength of her patriotism would be equated, for all the class to see, with these grubby, twisted woollen rags, hopelessly tightly knotted in some places and with great, loose loops in others, which were to be her contribution to the class afghan. Nor was she disappointed in her dread. Her squares, when she at last turned them in, after no amount of stretching and pulling had succeeded in making them look more like squares, were received by her teacher at fingertip's length and there allowed to dangle almost indecent in their limpness, like living creatures only recently deceased. There was that subtle something in her teacher's expression that Hoda had learned to know so well, a certain sucking in and holding away of the self which showed, more clearly than words, that some immigrant children imposed a considerable strain on western hospitality.

"Two more squares for row four, from Hoda." Teacher held them up for all to see. "Honestly," she had a nice, friendly way of saying things that were going to make you feel bad, "honestly I don't know whether to add or subtract these from your score, row four. Perhaps it might help the war effort more if some people simply stopped knitting. The war might end sooner and our boys come home!"

The class tittered. Teacher waited a moment, then she said sadly, "It's not funny." The class was silent. Everyone knew that like many other teachers she had lost her sweetheart in a war. That was why she was the way she was. Not that she had ever taken any known generation of children into her confidence, but she didn't have to. They could tell. Her boy would never come home again. The only uncertain thing was what war he would not come home from. In past years it had been, according to class legend, the Boer war in which her sweetheart had fallen gallantly defending his king. For future generations it would be the First Great World War which had buried him, deep in poppies. One of the boys

Hoda was in love with, who talked to her sometimes, a wiry, bright little fellow, had passed on to her, behind his hand in history class one day, the theory that teacher's sweetheart must have been plucked from her in the wars of the roses, and was happy now wherever he was, to have been spared a fate worse than death. But on the whole the children were inclined to reverence in this serious matter. Hoda knew how she would feel if she lost any one of her three boy friends, and they didn't even know they were her sweethearts. How much worse it must be to have lost your only real true love, who loved you too, as no one would ever love you again. That was why you couldn't entirely blame teacher, when you were out of her reach.

But Hoda was well within reach, and aware now of a prolonged silence, with herself pinned at its centre. She had let the team down again. "I d-didn't kn-kn-know how to kn-kn-kn-it," she quavered finally, unable to look up.

"Neither did many others in the class," replied the teacher reasonably. "But they felt it was their duty to learn. And I suppose you don't know how to wash your hands, either? You were given a clean ball of wool. I can't even tell what colour these rags are. Class, can anyone tell me what colour this is?"

Yes they can, yes they can! Hoda knew they could. But no one spoke.

"No? Well, never mind." Teacher let out a mock little sigh.

"I do so wash my hands." The words were very deep and low from the effort of climbing past the tears in Hoda's throat. "Only," there was genuine anguish in her voice, "things get dirty anyway."

"So I see," said the teacher gently, and smiled. This time the class laughed louder and craned to look at the fat girl who

41

sat squirming in her rumpled, stained tunic and already grubby white blouse. Hoda opened up her quivering mouth and tried to pretend she was laughing too. The effect was grotesque and somehow irritated the teacher. She turned away abruptly. "All right, class, we've wasted enough time."

Helplessly, Hoda suffered, knowing herself to be lovable but in this place unloved and misjudged. It wasn't true, what her teacher had suggested, that she wasn't patriotic. She sang "God Save Our Gracious King" better than anybody else in class, and with a good feeling in her, because more than anyone else she secretly loved the young prince they called the Prince of Wales who was maybe even to be king some day, and anyway could marry anyone he liked and make her a princess. That was why her voice got loud sometimes, when she was singing, because her heart got so big in her when she thought of him. Only then the teacher always said "Somebody's booming again," and looked straight at her, so that she had to catch the music, suddenly, as it was coming out of her, and hold it back in her mouth, and just move her lips and pretend she was singing. Sometimes it was as though she would never be able to do anything right. That was why she hardly ever liked English school much. It was not hard to learn things, but something always made you feel bad. When they said nasty things that wasn't even the worst part. You could always talk back and get into trouble and Ma would have to come and talk to the principal again, or you could say hot things like "fuck you" under your breath, or "sticks and stones may break my bones but names will never hurt me." But how could you look back their looks when you didn't have the awful looking feelings that were in the faces they looked at you with? Some people didn't like you. No matter what you did they wouldn't like you. You couldn't be what they would like you to be because they didn't like you to be at all. How was the world ever going to be perfect then?

It would take time, her daddy said, but people would have to learn eventually not to be so mean. Sometimes when the kids were nice she thought maybe the time had come and now it would last forever, if she didn't do anything to spoil it. She tried to tell them who she was. In the schoolyard she stood, surrounded by her peers, and earnestly told how her grandfather, for twenty whole years now, and maybe even more, had served, was still serving, and didn't know how to get out of serving, our gallant ally the Czar. If it weren't for her grandfather the Russian army wouldn't have a pot or a kettle to eat out of. They'd all starve and lose the war. That's how important a tinker is. And he did other things too. He had been a soldier for longer than anybody. He had even been sent to fight Japanese soldiers once, though he didn't like it much. It was too far away from home. But it was his duty so he did it.

Hoda had discovered that "duty" and "honour of your country" were the things you said that made you feel patriotic and just like everybody else in English. In Yiddish the words that felt right when you talked of wars and soldiers were, "When will they stop killing each other like wild animals and come home and look after their families?" But the English feelings were good here, for all the children shared them and were looking at the warrior's granddaughter respectfully. She forgave them gladly for having laughed at her and called her names so often, and tried to think of something more to tell them.

"What did she say her grandfather was? A stinker?" asked one of the bigger kids at the outer edge of the circle.

"No, he's a tinker," Hoda explained. "He mends broken pots, and he can even make new ones, if . . ."

"Stinker, stinker! Hoda's grandfather's a stinker!" The circle was broken. They were scattering from her in all directions.

"Stinker, stinker!" The joke was too good to resist. "Hoda's grandfather's a stinker!"

"No he's not!" Outraged, she flung herself after them, now charging in one direction, now veering toward another taunt.

"Run, Hoda, run!" they chanted. "Hoda weighs a ton!"

They weren't nice. No they weren't nice. They spoiled everything. They didn't even seem to care if you had good feelings for them or not. Hoda cared about their good feelings. Why didn't her good feelings mean anything to them? They shouldn't be that way. Someday they'd see. Then they'd come to her. And she wouldn't be mean. She wouldn't push them off the snow castle, playing rough, no fair, all of them against one, jumping on her and rolling her all the way down, shoving her face in the snow, tearing her toque off and rubbing snow all over her cold ears and down her neck. No she wouldn't. She wasn't that way. Alone when they had gone at last she climbed, her exertions punctuated by sobs and sudden bursts of laughter. "You said you wouldn't let me but I am," she crowed. And sobbing, "I hate you fuck you I won't play with you either."

Catching the echo of her own voice in the crisp winter air she paused a moment, apprehensively examining the shadows that played between the street lamps and yellow-lit windows of the houses across the street from the school. She was sweating again, no longer so cold as when she had stood and begged, at first at the foot of the snow castle and then, after she had laboriously crawled nearly to the top when she thought they weren't looking, but they were really waiting to grab her and throw her down and jump on her, when she had got away from them at last, and stationed herself over by the street lamp, so she could duck behind it when they threw snowballs. Then she had stood, stamping her feet and growing hoar frost all over, and little burning icicles inside her collar, and around the edges of her gloves her skin onfire, and wet socks itchy inside her moccasins, and answering their taunts, "You can't!" with her own frost-steaming bawl, "I can so! You can't stop me!"

"We dare you!"

"I will when I feel like it!"

And she had outwaited them, standing alone finally, under the street lamp, snuffling and muttering to herself when they, having long tired of chasing her off and now tiring of their snow game, wandered home to where their mothers would scold them for lateness and soaking clothes while they endured the brief agony of thawing out before supper. Now she climbed alone, slipping occasionally, and sliding down as a fragile jut of snow gave way beneath a hand or foot. She had outlasted them into a fearsome, never-been-out-so-late-before evening of glinting air and blue shadows and a looming dark school filled with ghosts of shrieking teachers who'd gone crazy mourning lovers lost in ancient wars. Occasionally, no less ominous, crunching through the snow came a mysterious, humped over grown-up she mustn't talk to if he stopped.

Almost at the top now. *I'll show them.* Hoda heard her mother's anxious voice calling from a distance. "Hoda? Hodaleh? Hoda!" Her mother's voice, treble, trembling, thin with misgiving, banished fear and relieved her of the lonely evening.

A final heave and Hoda scrambled to her feet, higher than anybody. She could see her mother, half a block down, at the other end of the schoolyard. Flinging up her arms, Hoda blared out proudly in her loudest voice, "I'M THE QUEEN OF THE CASTLE!" And she waited, triumphant, watching while her mother, holding on to her stomach with both hands, broke into a panting trot through the snow, as though afraid to continue to walk lest the child should disappear into the evening again. Hoda's impulse, after that victorious cry had been rescued from loneliness, was to jump and slide down and run to meet her mother. But her mother's voice had already changed. Angrily, she was calling out as she bobbed her crooked, hurried path across the schoolyard. "What are you doing here this time of night? Why didn't you come home from school? Why didn't you go to Jewish school? You'll catch pneumonia!"

"I'm the queen of the castle," Hoda reiterated once again from above, trying to communicate, before it disappeared entirely, the fast-fading glamour of her reign. "They wouldn't let me play before. I said I would and I did! I wasn't even afraid, hardly."

"Come down from there. You're all wet. I've been in every house in the neighbourhood. Your father wanted to call the police. Come down this minute!"

Hoda hesitated still on her hard-won height.

"Are you coming?" Rahel's voice was sharp, her face very pale and tired, though the child saw only the anger.

"But they wouldn't let me play with them."

"You come down this minute. Now is not the time to play!"

Hoda came, finally, and let herself be dragged along home by a scolding mother who punctuated her lecture with an occasional, ineffectual swipe behind, crying out each time she struck, "Oi, frozen! Oi, icicles!" as matted lumps of snow dislodged themselves from Hoda's coat. Well, so what. Even if the kids did call her fat and didn't want to play with her; even if her mother, disappointingly, cared only about how wet and frozen she was, he would know. The Prince of Wales would know who was born to become his queen.

And he wasn't the only one who would know what she was really like, under the spell of fat she couldn't escape and sloppiness she couldn't control, like the Frog Princess and Beauty and the Beast and the Ugly Duckling and Cinderella too. All kinds of girls who thought they were the fairest of them all would get a surprise some day, when the young prince who was ripening in his long-chinned, pale-eyed, non-descript, special kind of noble beauty would come from over the seas and not even notice them at all.

To Hoda it was like a promise of all the good things to come when she was finally promoted to a class where the teacher actually seemed to like her. Miss Flake even said to her once, "You have a good head, Hoda. If you apply your-self we may hear great things of you." She was the only teacher who had ever guessed it so far, and Hoda figured it was probably because she was just freshly over from what she too called "the old country," though her old country wasn't Russia, it was really *the* old country, the dear little island. When she spoke, if you hadn't seen them riding around out there on top of her big, knuckly gums, you would have thought that her teeth were running around loose in her mouth, and she was trying to hang on to them at the same time that she was pushing the words out past them. You had to listen carefully to understand her, but it was worth it.

"Some of those dumb kids make fun of Miss Flake because she spits when she talks and you get sprayed if you sit in front of her," said Hoda, laughing a little in spite of herself when she told about it.

"That's not very nice," said her mother. "She probably can't help it."

"I know. That's what I say. I think she's the best teacher

47

in the school, even if she does spit and even if she's funny looking, with hair on her chin."

"These are things a person can't help," said her mother.

"That's right," said Danile. "I never pay attention to what a person is supposed to look like. I ask myself, 'What is this person really like inside?'"

"Well she's nice. She's so nice," said Hoda with a rush of enthusiasm, "I just love her. She knows everything. She's even seen the whole Royal Family, more than once. She waited outside the gates of the palace for hours, and they came." The Royal Family had never disappointed Miss Flake, not once.

"If you wait long enough, they'll come," she told the class. "Indeed, once I was very nearly discouraged. I thought, 'Surely I have been misinformed,' and I was tempted to leave. It was a very wet day. But . . ." and Miss Flake's equine face was suddenly broken open by a convulsive smile, which was not entirely lacking in charm in spite of the fact that her eyes squeezed shut and her teeth, riding recklessly high on her gums, reared up and threatened to leap right out of her mouth. "But I stayed on and they did come after all, you see. Perseverance." Miss Flake smilingly emphasized the moral of her lesson with another reckless charge of her teeth and a haphazard spray of spit and sibilants across the front of the class.

Of course they came! Miss Flake had not, would not, could not be disappointed, and Hoda felt that her words had anointed her own awed face with special promise that she too would not be disappointed. For Miss Flake loved the Royal Family not with an exclusiveness, like some of the other teachers, as if they were the only ones who had a right to and really knew how. She knew more than all of the other teacher put together. She could tell you what was really going on over there. Daddy himself asked Hoda every day if Miss Flake had any news or opinions about the way the war was going. She really knew things. The Kaiser, for instance. Miss Flake disliked the Kaiser on personal grounds, on the grounds of his bad character. For a man to make war on his own cousin, she said, was very poor form, inexcusably bad taste, caddish, greedy, degenerate behaviour. Miss Flake was very serious about family responsibilities. She had had to look after an idiot brother until he died, or she would have come to settle in the new world long ago. No one had ever heard her actually tell about her idiot brother, but where extraordinary homeliness ruled out a sweetheart killed in a war, good nature and strong family feeling suggested an idiot brother as a logical alternative. And so an idiot brother there had been, as all the children knew.

As Miss Flake saw the war, it was the result of a family quarrel between the three cousins, Czar, King and Kaiser, and the Kaiser had had the poor taste to carry his quarrel with his cousins to this public extreme. A family should show a more united face, and if families did the whole world would and there would be no more wars. All that was needed was for each member to know and to do his duty. In the discussion period after Miss Flake's current events class Hoda waved her arm about importunately until Miss Flake gave her a chance to speak. Then she heaved herself up from behind her desk and testified that Miss Flake was right and she knew it because she knew some people who had a rich uncle here in this very city and he wouldn't help his poor relations hardly at all, and they were very poor and everything.

For some reason not entirely clear to herself Hoda refrained from identifying those poor relations and their rich uncle. She would have liked to, in a way, and if anyone had questioned the truth of her testimony she was ready to blurt out an admission, as positive proof, happy to be able to reveal a truth about her special case that proved her to be linked so significantly with kings against kaisers. But she was learning caution, and though she knew from her father that there was nothing to be ashamed of in their poverty, she knew also from her mother that the whole world didn't have to know about it.

Miss Flake required no additional proof. She accepted Hoda's little example and with a sigh and a shaking of the head, went on to talk of troubles in the family of nations.

"Maybe your Miss Flake will come and have a glass of tea with us sometime?" suggested Danile daringly, one day. "She sounds like a really intelligent woman, someone you could chew a few words down with."

"Here?" asked Hoda, startled. It had never occurred to her that Miss Flake could like her well enough to want to come to her house. The idea made her a little afraid. "She doesn't speak Yiddish."

"That's true," said Danile. "But you could translate for us. And your mother understands a little English."

But her mother did not seem to be impressed by Miss Flake's political theories. "If they want to fight why should we have to get killed?" asked Rahel.

"Because we're their loyal subjects," explained Hoda patiently, not for the first time. She knew her mother harped so on the subject because she was worried about grandfather Shem Berl the soldier. It was a long time since she had heard from her family, and she didn't know what ditch he might be lying in now, the gallant Shem Berl, a martyr to these cousins' wars.

"In my family," said Rahel, with bitter dignity, "we don't fight very often, but when we do we do it ourselves and don't make others go out and fight for us."

"But Miss Flake says we're all in the same family," said Hoda stoutly, hoping her mother wouldn't argue more and spoil it.

"Sure, for fighting and getting killed," replied her mother. "For living and letting live and earning a crust of bread and holding our heads up in the world we belong to another branch altogether."

"I dunno," muttered Hoda rebelliously, "I dunno."

"I would like to know what a nice one of them really thinks," said Danile wistfully.

"You could have plenty of opportunity to, if you wanted to," Rahel shot out at him tartly.

Danile was silent.

Hoda looked uneasily from one to the other. Of late there had been a curious feeling that ran with rough edges between her father and her mother, cutting them both. She could sense it in the words they said to each other and the way they said them, though she had never heard them quarrel. It wasn't there all the time, just sometimes, spurting from her mother to her father in a few incomprehensible words, and slashing across his suddenly somehow naked face; and whether or not he answered her, with his low-voiced plea of "What do you want from me?" Hoda could see that feeling spurt right back at her mother, stinging in her eyes. Hoda didn't want to know what that feeling was, that made them both look so miserable, just as she didn't want to know that what her mother said about the things she learned in school was true. She tried to dispel the feeling.

"Can I invite her, Ma? Can I invite Miss Flake?"

"Maybe sometime," said her mother, absently.

"For my birthday, maybe? If I have a party this year?"

"If you have a party," echoed Rahel non-committally.

"Oh boy!" said Hoda. "Oh boy, Daddy!" she repeated. "You'll like her too, Mama. You really will."

"If you like her I'll like her," said her mother, in a half-suffocated, brushing-aside kind of voice, as though she was listening for something else.

"Who knows," said Danile heavily, "I might develop a taste for meeting strangers."

"Oi Danile," said his wife quickly, "Oi Danile, I'll live to tease you for your shyness yet, when you go rushing off, with no time for us anymore." Her mother's voice had filled with life again, as though something had been said that she had yearned to hear.

"Oh boy!" said Hoda, once again. She could hardly wait to tell the kids in school that Miss Flake was going to come to her birthday party maybe. But what if one of them went and asked teacher to a birthday party before she did? It wasn't fair; it was her idea. Well then she wouldn't tell them! But she wanted to tell them something. All right, she would tell them she knew a secret, all about Miss Flake, Miss Flake and Hoda herself, yes, and her mother and father, all in a secret together. But she wouldn't tell what it was. Even Miss Flake wouldn't know yet, because her birthday was a long way away. It would be a long secret and everybody would wonder about it and they'd keep on asking her. Well so what; she didn't have to tell.

Rahel could not have done better than to call that feeling shyness, which she had grown to suspect was, in Danile, simply fear. She was no less grateful than he for the inspiration that had come to her in a word, before it had even passed through her mind. Now they could speak warmly of his shyness during those long, muttered arguments in the bed to which, for the sake of the child, they confined their quarrels.

One could cope with shyness, be persuasive about, argue, rally, insist, all without coming too dangerously close to hurting too deeply, as she had already done out of her own pain and fear once or twice. And all for what? Rahel was past knowing whether the course of action which she had determined for Danile was equal in value to the importance with which she invested it. Suffice that it was the only thing she had been able to think of. Had he agreed without fuss it might never have taken on the force of an obsession with her. But because she recognized Danile's resistance as symptomatic, she threw all of her remaining energy into overcoming it.

"But what if I can't learn?" he asked her, as they lay together in the equalizing darkness, on the night when she had accidentally created the theory of his shyness. "What if I can't learn how to make baskets? A basket has to be made well. How can a blind man make a basket well?"

"They do," she replied weakly, for the pain had come on her again as soon as she lay down, so that she did not know which way to turn for ease. "I've seen them. They make beautiful baskets. They teach you."

"How can they teach me?" he insisted, with a curiously plaintive note in his voice.

"With their hands. You learn by feel. And they explain."

"I don't speak English."

"That doesn't matter, I told you. If they have to, the lady told me, they'd get an interpreter."

For a while he lay silent. "And they sell the baskets?" he asked finally. "And you earn the money? And they let you keep it?"

"Yes," said Rahel. "They get the materials cheaply and once you start selling you pay for them. You won't earn much at first, of course, but . . ."

"Baskets are very useful," Danile was musing. "I remember my mother, when I could still see, she had a beautiful basket, yellow straw colour and there was red on it and green, and black. It was so big I even used to climb into it and crouch down, I remember, when I was little, and ask her to take me to market. It was a beautiful basket, now I think of it. Could a blind man have woven that?"

"I don't know. But here it's a thing they do to help the blind. And they teach you to fix wicker chairs too. People bring them to be fixed. They pay . . . not much, of course, but . . ."

"Not much and not much makes how much?" asked Danile, suddenly playful. "Out of much not much a man could work himself into a living. You really want me to go, Rahel?"

There was a pitiful note, still, a plea behind the question. She felt herself harden in her pain. "Yes, you must. Not because I want you to, but in case, in case something happens to me . . ."

"No," said Danile, quickly, refusing as always to recognize this argument. "I will go, but only on condition that nothing happens to you. Once and for all that's final. All right?"

"Oi, Danile."

"All right. It's settled. Here is coming into the world the first great basket magnate of the West. I will make baskets of every shape and pattern. My fingers will nip in and out among the straw as though they had a seeing eye at the tip of every one. My baskets will be so finely made, so strong, so perfectly woven that people will speak of them with wonder. 'Danile's baskets?' they'll say. 'There's something magical about them. They are the first authentic bottomless baskets. Why, they could contain the entire universe without straining a fibre. Not only that, they'll even hold water!'"

Rahel, for the first time since she had initiated those obsessive, interminable arguments over whether or not he would consent to go out and become a weaver of baskets, found herself relaxing a little, and even smiling at his nonsense. He was such a child. How little he understood. She allowed herself a momentary doubt. Was she right to force him out into the world? But where there is no choice doubt is a luxury.

Danile was making plans; ". . . and those few cents I earn will give you that much more time at home, to rest. Comes a time I'll earn more, you'll stay home and rest more. Someday, maybe, you'll stay home altogether and I'll earn our bread all by myself. Or else I can have a shop of my own and you will take care of the customers, and when business is slow you can sit all day in one of my wicker chairs and let my skill comfort your beauty."

He had lowered his voice to a whisper as he allowed himself this playful coarseness by way of a prelude to intimacy. As he waited for a response he became aware of the faint whisper of a groan in her breathing, and aware also of the fact that she often breathed this way nowadays; in fact, that it had been a long time since he could recall a night that was entirely free of these sounds. They were what he had fought against with his blind and stubborn panic of "no's" to all her long arguments. And now he began to realize that even by acquiescing to her wishes he had not been able to exorcise these illicit, impersonal groans that rasped out a ragged, insistent rhythm, counter to the rhythm of her life. Something was there; Danile could hear it now with his preternatural ear; whatever it was, it was comfortable, counter and alive, feeding on the life beside him, inextricably involved; who knew what you were touching when you put out your hand to caress? For one sickening moment he understood completely, in his flesh, what he could not bear to know. His flesh shuddered. Rahel mistook his spasm for another expression of his fear of the world into which she was forcing him. She wanted, with all her heart, to comfort him. But when he felt the gentle pressure of her hand creeping along his arm, in response to the sudden convulsive griping and recoil of his own, it was a long moment before he was able, in his horror, to turn to comfort her.

Yet human beings are, after all, able to comfort not only each other, but themselves as well. Danile flung himself into his new career of basket-making magnate. He learned, at his own insistence, to tap his way alone to the streetcar stop several blocks away. He learned to change cars twice before he descended finally at his destination, and after his lessons, he learned to find his way back. The streetcar conductors learned to expect him, and before long he was travelling through the city with hardly any anxiety about losing his way at all. The only thing that caused him consistent anxiety was his feeling that he must learn and succeed in a tremendous hurry, for only so would he enable Rahel to ease up on her own work. If she had enough rest, and perhaps, at the very worst, that operation that the doctor had talked about, well then, probably that was all that would be needed. In fact, rest itself would probably suffice to stifle the groan which he fancied was now far less audible than when it had first forced itself on his attention. The very fact of his own activity was beginning to have its effect around him. Danile blamed himself for having resisted for so long. Coward that he had been, afraid to venture forth. Why, he could probably have had three basketry shops by now. Where had he spent his life? But he would make up for all that. He had begun to make up for it already. There was not a single one among the elderly men with whom he used to spend a great part of his days at the synagogue, who was not impressed by the first basket he brought to show them. He knew they could hardly believe that a man like him could do such work. Danile was not used to the compliments he felt were simply pouring over him. He was overcome with gratitude and with the desire to give them something in return for those rare and lovely words of praise.

"I'll make you all baskets," he promised fervently. "First thing my good friends. I'll make a beautiful basket for each and every one of you. Tell your wives, tell your daughters, you can even choose your own colours. Yes, you think I can't tell the colours apart?" Danile laughed delightedly. "Every profession has its secrets. Never mind, just tell me the colours you want and leave the rest to me. With God's help I'll blunder along."

Never did he look or feel less like a blunderer than when Hoda, through force of habit and because she enjoyed talking to the grandfathers, for Danile knew his own way home, came to fetch him for supper from the synagogue that evening. He strode along, tapping the sidewalk smartly with his cane, more out of habit than out of any need to feel his way. In fact he knew exactly, to the fraction of an instant, when to swing his cane with a debonair flourish and tap each elm affectionately across the bark, as he passed. And like a little boy he ran his cane rattlingly across the slats of the wooden fence in front of Thelma's house. Some of the stranger kids from the other blocks thought he was doing crazy magic things, if they happened to come by when he was striding so actively along. They skipped hastily across the street, and, because they were afraid of his magic, hardly ever threw stones.

This evening he let Hoda carry the sample basket. He had made it for Rahel, to replace the tattered kerchief in which she still carried her effects to work. "But the next one's for you, Hodaleh, to carry your books to school in." He could hardly wait to tell his wife of the compliments he had received in the synagogue. Right through supper he talked of it, repeating every word every one of the old men had said, imitating their accents, and describing how he had had a hard time maintaining the pose of modesty which it was only right for him to assume when what he had really wanted to do was dance and sing and cavort about for sheer pleasure.

"You say you have orders for baskets from every one of them?" asked Rahel. "How much are you going to charge them?"

"How do you mean, charge them?" said Danile, puzzled.

"For the baskets you're going to make for them."

"I can't charge them," Danile explained. "They're presents. For my friends. When could I ever afford to give gifts to my friends before? And . . . and . . . and . . . besides, it was right in the synagogue. They were admiring my work. I can't do business on holy ground."

"But Danile!"

"And they liked my work so much, I told them, because we're brothers in the same congregation, and they're poor men too, most of them, so I said I'd make them little gifts, since none of them knows how to weave. That's why it's called a gift, Rahel; when you discover you have a gift, it means you have been given a gift, and it also means that you should give your gift. The whole idea of a gift, by its very nature, implies something that should not be hung on to but can only be kept alive by being passed on." Danile was thinking and speaking very quickly, and finding his train of thought so felicitous that he knew his wife could not fail to follow.

"But what about making a living?" Rahel interrupted.

"Thank God I'll be able to now. The more people see my handiwork, the more will come to me for more. After all, you don't think I promised a basket to every single member of the entire congregation, do you? Not all of them by any means." Danile laughed. "Just a few I pray with all the time, only about eight or ten, yes, well, make it ten. It might as well be a minyan. That's a good sign before God."

"Only ten!" Rahel groaned a healthy groan. "And with coloured straw yet too, so it should be more expensive. Oi Danile, who will look after you?"

"We have nothing to worry about, now that I am becoming an artisan. My father, bless him, always said, 'No matter how learned a man is, he is an ignoramus who doesn't have a trade. A hungry scholar is as helpless as a hungry idiot.' Unfortunately, in the old country we were too ignorant to know that there was something even a man like I could learn to do, besides beg in the streets. But don't you worry, once I get going, once I've started my little business, my wife is not going to crawl on floors any longer. I will learn to do very fancy work. The rich will come to us with special orders. We will be very well known. I may have to take an apprentice. I could even teach you; it's not strenuous. Ah Rahel, what would I do without you and that head of yours full of ideas?"

Rahel was silent, wondering too, but he continued enthusiastically. "Wait wait, when we're on our feet, the things we'll do! We'll take the child to the beach in summer, like other people. We'll invite our uncle to dinner on Friday night and show him that we too can spare meat from our table on the Sabbath. We'll begin to live!"

She listened uneasily while her husband dreamed on. Yes yes, let a half of it come to pass and it would be enough, for now. She had begun, finally, to think of the operation as the only alternative to attacks of pain which she could no longer bear. There were now long moments during which, as she afterwards realized with horror, she no longer cared, not only about what happened to her, but about what happened to these two, her only link with life. And if she no longer cared then what did it matter? The knife was as good a way as any, and more final than those lingering spasms, to cut short a state which horrified her.

But it wasn't true that she didn't care, she told herself as she listened to him now. Indifference was a kind of sickness imposed by physical pain, which was itself an indifferent and inhuman thing. It was alien and disappeared with the pain, and left the nerve of caring so rawly exposed that she could hardly bear to realize now, for the first time, by the very fervour of his reaction to his new career, that her husband was not, as she had often imagined, a stranger to humiliation. She recognized it now and wondered greatly at the species of pride, or the species of ignorance, that had endured without naming, had submitted without surrendering, to the kind of indignity which had embittered so much of her own life.

"When I come back from the hospital," she said, not resisting the strong desire she often had of late simply to lay her hands on him, "we'll make plans. As soon as that's over with we'll really plan, won't we, Danile?" She moved her hand over his hair and down his face and against the flesh and bone and sinew of his neck with a kind of searching eagerness, as though she were the blind one and he an unknown dearness.

"That's right," said Danile. "The sooner the better." He took her moving hand and held it against the nap of his cheek. "Go and come, you hear me? And no loitering."

"No loitering," murmured Rahel.

But in the end they had to take her, to carry her roiling

on a stretcher, in a screaming ambulance down the street into which Danile had stumbled, in the middle of the night, to call out to their neighbours for help. They pushed Danile up into the ambulance with her, and he crouched, his hand paralysed in her grip, whispering her name over and over again.

One of the neighbours had run to fetch the doctor. He and his wife and another neighbour, who complained he was a light sleeper, stood for a few moments in the dark, after the ambulance siren had faded away, shaking their heads and muttering sombrely. Then they dispersed, eyes downcast and yawning discreetly.

They forgot about Hoda. The child had been wakened some time before by her mother's screams. The house was partitioned off so that directly you entered, to the right, was the little cubbyhole that was the master bedroom, with a window onto the verandah. Next to it, straight ahead, was the bathroom, and just beyond the bathroom, also to the right was the cubbyhole that served as a bedroom for Hoda, with a window looking out to a neighbour's plank fence. Beyond Hoda's bedroom door and directly facing the front door, was the back door of the house, which led onto the lean-to shack which they called the summer kitchen. The rest of the house, to the left, was one large room, which served as kitchen and living room. Hoda had been given the room at the back because it was partially insulated by the summer kitchen, and also because it was closest to the wood stove which stood at the back of the kitchen, and was supposed to heat the entire house. Usually, if she awakened, it was still early evening, and she was comforted by the murmurs of her parents as they took their late evening tea or sat and warmed themselves by the stove. Her mother always left her door open a crack so that she could see the friendly streak of light slipping through the door and lying on her bed and climbing up the wall. But now it was pitch dark when she awoke and an animal was screaming in her mother's voice.

She lay rigid in her cot, straining to hear. The screams came again. It was her mother. No it wasn't. It was. "Mama?" she whispered, afraid to be heard. But the voice was worse than a stranger's, impersonal, inhuman. Indistinctly, she made out another voice, her daddy's, but he also sounded funny, less frightening than frightened, and so almost more frightening still. There were movements, scuffing, bumping sounds. She waited in the darkness for the lights to go on, but the darkness remained. Only Daddy was moving about. She heard his familiar step in the kitchen.

"Daddy?" she called. "Daddy?"

"What?" his voice came, distracted. "What? Go to bed, Hodaleh, sleep; it's nothing."

He was interrupted by sounds of suffering from the other room. "Sleep, child," he whispered hurriedly, and shut her bedroom door.

"Don't close my door, Daddy!" She was too late. Now the darkness was closed in with her, but the screams, when they came again, were not shut out. They seemed even louder, perhaps because she was listening so hard for them. Then she heard her father's voice again, calling out, distractedly, "Wait wait, I'm coming! I'll be right back. Wait. Don't cry. I'm coming!" But he wasn't calling to her. The front door slammed. Terrified, she lay in the darkness, waiting, listening for the intermittent madness of her mother's voice. For ages she waited. Once, she almost screwed up her courage to the point where she was ready to creep out of bed and stand by her bedroom door to try to hear why it had grown so frighteningly silent beyond, but the animal sounds broke out again, to her terror and relief.

At last she heard outside noises: the front door, strangers' voices, calm, low-pitched; her father's voice. She could not make out any of their words. They were in her mother's room now. Hoda jumped out of bed, held her hands before her in the dimness, till she was pressed against the closed door, wanting to open it, but afraid, afraid of looking, of seeing, of finding out. Once again her mother's voice rose, riding high on a scream, and toppling crazily off. It was the last scream she heard. After that, murmurs, brisk voices, movements, a light stabbing at her nightgown through the keyhole, instructions being called back and forth, shuffling, the front door opening, more movements, the front door closing, then the front door opening again and a stranger's voice calling out, chillingly, "Just a sec, I'd better turn off the lights in here." Brisk footsteps now, the stiletto of light suddenly withdrawn, like a part of her, from her nightgown, while she stood, unable to call out; the front door closing again, and silence, silence, and the sudden shattering of silence by the wild, shrill, impersonal keening of a siren.

"Don't go away!" Hoda screamed, wrenching the door open at last and flinging herself into the larger darkness of the living room. It was true; they were gone; she could feel it in the darkness. The house was empty, they had taken Mommy, this much she understood, from the fragments of conversation she had heard through the door. They had carried her out, calling out to each other to be careful, to step this way, through the door. But where did Daddy go? He was helping them. He would come back in a minute. She shouldn't be afraid. But why didn't he come? That was a long time ago. Why didn't he come then? Where was he? She stood very still in the darkness and moved her head slowly about on the axis of her neck. Almost, in the thickness of the silence, she could hear her neck creaking. Afraid, she stopped moving it, holding her head stiffly at an awkward angle, while her dilated eyes craned into the void and ominous darkness of her mother's room. Darkness and silence; silence that was different from simple quiet; darkness of predators, there, in her mommy's bedroom, and straining at the latch of the summer kitchen door behind her, where she daren't turn to look, and there too behind the stove. Hoda turned and flung herself back through her bedroom door, slamming it shut and flattening herself against it, while the whole house echoed with feet running to get her. It wasn't enough to push against the door this way. She could never keep them out, all against one. Hide. In the bed. No no. They would rip the covers off her. Where then? She daren't look up. They were outside the window too. If she stood very still . . . but they could hear her, could hear her heart, thunking wildly in the stillness. A sudden creaking from somewhere close by sent her, with a crazy little moan of fear, down onto her hands and knees. Under the bed! There, in the farthest corner of darkness to escape them. Sobbing, she scuttled, flattened herself and turned her head sideways, scraping her ear on the floor, in order to get her head under the iron tube that braced the cot. Head in safety, she wriggled and bumped and scraped her shoulders on the iron, hurting them. It pressed down tighter on her shoulder blades, but in spite of the pain, gasping and panting, she wrenched them through. Now the bar was pressed down on her back and her stomach was squashed and she couldn't move. She could hardly breathe. She lay for a moment, very still, gathering breath, then, flattening herself as far down as she could, she pulled, strained and tugged, frantically. But it was no use. She was jammed. She jutted out too much behind. Her stomach was too big. The rod had pinned her down, half under the couch, half exposed to what was fumbling at the doorknob. Panicky, she tried to raise herself up, lift the bed, but it was too heavy for her to budge. She tried to wriggle out again backwards, the horror of entrapment driving other fears for a moment from her head. But that part of her stomach which had managed to squeeze under the bar had somehow swelled up again on the other side. She was stuck. "Daddy! Mommy! Help me!" she screamed. "Mommy! Please! It hurts! It hurts! Help me!" she sobbed, wriggling her nether half frantically and trying to squeeze it small so that the killers might miss it when they came to get her. She could no longer keep silent or try to control her sobs, though that brought them closer and closer. "Please, please Mommy! Come back! Don't go away! Don't leave me! Daddy! It hurts! Please!"

But no one came. No one would come. Forever; she was stuck forever. She would die here. They would kill her, they, it, all of them. They would do horrible things to her. Despairing, she closed her eyes tightly and pressed her hands against her ears, so as not to see or hear what they were going to do to her. The dust under the bed had crept up her nostrils and exploded suddenly a chain of sneezes, each one of which jerked her painfully against the bar. Exhausted now, she lay quite still. The bar didn't hurt so much when she lay still.

Gradually, her sobs turned to whimpers, her whimpers faded to little moans and at last, with a sigh, she fell asleep. Blessedly, she remained that way, though not long afterwards daylight cast its punctual gleam through the window, brightening cheerfully on a pair of plump legs, a rolled-up nightgown, and twin rounds of great soft, rosy, vulnerable, innocent bum.

She was still lying thus, cruelly halved and wholly asleep, when Danile poled his way heavily up the verandah steps and into the silent house. It had been a night immeasurably long and inconceivably short, a night of ungraspable dimension, the abyss discovered by the sundering of lives. At the hospital he had sat huddled for a long time after the doctor had come down from the operating room, and had told him, and had expressed his regret, and had gone away. No one came near his blackness to put a hand on his arm and lead him away too. So he sat on. They had forgotten, when they dispersed, that he was a blind man, and that perhaps he might not know his way home. When a new nurse came on duty in the emergency room she must have thought that he was some tramp who had found his way into the waiting room and was dozing quietly on the bench, for she came up and spoke to him rather crisply before she noticed the white cane lying beside him and realized from the way he raised his head and looked at her with infinite blindness that he had not been asleep. She found some one to take him home.

He went straight to the child's room, opened the door gently, stepped in, and stumbled over her prostrate form. There was a muffled bellow and a violent kicking out of legs which prevented him from regaining his balance, so that he fell forward onto her empty bed. Somewhere below him she was screaming her newly awakened fear and pain. "It hurts! Don't jump on me! I'll tell my daddy!" and a further torrent of unintelligible words, accompanied by a frantic kicking out of her feet.

"Hoda? Where are you?" he felt about on the bed. "Don't cry, I'm here, where are you?"

At the sound of his voice the frightened gibberish resolved itself into a long wail. "I'm here Daddy; it hurts; I'm stuck under the bed!"

Something in Danile gave way and he began to cry. He cried as he heaved up the bed and held it with one hand while he helped her pull her cramped and painful body out from under it with the other. He wept as he gathered her up, big girl that she was, and held her blubbering in his arms. He cried with her as she told him how she had been left alone and they had chased her under the bed and she had got stuck there and how it hurt her now all over. He wept and rocked her gently, so gently that she could not know that he was weeping in anger, a desolating anger such as he had never known before. For a long time he rocked her and comforted her with his tears. And finally, when he thought that tears and anger had already drained him utterly, and she too sat quiet in his lap, she stirred and asked about her mother.

THREE

Uncle was angry. Right from the beginning he had conceived a dislike of Rahel, whom he referred to simply as "the sack." He disliked her not only because he felt she was somehow responsible for their intrusion into his life, she and that clever family of hers back there, but also because he didn't like a certain way she had of looking at him.

"I don't like that sack and I don't like what peeps out of that sack," he told his wife, whenever the infrequent occasion arose when his mind was forced to turn away from more important business, to consider his unfortunate relatives.

"That's my family," he would declaim bitterly. "My sister, healthy as two women, almost as big as I am, has to let herself get dragged off by the cholera. What does she leave me? The only family I have to turn to in case I should need them, heaven forbid, my only connections that I brought all the way over myself so they could set up a life for themselves like a brother should do for a sister's child. And what did I want from them? What do I ask for? Nothing! My children should know their own and I should have someone to talk to sometimes. She never wrote me he was blind! Always 'my sweet Danile, my clever little Danile. Thank you for the money; Danile thanks you too.' I thought she had a prodigy there. I thought we might even be able to train him for the business." At this distance in time Uncle could reconstruct touchingly the fine intentions which had been disappointed by his relatives. "So what did they send me all the way from over there? Three sacks." Uncle had something of a poetic streak in him. "An empty sack, a lumpy sack and an over-stuffed sack."

But of the three Rahel was *the* sack, and he was furious, as though she had aimed the blow directly at him, when he heard from the hospital that Danile had named him as the man who would take charge of the situation.

"The sack is dead. I have to go bury her," said Uncle when he heard.

His wife, who listened to everything he said with the same injunction ready on her lips, let it drop without even hearing herself. "Don't spend money."

Uncle Nate saw Rahel's death as an act of personal malice toward himself. "Not enough she had to embarrass me before the whole town by crawling on floors, she has to go and die on me too. On my back it's easy to lie down. What's Uncle Nate? A broad back to carry sacks. Come on, tell the whole world, 'send your cripples to lay their burdens on me.' God knows I never wished her harm! I signed for them. I welcomed them. You want to make your own living? Be independent then, and my blessing on you. Climb strangers' walls with a rag in your hand. Never mind your uncle has a name in the community. Let the world laugh. You don't like Uncle? All right, Uncle doesn't ask you to be grateful. You live your way and he'll live his. But die? Who wanted her to die? What does she mean by dying? What will I do with them now?"

Annoyed though he was, Uncle Nate was nevertheless still a man of the community, and he knew the rites of sorrow. He came, for a short period every day, through what he called the "jungle wilderness" of their front yard, up the rickety steps and across the lilting verandah, with his wife close behind him. He sat barefoot on a piece of sacking in Danile's living room, and with a large and impressive coarseness which had repelled Rahel in life, managed, even from that position, to exude his sense of worth and his consciousness of the great honour he was paying the broad floorboards of this humble house, by enthroning himself so graciously near.

People said, "Ahaah! See, though he's rich, he follows the way of the land; he shows respect!"

And other people said, for some are never satisfied, "It is easier for him to do it now she's dead than when she was alive."

And even Danile, who sat for the most part wrapped in his darkness, rapping on his darkness, rapt and listening in his darkness for an explanation of this further extension of his void, thought in a corner of his mind, "Now Uncle sees that we too are of some account. Not once have we fallen short of a minyan for the prayers."

Uncle was, indeed, a little surprised, for the old men seemed to have brought the atmosphere of a synagogue to the shack, and they and their wives behaved as though they were mourning someone of note. Food was plentiful, brought daily by the old women, and even uncle's wife, sitting with the women, but for a while, at first, somewhat aloof, finally broke down and joined in conversation with the others, some of whom had once been friends and acquaintances, before the bliss of financial fortune had proved her of superior clay. She even deigned to ask after their families and mention her own grown children, once she had allowed herself to relax, and was pleased at their simple gratitude that she hadn't forgotten those whom she had once known. Once the barriers were down she could also, with a few compliments, bring the conversation around to one or two delicious things she had been tasting, and to ask, with the air of conferring favours, for the recipes. The old women were delighted to have something to give to the grand lady, and freely parted with their pinches of this and handfulls of that. In return she was persuaded at last to tell them the secret of the cake which she herself had brought, and was even candid enough to confess, rather touchingly, that though in making the cake, she usually used a dozen eggs for it to be really successful, she had unfortunately, this time, run short of eggs and had used only nine, which explained why the cake was not quite what it usually was. Still, she had left herself without an egg in the house, rather than scant more than three.

The other women assured her that her cake was indeed as good, every bit as good as though it had the required dozen, that the trick was always how you handled the materials, and not exact amounts, and Auntie allowed herself to be persuaded, and gave them the recipe all over again, going through all her magic cooking gestures as well, and received many compliments all over again. When she left, the old women expressed their delight at having discovered that rich though she was she was still as stingy as ever. Imagine cheating a cake of three eggs! It was enough to reconcile you to your own poverty. She had obviously never put a whole dozen eggs into a cake in her life, even for her rich guests, though her husband probably picked them up for nothing while he was out robbing the farmers of their grain. And who believed there were even nine eggs in her cake, anyway? Whom did she think she was fooling? One particularly virulent little old lady, who had parted, in a flush of good feeling, with her favourite recipe, defied anyone to try to tell her that there were more than four eggs altogether in the cake. In fact if there were four there were a lot. Why, the sawdust was hardly holding together! Still, for all that she was stingy and a bit of a fool with the airs she put on, she wasn't a bad sort. And she hadn't been so foolish it turned out, to take big Nate with his warty hands after all, when no other girl would look at him. Not that he gave her much of a life, from what you heard, but she was no great bargain either, so they were probably well matched.

Hoda, who had seldom seen her great-uncle and aunt in her life, felt that she ought now to show her disdain by some act of rudeness which would make them realize that she knew all about them. But when it came to it she was too frightened, too much intimidated by something real that they represented, something which, she could tell by the attitudes of those about her, really worked in the world. So she smiled eagerly whenever Uncle looked her way, pulled in her stomach and answered demurely when Auntie remembered to speak to her, was sorry when they were leaving because everyone would act more ordinary again, and was sure she hated them twice as much when they were gone. She consumed nearly all of Auntie's dry cake all by herself, telling herself as she ate that they were lucky that she didn't want to be mean during mourning, or she'd have shown them she was somebody and maybe they'd be nicer to her and Daddy after that. Maybe now they'd be nice anyway, because they were sorry they never helped and Mamma had to die.

Hoda ate an enormous number of good things that week. Every time she thought of her mother she went and ate something. There were things to eat she had never even tasted before. With no one to regulate her, even in the very minimal way that Rahel had taken to doing, because the child herself had sometimes complained that other children made fun of her because she was fat, she preyed on the food. Altogether it was an exciting week for her. There were people in the house all the time, more than had ever been at one time before. Everybody was nice, and very solemn when they remembered where they were. Only she herself, Hoda, was afraid that she wasn't showing the right feelings for the occasion. They all looked at her with such long, sad looks and shakings of the head and said things like "Poor little orphan," and some of them turned red around the eye rims when they said it and put their handkerchiefs to their eyes, and she felt that she ought to cry too when they did and feel terrible, and sometimes she did, she really did, but sometimes, though she tried to squeeze the right feelings out of herself at the right time, she couldn't find them, and pretended, and felt just awful about it. So she forced herself through elaborate mental contortions, trying to feel what it was like to be dead, to be like that mound that had lain under the cloth in the living room the first night, with candles at its head and Daddy and everybody sitting around it and Daddy and his friend the shahmus sitting alone beside it all night long, and she had been glad and hoped they wouldn't fall asleep because if they did it might get up and walk right into her room and she'd die of fear and scream for her mamma, and then what would it do? Would it say, "I'm your mamma!" And would she have to put her arms around it? Yes, she would have to; she ought to be glad to. You have to love your mother even when she's dead. What would it feel like? But her mother wouldn't do that, she wouldn't come; *"please mamma, I want you I do, but . . ."* Her mother didn't want her to be scared.

What would it feel like anyway to be dead, cold, still, without breathing or anything? Once or twice she managed to frighten herself thoroughly, when, after much concentrated imagining, she caught a glimpse of her own cold corpse with herself not in it. She didn't want to be dead that way! But her revulsion was an insult to the dead, an insult to her mother. She must be a bad, an awful person, because only briefly, at scattered moments, did she really have a terrible feeling, the realization in her stomach that her mother was lost and gone, which she recognized as grief. She tried to hang on to it when it came, for it was a right way to feel though it was awful, but as soon as she sought to reassure herself and others by showing its presence, it was gone, and a kind of gladness, because she was feeling the right way, was there instead. So she caught herself in her own badness again and felt wretched and went again to have something to eat.

By the time the last day of mourning came she was terribly bound up. She spent a good part of the forenoon locked in the closet, bellowing for her mother with utter sincerity. When she was through she was too embarrassed to come out, and was, unbeknownst to herself, the cause of a humiliating accident to one old man who had waited patiently and too long, for her to vacate the bathroom. As a result, just as he had finally bethought himself of an alternative, and had taken a hasty few steps toward the door of the summer kitchen, he was caught short, and had, after a helpless pause, without stopping for goodbyes, to shuffle his way uncomfortably out of the house, leaving his wife to mop up while the other old ladies, eyes tactfully averted, muttered sadly about what becomes of us all.

When Hoda did emerge finally, it was at the prompting not only of the soothing, motherly voices of the old ladies on the other side of the door, and their reminders that it was lunch time, but also of the defiant thought that anyway they could tell from the way she had been crying that she really did miss her mother.

They were surprised, the old ladies who came to show her how to cook, at how well she could already do things. Because her mother had taught her, that was why she already knew, so she could take care of Daddy when her mamma went away to the hospital. She knew all kinds of ways to stuff all the nicest parts which were also the cheapest, because some people didn't know what to do with them, like spleen and lungs and guts and how to make soup from fish heads and bones they gave you cheap because they had to throw them out anyway. Her mamma had thought of everything. Even Uncle was surprised, when Danile tried to press on him, once the shiva was over, a small wad of dollar bills.

Uncle didn't laugh right in Danile's face; it would have surprised Rahel to discover that he was not quite so coarse as that; but, as he told his wife, he almost did. "It's good to be blind, I can see!" said Uncle. "He actually thinks that couple of dollars of his is enough to pay the expenses! He says she was saving it for her operation. A tooth she could get pulled, maybe, by a butcher-dentist, for that coupla bucks."

"Did you take the money?" asked his wife who had little sense of humour, which was one of the many things he disliked about her, though what he disliked most was the fact that she had accepted him when three more attractive girls had turned him down, and proved thereby that she had a far shrewder business sense not only than those three others, but than he had himself. If he had had more sense he would have waited till he could afford one of the others. Well, at least she had appreciated his worth. And about money, anyway, you could talk to her, though she always wanted to know too much.

"What do I need his pennies for?" he snarled. "I told him to keep them. He'll need them. He's my nephew, after all. His mother saved to send me here, before she married that rag-and-paper tailor scholar of hers; a fine, strong woman like her has to go meddling with the Torah and Talmud types to bring cripples into the world." Uncle had actually been rather proud of his sister for marrying a learned man, until the scholarly Benyamin first gave hint of some basic inadequacy by dying young and leaving Malka a widow with a son to raise. But it was not until he'd had the shock of meeting Danile that Uncle realized what thinning of the blood by coupling with a word-niggler can do.

His wife knew better than to argue when he began to rant about in one of his moods. "You know best," she said, with enough lack of conviction to infuriate him.

"That's right!" he stormed. "I know best! Who else knows best? Somebody else around here knows best, maybe?"

She was silent.

"About my headaches I know best," he muttered gloomily.

"I wish my children had eaten as well," she remarked tangentially, applying the needle with skill. "We were too poor to provide banquets for them all day long."

But Uncle was not in the mood to be pushed. If he allowed her to antagonize him he might do something to spite her that would be against his best interests. "Listen here, you," he said, "you open your yip once more and try to tell me that I haven't been a good provider, plenty, over your head when others didn't even have the taste of saliva in their mouths, and I'll hand you a reminder you won't forget. Are you trying to call me a poor man because all your life you'd rather feed the bank than your own kids? You think I don't know you? You and your whole damn skinny stingy family. Just let me hear you open your mouth once more about my family, go ahead, and I'll put such a rose in it you won't be able to chew around the thorns for a week!" Uncle was not really a physically brutal man; he didn't have to be; he had discovered long ago that all he had to do was threaten, and she would retreat with gratifying haste. He enjoyed threatening, was rather vain about his skillful turn of phrase as a threat maker. That shut her up good! What he never realized was that once she had pushed him to the point where he was making threats, she felt no need to continue, for she knew she had planted the right feelings to counteract any foolish impulse of his that might incline him to make a generous or otherwise unbusinesslike gesture. Some prickly plants grow best on very little water, and she knew that she didn't have to, even had she dared, remind her Nate too often that she had advised him against bringing over his nephew and his family in the first place. Nate was not a man you had to remind of his mistakes. Just put him in the right mood and he would remind himself how he had been taken advantage of all his life. And it was not hard to put him in the right mood. She knew her husband. *Oh yes,* as she often told herself, *I know my woes.*

Uncle's problem now was pressing but really very simple. Some money would have to be spent; he was reconciled to that. The question was how to get the most out of that money. His wife maybe thought he was a damn fool, even after all these years of watching him perform his magic trick of sacking grain and ransacking gold. No, you couldn't talk to a woman like her after all. She didn't understand that there are other kinds of profits a man can look for in the community, once he has his dollar in his pocket. Uncle Nate was a man who measured his own felicity by what he imagined happened to be the state of mind of the great segment of the community whom he felt were his enemies. For his enemies to know that he could match anyone dollar for dollar, that was sweet; whatever else they said about him, he knew they had respect. But he was capable of a bolder ambition that promised even sweeter rewards. What would the world think of a man who could buy songs of praise for himself on earth and in heaven by giving more money away than his enemies could afford?

If Uncle had a dream that was still precious to him it was to reach that point of security in his wealth someday, when he would be sitting at a banquet in the company of the wealthiest men in the community. It would be a big welfare drive say, or maybe a building drive for a new synagogue, like the one they had a couple of years ago, that had raised from the crumbs and spots on the tablecloths enough money to buy and to renovate the big old house that was now the only Jewish orphanage for nearly a thousand miles in any direction. Speeches would be made by all the recognized leaders, all the big talkers, some of whom could hardly jingle two pennies together in their pockets. He himself was no big talker. He'd sit quietly. Then the pledges would begin. The chairman would read off a few prior pledges to start things off, a lot of little fives and tens from people who couldn't even afford to come to the dinner, and then a twenty-five or two, and then the real giving would begin. So-and-so pledges fifty, so-and-so a hundred, so-and-so two hundred and fifty and he's sorry he can't be here to take part. Well, so are we, so let's give him and his missis a big hand so they should hear us all the way to Philadelphia where they're probably playing with their brand new grandson now. Applause would break out in tribute to the absent beautiful ones, their generosity and the new proof of the continued vitality of their line. Everyone would be in a good mood now for the pledging from the floor. Someone would call out a pledge from one of the tables and would promptly be matched by someone else across the hall. Yet a third voice would match the pledge and alert the company to the fact that the business behind the voice was doing better than had previously been imagined.

Now a new number would vault, inspired, across the tables. "Three hundred!" the chairman would repeat admiringly, while a ripple of appreciation would run through the hall. "A pledge from Mr. Jerry Loshn over there for three hundred dollars!"

"That's mamma-loshn!" a wit would quip, and Jerry Loshn would sit back, grinning modestly, with one hand held up as though to brush aside praise as the assembled company applauded and those lucky enough to share the table with him all grinned at him and shared the warmth, and everyone agreed, except maybe one or two of the speechmakers with golden mouths but nothing but wind in their pockets, that that certainly was mother-tongue talking.

Then the pledging would be taken up in earnest, while the beautiful few for whom the whole hall waited one by one paid for a brief moment of glory on earth and improved their accounts with the everlasting above. After Jerry Loshn, all the men who could show that they were as rich and generous as he would make their pledges, each after his own fashion. Some, like the aforesaid Jerry, would call out their pledges, either boldly, with the gesture of a poker player flinging down a golden hand, and eyes flashing challenges to those about them, or casually, as casual as it is possible to be while yet making yourself heard in a large roomful of excited people. Some would call loudly, under the pressure of an impulse still struggling to free itself from a counter-impulse to shut up and think it over. Some, more restrained, would pass up their bids by way of mouth-to-mouth whispers all the way to the chair. This was a generous, gratifying method, by which the giver was able to share the sweet words with a dozen pairs of lips eager to have the joy of being able to repeat a pledge which their owners would never be asked to make good. It was a method, however, which had lost some of its charm since the time when, either through an accidental mishearing, or through waggish malice on the part of someone in the chain of whisperers, a pledge which had left its owner's lips as five hundred dollars, surely a generous enough amount, reached the chairman and was carolled forth in an ecstasy of gratitude as fifteen hundred dollars, the shock of hearing which, it was rumoured, had brought on the next day the first of a series of heart attacks which had seriously undermined the health of the donor, who could not, nevertheless, renege on a public pledge on the flimsy grounds of having been misheard.

Some of the older wealthy, who considered themselves the apostles of good breeding and manners in the community, disdained to call out their pledges or pass them by word of mouth at all, but sent them up instead, in modestly folded little notes, and one or two, with tantalizing insolence, did not even deign to identify themselves publicly, writing down simply that one or three or even four thousand was pledged by a friend. Auntie Gusia pointedly doubted the good intentions of these anonymous donors, but Uncle Nate knew that the pledges would be made good, that those who counted knew who had made them, as indeed, by a rapid process of elimination, anyone could guess.

It was as the last and largest of these donors that Uncle Nate dreamed that he would one day stand. Even as he shouted out, in the early stages of the pledging, his fifty-dollar promise, carried away by the excitement of it all to the point where he could ignore his wife's continuous complaint about them charging twenty dollars a plate and expecting more donations yet; even as he allowed himself to make this premature pledge in order to forestall, as his wife knew very well, any later impulse to pledge some really preposterous sum, he dreamed that someday he would bring himself to wait, to wait past the hundreds and the five hundreds, to gasp but not cry out among the early thousands, to wait without fear or regret for the cries of admiration that would follow those last two anonymous notes, to wait, even, until the wealthiest of the wealthy, man and wife, made their preeminent way past the chairman and paused briefly, riveted by every eye in the room, to whisper, as though in afterthought, a few words which would electrify the hall as the chairman repeated them incredulously after their casually retreating backs. Then, at this signal that the banquet was over, in the brief instant before the backs of the most superior had quite disappeared through the door, Nate would make his move, big Nate with the warty hands and neck which had long ago been treated surgically though the memory still remained with those who had known him in his youth. Then Nate would indeed make his pledge, and a new head would be crowned in the community. Someday, someday. And he wouldn't shout it out either, if he could help it, though he loved the idea of his voice bellowing out a hair-raising sum. No, he'd do it the dignified way, on a slip of paper to pass up, or maybe he'd come pounding past the tables before the big breaking-up, to climax the climax. Someday, someday, his time would come.

Meanwhile it would not hurt for him to begin to be known about the town as a benefactor of causes to which he had hitherto paid only token attention. "Never mind;" Uncle remarked kindly to his wife, mollified by the rehearsal of his dream; "you'll find your old man's not such a fool in the long run after all."

His wife knew better than to press him for explanations at this point. And it was a good thing, perhaps, for her peace of mind, for it might have troubled her to hear that her husband was planning to become a philanthropist, and she might have earned herself some stormy scenes by warning him in advance that he would get no thanks.

Nor did Nate find it necessary to clarify his remark any further. Once he had formulated a scheme of action it was not his habit to make unnecessary consultations. Only, in fact, when he was not completely sure of his way did he take the trouble to test it by initiating one of those discussions with his wife which he found so infuriating but which, though he was incapable of admitting or perhaps even realizing it, helped him to make up his mind. It would have occurred to him even less, in this instance, since he felt the responsibility was completely his own, to consult those most nearly concerned with his plans.

While Uncle waited, or whatever it was he was doing which prevented him from coming, Hoda waited too, with active impatience. She had listened to the speculations and assertions of the old people during the mourning period, and knew that Uncle should come to their assistance soon. Every day when she came home from school she asked her father, first thing, "Did Uncle come? Was Uncle here?" She hesitated to elaborate her query because she remembered that her mother had never even wanted to think of help from that source. Nevertheless Uncle ought to help them. Everybody said so. He could afford it. When she grew up she would pay him back, every cent, so it would be only a loan anyway.

She spent much time privately guessing how much

money he would bring, what the bag would look like that he would bring it in, and where she would hide it in the house so no one would be able to find it and steal it away from them. He would no doubt bring it in a bag because that's why rich people were called moneybags, unless he brought it in a pot, because Miss Flake said that some people had pots of money. But pots were something like in the fairy stories, that she used to read when she was a kid, that you found in caves and were filled with gold and jewels. Her expectations from Uncle were somehow more modest. Bags were more of a natural graduation from where the money she knew came from, tied in the corners of handkerchiefs. And anyway, she'd heard the old women say that he had "sacks" of money, which were more like bags, really. The sacks came from him being a grain merchant, and exchanging grain for money, a transaction which the old people viewed, on the whole, with mistrust, as it was too successful to be honest.

But Miss Flake knew better about things like that. That was another reason why Hoda was anxious to see Uncle again. She hadn't known before how important he was, until Miss Flake explained about the grain exchange, how it was one of those key institutions, like the stock market, which kept our country alive. Miss Flake had drawn a seed of grain on the board and spent a whole lesson explaining that the economy of our country was firmly balanced on this sand of grain. On such sands of grain our country stood tall and firm like a prairie elevator, and fought bravely in the world overseas. The children couldn't help but be moved when Miss Flake uttered beautiful phrases through her earnest teeth and every now and then flashed her radiant, luminous smile at the class, which made them all feel like standing tall and proud like prairie elevators. Miss Flake had a gift for the hectic metaphor, and when she was really moved to throw herself into her teaching, so the children would never forget what she had to say, she used it extravagantly. It was this very gift for passionately conceived and stirringly delivered litters of metaphor which fascinated the children and helped to earn her the reputation of being one of the best teachers in the school.

No wonder, then, that Miss Flake's lesson on the grain exchange was a revelation to Hoda. She was surprised that no one had given her to understand the significance of Uncle's profession before. She had not known that being a grain man meant being in the grain exchange and so important, and she surged to her feet eagerly in class to testify that her uncle, her daddy's very own Uncle Nathan, who had come to her house every day during the mourning, was himself one of those same men who kept our country alive, and for a moment she felt as though she had restored some of her family's lustre, which she feared had been somewhat dimmed in her teacher's eyes of late.

Not that Miss Flake hadn't been nice to her when her mother died like that. She had really been very nice and kind. She had even, once, put an arm around her and rubbed her bristles against Hoda's forehead, and Hoda would have liked to respond with a distinguished display of grief, but all she could feel was a momentary gratitude, and an itch in her forehead which she couldn't twitch for fear of offending her teacher, so she sucked her lip instead, and Miss Flake gave her another squeeze around the shoulders and said tenderly, "That's it! Stiff upper lip!" And she could see the other kids were looking at her in a particular way when she went to her seat, and they really were nice to her and talked in special soft voices to her all during recess.

If they only knew! Well, they ought to know. They were

nice to her now. Maybe they would be nice from now on. But if they really knew they would never be mean to her, ever again. And Hoda began to wonder whether she shouldn't perhaps tell Miss Flake and the rest of the class how much more there was to it than they could possibly imagine. She would have liked to let them know somehow, especially now, since the Russian people had let the team down and Russia was doing so badly in the world picture. The Russian army had turned against our noble ally, the Czar, and was even trying to desert the family alliance against the vile Kaiser. Hoda had never been so confused in her whole political career. Not that Miss Flake had ever said anything to indicate that she blamed Hoda or her family in any way, but Hoda felt that her stock had fallen, somehow, by implication. One part of her was not really very surprised, however, because in one part of her she had known all along how people felt about the Czar. Her mother had always said he was no good, and even her father, while he was inclined to agree that the Czar's family feeling in his relationship to his cousins the King and Kaiser might be unexceptionable, felt nonetheless that when it came to Jews and ordinary people the Czar somehow did not have the right attitude. But then, of course, he was surrounded by all sorts of evil advisers and you really never could tell how much he even knew of what was going on. But now he was gone altogether, and nobody knew where he was or the princes or anybody, and Miss Flake prayed for them and talked bitterly of going it alone without the Russians, and Hoda was no longer at all sure of her own position in the world of Miss Flake's values.

She didn't even know what side to have her grandfather Shem Berl fighting on any more, because Daddy's friends all felt that the revolution served the Czar right, and her teacher at Jewish school was so happy he rushed around crazily on one spot acting out the worker's struggle and the Red Army and freedom for all the nations of the world. At the same time wouldn't Miss Flake feel it dreadfully disloyal of Shem Berl not to stand by his Czar unto the death? How she longed to jump up in class and comfort Miss Flake in her disappointment, by crying out that her grandfather, Shem Berl the warrior, for sure had leaped into the breach and sunk, gallantly defending his lion-hearted Czar, taking at least a dozen of the treacherous traitors with him to heaven before going back to the mending of his pots for the proud and free new army of the workers of the world.

One day Hoda asked her father what side he thought that grandfather Shem Berl would be fighting on and Daddy said he didn't know; it depended on who forced him; and anyway it was so long since they had heard, for all he knew Shem Berl might not even be alive anymore, but even if, as he hoped, the old soldier was still alive, surely his fighting days were over. That was what the revolution was for, to see that such injustices as this dragging about of old Shem Berl and his pots from war to war should be put to an end. Well, that much was a relief, to find that she could honourably retire him from the line of battle, without having to subject him to a political choice which might upset Miss Flake. And her mother would have been happier about it too. Her mother was more right than Miss Flake, Hoda decided, about a lot of things. If her mother had lived, and she had been able to have her birthday party, in a couple of week's time, Miss Flake would have come maybe and her mother would have told her the truth about a lot of things, and her father would have told her about a lot of things she didn't know about either. Perhaps now it would be up to Hoda. Particularly when the kids began, so soon, to forget that they ought to be nice to her, Hoda began to wonder whether she shouldn't enlighten them once and for all. But she hesitated, even though Daddy told her about it again a lot nowadays, and reminded her of all kinds of things she had almost forgotten. She hesitated because it was her special knowledge and it set her apart from them inside, where she could get away from them all whenever they were mean. Sometimes she thought, *if they knew they'd never be mean again;* but she wasn't always so sure, and something inside her didn't want to use it on them as a weapon, but rather, wanted someday maybe to give it to them as a gift, when she didn't even have to, and they would always go on liking each other after that, forever.

Rich Uncle Nathan and his position on the grain exchange were something different. He belonged to the world of daily profit and loss that they all shared. So she could boast about him and show off a little about what he might give her and not even care what they said. They didn't have to believe her, she had the whole grain exchange on her side.

She even told the gentile ladies from the blind club all about how Uncle was going to help them, and maybe even give them money to open a little basketry shop someday, that time when the ladies came to find out why Daddy hadn't been to the basket-making class for such a long time, when he was even getting good enough to be promoted to chair bottoms.

That was a surprise visit. Danile had not expected it at all and was impressed by the courtesy of the Christian ladies. They came on a Saturday and Hoda ran to fetch him from the synagogue, where the other men were much impressed to hear that he had gentile visitors, and some of the older ones even made a point of coming over to say goodbye to him, almost as though they never expected to see him again, though they were somewhat eased in their minds when they heard that these were only two women.

When Danile, after his initial resistance, had resigned himself to venturing among strangers in order to please his wife, he had simply accepted the basketry weaving class and all it entailed as an extension of his area of living and had made himself as comfortable as possible within a situation which was even more severely limited than usual. Rahel had been surprised to discover, the first time she took him to his class, though she did not tell him, for fear of upsetting him, that the place into which she led him was the basement of a church. She sat through that first lesson with him uneasily, and with some anxiety, particularly when, for the entertainment of their little group, as the ladies explained, one of them sat down at the small organ and blew forth a hymn or two, and all those present raised voices in song. Rahel was relieved to note that her Danile did not react as though there were anything amiss in this, and even showed signs of a willingness to hum along. Since he neither complained nor asked for explanations, Rahel, who was herself made markedly uneasy by the engulfing organ tones and what struck her as rather lugubrious music, thought it best not to enlighten him about a fact which might, if Danile decided to balk, undo all her long efforts of persuasion. The main thing was that he was here at last, learning a trade, and since these people had been kind enough to accept him as a student, he might be left safely in their hands even in this place.

Indeed, Danile's incursion into their lives was more trying by far for the ladies of the guild than it was for him. The whole enterprise in social service was a daring foray, on the part of the good ladies, into the world of the flesh, their aim being to comfort and succour the blind in this life and to catch their souls firmly in the gentle net of piety, and to save them from straying, in their early blindness and despair, in a direction which might sever them eternally from restoration of the only light which really counts in the long run. Having determined their short and their long-range ambitions, the more indomitable spirits of the guild were loath to limit them when a strange fish indeed wandered into their net, through the accident of Rahel having heard from the Christian neighbour of one of her customers something of the practical side of the project. Danile's arrival as a member could fairly be interpreted as a test of their strength in God, and under the firm guidance of their pastor, who pointed out that after all the Son of God was one of Them, they set out, not precisely to proselytize, for that would have been difficult. As yet they had no technique for the proselytizing of a blind Jew who spoke no more than a few words of their language. No, they limited themselves to the more modest aim, for the time being, of making him feel at home in the basement of the Church of God, till such time as he might be deemed capable of further ascent.

Danile responded well to the music. It was natural to him to sing while he worked, as his father had done before him. In fact, the whole situation, in which he found himself increasingly more capable of performing a blessedly useful task with his hands, roused up in him memories of old songs not heard or even thought about for years. It even occurred to him after awhile, when he had begun to feel more at home in this place, that his companions might like to learn a new tune occasionally. Accordingly, he waited politely one day for a break in the organ music, and when he felt the appropriate time had come, he obligingly offered them a few Yiddish ditties in his not unpleasant cantorial tenor. His interpolated offerings were at first greeted by a shocked and embarrassed silence on the part of the ladies who ran the guild, though the other blind members smiled and nodded their heads in spontaneous response, and some even laid down their strips and clapped a little when he was through. The ladies were particularly uneasy about the possibly blasphemous content of the songs, about lutings too suspiciously gay, or complaints too foreign and even too sinister perhaps, to be heard in the basement of a church. Nor did they know, though wishing to be polite, whether it was the right thing to clap when his first "tumbala yahy-ti tahy-ti tahy-tums" and weird lutings of the voice had ceased. But Danile expected no particular attention as a result of his offering. He continued to hum away cheerfully, happy to imagine he was being allowed to make himself at home.

Unfortunately, some of the ladies felt that he was perhaps making himself too much at home. There was an activist faction among them which responded to his songs as though to a hostile invasion. One determined little soldier of God set herself to combat, single-handed, the possibly evil spiritual effects of the Jew's singing, by playing a non-stop marathon of hymns on the organ during the entire period of Danile's next visit. The campaign did not have quite the desired effect, however. Danile, who took this to be music particularly related to the blind of this country, and found it strange and sad, though sometimes full of life and spirit, and sometimes even comical in a way, was perfectly happy to sing along. It was not until the other blind got tired of singing and the little body at the organ played determinedly on, that the ladies were able to hear that Danile was fitting his own words to the music, which was, in fact, quite natural, since he did not understand theirs.

It was a lucky thing, perhaps, that Danile had no notion of the jarring effect it had on the ladies to hear their beloved hymns set to strange new lyrics. "Oiyoiyoi's" and "ayayay's" played themselves off against the solidly beating notes, with an occasional "Gottinyuuuu!" rising to a wail above the organ's hum. Fearful of a further incomprehensible blasphemy, the little warrior of the organ, urged by her sisters of the guild, gave up the battle finally, and let their Jew go back to singing his strange incantations to his own native melodies. At home Danile, as he sat practising his work, would sometimes burst forth with a tune which would cause Hoda to say in surprise, "I didn't know you knew that hymn too, Daddy. Grade four sang it at the concert."

To which Danile would reply, "Oh yes, it's a song of the blind. They play it all the time at our school."

And occasionally, as these things are wont to turn out, one of the more musically suggestive evangelical ladies would also burst forth in her own home with an exotic melody, accompanied by tentative vocables, daringly spun from her tongue: "die yay ti tie ein shneider-ing dee yoi yoi yoi yoi Gottinyu!" She would catch herself at it uneasily, uncomfortable in some vague apprehension that she and hers were not alone in heaven and on earth, and might even be seduced to make themselves at home anyway. She would remind herself again of what the pastor had said, about the Son of God having been one of Them. In some ways it was a good thing it had all happened so long ago, and the foreignness had had time to wear off.

It was therefore a relief to some when Danile didn't turn up at the guild for several meetings consecutively, but after a while some of the ladies on the follow-up committee became a little uncomfortable about his absence, almost to the point where they actually missed him and realized that they would miss him in the way of unfinished business until at least they knew what had happened to him. Perhaps the poor man was ill. Some gesture should be made. And so one Saturday two of their members adventured forth into the unknown north-end of town, pushed their way up a weedy path, mounted four rickety steps and picked their way across a skew-warped verandah to rouse from within the old shack a grossly fat adolescent with a fresh and eager face who invited them into the dark interior enthusiastically, then excused herself and thudded past them out the open door, across the creaking verandah boards, leaped, like some briefly airborne dirigible down the four steps, to land with surprisingly no crash on the path below, and trundled off with unexpected speed out the yard and down the street, to return very shortly with their familiar blind man in tow.

It was Hoda's first experience as hostess to total strangers. They were rather odd old ladies, stiff and unfamiliar, who spoke to you with squared-off words, like teachers, and with the foreignness of the majority, a little fearsome in that you could never rely on any balance of its shifting elements of ingratiation, condescension, confidence, contempt, and what sometimes even felt like fear. Maybe they were a little afraid, like some kids were, of coming into a blind man's house. But Hoda wasn't going to be afraid of them. They must be nice; they had come. Maybe they were hungry. She offered them some stuffed spleen and potatoes she had cooked up for supper. When they had refused several times, politely, without even allowing her to coax them over to the pot to show them how good it looked and smelled, she was disappointed. Nevertheless she told them all about her mother's ailment, and when they showed they were really interested she went into detail, including all the speculations she had overheard from the old ladies, for no one had bothered to explain to Danile what Rahel had actually died of. As far as they knew she had died of the operation. But the story of her illness was an impressive one, as Hoda told it, enough to have killed five women. The old wives had been free with their diagnoses. Hoda laid before her visitors, besides the old tumour big as a watermelon, the possibilities of a pustulent liver, a gangrenous gall-bladder, a suppurating spleen, and a digestive system which had turned utterly to stone, too much stone to be chopped away, alas, when they finally opened her mumma up. Hoda told all this in an eager, positive voice. The information was impressively mystifying to the ladies, since Hoda didn't know the English words for many of the hidden parts of the body she was naming, so she named them in Yiddish, the very foreignness of which gave the whole rendition, to the ladies, a medically authentic, if ominous sound. Hoda was not, in fact, quite sure of what some of the names referred to anyway, although when she got to the story of the disintegrating spleen she had an inspiration and this time succeeded in dragging them over to the pot on the stove to show them what she meant, at the same time contriving to reveal in a sufficiently offhand way, that she actually did know how to cook, in case they really were hungry and too polite to say so. She was unaware of the effect which the sight of the grey skinful of spongy, stringy purple stuff in the pot, well spiced-up, of which she was so proud, following hard on her medical revelations, had on her father's guests, for she was not much more than a child, after all, and was genuinely disappointed when they, even now, refused to sample her cooking.

Perhaps they'd have some tea, then?

Again the ladies, after an exchange of ambiguous glances, refused, on the grounds that they must be running along soon.

They had funny manners. Even when her mother used to beg her, when they went to visit, not to eat everything in sight as soon as it was offered, there was always a point at which it was the right thing to do to gratify your hostess, and almost worth all that hard self-control. So Hoda pressed them, again and again, to have tea, redoubling her pleas the more they refused, bringing out everything in the house, and realizing as she did so, that it was little enough to tempt a guest. Nevertheless it made her feel hungry, but she knew that she mustn't eat unless they did and she couldn't understand why they wouldn't touch anything, not even one little thing, and she began to worry that maybe they had noticed that one of her fingernails was dirtier than the rest, which she had only just now noticed herself. She tried to bury her hands in her lap and worked at the dirty fingernail with the thumbnail of her other hand. Meanwhile Daddy was urging her to tell them what a good student she was and how she liked to study. So she translated for him, modestly, and then with a certain resentful boastfulness in response to their too polite little ohs and ahs. Why wouldn't they take something to eat anyway?

"Ah, study, study!" Danile beamed as Hoda translated the pregnant words and he heard their undecipherable murmurs in response. How well she spoke their language. She could hold her own with them all. Clearly they were as impressed as he was proud, for the child was doing most of the talking.

If the ladies were, in fact, somewhat unpleasantly impressed, they were certainly too polite, as far as they knew, to show it. At a certain point they simply began to concentrate their combined longings and even the direction of their movements in their chairs toward the grey front door. They waited, with scarce concealed impatience, for Hoda's chattering hospitality to flag, signalling each other with minimal gestures but with increasing frequency, that the moment was now, in which to rise in unison and make their retreat. Their movements did not escape their young hostess, and perhaps it was as much her reaction to her own relief at the imminent removal of these ungiving presences, as it was her desire to draw from them some unequivocal acknowledgment of their value, hers and her daddy's, that compelled her to renew her gestures of hospitality and redouble her anecdotal flow every time they made a move to go.

Mixed though her feelings were towards these stranger ladies, they didn't crystallize to the point where Hoda consciously knew that her guests were recoiling from her. The simple fact would have been too hard to assimilate, for she did not know what else she could have done to make them feel at home.

As for the ladies, even had they been more analytically inclined, or perhaps less determined in their charity, they would have been unable, until the end, to put their fingers on any one precise reason for their uneasiness which they could comfortably accept. Hoda herself unwittingly supplied them finally with a formal shape for their discomfort. One of the kindly souls had actually just had the splendid idea of suggesting to the other members of the church guild that they ought to make some Samaritan gesture, such as perhaps fixing up a food hamper of decent, civilized food, to send these poor strange people. She was thinking warmly in this vein, that this was the first thing she would say to her companion if they ever managed to get out of here, when Hoda made the mistake of answering some polite inquiry with a vigorous and daring expression of her youthful sophistication. "Oh hell, no!" she said, in a grown-up, woman-to-woman way. Her ejaculation brought the charitable guest sharply back from the edge of the abyss which separates the saved from all those others. The visitors glanced horrified epistles and exhortations at each other. Hoda prattled blithely on, neither aware that she had shocked and offended them by referring with such blasphemous familiarity to the residence of the immortal enemy, nor that, in doing so, she had in fact put them finally at their ease. It is a relief to the righteous to know that their repugnance is God-given. They knew now why they wanted to escape. And they managed it now, firmly, but with a new spurt of cordiality, so that Hoda was assured that the visit really was a social triumph, and that she had acquitted herself very well, even though the funny ladies still hadn't eaten anything. They were especially effusive in their invitations to Danile to come and visit the class sometime, urging him not to make a stranger of himself, and of course to bring his daughter, too. There was much to be learned in their little centre, besides the weaving of baskets, much that could help give meaning to a young girl's life, for God is everywhere. Salvation awaits. The lost will be found. So much the ladies could still promise, courageously, even as they retreated from the abyss. Hoda, on her part, promised with enthusiastic and only partly recognized insincerity, that she and her father would certainly return the friendly visit. If people were nice, but they still made you feel uncomfortable, well, maybe it was because you weren't used to them that the things they said sometimes sounded creepy.

Good feelings arose in response to expressions of good feeling and finally the guests hurried away, bubbling with dreadful things to talk about. By this time Hoda was simply ravenous. Perhaps it was a good thing that she was never to know that she had succeeded in talking herself out of a new culinary experience. For the ladies no longer thought in terms of food hampers. Instead, the guild decided to concentrate on the succouring of two starved souls, and shortly afterwards, the first of the mysterious evangelical pamphlets began to arrive, which were to plague Hoda and her father for years, and were particularly irritating since Danile never found a letter in the mailbox without hoping that it might contain some news from the old country, and sometimes, before he learned to recognize the feel of the paper, he waited for hours for Hoda to come home, only to hear at last that it was just some more of that Jesus stuff. Hoda came to look on the religious tracts as hostile acts, perpetrated by an unknown and vindictive enemy that she swore she would someday publicly unmask. For a long time her suspicions were centred on some gentile neighbours down the street, who kept to themselves, she felt, in a guiltily secretive way. Accordingly, she never failed to seize the opportunity, if she thought any member of this family was within earshot, to express her conviction, as loudly as she could, that in God's eyes it was preferable to be a Jew above everything else, and that she and her daddy wouldn't dream of being anything else but Jews, and it was a pity some other people didn't know anything about being Jewish. These neighbours finally moved out of the neighbourhood, an action which Hoda saw as variously indicative of guilt and, perhaps more accurately, of defeat. When the tracts continued to arrive, even after the removal of the putative perpetrators, Hoda more than once darkly remarked that they were lucky she didn't know where they'd moved to, or they'd get a piece of her mind all right.

Had she known that the tracts were substitutes for real food, particularly at that tight and chancy time in their existence, and were the direct result of her own hospitality, she probably would have considered them even more bafflingly punitive. For she would never have dreamed of offending her guests. She would have died, for instance, rather than say "fuck" or "shit" in their hearing, at least at that time in her life. She had too much respect. One thing Rahel could rest in peace about, as Danile told himself that triumphant evening as they sat down finally to their meal. She had brought up their daughter well.

If only Uncle had been able to see that this was so. If only he had paid some attention to what they said, had tried to listen and to understand how they felt instead of right away getting mad and saying things like that in front of the child and getting her started that way. You can't frighten a child and expect her to act like an adult. It was true that he had been half expecting Uncle Nate, as the child had been too, though not because they needed help from him; Danile never allowed himself to think that he expected Uncle for this reason, although he knew that when Nate came, help or some form of concrete advice might also be forthcoming. The fact was that Danile had not, as yet, paid much direct attention to the practical implications of their situation. He was still unable to drag his thoughts away from his bereavement, tormented, as he was, by the conviction that he had not comprehended it fully, as yet, and would be sinning against God and his dead to turn away from her prematurely, without having found something in her death to understand.

But he had had a premonition, on that afternoon when Uncle arrived at last, an uneasy tugging at the heart, he didn't know why. Uncle was so pleased with himself, you could feel it in his footsteps. He simply knocked loudly on the door and walked right into the house where Danile sat twisting some straw in a desultory way and quietly conning his inner conundrum, and Hoda clattered about with pots and pans.

"Well Danile," he said, seating himself and sighing a perfunctory sigh. "The question is what to do now, eh?" Uncle sighed again, a pitying sigh which at once accused, forgave, and embraced these inadequates who didn't know. "Well, I've solved your problem," he continued, with such authority that Danile, for a moment, believed that even this might be within the scope of Uncle's mastery. But the feeling which responded to Uncle's words was unaccountably one of dread. It was as though his heart already imagined then what his mind could not conceive. Who would have believed that Uncle, with all his busyness and all his importance, could find room in his heart to hate them so?

For Uncle's plan, which he revealed to them as already set into triumphant motion, was to send Danile to the Jewish Old People's Home, where they also took care of a few cripples, and Hoda to the Jewish Children's Orphanage. They would be better taken care of than they could possibly care for themselves. Uncle could guarantee it himself; they would practically be waited on hand and foot. Hadn't he already personally promised those institutions the largest donations he had ever made in his life?

The last thing Nate had expected was resistance. Perhaps, because he was so taken aback, he was cruder than he might have been at first in brushing aside their misgivings, and later, with all the bull rage of his anger and frustration, in trying to break them down. His fury at their refusal to accept his plans would have been disproportionate, normally, which was perhaps what gave Hoda and her father the impression that he hated them so. Even when, in his rage, he revealed to them how he had overreached himself, because they understood so little the value of large sums of money, they were slow to grasp the enormity of what they were doing by refusing point blank to allow him to separate them. Uncle could not bring himself to tell them that the reason he was so upset was that he had been so carried away by his vision of himself in the role of pure philanthropist, that he had not taken the precaution to make his donations contingent on the entry of his relatives into the relevant institutions. He had made his offer of a gift as a free and generous act to each, motivated, as far as anyone knew, only by the goodness of his heart. If, after all this, these two . . . these two . . . he didn't know what to call them, this freakish pair, his curse, his unmerited punishment from a God who knew he deserved better; if after all this they refused to go, he would have no excuse to renege on his pledge.

Uncle had made his terrible mistake because the thought of generosity, per se, was so attractive to him. The thought of the man who gave, rising up from some dim dream memory of an impoverished childhood was, to him, as the thought of some powerful creature transcending his humanity through the most difficult gesture of all, an act of pure generosity. And Uncle allowed himself, because he was momentarily fuddled by his dream of generosity, a fantasy bad for a man of business, as no one normally had to tell him, though his wife often did, to commit a grave tactical error. A need for purity of motive had survived in him somewhere, and even thrown forth a stunted shoot in the darkness where it had lodged through most of his adult life. Now, choosing this moment, masquerading as vanity, or perhaps it was vanity masquerading as purism, or perhaps it was the offshoot of both that showed itself in him now, it sent him forth, inspired, not to one but to both institutions, first to see the Director of the Home for the Jewish Aged, and then to see the Supervisor of the Jewish Children's Home, to shake hands and sit large and imposing, and to say, after a pause long enough for the trimming of a cigar, portentously, to each in turn, "I've been thinking seriously about this place. I think you're doing good work." And then, containing himself, and allowing himself to be led and shown and told about the good work, hardly hearing, hardly seeing, but waiting for the right moment, savouring the instants till the time came irresistible, and tore from him, untrembling, the words, "I want to make a donation," and, watching for the gladness in his listener's eyes and judging it insufficient, to elaborate, with succinct eloquence, "I mean a *real* donation," and to remain silent, demanding, drawing forth from the other's riveted eyes the first dawning gleams of recognition, of real respect, signs of a certain flinging of the very soul of the man to his knees, where it would remain, doubly and triply humbled by the power of the sum, the life-giving sum before the manifest glory of which no director or supervisor of a charitable institution could help but fall down and weep, figuratively speaking if not in crude, physical reality, while counting off in dazzled gratitude the palpable benefactions this vibrant wad of energies represented to the lesser beings, his unfortunate charges, the unwanted old or the unclaimed young.

It was this purity of response to his gesture that Uncle wanted to preserve as long as possible, the purity of assumption that he was to do all this simply out of the pure and simple generosity of his own naked soul, *for nothing,* as one side of his nature suggested to him sardonically. *They want me to give away my hard-earned cash for nothing, just like that, as if I owe it to them,* while at the same time something in him expanded too, and glowed at the enormity of such a transgression against all that he had worked and schemed and clutched and grasped for. What the hell! Something in him actually, some fugitive impulse actually took joy, briefly and vaguely, in the idea of feeling contempt for what he was bound, by a whole lifetime's dedication, to adore. But he knew too much. Sure, give it away, give way once and entirely to that extravagant impulse to free himself of that self's way of looking at the world, and what would happen? He could see ahead. Here he would stand, in this same place, destitute, without a cigar even, begging this same little hand-rubber to give him shelter too. Whose soul would be forced to its knees then? Let those who didn't have it adore it, and adore, too, him who had it to give away and had the sense to be judicious in the giving.

But the sensation of abandoned giving was sweet, and Uncle found himself, for the time being, incapable of reducing the effect he felt he was producing, by explaining that he intended his donation to be contingent on the acceptance of his destitute nephew and grandniece, each into the relevant institution. His donations, looked at from this vantage point, would not, indeed, appear to be such extravagantly munificent acts, though no doubt perfectly acceptable nevertheless. But Uncle was too hungry, as he rushed, from one institution to another in a single afternoon, fit of the poet on him, for yet another glimpse of himself perfected, to do more than meet effusive gratitude with the cryptic remark, "We'll go into the details later."

But it was the details which proved intractable, hollering and pleading and weeping and deaf to the fact that they were either going to force him to make a fool of himself and renege on a solemn pledge made voluntarily and with large gesture, or give away, lose right down the drain, a lot of money for absolutely nothing.

"I don't want to!" yelled Hoda. "You can't make me leave my daddy!"

— *Grotesque,* he raged internally, fighting the impulse to do violence to all this blubber, grotesque offspring of that cunning little hunchback whose eyes still defied him from the grave in these grey living eyes. But Uncle's rage wavered slightly before the yammering of this four-square creature. There was something of his own in her, something of the largeness of mother and sister, dimly remembered worlds of another self. Nor was the face ugly, and the skin, so much of it there must be to cover all that bulk, what he could see of it was fresh, the face tear-runnelled but glowing.

"Wipe your nose!" he yelled, out of an obscure impulse to protect that skin. But the impulse was momentary. Hoda, frightened by the shout, responded by throwing a temper tantrum, yelling and screaming and howling so that Uncle himself was amazed and taken aback both by the passion of her feeling and the bad language of the natives which she, mere child though she was, had amassed, through which to express it.

"Shame on you!" he roared back indignantly, infuriated by the fact that he was fighting, concretely, not his nephew so much as this yelling, swearing, fat adolescent with the ghost of his mother and sister in her flesh who reduced his firmly based decisions to a mutual temper tantrum of threats and insults in which he finally made a move toward her, to prove he would carry out his threat to thrash her for her insolence if she didn't shut her mouth this instant and she, screaming, flung herself to her knees before her father, wrapped her arms around his waist, and threatened incoherently into his lap, that she would kill Uncle Nate if he took her away from her pa, while Danile stroked her head and murmured distractedly and smelled apprehensively toward the whiffs of cigar smoke that puffed at him from all directions while Uncle raged to and fro, glaring at the great mass heaving and blubbering on the floor, with her head in her father's lap, and beginning to foresee, in unbelieving astonishment, his own defeat.

"Please Uncle," Danile begged.

"Please Uncle," Hoda echoed from his lap, in her still childish bass, thoroughly frightened now at what he would do because of her outburst. For the two of them thought that if Uncle really wished he could make them go; if he insisted on carrying through this proof of the terrible enmity he had now revealed to them, he would really be able to separate them, because he would have everybody on his side because he was rich and one of the indispensable members of the grain exchange on which the whole country rested tall and proud like prairie elevators. Oh, what had she found to boast about there? Why couldn't he have been someone else's uncle? One thing he couldn't do, anyway, and she had told him so when he had threatened to, which was what made him even madder. He couldn't send them back to Russia. "Oh no, you can't!" she had yelled. "There's a war on! That's why!" But they'd all be on his side; for the first time Hoda began to understand that feeling she had felt in people during the mourning, when Uncle was around. It was all a lie, all those other things people said; her mother had known it. All you had to be was rich, and Uncle knew it; he could make the police and the government and everybody come and punish her and her daddy because they were poor and drag them apart and take away Daddy and put her in an orphanage and put him in an old folk's home when he wasn't even old and they wouldn't even know how to walk with him in the way he liked so he could know where to go himself because he hated being led. And Hoda, who was so afraid, knew one thing for sure, that she hated them all.

"Please Uncle," she heard herself choking out once again, begging, and knew she hated herself too.

Uncle didn't give up easily. He kept on trying, but nothing he could say or yell or threaten would convince them that he was not trying to separate them through enmity but for their own good. Finally, Danile, weeping, cried out that he was glad that his mother was dead so she would never have to know that her beloved little brother had, among strangers, contracted the strangers' disease of inhumanity. Uncle was nonplussed and insulted and yelled and threatened some more, and kept talking of all the money they were going to cost him for nothing, and Hoda, raising her swollen, stained face from her father's lap, asked him why he didn't just give the money to them, to which Danile said sternly, for him, "Hush, child, you don't know what you're talking about. We don't need it. We don't want anything." And all the while he spoke Danile was conscious of his terror. All he said sounded false, false his arguments, false his assurances that they would get along, false and puny arguments to pit against Uncle's large and angry conviction that they had no business to make an inconvenience of themselves to others in the world, and at the same time to demand to have their own way.

And finally Uncle said, "All right. You don't need help from me. I promised them that money and nobody's going to laugh in my face. When you get some sense in your heads we can talk about it then. You'll come to me yet with another song on your lips, and you'll see if I'll turn you away then, even though you have to learn I'm right the hard way. You'll see if I'm your enemy then." This last was said in an aggrieved tone and aimed at Danile, whose reference to his sister stung. And besides, though Nate could see that starving them to submission was the only thing to do now, he wanted to leave them an opening for a reconciliation soon. They could whine all they liked about how they didn't need or want any help, but who would be blamed by the world if word got around that they weren't getting any?

The fact that he left them finally still weeping in each other's arms was of minor comfort to Uncle in his frustration. For months after, every time he thought of that scene, he nearly had a fit. At first he determined not to tell his wife what he had done. He tried at first simply to keep quiet about it and yell at her about everything else that now irritated him more acutely, but it was too hard. He needed her disapproval of what he'd done to yell against, just as he needed the release of making his confession. When he told her, finally, Auntie Gusia went into a shock of mourning, and ran to tell her married children that their father had fallen into his second childhood and was squandering their inheritance. She consulted frantically with them and with the light of her eye, her bachelor son, whether it was legally possible to put restraints on him. Her reaction, and the effect which his gratuitous generosity began to have in enhancing his name in the community, were, however, ultimately so gratifying, that Uncle gradually began to recover his confidence in the uniquely favourable fate which sponsored even the apparent errors through which his virtues were at last to be made manifest to himself and to the world.

FOUR

There was a point, during the argument with Uncle, at which Danile lost touch with the words that were being uttered, and heard only bull cries of rage and treble screams of fear and defiance, his own voice wailing uncontrollably in unintelligible concert with theirs, the feelings working against the words, smashing at the formal combinations of sound which tried to give them shape, cries merging with unheard cries, emotions dissolving in a chaos of emotion, the three of them baying in deaf unison of distress. And it seemed to Danile that the three of them were no less helpless than those two other screamers whose anguish had obsessed his mind these past weeks. Why was it that both of the women who had loved and taken care of him in his lifetime had been taken screaming from him? How often since it had first appeared, unbidden in his mind, had the question recurred, its very persistence a denial of irrelevance. Screaming, why did they both have to scream so, each in her terrible way? What could there be behind such screams as theirs but a whole universe of pain? Such thoughts frightened him, for he knew he stood on dangerous ground for an ignorant man. But he could not help remembering those inhuman screams of his wife, echo or continuation of the anguish of his mother, could not help conjuring them up in his head, telling them over in his mind, reliving his helplessness.

What if he had listened to Rahel, had gone sooner to learn to make baskets? Would that have made any difference? Was that what her screams had been trying to communicate? An accusation? Almost, he wished it were so, to keep it personal, between himself and her, to deny the indifference. Over and over he forced himself to listen to those screams in his mind, until the sound of Rahel's voice, so recently heard in life, began to fade away altogether. When he suddenly realized that he could hardly even conjure up the sound of her voice anymore, Danile became even more frightened than before, and forgot why he had been trying to summon up the memory in the first place. Could he then lose still more of her, who was already gone? Gentle Rahel who had girdled his life with warmth of sound and pleasure of touch; was he so leaky a vessel that he could not contain even her memory for long? Urgently Danile had turned to his daughter, had poured out to her once again in a fever of recall the memories of his life with Rahel, the large and the little miracles that proved, surely, that even though she was gone from them the largest miracle of all, the miracle of her existence, had really and significantly taken place. Yes, her existence must have meant something, though he could feel the death of all meaning implicit in the senselessness towards which their own screams and shouts and incomprehensible attempts at self-justification in this battle with Uncle appeared always to be striving, beneath all of those words, pushing always towards that long scream of terror and pain and indifference into which wife, mother, and now self as well seemed about to dissolve.

Long after Uncle had stormed out of the house, making a great clatter as he stumbled over the warped planks and was forced to descend precipitantly down the stairs with quick little steps in order to maintain his balance, the sound of which clumsiness elicited from Hoda a derisive snort through her tears, he sat and listened to the echoes of all their voices merging and emerging and merging again. Late in the night, still, long after Hoda had told him that it was time to go to bed, for nowadays if she didn't tell him he was apt to simply sit on through the intenser stillness that she knew as night, when Hoda lay sleeping deeply after her struggle with Uncle, Danile listened, until his head grew empty of sound and his own long sigh seemed to sweep it through like the prairie wind. Then it was that memory stirred, of itself, and he remembered that Rahel had foreseen this. Rahel had warned him, and tried to prepare him. Rahel had tried in advance, wise, persistent Rahel, to fortify him against the worlds of screams and frightening silence. And he in his stupidity had resisted, had clamped his lips shut and turned his head this way and that, like a child trying to avoid a bitter mouthful that the doctor has prescribed, while its mother darts after his lips with the spoon, patiently coaxing. Blessed Rahel, had she foreseen it all? foreseen Uncle, foreseen even her own anguish, and sought to fortify him, in his ignorance, against this impotence of despair? If this was so, and he could not doubt it, as no other avenue opened itself to his mind, he knew what he must do.

It was not in Danile's nature, once he felt that his path had been revealed to him, to cling to despair. Then and there he made the first move toward the time when he and Hoda would be able to reconstruct from the shambles of that visit the great myth of their heroic resistance to Uncle. Moving quietly, so as not to awaken the child, he slipped out of bed and made his way to the materials through which his wife had prepared their salvation. Lovingly, he ran the lengths of prepared straw through his fingers, felt, measured, twisted, plaited, worked, shaped, and before long had caught himself even beginning to hum. This would not do. He might awaken the child. He made several trips, gathered all his materials, transported them to his bedroom, shut the door carefully behind him, arranged himself comfortably, and set to work. For the first time in a long while he did not think of screams. In fact he had to check himself, occasionally, remembering that he must not sing too loudly, even here, for fear of waking the child. But he soon forgot, and Hoda, awakened, came thudding along the floor to ask, in a frightened voice, what was the matter? Why was he praying in the darkness when it wasn't even today yet? She didn't realize, that first night, that he was already shouldering his responsibilities. He assured her gently that all was well, and sleepy, she stumbled back to bed without having thought to turn on his light. But a night or two later, awakened again, she had come into his room and switched on his light to find her daddy fully dressed and sitting cross-legged, plaiting straw and singing to himself. It was such a shock to see him so, as though all sorts of things went on in the dark where only dreams and shadows were supposed to live, and you could never be sure what would happen if you turned on the light. But she got used to it, and before long she no longer even heard him singing in the night, but slept soundly as before, or perhaps even more soundly, at least for a little while, comforted as she was by the knowledge that Daddy really was going to show Uncle that he could take care of them by himself, even if he had to work day and night to do so.

Hoda helped her daddy as much as she could. She printed signs, "STRAW AND WICKER WORK," "BAGS MADE" and "SEATS FIXED," which she hammered onto big tree trunks in the yard, facing the street. She also made a little notice to put in the grocery window, and one which Yankl the butcher was glad to display in his window for her too. Yankl said that when her daddy had made enough baskets, he'd even take one or two and keep them for sale in the butcher shop. Yankl was always nice to her.

Uncle would find out they didn't need him. God would help. Daddy said it and Hoda believed it. Hoda, however, was young enough to take future miracles for granted, while at the same time she was getting to be old enough to worry about everyday things. How did it work when God helped? Did the breadman, the grocer, the milkman, the butcher help? Of them all the butcher was the only one Hoda knew for sure would help, at least on a barter basis. Not that the others were mean; they had all liked Mamma. Yet they never indicated to her that they would like to make a trade like Yankl the butcher, though she watched for it pretty carefully and was nice to them. She was too shy to offer openly, because she really was not quite sure that it was completely all right, though Yankl always said "What's a little feel, eh?" in his heartiest voice afterwards, as he threw piles of bones and bits and pieces of meat scraps into a paper for her, enough so she and Daddy would have meat and soup, and marrow to suck, for a week.

Yankl himself didn't seem to think it mattered much afterwards, and when she was behind the counter with him he acted as though it was just something that happened to happen while something else important, like cleaning the counter top, was going on, even though he really showed he liked her when he was coaxing her. He didn't even look at her when she did what he'd begged her for, and talked rapidly about all kinds of different things as though he were talking to himself, and rubbed vigorously at the hollowed-out wooden chipping block, and kept glancing angrily at the door, so that every now and then when he said "hard" in a sharper voice, if it weren't for the particularly urgent sound of it she wouldn't have known he was giving her an order. She never talked to anyone about it, of course, because Yankl said it was a secret. His wife wouldn't like it if she knew he was giving meat scraps away, because she liked him to bring them home; but if someone had asked her Hoda couldn't honestly have said that she minded the feel of it; on the contrary, though it disturbed her when it went down like that, suddenly, after all that. But Yankl liked it so it must be all right. Anyway it was worth it to have him for their friend. Besides, she felt sorry for him. Once, she saw him walking down the street, only he didn't see her where she was, and she almost burst out laughing. Just from the expression on his face, his eyes looking around absently, angrily, and the way his hands were moving in the air, and the way he was walking, especially since he didn't have his big apron on, she could tell he was in the same place he went when she was behind the counter with him. She even bet he wished she were there with him, and thought that maybe he really liked her a lot. But he was so old, and married, and even had big kids, to be one of her real sweethearts. So she forgot about it after she got home each time and washed her hands, and thought about cooking supper instead. If he liked it it was his business.

She had more important secrets to think about, especially all that about how a lot of the boys liked her better, sometimes anyway, even than they liked the girls who thought they were their girl friends, because she was nicer than them.

And they didn't care that she was fat, either, when they were liking her. Even though those three big boys from the dumb class, who followed her home sometimes, called her Fatso, they really liked her because they kept talking like that about her things that they couldn't even see naked under her clothes, though she herself could feel them all separately swelling up when they talked that way. But she wasn't going in the back lane with those boys like that dumb Seraphina in their own class used to do all the time before they took her away and put her in a nun's school, and then the boys laughed about her and pretended they had never liked her even though they had all gone in the back lane with her, sometimes even five of them, and wanted to every day. Hoda knew it for a fact because Seraphina had told her herself and had showed her a nickel a man once gave her. Seraphina told her because Hoda was nice and talked to her when the other girls said she was awful and they wouldn't have anything to do with her. They were jealous because the boys they liked did that with Seraphina. They all said it was a bad thing to do, even though they kept talking about it and who did it and read those poems the boys passed around and giggled and said they were awful even though they could make Hoda feel good for hours. Why did they say it was bad when it made you feel so good? Maybe because they weren't as fat as she was they didn't have room for as many good feelings all over them. But Seraphina was skinny. She was just too dumb to pretend something was bad when it felt good. Hoda could pretend; she was just as smart as they were. But she wasn't going to pretend if she didn't feel like it; why should she squeeze all her good feelings down and be left with only mean feelings instead?

When those big boys followed her home and they came to the corner where they usually turned off to go to their own houses, though they always said they would come with her all the way home if she would take them in her shed for a little while, Hoda usually slowed down a little so they wouldn't go so soon. She wasn't afraid, even that time when they rushed her and backed her into the fence, all three of them, and said they'd drag her in the back lane, and grabbed her all over with the big hands they all had except for the pale, thin one with the long fingers that she put her own hands on hopefully when he touched her; she tried to look deep into his eyes, because she knew that princes had long, slim fingers and he might even be the Prince of Wales himself disguised as a dumb yuk.

It always seemed funny to Hoda that you had to love each other in such strange disguises before everyone became nice and everything turned out all right. Wouldn't it be nice if that mean, conceited boy Stanley, in her class, the one she really loved, really loved her too, secretly, and was just pretending to be mean until the time came when he could show it? Maybe he didn't even know yet himself how nice he could be and how nice it would be if he were nice. What if Stanley were to follow her and put his hands on her that way? And what if he begged her to come to the shed? Well she wouldn't! Not after the way he acted in school! Anyway if he were really nice he wouldn't tell even if she did. Not that she cared what they'd say if they knew, all those girls who liked him, even if they were prettier and looked nice in their tunics and were always neat. She could do what she wanted. Some of the girls thought she did it with boys already just because she was friendly with Seraphina before she got sent away and hung around and kibitzed with those rough kids after school sometimes. So what, she wasn't afraid of any of them. But she wasn't going to be like Seraphina. She wasn't going to give Uncle a chance to get her sent to the orphanage like they sent Seraphina to the nun's home. Not that Uncle had to know about what she did. She'd fix anyone who squawked. Any way she was not like dumb Seraphina. Just let them try to send her anywhere and they'd find out.

Think of Stanley instead. Maybe she should try to clean out the shed a little so it wouldn't smell so bad from dampness and rotting old stuff. No, why should she? If somebody really loved you they wouldn't care. They'd know what you were really like. They'd see you weren't really just fat and sloppy with holes in your stockings and stains on your tunic. Those other girls didn't know how it was when you were so poor and didn't have enough time in the day to do all those things you had to do, like keep the house clean and cook for Daddy and wash his stuff too, and sheets and things, and you never had enough mended clean blouses and pants to change to, and the ones you had kept coming apart because they were old and you were growing. They didn't even know how to take care of their daddies, and even if they did, they'd want to play outside sometimes too.

What would happen if she were to let those big boys take her in the shed? She could if she felt like it. Then the boys would come and hang around her yard in the evenings maybe and she wouldn't have to go for a walk just to pass by the house of one of the popular girls where the kids collected on the verandah in the evenings and they always laughed a lot and had fun. They never exactly invited her and Hoda had to pretend to be surprised to see them sitting there, and say "Hi!" as though she never expected to run into them though the way some of them looked at each other she could tell they thought she had really followed them. Well so what, they couldn't prove it. It was a free sidewalk. She could stand there as long as she felt like it, and she did, trying to think of things to say to make them really notice her and keep them interested so maybe they might ask her to come and sit on the verandah too. She knew better than to ask right out if she could come up with them, because that would start all the jokes about the verandah collapsing. Sometimes, though, they were friendly, and let her come up, but mostly she stood on and on, moving her hands over the rough slats or paint-chipped wire offence or gate, laughing loudly in her strident voice if she happened to hear part of a conversation that was funny, never able to figure out how to trigger that gesture of friendliness that would bring her in among them for good.

She had things to do at home anyway. When they all pushed indoors like they did, suddenly, as though someone had given a secret signal, and disappeared to eat or play games in there, even though she had tried to keep them talking because she always had a feeling when it was going to happen, as if they were trying to get away from her, and they left her still standing there, without anyone saying anything to her so she could feel invited and come in too, she felt sorry for them. She wouldn't act that way. And she knew who the ringleaders were too, the ones who didn't want her, and the way the boys acted around them you'd think they were like that too. But Hoda knew better. They weren't, not all the time. But one thing Hoda knew when they acted that way. She wasn't going to clean up the shed for somebody who acted like that Stanley did. If they wanted you to have a clean shed they'd darn well come and help you clean it up, that's what they'd do, if they wanted you to believe they really cared about you enough to get you to go in there with them in the first place. And just to test them out, when those boys asked her again if she'd take them in her shed she teased them right back, "Sure, if you guys want to clean up my stable it's okay by me! I'll come and inspect!" Of course if one of them really wanted to, she wouldn't really make him do it, but then she'd know it was really he, and she'd clean up the shed herself just to show him she really loved him too.

And for a while it became the thing for any boy who wanted to get a quick and easy feel of Hoda, to banter with her in the loud, excited way he couldn't help in spite of the fact that he thought he was whispering. "Hey, Hoda, come over here a sec, naw, a little closer, I want to ask you something in private." And when she came, half pretending she didn't know, half hoping for she didn't quite know what, he would shout hotly in the general vicinity of her ear while his hands tried to rove and maintain a permanent grip at the same time, "Hey, you want me to clean out your stable for you?" And Hoda would tease, giving back chaff for chaff, with a hard-to-control feeling of exhilaration and even, when she got happy enough all over, patting the boy, as she pushed him away, in such a way as to make him spring right back again as though not of his own volition, a bouncing ball, over and over again. That was when they really liked her, and even begged her, and some-times even offered to give her money, and that was how she knew for sure she really wasn't like all those others; she didn't like to say no. It really hurt her to be mean, even though they were mean to her sometimes. She didn't like to see them look that way, when they really weren't joking, their eyes soft and sick and miserable, as though it was all her fault. And it wasn't, either; they started it. They didn't have to come after her if they didn't want to; and besides, they never even said they really loved her, anyway. Maybe they were waiting for the truly right time too, the time she knew must be coming soon, to make up for all those times when she felt so badly. With all her heart Hoda looked forward to those coming times when things would be all better and she would swim around in good feelings always and forever after, instead of feeling so badly so much of the time. She knew the time was coming, knew it even in her bad feelings, which were so awful you couldn't hold still with them. But the good feelings were there too, right under them, struggling to get out. More and more she knew it had to happen soon, and those strong, dense, concentrated, persistent sensations of sweetness that waited to enwrap her with urge and promise through all those many less pleasing moments of her day, let her know, in their own way, that joyous events can commence in humble places, even a smelly old backyard shed for instance, just for instance, and it wouldn't be bad, either, the way some people always said it would because somehow it would turn out all right and you'd get married and he'd be rich and noble and would take care of you and Daddy and get more people to buy Daddy's baskets.

Sometimes Hoda had so many feelings all going on in her at the same time that she felt as though she would burst, and all those feelings that were churning around that way inside of her would come splattering out in all directions like her blood and guts were supposed to in that song the kids had once made up about her eating so much she was going to burst. The feelings were so thick in her they even sometimes pushed up into her mind, somehow, without her even wanting them to. The things that got said in her head, some of them were just awful! An awful thought would pop into her head, without her even wanting it, and she'd have to say in her mind, "No, I didn't mean it," over and over again, to chase away the bad thought and make it all right. Sometimes her thoughts were just opposite to the thought she really meant to think, and they made her feel bad too, because she must be a really awful person to think things like that about wishing people were dead and other bad and scary stuff like that. She didn't know how those ideas even got into her head. She just wanted everyone to be nice to everyone else and the lovetime to hurry up, and people to come and buy Daddy's baskets so there would be money for rent and wood to heat the stove and a new tunic for next fall and maybe a dress or something for now because she wasn't very good at sewing and Mamma's housedress looked funny on her the way she had tried to sew in an extra piece to make it fit. Of course, when the really good time came she would be thin and beautiful like everyone else, and have plenty to eat anyway. If only people would hurry up and begin to buy Daddy's baskets.

It didn't seem to bother Daddy much; he said they had to be patient, but Hoda was surprised and disappointed that all the people for miles around hadn't come rushing in to buy as soon as she had hammered up her signs. Why were they so slow? Once the school year was over, and Miss Flake had bid them all a moving farewell, wishing them good luck, each and every one of them, and bidding them pray for all our sakes for a quick Allied victory, and sending them off, after spraying them with her final benediction, "Have a simply splendid summer," Hoda set out to make sure that people had a chance to get better acquainted with Daddy's handiwork. She took a whole armful of samples out to sell by herself. She walked all the way to the busiest street in the district, where all the people went to shop, and she walked up and down, all the way up to the farmer's market and back. The second time she even wound in and out of the aisles of the open-air farmer's market, beaming broadly and offering baskets and straw bags to everyone she saw. It was fun. You talked to people and people talked to you. Sometimes they shoved you aside and wouldn't listen, but there were always new people to go up to, so you didn't have time to feel badly. More important, she actually sold a straw bag, sold it to a farmer who would only pay half the price she asked for it, though he threw in a couple of tomatoes, but the rest was real money he gave her. And then when she was coming back down the main street and stopping people on the way, that cop came and told her to get away and stop bothering people, because she didn't have a licence to peddle. She wanted to argue with him. This is a free country, isn't it? Some free country! Only what if he took her to the station like he threatened to when he caught her the second time, and they took away Daddy's baskets, or worse still, if they found out who she was and Uncle told them to put her in the orphanage or she would go on breaking the law? Well they'd have to catch her first. Next time she saw a cop she'd scoot before he saw her. Someday she'd tell those police what she thought of them and their free country where they chased you around when you weren't even doing anything wrong but only trying to help your daddy.

It was while she was standing with her baskets in front of the bicycle shop, in the shade under the awning, partly to shield herself from the summer sun, and partly because some boys she knew sometimes came and hung around the bicycle shop window, that a lady who knew her, because Mamma used to work for her, came up and asked Hoda if she wanted to come clean her house sometime like Ma used to. She wouldn't pay so much at first till Hoda got experienced on the job, but if Hoda was a good girl and worked hard and was honest like her mother, she might even get to earn as much as a grown-up someday. The woman's name was Mrs. Pankess and she warned Hoda that the last cleaning woman she had was lazy and used to drink the cream off the tops of the milk bottles if she left her alone in the kitchen, even for a minute, and that kind of thing didn't go with Mrs. Pankess, she wanted Hoda to know right from the start. She turned her milk bottles upside down on cleaning days now so the cream rose to the bottom.

Hoda assured her eagerly that she wouldn't dream of stealing anyone's cream. Her mummy had taught her never to drink from the bottle anyway. And she wasn't lazy; Hoda was sure of that. Not that Mrs. Pankess listened to her protestations. She was too busy telling Hoda all the awful things that cleaning women had done to her. Hoda hadn't realized how things had deteriorated since her mother had died. They just weren't the same anymore. Almost, Mrs. Pankess talked as though she was mad at Rahel for having died and betrayed her personally into the hands of the inferior new breed of cleaning woman. Hoda hadn't realized how important her mother was. She would show this lady that it wasn't true there was no one left to be trusted. She would work hard. She would prove she wasn't lazy. And she would earn a lot of money, all summer, while Daddy was gradually building up his basket business.

After the first time she went to work for Mrs. Pankess Hoda wasn't so sure herself that she wasn't lazy. Could this be laziness that she felt, this ache in all her bones from scrubbing walls and pushing furniture and washing floors in the summer heat for thirteen whole hours and more? Maybe it was, for she had thought she was through with her work and had been eager to go home hours ago but every-time she had wanted to leave Mrs. Pankess kept giving her new things to do. And though she did all those extra things that hadn't even been mentioned before, she was not at all sure that she had convinced her employer that she was really as industrious as her mother had been. Mrs. Pankess complained all day, as Hoda worked, and acted as though Hoda were taking advantage of her as she reluctantly counted out the girl's meagre payment into her eager, reddened palm. But Hoda knew she couldn't have failed entirely, because in spite of all her criticism, Mrs. Pankess said that she would, after all, call Hoda in the next time she needed to give the place a real going over.

Tired and hungry though Hoda was, because her allotted time for lunch had been brief and her allotment of food minuscule, from her point of view, and she had made the mistake of gobbling down the two sardines and the chunk of stale bread very quickly, not realizing that there would be nothing to follow, she was nevertheless elated. Not only was there real money in her hand, but if one woman wanted her and would pay, why not some of her mother's other old customers? Maybe they weren't all as stingy as Mrs. Pankess. Mamma used to talk about her and her stinginess and fussiness, though Mamma had certainly never mentioned the contrasting generosity of Mr. Pankess, well, probably because he wouldn't dare do that to Mamma. Maybe that was why his wife kept calling out all day, from wherever she happened to be in the house, "Manny, where are you?" to make sure he didn't have much chance to do that to the cleaner. Poor old man, with that funny shuffle and stiff arm and buggy-out eyes and mouth drooping down one side; she hadn't even heard him coming up behind her while she was standing on tiptoe on the fourth rung of the ladder, steadying the pail with one hand and scrubbing the wall with the rag in the other, and really scared because the ladder-step jiggled and she didn't like to be up so high. And then when she felt something touch her behind that way, when she wasn't even expecting it and didn't even know he was there, she couldn't help it, she let out such a yipe! and nearly fell off the ladder.

That sure must have scared him, when she let out that yell, because when she looked around, tugging her sweat-wet dress down again with one hand and clinging to the ladder with the other, he was standing there trying to say "shh shh!" out of his droopy mouth, only it came out "sss . . . sss!" And his eyes nearly fell out of his head when his wife called out, "What? What did you say? Manny where are you?" from the kitchen, and he frantically felt in his pocket with his good hand and brought out a dime and pushed it into Hoda's hand, begging her, with his buggy eyes and wordless movements of his slack, stiffened mouth, to be quiet.

"Nothing!" Hoda yelled back to reassure Mrs. Pankess. "I didn't say anything. I was just singing." And she felt like singing, too, the rest of the day, with all that extra money to add to her wages. All that money for just a little poke! Husbands were more generous than wives, that was for sure. She couldn't believe that he didn't intend to try some more, just to get his dime's worth. What if he sneaked up on her again? Why didn't he wait till she was washing the floors? It wasn't fair while she was on the ladder. A person could fall. Hoda could sense his lurking presence in the background as she worked, shuffling about, awaiting a second chance. Once or twice, as she paused to wipe her sweaty face or tug at her clinging damp garments, she caught his glossy eyes on her, and lowered her own modestly and heaved herself back around to her work. It gave her something to think about as she crawled about the house. It also gave her employer something to complain about. "You're slow," Mrs. Pankess commented, at one point. "And why do you keep looking around all the time like that? You'll never get your work done that way. I'm not paying you to play."

Hoda tried to work more quickly. No, of course he couldn't have done it with that stiff arm that hung down at his side. The thought made her shudder, though almost simultaneously she wanted to giggle, at the idea that flashed through her head, that maybe the only times the arm stopped being paralysed was when he saw a girl with her back to him on a ladder. Then it went shooting out suddenly, jab! A whole dime, just for that!

Hoda tried to concentrate on her work, but still she couldn't help wondering at how easily money could fall into your hand sometimes while at other times you had to work so hard. She felt sorry for poor Mr. Pankess, sorry because she was repelled by the look of him, and a little scared, which was a mean way to feel because he couldn't help it, and sorry most of all because he really must have fallen passionately in love with her at first sight, if he couldn't resist coming at her that way. Seraphina only got a nickel for letting that man really do it to her. In a way she was sorry that Mr. Pankess never got a chance to get another feel in that day, not just because he gave her a whole dime, but to make up for the fact that she didn't love him.

That summer was not as busy with cleaning work as she had hoped it would be, though she did manage to get a few women to overcome their distaste for letting a mere child do heavy physical labour, and allow her to help clean their houses. In her favour was the fact that Hoda was so big and fat that it was somehow easier to forget that she was just an adolescent, at least some of the time. She needed close supervision, though, the women said, and sometimes when she opened her mouth she wouldn't close it; that was where the childishness showed. You had to be firm with her. If you didn't keep your eye on her and remind her occasionally of what she was supposed to be doing she tended to moon and dawdle, and given half a chance she would stop work altogether, and with a big, friendly grin on her face follow you around and try to keep you in conversation for hours, talking all kinds of nonsense her head was filled with, poor thing. But she was good-natured, and willing; if you told her to do something she tried to do it, though you did have to watch her. Well, don't you always have to watch them? If only she didn't talk so much! When she caught your eye on her she thought you were trying to be sociable, and it would begin all over again, with her daddy this, her daddy that; such a great, clumsy-looking creature with a bust and belly at that age already that could be hiding twins, heaven forbid. Poor orphan. Well, she was stronger than her mother, that was one good thing when it came to moving the furniture around, though sometimes she was a little too enthusiastic in her movements. You had to keep telling her not to be so wild; she might break something. And the way she wolfed down her lunch it was as though she had come straight from the hungry land. No matter how much you had prepared it made you feel like such a cheapskate to see her dabbing her damp finger on the tablecloth and in her empty plate, to pick up crumbs to lick. Not that she asked for more, but in spite of yourself if you had any heart in you you felt compelled to ask if she was still hungry. And she always was. Well, once you'd asked and she said yes what could you do? You could tell her it wasn't good for her to be so hungry all the time, with all that ugly fat on her, but that was where the childishness showed too, in the sudden rapid blinking of grey eyes that were suddenly watery, as if you were begrudging her instead of telling her for her own good as her mother would have done. So before you knew it, just to prove you weren't begrudging her, you'd almost emptied the ice box. Well, she was an orphan and just a child, practically. It was a good deed to feed her, and people couldn't go around then trying to say you were taking advantage of her, just because you were letting her earn a few pennies.

Hoda herself did not in the least realize that she was being so well fed. But her appetite was not helpful to her aspirations as a professional cleaner, since some women who would have been inclined to overcome their reluctance to hiring a schoolgirl for hard physical work, retained their prejudice against such exploitation in view of the uneconomic aspects of such an appetite in a menial. Anyway, a Jewish girl should find something better to do. Some of the women lectured her, as they followed her about the house, interspersing instruction and criticism with well-meant advice. "Enough your mother had to slave her life away. You think if she were alive she'd want to see you crawling after her up the walls? More to the left there, a little higher; you've left a grey streak. Watch out, you didn't wring out the cloth enough. It's dripping down. Make sure you get all the soap out. What kind of future is there for you? Your mother worked, poor thing, so her daughter shouldn't have to have swollen knuckles. Be careful, you'll tip over the ladder. Isn't it time you should change the water? It's thrown-away work to wash black with black. She had to do it, poor thing; well, her case was different, an immigrant, a cripple. What choice did she have with a husband who was nothing but a burden? But you're a young girl. You can study. You can learn to do something more fitting, so your mother shouldn't have to weep in heaven."

"That's what my daddy says," Hoda would try to express her agreement, though she didn't like it when people called her mother a cripple, right out, just like that, and her father a burden. What did they know about it? "He and my mamma always wanted me to study and learn and stand up in the world like a real human being, and have something to say so things will get better and better for everybody."

But the people who hired her only wanted to talk, not listen. They hardly ever let her finish saying anything. "That's another story. Take my advice. For a young girl you have a little bit too much to say. While you're working it's best not to have too much to say because you'll never get your work done. When you're working, take my advice, it's best to listen and not talk. Didn't I tell you a long time ago to change the water? It's thrown away work to drip that filth on the walls. Get down, get down, I'll hold the ladder. Oi, where did you get such a behind? On a young girl, it's the first time in my life . . . your mother was such a wisp. You should gobble less food, take my advice. What man will marry you? Gogmagog himself would be baffled. It slows down your work, too. Why would anyone want to lug around such a carcass?"

Hoda didn't want to lug around such a carcass. She was used to being told in less than complimentary terms about how fat she was, and she didn't care, really she didn't. But when, interlarded with all that other stuff that all seemed so kindly meant, people said all those mean things, as if she had no feelings and she mustn't open her mouth to say anything, when she was working so hard to please them, as if it was her fault that she looked that way, she could feel the water line rising in her eyes, and she had to keep her head tilted a certain way to prevent it from spilling over and also to prevent her employer from noticing it. That was why she was slow in coming down from the ladder, not because she was so big. She just wished Mrs. Shmantz would go away, though she knew she was right about some things. Hoda didn't want her mother to weep in heaven. Hoda didn't want to climb on walls all her life, and come home with her whole body aching so much she didn't even feel like going out to have fun, and then when she tried to join the girls her age, to discover they all knew she was a cleaning woman, all the kids, and laughed at her as though it was something dirty. Mrs. Shmantz was right about that all right. Hoda wasn't going to do this all her life. But if Mrs. Shmantz didn't like a fat behind coming down at her from the ladder, well, she knew what she could do. Miraculously, Hoda didn't say that last thought, though it was swinging on her tongue and kicking at the door of her hastily shut mouth. Hoda remembered the wages she was to receive and had to let herself be satisfied simply with the thought of uttering that rudeness. Furthermore, if she wanted to lug a big fat carcass around it was her own damn carcass, and Mr. Pankess hadn't complained and maybe Mr. Shmantz wouldn't either, if he knew her.

In spite of the Mrs. Shmantzes Hoda didn't have a bad summer, all in all. It was a busy time. She paraded her baskets up and down the main streets, ever optimistic about making a sale in just another minute, though sometimes days and days went by without one. She became a familiar figure where people congregated to buy and sell, and as such, was at least tolerated by the other regulars, though some found her a nuisance and were irritated by a presence which was more than merely physically obtrusive. For it was not easy for Hoda to endear herself to people, though she tried. There was, perhaps, too much naked hope in her glance. People recoiled, and sought and quickly found, in her looks and manner, justification for their uneasiness. But for Hoda each new human being was an open possibility, and yesterday's people too, though inexplicably unfriendly, were renewed possibilities today. It was fun stopping people and talking to them, and it was fun having to feel alert and as though she had to have eyes in the back of her head all the time, in order to evade the cops, not that they bothered her all the time. Sometimes, even when she was sure a cop had seen her, he didn't chase her, if he happened to be a good guy, or in a good mood, or something. She talked to strangers; she got to know the farmers and the peddlers at the market. On busy market days after she'd walked with her daddy to the synagogue for his morning prayers, she went on with her baskets, straight to the market, where the farmers and peddlers sometimes let her help unload, and gave her things for it, slightly off vegetables and fruit that were only partly gone, all of which she put aside, except for what she couldn't resist nibbling, so that even if she didn't sell any baskets or bags her day wasn't wasted. By evening she sometimes had almost a full basket of stuff that would be pretty good once the bad bits were cut away.

Try though she did to earn enough money, when schooltime came again Hoda still didn't have a new tunic, just the old one let out at all its seams as far as it would go, and cleaned and steam pressed as carefully as she could. It took hours, but it still didn't look anything like a new one. Well, she couldn't help it. More important needs had swallowed up hers and her daddy's earnings as they had come in, and wide-mouthed debts stood waiting to snatch anything that happened to be left over. It was partly because of the tunic that Hoda almost didn't want to go back to school, because it looked so tight and shabby, and everyone else would look so nice the first day, and everything depended on the way you started off, if things were going to be different.

Hoda knew she was going to miss those market days, and the freedom to wander the dusty streets at will, but she was glad to be going back to school. She knew it was important for her to study and find out things, as her daddy kept telling her all the time, and she wanted to get that feeling back of being one of the kids again. But what about Daddy's baskets? And what about her cleaning work that brought in most of the money they could look forward to? She would just have to skip school occasionally when she had a job to do. She could easily catch up on anything she missed. Daddy wouldn't like her to miss school, but Hoda was afraid that she might have to go against his wishes for once. That didn't mean she disagreed with him, not at all. Hadn't they got through the summer all right, like Daddy said they would? Hadn't that seemed impossible when Uncle had stamped out the door and tripped down the stairs, and left them to their own devices, expecting them to come begging for him to put them away in institutions because they couldn't take care of themselves? Hoda had actually gone past those institutions that Uncle had given the money they needed away to, several times during the summer. She had smiled and said hello to some of the old people seated on benches on the verandah of the home. She didn't grudge them the money. It wasn't their fault. And she had gone by the gate of the orphanage, too, and tried to see if she could meet any of the kids to ask them what it was like. But the house was way down the drive, and she never saw any kids the times she went. In a way she was glad. Suppose they were mean, and called her "Fatso," because they didn't even know that if it weren't for her and her daddy they wouldn't have a lot of the good stuff they had? Daddy said the Almighty had used Uncle's badness as an instrument for the performance of His own goodness, and as a gift, because He had used them as His intermediaries, He would allow them the privilege, if they held out in their decision to defy Uncle, to know themselves secretly among the most philanthropic paupers He had ever created. But it had to be a secret, because it would be a terrible sin to humiliate Uncle Nate in public, and besides, philanthropy should always be a secret, because God knew and nobody else had to; besides in this case it was God's secret which He had revealed for their pleasure only. That was something Hoda bet that Uncle would never be able to figure out because he didn't know how God worked the way Daddy did. Too bad. He would sure be sore.

Well, Daddy was right; Hoda knew he was right, and when he was laughing and talking about it she even felt he was right, light and exalted all over. But she wasn't as good a secret philanthropist as Daddy was because all she wanted to do when she felt that way was fly right out of the house and tell everybody she saw. And then a little while later her feelings would change and she would think, even though she tried not to, that maybe this wasn't how things felt to other people, though she knew Daddy was right because this was how things had always happened to him. And then she would think, though she hated herself for it, well so what? What does it all mean? *He might be right but it isn't right, the whole thing; it just isn't right.*

But Daddy said they had to wait; they would know in time, just like all the other times. He explained it to her: "Where is the shape of a basket hidden before it is completed? In its maker's fingers? In his head? In the straw? To know the shape of a basket one must wait till it is completed." When Daddy explained it that way Hoda could not help but understand. She yearned to explain it to others in her turn, to show how unexpected wonders had already shaped their lives. For that, too, she knew the time would come, must come soon.

Danile was not surprised that the inner pattern of things was revealing itself to him now that he had found his own place again. It was not the first time that the fragments of a disordered world had snapped back into place for him, as at a gesture. Naturally, it was a little more difficult for the child to understand and accept the process whereby they had suddenly become the benefactors of the orphans and the old people in the community, while themselves becoming more impoverished than before. Perhaps it was natural that she should feel a little deprived. Who had encouraged her to expect so much from Uncle in the first place? But in time, Danile knew, she too would see the full beauty of it. Meanwhile it was amazing how much like her mother she could be. As his fingers moved contentedly among the grasses that he had learned, like the wind, to bend and twist and bow to his will, he mused, with pride and tranquil amusement, on the nature of this child of his. How seriously she took their problems, like an adult. How practical she was, like her mother, busying herself with schemes to try to solve them, all by herself, running here and there, taking on hard work, trying to function like a grown-up. And yet, how childishly impatient she was when things didn't turn out immediately as she wished them to be. What a child she was, really, with her hundred and one projects begun around the house, and as quickly forgotten as more chores, more ideas, more projects occurred to her, most of them centred around taking better care of her poor, blind daddy who spent half his days, meanwhile, cleaning up after her. If that woman who had come up to him outside the synagogue had realized how well he knew his own little girl, she would not have worried so. Not that he held it against her in any way; on the contrary, he was grateful. She had warned him with the best of intentions. Funny how people thought that blindness took away more than just the sight of your eyes. So the good women around town felt that he should know that his Hodaleh had been seen in bad company. And they were afraid that such company would turn his little girl wild. Rahel would have laughed. As it was Danile had thanked his informant for her concern, and pointed out with pardonable pride, what a good girl his daughter had so far shown herself to be. Nor had he dismissed the subject from his mind. That very day he had said to Hoda that he hoped she wasn't getting into bad company when she went out to play on the streets in the evenings. There were many dangers to a young girl who went out by herself: rough types, wildness, behaviour not befitting a Jewish daughter.

Hoda had answered him with typical, cheerful self-confidence. Daddy was not to worry; she wasn't afraid of any rough types, she knew how to handle them. A lot of them that seemed tough at first weren't even so bad after all. She would have brought these friends home sometime so daddy could see for himself, only some of them didn't talk Yiddish. That didn't mean she was forgetting she was a Jewish girl just because she fooled around with gentiles sometimes. It was like with the basket-making ladies; they were just people, and if you went to school with them or they lived in the neighbourhood you should be friendly.

Danile wished the woman outside the synagogue had heard that reply. Wild! If there were more such children as his around there would be less wildness the whole world over!

With this conclusion Hoda would have agreed, not out of conceit but out of consciousness of the boundless goodwill that was ready to flow in the universe, and of herself as a direct tap to the source, just waiting to be turned on. If people would only realize what she was really like she would somehow be able to become her true self, and all the badness she sometimes felt, inside and out, would wash away. Only they had better hurry up. No matter how hard she tried things just seemed to go along in the same old way. But she felt more impatient about it nowadays. It was not just that she was uncomfortable,

wedged between her seat and her desk in school, and sometimes there were titters as she squeezed herself in. Well to hell
with them! And it wasn't because she wanted to show off to
and make an impression on anybody, not even big Morgan,
the handsome boy with the back name in front, who had
failed grade nine for two years in succession, and this year had
been assigned temporarily to their class because there was no
room in the D class and the principal thought he might
benefit from the example of good students who knew how to
behave; that's what Miss Boltholmsup said in the sour little
speech she made before they sent Morgan in, when she
appealed to them all to help him as much as they could. Poor
Morgan! Hoda wouldn't want such a speech made about her
behind her back like that. How awful to come into a new
classroom and see all the kids looking at you pityingly, and
have the teacher introduce you in a special high voice as if you
were a bear she was trapped with and trying to keep happy by
feeding it a spoonful of honey in little drips. Hoda didn't have
to show off in front of Morgan, because he talked to her
anyway, because he knew her from before, and he liked to talk
to her because she wasn't goody-goody. Hoda knew something
none of the others knew about Morgan anyway; he wasn't
really like the way he seemed to be when he came in the first
time, red-faced and shuffling his feet, and darting quick looks
up from the floor while the teacher talked. Morgan didn't give
a damn what they thought of him; he was going to quit school
as soon as he got hold of some dough. He wasn't going to hang
around here for the rest of his life! And Hoda could understand very well how he felt. School had become so boring. It
seemed to her that she had somehow got even more separated
from the other kids than before, though she tried not to be,
and even felt a little afraid of her feeling of separation. And the

school work was just things to learn, and her new teacher was no Miss Flake.

Hoda had made a pilgrimage to her old classroom on the first day of school, to see her old class teacher, and Miss Flake had greeted her cheerfully and warmly and wished her the best of luck again, and then got very busy with all kinds of things she had to do, and obviously had no time to discuss the world situation, and then recess was nearly over and Hoda had had to return to her new class anyway.

Hoda's feeling about her new teacher's attitude to Morgan came very close to the truth. Had the children had the daring to put their stray intuitions into words they might have realized, as some of them vaguely apprehended at times, that Miss Boltholmsup was afraid of them. Miss Boltholmsup made her living by giving herself up, five days a week, relinquishing all hope, each morning, from the moment she awakened. In numb dread she went through all the habitual preparatory movements which led her halfway across the city and into the large, noisy cage that housed all the noisy little cages in one of which her personal immolation daily awaited. There she remained imprisoned for what to others, somewhere, must be the most joyous hours of dancing daylight, trapped with a suffocating complement of dangerous, unknowable creatures. At a longed for moment every afternoon, she heard the bell which signalled that she was once again briefly to taste the miracle of survival, prologue to tomorrow's renewal of dread. Like all who live in constant danger, Miss Boltholmsup in her cage was always alert, interpreting signs, picking up motions, working out new tactics, forestalling, soothing, guarding, doubling back, retreating, making plans, keeping them busy, keeping them diverted, above all keeping them under control. She was, in fact, considered by a respectful principal, to be the hardest working teacher in the school. His decision to try to calm down that flaming nuisance of a Morgan boy by putting him in Miss Boltholmsup's class was by way of a compliment to her. She, if anyone, could handle him. Nor did her protest that the boy would disrupt the work of the good students, which was as close as she dared come to admitting the terror inspired by having this additional penalty added to her cageful, divert the principal from carrying through his malignant compliment. Why her class? Why in particular one of those overgrown louts, physically already a man, who was, in some obscene way which was particularly frightening in the young, not as yet in control of his manhood? For Miss Boltholmsup was plagued, in particular, by the animal natures of her charges. "They mature so much more quickly in that district. It's where they come from, those backward places," she confided, occasionally, to one of her few friends. "Really, I sometimes think that's all there is to them, all they think about." It was not simple insolence, or even mere physical violence, that Miss Boltholmsup feared most from the inmates of her cage, but rather those profounder wounds with which their awareness of their physical selves so frequently assaulted her moral being. They were more than just wild, dangerous young animals, they were animals who were unclean, and still didn't know it, but like the gross creatures that they were, licked publicly and unashamedly the honey of their profane spring. The burden of knowledge was hers and hers alone, and it wore her out, wore her out with the strain of seeing and having, perforce, to pay no attention; wore her out with simply the effort she put in daily to avert the undefined disasters with which their presence filled her life.

Though she was usually disappointed, Hoda continued to hope. She daily carried with her to school the expectation that today something nice might happen, something really nice. And one day, as though she had been inspired by a power beyond herself, acting in Hoda's interest alone, Miss Boltholmsup announced that the time had come for the members of the class to get to know each other better, and she was going to give each one of them the chance to put his best foot forward. During the next few weeks, in Composition and Oral Expression period, everyone was going to get a chance to talk a little about himself, not just general things that people could get to know easily enough, but some special aspect of himself that he considered most interesting, like a hobby or a dream or an event that had most affected him. There would be points for posture and delivery and content and everything, and at the end they would see who got the most points and was the most interesting person in the class.

To show how it should be done and to prove that teachers are good sports and are willing to reveal something of their true selves to their classes, Miss Boltholmsup started things off herself. Standing with ramrod back and operatically clasped hands, she delivered a few roundly enunciated facts and anecdotes about her own hobby, some of which even poked mild fun at herself, delivered them bravely to the rear wall of the classroom. Her hobby was travelling. She began with daring candour, which she knew the class would mistake for humour: "As soon as the school term is ended I run away." She had prepared her talk very carefully and was, on the whole, gratified by the response of the class. They even laughed in some of the right places, though they also laughed once or twice, disconcertingly, either where they were not intended to, or with too much heartiness, which made her uneasy. Her final statement, for instance, which had been planned as a wistful and rather poetic summing up of her dreams of escape, "Who knows where the last of the

Boltholmsups will end up?" was received with a loud and inexplicable guffaw by some of the most dangerous elements of the class. It passed briefly through her mind that of course it was too much to expect that these young people should have any appreciation of the significance of tradition, or of the fading away of a family, since they came from nowhere themselves. But the thought was outweighed by the gratification of experiencing what for her was a rare pedagogical thrill, that of having introduced a project which would keep them busy for several weeks and at the same time enable her to discover useful little things about them which might help her keep them successfully at bay for the rest of the year.

The class appreciated teacher for leaving herself open that way by telling funny stories about herself. She sure was lucky to get to travel like that. How come it was always dull old people like teachers who travelled so much anyway? They must get paid plenty, so what were they always so sour about? She didn't have many real adventures to talk about, though; some of her stories were pretty corny, and they laughed more to make her feel good than because they found them funny.

Though Hoda had listened to teacher's speech with an apparent intensity of concentration that was revealed by the rapt and dazzled expression on her upturned face, and though she laughed with the class, automatically, at the appropriate and inappropriate times, she scarcely took in a word. All she heard was the surge and counter-surge of "yes, I will" and "no, I won't" within her, as her feeling fluctuated, first with a radiating joy at the sure knowledge that the time had come to reveal herself at last, and then with a dreadful, inexplicable fear that something would go wrong if she did. The "yes, I will" and "no, I won't" continued for a couple of weeks as Hoda awaited her turn. Teacher had scrambled their names and assigned them each speaking times, and Hoda had to wait while more than half the class, two a day, got up and told about themselves or their hobbies. Teacher sat at the back and pretended to be a student. After the two students had spoken teacher made some comments, and then if there was time there was discussion and the class had a chance to make comments. Then teacher summed up and reminded the kids who were speaking next day to be ready. After that they went on to the next lesson. But as far as Hoda was concerned this was the only lesson in the day that meant anything, because each day's two students brought her day that much closer.

None of the other things which normally would have disturbed her, slight or misunderstanding or unpleasantness, had the power to touch her nearly now. It was not that she didn't notice them, rather that she saw them now as from a great distance, as anachronisms, prehistoric, soon to be extinguished squibs from a time that was already dead. Not that, now that her turn was rapidly approaching, she was yet sure that she was actually going to give the speech that she had been preparing and revising and practising out loud by herself in the shed for hours and hours. She was only preparing it just in case she decided, at the last minute, to give it after all. The trouble was there was so much to tell she didn't know how to keep it short enough for the time allotted and still explain all the important things. Daddy would know what could be left out, but she wasn't going to tell Daddy, not yet. That was why she practised in the shed, though Daddy wouldn't have understood most of the English anyway, if he heard, and anyway, even if he understood and caught on to what she was doing, he would probably be terribly proud. But he mustn't know till afterwards, not till after she had actually done it, and carried home her triumph to him, all the wonder and the admiration and the respect and the popularity and the affection that would be the natural crop of her revelations, as well as at least forty-one, counting teacher, orders for bags and baskets that the whole class would make their parents buy to begin with, which was peanuts compared to the rush of business that would come later, when the story got around, and orders came in from the whole school.

Yet time and again she changed her mind and decided that when she got up there in front of the class she would just say anything that came into her head, or tell a lot of jokes on herself, like Jerry, who thought he was imitating teacher, or pretend she had got stage fright like big Morgan really had, who couldn't say a word once he got up front, which gave teacher a chance to talk about how much he had to say from his seat when other people were trying to talk, while he stood there shuffling his feet and getting redder and redder. Teacher really had him nailed there, though she wouldn't have liked what he had to say afterwards about what he'd like to do if ever he got Bottoms-up alone some dark night.

Hoda wasn't used to getting low marks but there were times when she knew that she would rather fail than risk telling them, that she wouldn't mind even if Miss Boltholmsup gave her a big fat zero for her mark in the project. But Hoda knew that she wasn't a big fat zero. Far from it! She was glad that Strawberry Gertie was speaking before her, because then her talk would be freshest in everybody's mind and the kids could start asking questions right away, and Miss Boltholmsup would let her answer the questions in more detail than she could put into the story itself because of the time limit. Maybe teacher would even let them run on into the next period this time, because it would be so interesting, and the next period was only music.

Even as she pulled herself out from behind her constricting desk, tugged her tunic down all round, and moved, somehow footlessly, to the front of the class, Hoda rejected the ungenerous temptation to let them go on thinking what they thought in ignorance. She owed them the opportunity to know, all those kids and the teacher who were even now waiting expectantly, with no idea of what they were to hear, owed them the opportunity to trade unqualified love for love at last.

Hoda cleared her throat, smiled tenderly, and at the same time reached both hands around her bosom to clasp each other on the ill-defined differential line between it and her belly, in imitation of teacher's speechmaking stance. She could see by their grins that some of them thought she looked pretty funny that way, and to protect them from feelings they would later be ashamed of she plunged quickly into her speech, though even as she heard herself begin to speak she had a strange, twisty feeling in her heart, as though for some reason someone in there was wringing her hands. But she didn't even want to stop now.

"I want to tell you how my parents were married and saved the whole village from the plague and the pogrom and even though they lost the first baby they didn't give up, and thank God I was born." Hoda had worked for a long time on that opening sentence. She knew that right from the start she had to establish the importance of what she was going to tell them, so that they would listen, really listen to what she had to say, because it was so significant and there was so much she had to leave out. But somehow it didn't sound the same as it had when she had practised the sentence in the shed, over and over again, large and portentous and serious. She did not quite understand why it sounded different; it had somehow got dissipated among all those faces in front of her. Were they feeling it?

"You see," she continued earnestly, her eyes scanning their faces eagerly as she spoke, "my father has been blind for most of his life, since he was a little boy, and my mother, well, she had one shoulder higher than the other so she looked a little hunchbacked."

From her seat in the back row Miss Boltholmsup heard about blind father and hunch-backed mother while she was still trying to assimilate the fat girl's breathlessly delivered opening sentence. So far there had been no trouble from this one; a certain blowsy eagerness, a super-abundance of physical presence, she was one of those bodies you felt was impinging on all your senses; you might not actually be able to, but you felt as though you could even smell her at a distance. And wasn't there a certain reputation, shrugged away by some, but hadn't there been a revolting story about this one and some of the boys last year, that had spoiled her tea in the staff room one day? Miss Boltholmsup leaned forward across her desk, a movement immediately noticed by Hoda, who realized with a thrill of relief and pride that teacher was really interested. She addressed herself directly to Miss Boltholmsup now, eyes on her eyes, words aimed at her ears, watching for the circuit to be completed that would tell her that teacher heard and truly understood, searching for the light that would go on in her eyes, and stay on, shooting rays of sympathy and wonder. It was hard, though, to be sure if those were lights in somebody's eyes when you were staring at them, because your own got slightly glazed and teary with the effort of looking in, and you lost the rest of her face in blur, and after a while you lost the feeling of your own face too, and had a hard time remembering the next words in your speech. But Miss Boltholmsup's eyes stayed glued to her own and Hoda was certainly not going to insult her by being the first to reject the preferred intimacy and look away. Wide grey eyes staring gamely into blue eyes that glared helplessly (for how was Hoda to know that teacher felt trapped there?) the girl continued, telling all about how "my father and mother, they never even knew each other, even though they grew up in the same town in the old country, not until the plague came. Maybe it was because my mother was a little older than my father, just a few years. She was sorry about that, but my daddy didn't mind. And nobody else did either, when the plague came. The plague is a terrible disease and people die all over, but some good things can happen, if God wants them to, even in a plague. For instance if the plague keeps on getting worse and worse and everybody is sick and dying, and it really is a dreadful kind of sickness;" here Hoda, to emphasize her point, just had to make them realize how bad it was, because she really was afraid that she wasn't making them feel the way Daddy made her feel about it when he told it, the whole holy horror of it. So she digressed from her planned account to give a graphic description, vividly detailed, of what happened when people were dying of cholera. They really were listening now. Little shudders ran around the room, though there were some funny little giggles too. Unfortunately Hoda couldn't resist the temptation to glance around and see the effect of her description, and in doing so she lost the connection with Miss Boltholmsup's eyes. She sought it again contritely, but Miss Boltholmsup had her eyes on the sheet of paper in front of her now, on which she appeared to be writing something. What interesting question or comment was she preparing? Hoda had no time to speculate.

"At the same time," she continued confidently, "the Christians in the neighbouring towns and farms were mad because the plague was killing more gentiles than Jews, so they blamed the Jews and said they were sending the plague, and wanted to kill them, because Christians in the old country didn't know much about Jews or anything. My mother said it was because Jews washed more so the plague germs couldn't get them so easily."

Miss Boltholmsup heard these assertions with hardly more astonishment than she already felt. Her momentary weakness, the paralysis of will which had locked her eyes in baffling parody of communication with those of the fat girl, a contact which repelled and yet seemed to draw her like an obscene demand of the flesh, had alerted her to danger.

One way or another Miss Boltholmsup always recognized trouble in the bud; her instinct had never failed her. She did not have to ask herself now why this creature was mouthing these morbid distortions; her question, more germane, was where, where was the fat girl going? What was she leading up to? She was too pleased with herself in all this, was rushing ahead too eagerly not to have something worse up her sleeve. Those insolent eyes which had tried to outstare her a moment ago, they had been speculating, daring her, trying to gauge how far she would be allowed to go. There was more to come; oh yes, she could hear it in the voice, the husky, coarse voice, speaking more loudly than necessary, a voice gross like the body which Miss Boltholmsup could feel in front of her, though she could not, as yet, bring herself to look up from the sheet on which she was pretending to write, knowing that the eyes hovered on her face, waiting to entrap her again. But she could not prevent herself from hearing the words which assaulted, like crudely wielded weapons, though she was not as yet sure of which part of her being was most endangered.

"So if the plague didn't stop soon all the Jews were going to be in real trouble, because those Christians were killers in the old country." Hoda had made sure when she prepared her speech that she differentiated between the murderous Christians of the old country and the few potentially civilized Christians, including teacher, who were part of her audience. The last thing she wanted to do was hurt people's feelings. She wished teacher would look up again. She wanted to smile at her to make sure she understood. She noticed at this point in her talk that some of the Jewish kids moved uncomfortably and threw some timid glances at the gentiles, but she hurried on earnestly; there were more important things to bring to their attention now. "So you see they had to act fast to get rid of the plague. And that was where my mother and father came in; they were chosen to save the town, and even the Christians, too, from more plague and more dying."

It occurred to Miss Boltholmsup that there were a lot of Jews in her class, occurred with a new vividness, though she had always known it as part of her ordeal, yes, and an awful lot of them in the school, in the city more and more of them, and nobody doing anything about it though suddenly a person could find herself surrounded by fat presences with loud voices and demanding eyes. She risked a quick glance at the speaker, who had paused briefly, and experienced a sinking sensation as her eyes were snared once again in Hoda's ardent orbs of light. Captured. But no longer helpless, no; knowing the danger she could no longer afford to be helpless. But she had to proceed carefully, gauge the temper of the rest of them, find out whether this was an isolated instance of insolence or the signal for organized disruption of the class. Oh yes, there was more in it. Miss Boltholmsup steeled her eyes and stared hard, trying to will a warning.

"Everybody knows that there is one sure way to chase the plague away, if you're really desperate." Hoda said it that way deliberately, though she knew in her heart that probably very few of them knew, though Miss Boltholmsup might, being a teacher, and she smiled confidentially at teacher, who looked so serious, and had surrendered her eyes to Hoda again, as she realized tenderly, in token of her complete absorption. *Dear Miss Boltholmsup, I never knew you were so nice.* It gave Hoda such a buggy feeling, having to keep her eyes hooked in one place that way, when she'd rather just cross looks occasionally. But for teacher's sake Hoda clung, hard though it was to fulfill the responsibility of reciprocal love.

"If the plague gets so bad you don't know what else to do and the goyem are after you too, so you just have to do something or else stay barricaded in your homes and wait for them to come and get you, and you've tried everything else, there's just one thing left to do. You have to start a life thing happening instead of a death thing. The way to do that is, you have to get two very poor people who can't help themselves, especially if they're crazy or cripples or something, though my parents weren't that way exactly, and it's a lucky thing for me. And you have to take them to the graveyard, the Jewish graveyard. And if they're the right special people and if God wants you to get rid of the plague, He makes them fall in love and He tells them to get married right away, and they get married, right there in the graveyard, with everyone watching. The town didn't even want to pay for a baby too, or anything, but God wanted it, and they had to make those two people get married then and there. It was their only chance."

What did she mean by "married"? What exactly did she mean? Light and heat flooded Miss Boltholmsup's brain simultaneously. Suddenly she knew exactly where Hoda was leading, saw in disgusting detail the whole obscene picture, the wretched couple of cripples copulating in the graveyard while a bearded, black-robed, fierce-eyed rabbi stood over them, uttering God knows what blasphemies and unholy incantations, with the whole, barbaric townful of them avidly looking on. Miss Boltholmsup was positively sick to the stomach with the vividness of it. She had to shut her eyes against the nausea.

"It happened this way. They made my mother take a special bath first to see if she was alright. Then when they brought Daddy to the graveyard they had to practically carry him at first; my daddy was very frightened, but suddenly he saw he was . . ."

"Hoda that's enough!" Teacher's voice rang out, very high in the air. Hoda jumped. She had seen that teacher was moved, by the expression on her face when she released Hoda's eyes at last to shut her own. And no wonder! Hoda could feel her own excitement mounting with the unbearable poignancy of it as her father and mother took on their holy roles. But that teacher's eyes should spring open again so suddenly, glaringly, as if at something dreadful she had seen within, and be accompanied by such a shout, high, like a scream; half the class jumped too.

"Hoda, that's quite enough," teacher repeated, more quietly now, and got to her feet. *Quietly, don't show anger; don't get them all excited; calm; don't overstress; puncture quickly and move to other things; divert them; don't lose control; don't show too much; oh God, help me! help me! How? How?*

"But I haven't finished." Hoda still stood there, eyes rapidly blinking, suffused, voice no longer confident and assertive, curiously childish, rather, even in its huskiness. "I haven't finished," she repeated.

"Haven't you?" Miss Boltholmsup moved forward, and even managed a tight little smile in Hoda's direction, as she sought desperately for the right words. "I think we can say you've said quite enough for now. Take your seat." Miss Boltholmsup had reached the front of the room and pointed insistently to Hoda's desk, to which the hulking girl was moving blindly at last.

Miss Boltholmsup daringly waited till the girl was quite seated, and noted with satisfaction that the rest of the class waited quietly too. "Now class, I want your attention." The authoritative voice sliced, just on time, through the sigh of incipient murmurs which arose uneasily as Hoda sat. "I have something to say. We've just been hearing a very interesting story." Miss Boltholmsup spoke quietly, slowly, feeling her way. "But it's a perfect example of what I've wanted to discuss with you before, class. You young people have to learn not only what to say and how to say it, but you have to know what not to talk about, and in fact, at your age, what not even to think about, if you can help it. All of this is part of growing up. People get married. It's nothing to snicker about, nothing to be crude about. People have a right to their privacy. Even if, in more primitive times and places, they have taken part in curious rites, and of course I don't know the degree of truth in this case, but even so some things are best to remain buried in the past, together with certain accusations and prejudices which, at this time and distance it would be foolish to continue to brood over. We have no right to judge."

"But it's true!" Hoda didn't understand what Miss Boltholmsup was saying, or what it had to do with her talk, but she knew that somehow she was being attacked, and it must be because teacher didn't believe her. "I never made it up! It's true, every word," she protested desperately. And it wasn't true what Miss Boltholmsup seemed to be saying, because it didn't make sense. Why did she talk that way? Tears, uncontrollable, were running out of Hoda's eyes and down her cheeks and nose and plopping on her desk. "It's true! You can ask my daddy!"

"You needn't yell, Hoda," replied Miss Boltholmsup reasonably. "We can certainly all hear you when you speak. You don't exactly whisper, you know." Her words drew some uneasy laughter from the class. "I'm not accusing you of anything. In any event we'd have had to cut it short soon. You were running on too long. I don't know about the rest of the class, but I for one could hardly follow. And I did have something special planned for music period. But I would like to say a few general words to the class first, seriously. I had meant to save all my general comments till after the last of you had spoken, but now does seem to be as good a time as any." Miss Boltholmsup was improvising, but thank God they were listening quietly, curiously. Now to lead them away, gently gently . . . She could feel that they were, some of them, far from pacified yet.

"You have, on the whole, been very quiet and attentive; I've meant to mention this before. In any public speaking situation so much depends on the audience, and I've noticed throughout the past few weeks the class has been, on the whole, exemplary in attention to the speaker, in courtesy, and even though you've sometimes been a bit harsh in your comments, on the whole a spirit of fairness has prevailed, a very nice spirit. I must say I've often found it to be so since I've taught in this school, the spirit of fairness, of cooperation, of consideration for each other that the children in this district have, the desire to learn, to adjust to the new world and break away from backward and old-fashioned ways and ideas and superstitions, to get ahead, to be good citizens, I've found them all here. Each one of us here is lucky to be here and to have this opportunity to be a part of a great new civilization. We should realize and appreciate this, and try not to fight old battles over and over again. But the main thing I want to stress is fitness. If you want to fit in with people what you say should fit the occasion and the audience. Don't think you can really make a significant impression on people by shocking them, by offending them, by bringing up subjects that aren't discussed in decent circles.

"Now I want particularly," Miss Boltholmsup was inspired, suddenly, "what I want particularly to close the subject with, is an expression of gratitude to you, Hoda." It was now Miss Boltholmsup who probed past the tears and fixed her eyes firmly on Hoda's fast-blinking watershed. "I want to thank you, Hoda, on behalf of all of us, for reminding us once again how lucky we are to be here. I think that in the back of your mind that may have been your real purpose in telling us your story. By a very strange coincidence," Miss Boltholmsup found herself covering up an earlier lie sublimely, "I had actually planned a more relaxed music lesson than usual for today. I thought we might have a sing-song for a change. Thanks to Hoda I think we're all really in the mood for a few songs of thanks. Shall we put the plagues and the . . . how do you say it? . . . the programs? behind us and begin with 'The Maple Leaf Forever'?"

"Pogroms," said one of the boys.

"Ah, pogroms, thank you," said teacher courteously. "Shall we sing?"

The class rustled assent.

"Yah but what I don't get," said Morgan, "is how did it stop the plague for them to get married in the graveyard?"

"God knows, Morgan, as Hoda has already told us. And I think we'd better leave it to Him," said Miss Boltholmsup with witty finality. "Now do be quiet while I give you the note."

Hoda heard the relieved ripple of amusement with which the kids responded to teacher's reply to Morgan as through a veil, which, like the veil of tears which filmed over her eyes, gave a blurred quality of distance to the patriotic songs which now rolled through the classroom. After a while her tears stopped flowing, but she didn't notice. She remained isolated in her astonishment. She did not understand, could not even reconstruct what the teacher had said. She remembered that something in her had all along been reluctant to speak, but she could not now remember why, certainly not because she had remotely imagined that something like this could happen. But what was it that had happened? That was what she couldn't understand. First teacher had not even let her finish and then she had simply reduced everything that she had tried to say to nothing, somehow, without questioning her or even directly criticizing. She had just, simply, thrown it all away, dismissed it as though it meant nothing, had even tried to hint that it had never been, or if it had that it had been something unclean and uncivilized and best forgotten by those who wanted to sing "The Maple Leaf Forever." Was Miss Boltholmsup crazy? And the kids, why hadn't they said anything, all except Morgan, who was supposed to be stupid but wasn't too stupid to ask a question at least, while they all just sat there. Hadn't they heard anything at all? Maybe she hadn't told it right. How could they fail to see that it was going to be beautiful and holy? How could they all just sit there singing those dumb old songs and not even care what had happened?

That was what Hoda felt worst about, as though she had somehow betrayed what had happened, had taken a precious and beautiful and private thing and sneaked it out of the house where it belonged and everybody loved it, and showed it to all kinds of people who didn't even know what it was, and they smudged it with their dirty hands and hardly even looked at it and threw it away. She hadn't even had a chance to finish, but now she was beginning to be glad. They didn't deserve to know, even if they ever wanted to now. And Daddy didn't have to find out about what she had tried to do and how they were acting; she didn't have to tell him; and if he didn't know it wouldn't be any less precious; he would never know it had been in the dirt. She was stupid for having tried to tell them, that's all. And treacherous old Bottoms-up with her friendly-for-pretend eyes, who did she think she was anyway? She didn't know anything, and she was up there pretending she could teach you something. At least the French teacher taught French and the Latin teacher taught Latin. If Hoda had got up there and told about some silly vacation she never had or how her dog could crap standing on his hind legs, oh goody goody! yummy yummy! Inside of herself Hoda couldn't really believe it was all over, just like that. Miss Boltholmsup must have made a mistake. She had to let her know; she didn't want to do it but she had to have another chance, and give Miss Boltholmsup one too, though now she could hardly bear to look at her.

When Miss Boltholmsup finally dismissed the class she realized that her ordeal was not yet quite over. Hoda was still fiddling at her desk, though the classroom was empty. Miss Boltholmsup picked up her ruler to help quiet her nerves, as the fat girl came down the aisle toward her with dogged step. Hoda's face was set rigid with determination. Miss Boltholmsup clutched the ruler in one hand and pretended she was busy collecting her things, which were actually all collected and waiting for escape time, with the other. Hoda stood by the desk, enormous and silent.

"Yes, Hoda?" said Miss Boltholmsup finally, when she realized that the moral and strategic victory she might win by outwaiting the girl and forcing her to speak first might delay her long enough to make her miss her streetcar connections.

Hoda remained silent for another instant, gathering force to burst through teacher's curtain of remoteness. "I didn't lie," she blurted finally. "It's all true. My daddy can prove it. I worked hard; only you didn't let me finish!" Hoda stopped; her throat was all clogged up, her eyes were awash again, she hated herself for her weakness and she hated Miss Boltholmsup, who smiled.

Miss Boltholmsup smiled with relief. A crying adolescent is a less dangerous one. "Now now," she remarked crisply, "you weren't listening to me, Hoda. I never said you were lying. I'm sure if you say so it all happened, though I'm sure there are other explanations and other points of view. But . . . no, don't interrupt, listen to me. What I was remarking on was . . . appropriateness. A public utterance should be appropriate. I'm sure you don't like to make a fool of yourself, nobody does. No, I don't want to discuss it with you; I want you to go home and think about it. I think you and I can be friends, yes, I really do. I feel that way about most of you young people, that you are a new generation; I have a great deal of faith in you. But just look at you. When you got up in front of the class I was appalled, yes I was, and embarrassed, for your sake. Look at your tunic. You know as well as I do that school board regulations specify your tunic length must be no more than six inches above the ankle. Well, look at yourself. What is one to think of a girl who wears her tunic almost as short as her knickers? That is what I meant by appropriateness. Your whole display this afternoon was inappropriate. And if I tell you so it's because that's what I'm here for. I don't like having to do it any more than you enjoy being told. But somebody has to teach you. And you'll notice," Miss Boltholmsup couldn't help pointing it out to the still sullen girl, "that I refrained from mentioning this to you in front of the class. Now do as I say, run along and think about it. You don't want to make a vulgar display of yourself. You're getting to an age where a young girl's reputation is valuable. No buts now!"

Teacher's tone was final. Hoda was forced to retreat. Miss Boltholmsup felt, on the whole, that she had handled it rather well, so well, in fact, that she couldn't resist a test of strength. "Good afternoon, Hoda," she called after her, as Hoda turned wordlessly away.

"I said good afternoon, Hoda!"

"Good afternoon." From the shapeless, retreating back, came the shapeless mumble, reluctant, but a token of submission nevertheless.

Wretched girl would come to an evil end; if ever Miss Boltholmsup had seen the signs they were here. *Only not in my class, not in my time if I can help it. Another one to watch.* Miss Boltholmsup didn't honestly know how it was humanly possible to go on being as alert as she knew she had to be. She didn't notice that she herself was being watched as she hurried from her greater cage into the air of an early autumn afternoon at last. Survival! Miss Boltholmsup rushed off to catch her streetcar.

"What did she say?" asked Morgan.

"My tunic's too short," growled Hoda.

"So what are you bawling about? I don't mind," said Morgan, and the other guys laughed.

"You shoulda heard her story, though," said Morgan. "Creeps dying all over the place, and she got born in a graveyard. Bottomsuck jumped in and stopped her in the middle, just when it was getting interesting."

Hoda was about to jump in hotly and protest that she was not born in a graveyard. That wasn't what she'd said at all. But she remembered and stopped herself in time. Nobody was going to get another chance to spoil it. Let them be as dumb as they couldn't help being anyway. At least Morgan didn't mean to be mean. But she couldn't help being a little glad when Hymie said to Morgan, "I heard you weren't so happy either, when your turn came." Hymie was a big guy who hung around with them after school, and played crap in the schoolyard with some other big guys who had quit school already, though they didn't have steady jobs yet, because all the soldiers who were coming back had to get jobs first. Morgan liked to show off to these big guys though they teased him because he was still at school though he didn't want to be, only his dad wouldn't let him quit.

"Yeh, Morgo," said the guy they called Popowicki Polack. "They say the cat got your tongue and all you could say was 'meow meow.'"

"Sure," said Morgan. "I was afraid to open my mouth all right. All I could think of to tell them was about the time grandpaw caught his balls in the bedsprings. He sat down this funny way, see? It was a tight pinch. Yow!"

"Yow!" the guys chorused, wincing and laughing. Hoda said "Yow" too, and winced and laughed.

"Wasn't funny," said Morgan. "Granmaw cried for a week."

"What are you yowing about?" said Popowicki to Hoda.

"Business," said Hymie. "I'd rather give her the business than the bedsprings any day. How about it, Hoda?"

Hoda laughed with them. They were all right guys.

Bugger Miss Boltholmsup. She didn't even want to think about it. And most of all she didn't feel like going home yet.

"All right, boys," said Popowicki, "let's get rolling. How much doremi you got?"

"That's right," said Hymie, "artfing time's over. I want my dime's worth. Let's shoot."

"Hey, shut up; can it I say; can't you see there's a lady present?" said Morgan gallantly.

"Yeh," said Hoda, "can it and sell it."

"I tell you what," said Popowicki. "How about we play this way today. Whoever wins the pot, and I mean we'll shoot for the works, and whoever wins he turns over the pot to Hoda, see, and she turns over for him. How's that? Fair sport, hey Hoda?"

"Aw come on, climb off me," laughed Hoda.

"Say, you know, how come I never noticed, her tunic is too damn long!" laughed Popowicki, measuring in close.

"Get away from me, you Octopotz!" Hoda swung at him.

It was just kidding around and Hoda didn't mind it, even though they got a little rough sometimes; mostly it was only lip-rough anyway. They diced and kidded for a while until they got hungry, then they decided to go for supper and meet back under the enclosed arch of the front stairs of the school after they'd eaten, to try to finish the game before it got too dark for them to see the dice. Hoda promised jokingly to come back too, to see which guy she was going to belong to, since they were still kidding about Hoda being the grand prize.

So she had to go home, but she had an excuse ready for making and eating supper in a hurry. She told Daddy she'd promised to meet some kids, and she really had, hadn't she? She just couldn't stand it when he asked her how school was today and what she'd learned. She was afraid if she said anything, even if she just started to talk, she'd have to tell everything, it would all come out, and she couldn't bear it. So she pretended she hadn't heard him, and when Daddy repeated the question she almost wanted to yell at him, she felt so impatient. But she managed to put him off, and got out of the house as quickly as she could.

The guys knew how to fiddle the lock the janitor put on the gate that he drew across the front of the enclosed stairs that led up to the front doors of the school. It was cosy and private in there under the enclosed arch, and the boys got down to finishing their crap game while Hoda kibitzed and flirted with them, and every now and then one of them tried to cop a feel of her, pretending that he was looking for inspiration to win the game and the prize. Hoda played along, even to the end, when Morgan had cleaned the other guys out. Not that there was much money, but Morgan counted out the pennies and nickles and three dimes and spread them carefully and lovingly out on his big palm before he gallantly held them out to Hoda.

Hoda laughed and said, "Come back when it's longer or greener."

But Morgan wasn't so dumb about some things. "It's getting longer all the time," he cracked back, and they all laughed. "Scram you guys!" said Morgan to the others, and they kidded around some more, till the other guys slid outside the gate, each with a parting shot, like "May the best man win next time," and "I tell you it's money down the drain."

Not that Hoda had any intention of letting it go too far with Morgan. He was neither a Jew nor, she was pretty sure, a prince. But he was nice to her and Hoda didn't want to go home yet. Morgan spread out the money on the step beside Hoda. "Here," he said hopefully, "it's all yours. A bargain's a bargain."

Hoda wondered if he really meant it. Would he give her all that money? Even the seven cents he'd started with? How did she know he wasn't a prince anyway? The way they'd played for her, all three of them, like in those stories where a whole bunch of knights and princes and dukes and things went out to fight for the fair lady, and the best one won. Wasn't it the same thing, only with them shedding their money instead of their blood? Wouldn't any princess rather have it that way? What good was a bloody prince? And Morgan had won and laid the whole purse at her feet. Wasn't that love?

They kidded around some more, but Morgan's hands were blurring the limits for Hoda. Teacher was crazy. At this moment Hoda's tunic was really too long; her blouse had too many buttons, her bloomers were pulled up too high, and her belt was too tight for all those swelling feelings. But Morgan's hands were fixing all that. To hell with everybody; right here under the arch of the stairs of the school her tunic had suddenly got so short it was nearly strangling her. "Morgan! Morgo! No!" Hoda laughed. It was like a dirty joke she knew. "More! Go! Go! More!" She couldn't help saying it. "No! No!" She had to grip him tight, to hold him off, after she said that. Morgan fought, trying to roll on to her. Lucky for her she was fat.

"Ah come on, Hoda, please. Hoda, ah come on!"

"No no, that's enough Morgo. Don't!"

"Come on, Hoda, be a sport, come on!" He was very strong and he had fought for her, hadn't he? And he had won. And he had given her the money. And she should shove him away for good now, before her arms gave way. "No! No!"

"Please!"

She summoned up all her strength, holding him off.

"Please!"

"Then say 'I love you!'" cried Hoda. "Say 'I love you!'"

"I love you I love you I love you!" gasped Morgan.

And he meant it! He really meant it! She knew he meant it! She could feel he meant it, tearing through her, repeating and repeating and repeating "I love you! I love you!" till suddenly, those great hearty gusts of something like laughter burst from her, unexpectedly, shooting out from somewhere way down there in the very centre of her.

Morgan was kind of mad about her making so much noise like that, and got himself buttoned up fast, because he was afraid maybe the janitor was still around and if he heard might come after them from inside the school. Hoda was surprised and a little disappointed that Morgan was afraid of a little noise, after all the trouble he'd gone to, gambling for her and wanting her so much and how good it felt and everything. He hardly even wanted to wait for her when she was straightening her clothes up and down again. He didn't even act as though he remembered he'd said "I love you" when he said "so-long" to her on the corner where she turned off to go home.

Hoda felt let down, and she felt uncomfortable walking and unclean. But she didn't start really feeling awful till she came into the house and Daddy said "Hello Hodaleh!" to her in his cheerful, happy-to-have-her-home voice. Then she began to wonder what had been happening to her and what she had done. And she almost couldn't remember, except that she felt awful, and there were reasons why she felt awful, and she didn't even know how far it was her own fault. She hardly noticed what she said to Daddy. She only knew she had to get away from him and from talking, and somehow she did get into her room and into her bed at last.

And then all the events of the day began to swarm over her like ugly, crawly things, in little bits and pieces of memory and sounds of voices and fragments of feeling, and she couldn't shake herself free of them, till at last, to try to make herself feel less awful she tried to think of the nicer things about what had happened tonight, about how they had diced for her and she was more important than the money to them, and it was a little bit like in stories, and how Morgan had really said "I love you," more than once. It was hard to conjure up again how good she had felt because now she was all sore down there. She was so sore she was almost afraid the good feelings had got rubbed away forever. Then there was the money Morgan had given her; that was another good thing. She and Daddy could use that all right. But had she done it? Had she really done it? What was it she had done? Is that what it was? Would people be able to tell? Was this all the difference between before and after? Well so what! Big deal! To hell with Miss Bottoms-up, who probably didn't even know what it was like in spite of her name! Who would want to shoot crap for her anyway? To hell with any of them who didn't like her. To hell with Morgan, even, if he didn't like it just because she made a little noise when she couldn't even help it because he was making her feel so good. If she felt like it she'd go on doing it, and if she didn't feel like it she'd quit. Nobody was going to tell her what to do. If she wanted to she'd even fuck them all! Only Daddy wouldn't like it. And Mamma. Hoda knew that Mamma wouldn't have liked it at all. The very thought of Mamma knowing it made her feel just sick and awful. Well, what did she have to go and die for, and leave her that way, with Daddy to look after and everything. Did Hoda tell her to go and die? Why should she expect Hoda to do everything just as she would have liked it now, without her even being around? What did she know about Hoda being picked on by the teacher and made fun of and everything dirtied up? Why did she have to go and die anyway? Other kids' mothers hardly ever died. Was it Hoda's fault she had to die? *I'm sorry, Mamma, I won't do it again. I'm sorry. Really I'm sorry.* Hoda wept. *Honest, Mamma, I'm sorry.* And she was, too. They could just go on playing crap and begging her. Next time she wouldn't do it, not for anything. She would never do it again.

FIVE

Well, anyway, she didn't do it very often, at least not at first, and at first only with Morgan, because he was the one she'd already done it with and if she did it with him again it was less like doing a new bad thing and more like just doing an old bad thing over again. And was it really so bad? Once a thing was done it was done and maybe sometimes you just felt like doing it some more. At first she had to quit hanging around with the other guys after school, because she said she'd only do it with Morgan when he won, and not with any of the others. So they said all right then, if she wasn't going to be a sport she could scram. And she had to scram, only when Morgo won he came and whistled in the yard and when she came out he got her to sneak round in the back and go in the shed with him. He didn't care that she hadn't cleaned up the shed yet. But afterwards he kept arguing with her and trying to persuade her to do it with the other guys too, because she was being a poor sport, and they were even sore at him the way it had worked out, when he took their dough and left them with their hardons, and they didn't have a chance to really be winners when they did win.

Morgan wasn't supposed to feel that way if he really loved her like her one-and-only that he was supposed to be after he said "I love you," and for a little while she grieved over this failure in him. But she really didn't love him all the time either, like she had loved Stanley, for instance, last year, and like she would love the Prince of Wales forever, when he came. If he came she wouldn't ever do it with Morgan any more either, would she? So what difference did it make if it was Morgan or one of the other guys who loved her in the meantime? Morgan said that the other guys, even when they lost at crap, still had some money left over, usually, and they'd pay her too. Each one of them would put something extra in the kitty if she'd let them all do it to her, and she'd get a lot more out of it.

If she let them all do it, one after the other, would that make love stay longer? Was she being mean not to give it a chance? She knew how it felt to want something and not get it, and she blamed other people when they were mean to her. If she wasn't going to be nice when her turn came, how could she blame other people when they were mean? Somebody had to start off being nice, at least a little. And those guys weren't even asking for something for nothing, like some boys did. They were sports and she should be too. Maybe this was only in-the-meantime-love, while you waited for the real forever-love to come along, but Hoda liked it; she really liked love, now that she had found out exactly where it lived and how it worked. Love lived where it couldn't help itself, had to say yes, couldn't resist and had to give in, couldn't think, couldn't hide, couldn't pretend, like Morgan couldn't when she had made him admit it. Love lived where it had to be, where it made you have to be, even if you didn't want to, like Morgan didn't, afterwards. It might not stay but it always came back, like

Morgan came. No matter what they said Hoda had found out where love lived, and once you knew how it worked, knew exactly when was the time you could trust it, where the place you could enjoy it, that was when you could begin to have fun, and why shouldn't you have some fun while you waited for your forever-one to come along? Hoda knew she would recognize her forever-one, all right. She'd know him right away. She wouldn't even want him to pay her, or if she wasn't sure at first she'd give him his money back as soon as she was sure, anyway. And he'd say, "Keep it! There's more where it came from!" And when she found him he wouldn't mind it that she'd looked somewhere else first, and tested other love so she could tell that his was best. He was maybe making some mistakes while looking for her, too, like that guy with the glass slipper and all those dumb sisters pretending it was a good fit. He'd know who was the right fit all right! And he'd understand how she needed the money, at least until Daddy's business got better.

That love thing that she got into when she was with Morgan and the other guys, that was what it would be like all the time with her real guy. It was kind of like a foretaste and a reminder so she wouldn't lose heart and would go on searching. These and other things Hoda figured, at different times, while she tried it with the different guys, sometimes separately, and then when they finally talked her into it, when she let them shag her one after the other. You really felt sore afterwards, the first few times, especially if there were more than five of them one after the other, and some more than once, but it was fun to be popular, and the money was worth it.

One thing Hoda knew; that money wasn't going to be wasted on any new tunic. Nuts to all that. Not that she ever actually thought of quitting school. They couldn't make her quit! She just gradually stopped going, sort of, not altogether at first, and not right away, either, because she didn't want them all to think it was because of what Miss Boltholmsup had said about her speech. They didn't have to think she cared that much or feel sorry for her either. After a while she just got sick and tired of bringing notes to explain her absences. It was not trouble getting Daddy to sign, but why should she have to bother making up excuses to that old bag anyway? She wasn't learning anything there. If she kept on going she knew that one day she was going to tell old Arsendup off like she'd never been told off before. If they wanted her to come to school they could damn well come and get her. Only they'd better not try. They didn't have any right to send a truant officer to upset her daddy after the way they acted. If she came home and found one waiting for her she'd tell him off too. Just let him try to send her to the orphanage. Just let him try! But for some reason the truant officer never came, and Hoda figured all right, if they didn't want her she didn't need them either. But she never quit. She would go back if and when she felt like it. Right now all she wanted to do was stay away, and she didn't have to explain to anybody either; she just felt like it, that's why. She didn't have to go to school to learn things. She could teach herself, in her own way.

The trouble was how to explain it so Daddy would not become alarmed. Once, when Daddy asked her how she was getting on in school, she just couldn't help it, she didn't intend to but she just found herself cutting loose at him about how she hated it and how her teacher didn't know anything and she knew five times as much as old Bottoms-up, even with her hands tied and lying on her back too. She didn't know why she said that and afterwards she was afraid that he might think it was a funny thing for her to say, but Daddy didn't seem to notice what she'd said about lying on her back because he was so upset that she was hating school so much. He was so worried he even suggested that maybe he should go down to the school himself and talk to somebody, like Mamma had done once or twice. Hoda knew that it was not beyond her father, if it was a question of her welfare, to go tapping his way to the school to find out for himself why it was that the teacher had set herself against his little girl, and the thought of that humiliation she simply could not bear. He would hardly be able to talk to them in their language, and they would be exasperated and roll eyes at each other and throw up their hands and laugh, and say no wonder this and that about Daddy and about Hoda, and think they understood everything there was to understand just because they couldn't understand anything at all. No, her daddy was not going to learn his first lesson in that school, not if she could help it, particularly since she hadn't been there herself lately, and her name might even be struck off the roll by now. Once, she had heard from Morgan that Bottoms-up had asked about her, and she told Morgan to say next time she asked that Hoda was doing jobs and was too busy with more important things to waste time in school, though if teacher needed her help she'd drop in sometime to give her a hand. And Morgan went and actually said it, and the whole class laughed, and he got lines to write out because of it: "I must not be a smart-alec," five hundred times, but it was worth it, and it was, too, because he got Hoda without having to win her at crap that evening.

Danile was able to figure out what was bothering Hoda without having to go to see her teachers about it. Unwittingly, the child had revealed it herself in her complaint that she wasn't learning anything in school this year, because she was so far ahead of class and teacher. He could understand how frustrating it was to her to be so far ahead of the class, and of the teacher too; every time she mentioned the teacher it was with such exasperation. How could they allow such a totally ignorant woman to teach in a school? Danile also realized why Hoda was gobbling up the English books so quickly this year, and getting ahead of everybody else. It was because they hadn't been able to afford the Yiddish school in the evenings, though their friend Mr. Polonick the best teacher in the school, had come and offered to get her in at a very nominal rate, because, as he had timidly explained, she was quite a clever girl (as who could fail to notice? a real teacher certainly didn't!) and it would be far better for her to spend some of the evening hours in class, that she might otherwise waste in hanging about the streets. But though Hoda was very shy and respectful, and hardly spoke at all when Mr. Polonick was there, after he left she said no and emphatically no again, when Danile urged her to accept the offer. Daddy himself knew very well, she argued, that they had no money, and with winter coming on they had enough to think about without having to worry about school fees as well. And even if, as Mr. Polonick had suggested, in the case of absolute necessity, the school might waive the fees altogether for the time being, Mamma had never liked charity and Hoda didn't either, particularly since it wasn't, in Mr. Polonick's own words, an 'absolute necessity' for Hoda to attend the school. She could really go on learning Jewish things by herself. Didn't she learn things from the Yiddish papers that the shahmus of the synagogue saved for her to read to Daddy? With Daddy's help, and the help of the One Above, she didn't really need the parochial school. Hoda was a little uneasy about the way she had thrown God in, just to weight her argument. Not for the first time lately, she hated herself, too, for being glad, for an instant, that her father was blind. Well, even though she had said it that way on purpose, it wasn't entirely a lie. She was perfectly willing to learn whatever God wanted to teach her, as long as it left her evenings free. It was for Daddy's good as well as her own. Could Mr. Polonick make it as worthwhile for her to come to the parochial school as the boys did sometimes for her to stay away?

Danile was amused. It was right, he supposed, after all, that the young should be able to out-argue their elders, if there was to be any progress in the world. Common sense she certainly had, his little one, far beyond her years. And full of her mother's pride she was, too. If only his business would improve more quickly, so these sacrifices shouldn't be necessary. Any increase in sales that had taken place lately had been solely due to Hoda's efforts. She had even taken to peddling her wares in the evenings, and on the pretense that she was meeting her friends, had gone out again and again and returned triumphantly to count her profits into her daddy's hand.

"More money? Where did you get it?"

"I earned it."

"Hodaleh, you don't have to go out with the baskets so late. Like you say yourself, why shouldn't you spend a little time enjoying yourself with your friends in the evenings? The baskets will get sold. The One Above will take care of us."

"Don't worry, Daddy. I enjoy myself."

For all her clever argumentation that she thought he couldn't see through, that was probably the real reason why she didn't want to go back to Yiddish school. She had found that the evening was a good time to sell her baskets. Perhaps people, relaxed at the end of the day, contented after their evening meal, found it easier to appreciate a fine piece of workmanship, and had more time, too, to appreciate the intelligent, appealing little girl who couldn't fail to convince them to buy.

Danile suspected why, except for Hoda's special efforts, his basket business was moving so slowly. The trouble with his business was, oddly enough, in the baskets themselves. What happens when a man does his work too lovingly, too well? The workman could, under certain conditions, quite conceivably starve to death, – if it were not for the watchful eye of the One Above, that is. Take his own baskets, for instance. He knew, it was not immodesty on his part, that they were handsome. He also made sure that they were strong, not flimsy. They wouldn't easily fly apart. Therefore, a customer who had one of his bags or baskets was not likely to come back for another to replace it, for a long time. So fine craftsmanship can defeat itself as a means to making a living? A nice thought. Should a man then make worse baskets in order to make a better living? Not only the product but the man is reduced thereby. Does it then take a worse man to be a better provider? Ha ha! Around and around one could follow the thought, and Danile had propounded it to his friends at the synagogue, as a problem worthy of attention. They had debated it, off and on, for weeks, and every now and then someone brought it up again for examination anew. Ideas buried for a while in the mind sometimes reveal unexpected facets when examined afresh. He listened to cleverer and wiser men than he argue the question many ways, but inside of him Danile always knew how mortifying it would be to have his customers come back too soon.

Of course, Hoda's sensible solution was to go ever further afield in seeking new customers. But it was wrong that the child should take on herself all the responsibility of selling his wares. They had already discussed the question of sharing that burden, and Hoda had convinced him that if he wanted to go out and peddle sometimes too, he had better wait till spring, because winter was coming soon and winter was no time for him to go wandering about distant, unfamiliar streets. And besides, what if someone came to the house to buy while they were both out? She told people, wherever she went, where they lived, and a lot of people had promised to drop by if they needed anything in straw. And if they came by once and found no one home they might not feel like coming back again, and they might lose a sale, whereas if it were spring or summer people didn't mind coming back again. The child thought of everything. No wonder she was dissatisfied at school, if, as she complained, they really treated students like herself as though they were mindless creatures to whom fragments of knowledge were to be doled out in small doses. Naturally, because she was denying herself the Yiddish classes, and Danile did not fool himself that he could take their place, though he prayed fervently that God would find some substitute, her hungry mind was devouring twice as avidly what they set before her at the English school. With such an appetite for learning, who can sit still for hours and days before an empty plate?

Danile tried to caution his daughter against showing the disrespect which she clearly felt for her English school teacher. Rahel would not have liked it, even though the child were in the right. He must try to turn Hoda's complaints around, somehow, so that she would learn something, even from them.

"When you see that your teacher is ignorant, doesn't that make you realize what a terrible thing ignorance is?"

"Of course."

"And don't you feel, then, that you want to help the ignorant so they should be less ignorant? Don't you want to teach them to know better in the future? Great rabbis have been known to sit listening, humbly. Even a teacher can be taught, without realizing, sometimes, how much she owes to her students."

Hoda had tried that already, and it didn't work. They didn't want to know anything, any of them.

Had she been patient? Had she tried again? A teacher must try to make her pupils want to learn. If you were ahead of others, it was your duty to try to help them catch up. A teacher must never give up. Look at Mr. Polonick, her old parochial school teacher, who had come unbidden to make a special offer in order to coax a promising student back to her books.

But Hoda, though she liked Mr. Polonick, responded nevertheless with a surprising tirade. Mr. Polonick didn't have any right to try to interfere in her life; she'd be friends with anyone she liked, and she didn't care what he thought about it! So what if he had seen her talking on the street; she wasn't doing anything to be ashamed of; he didn't see her do a thing, and anyway, what business was it of his if she hung around with her friends in the evenings?

The uncomfortable knowledge that she was not being strictly honest with her father made Hoda yell a little, to show she was in the right. Old Polonick didn't have to come hinting around to her daddy. All his visit did in the end was upset Daddy, who wanted her to be a teacher or something when she grew up, and force her to further lies in her efforts to soothe him and divert him from dangerous ground.

"Sure Daddy, I'll bet I could be a teacher. I could teach what I've learned so far. All kinds of kids have trouble, like my friend Morgan, for instance. He's the dumbest boy in the school, but I've taught him plenty already. I don't even have to go back to school to be able to teach what I know. I could stay home and give private lessons maybe." She left it at that for the time being, hopefully, not daring to go on, not quite sure of what she was going to go on to. In a way she had told him, hadn't she? when she had said that about "going back" to school? You couldn't go back unless you'd been away. And then if you said you didn't have to go back and Daddy didn't say anything, he was kind of agreeing with you, wasn't he? It was almost like getting permission. It was almost like telling him. It was getting him ready to know. What was the use of worrying him with any more all at once? And besides, she probably could be a teacher and give private lessons, a far better teacher than old biddy Bottomsuck. And maybe she would, too, someday.

But meanwhile, as long as Daddy seemed satisfied, and she was having some fun, she tried not to think about worrisome things. Leaves fell. Indian summer came and lingered. Intermittently, in between cleaning jobs for bossy ladies and her troubles with the basket business and other money matters, Hoda tasted freedom. For long days she wandered about, pacing the flat platform of earth under pouring blue sky, smiling into the air, her mind so filled with pleasant snatches of thought and feeling that she hardly knew she was alone. Wherever she turned the horizon was low, just at the bottom of the street, and she fancied herself walking off into the air, heavy Hoda, lighter than air. But she didn't have to walk off. Most of her was in the sky already. Only the soles of her feet kept contact with earthly things. While they plodded dutifully along wooden pavements, mud walks, gravel ways, and sometimes even got so far as the newly paved streets of the rich, with their clean, hard cement sidewalks and asphalt roads, the rest of her swam through oceans of friendly sky, crisp and autumnal smelling, and faintly cloudy with her breath. When she felt like it she peddled baskets; when she felt like it she kicked stones; she felt good or bad, when she felt like it. She was free to dream her day through. No one could tell her what to do. There was no one she had to try, fruitlessly, to please, no one to criticize her constantly, no one to squelch her or laugh at her, no trap to be caught in where she would be forced to stay even if they made her feel bad all the time. Freedom was fun.

Between the public park and the Anglican graveyard, down towards the river, there was a quiet road with deep ditches beside it and high bushes and old trees. No one had bothered to clear away the autumn leaves here. Here the boys built a ditch fire one evening, out of twigs and leaves and some wood they'd pinched from the woodyard, and they roasted potatoes, and Hoda ate the charred black spuds, smelling them deeply, tossing them from hand to hand till they cooled off, smelling and licking her fingers afterwards. And then she lay on her back on a pile of leaves in the ditch with her dress rolled up, and the leaves crunching as she squirmed and sank deeper, as boy after boy rolled on her while his buddies raked the embers for the last few spuds, and in between boys she lay watching the early evening stars and smelling the smoking leaves and sucking the black burnt potato peel-leavings off her lower lip, and resting, and then she took the boys again and she couldn't help it, she laughed and laughed. But nobody cared much about the noise here. The park was dark on one side of the lane, and the graveyard dark on the other, and her laughter rolled over both of them, and upward to the stars. Nor did she even think to ask for money that time, nor did they think to offer to pay. But afterwards she worried about it and warned herself not to do it too often that way. If she didn't take payment, then it was as though she didn't have to do it, and was doing it for her pleasure only, and she didn't know if that was right, unless you were married and with your one-and-only. She was pretty sure that was the way it was supposed to work.

If only Indian summer would last forever, or at least till the really right things started to happen. But it didn't, not that year anyway. As the air grew colder people seemed to be less and less interested in buying straw things. Soon there would be no point at all in peddling from door to door. But the stock of baskets and bags was growing alarmingly, and Daddy was so happy at his work that Hoda didn't know how to tell him not to work so much. And soon it would be too frosty to fuck on the school landing under the arch, or in the ditches, or even in the damp shed. Then where would she get the money to rescue them from the constant need to which Uncle had doomed them when he had rushed out and gone tripping, spat over natty white spat, down the crooked verandah steps?

Persistently, she lobbied for more cleaning jobs, schooling herself to keep her mouth shut, because she knew that just because she stood up for her rights sometimes, those dames went around telling each other she was insolent. Who wouldn't get fed up with the way they nagged, and some of them even yelled at you, as if you were their slave, when you knew you were just as good as they were and perfectly free to go out and breathe fresh air and hang around and be happy, if only you didn't need the money for you and Daddy to live on.

She tried different places to get jobs, like the stores around the market, where she had got to know some of the people in the summer, but nobody seemed to need her, except to run a message or make a delivery sometimes, when the boy wasn't handy, but they didn't encourage her to hang around all day like she was willing to do, just in case they might need her. She wasn't dumb; she caught on to how they felt about her, and after a while she got so embarrassed she had to force herself to keep asking, because it made her feel so badly to be sent away again, as if now the person who had turned her down had some kind of mean advantage over her, because he knew of her need, and still he didn't want her around. So she tried to be flippant in advance, even in asking, so they shouldn't think it was so important to her anyway.

Once, she even walked all the way downtown to the factory district behind the City Hall to see if she could become a factory girl, but when she came into the long, narrow, dim room with machines going noisily all over and long tables and people all with their heads down, inhaling nothing but the sharp, cloth-dye smell all day, it seemed even worse than being in school and having to do dumb things all together, so when the man called her into the little partitioned office and asked her questions, Hoda let herself get pretty smart with her answers. Not that she said anything bad or anything; she just joked around as though they were already friends. If he accepted her this way it might not be as awful as it looked here. Of course she made sure she let him know she wasn't lazy. She wanted to work. Maybe it was because he reminded her a little of Hymie's friend Limpy the Letz, who looked pretty jerky but was a lot of fun once you got to know him, that she gave him the chance to show his human side. Just so he didn't think, as he seemed to, from the first few things he said to her, that he'd be doing her any big favour if he offered her a job in a noisy, smelly old place like this. He needn't expect her to kiss his feet. She'd just work hard and that ought to be good enough for him.

But instead of trying to do her any favour, he started to give her a lecture about how many kids came in begging to be trained, willing to work for nothing, so why should he take someone like her, who came in with a lot of lip, and was worried already first thing about how much money she was going to take home, when she'd never even threaded a needle yet. He practically yelled at her, and Hoda was taken aback. Almost, his words had begun to intimidate her; he was a grownup after all. But she realized, suddenly, that he wasn't going to give her a job anyway. So what was he yelling about? She didn't have to take it. She didn't have to bid him a polite goodbye! She was never going to kiss anyone's asendup again for nothing! So she let him know that she was not that kind of sucker, to work for nothing. Why should she be, when she had guys who looked just like him, only younger, begging to pay her? Only she didn't tell him that. Instead she thought of what her old teacher Mr. Polonick used to say about the capitalists and their slave labour factories, and she gave him some lip, all right, about that, and plenty loudly too. He didn't have to yell at her. And she realized suddenly that the noise of the machines beyond the partition had died down, so she yelled even louder about slave drivers and dirty capitalists who expected you to work for nothing. And then she got out fast, clattering down the stairs of the loft, chuckling because she'd got out before he could throw her out, which was what he was even now yelling up there, two flights up, yelling above the noise of the machines that he'd do it to all of them, throw them all out, if they stopped work on him again to listen to some crazy communist crank. They could hold their goddam union meetings on someone else's time, and heaven help them if he heard about it!

Hoda felt better about her failure to get that job than about any she had tried for so far. She felt so exhilarated she was tempted to go and apply to a few more foremen and managers and give them all a piece of her mind. Someday maybe just for the fun of it she'd do that. Afterwards, when she told the guys about how she'd sassed the manager, it turned out that some of them knew who he was because they'd tried to get jobs there too, only none of them had thought of sassing him, though he was a crud and paid starvation wages and probably turned them down because they didn't look starved enough. Well, what could you expect? He had shares in the business. Who wouldn't want shares in a business that could keep a hundred and fifty workers starving?

Hoda wouldn't, that's who!

The guys listened to her radical talk respectfully, though maybe they didn't entirely believe her, but she had a right to talk because she was the only one who'd had enough nerve to tell all those shares to go take a jump.

Hah! They should have heard what she'd said that time to Uncle!

Heartening though her failure to get the factory job was, it did not reduce their own starvation potential, and once or twice she wondered, briefly, whether she had behaved wisely. But slavery? Nuts to him! There must be other ways to earn a living. One by one Hoda tried those she knew, but with little success. One day, because she thought he might like it better, and consequently give her a more substantial ration of meat than what he'd been throwing in the paper package lately, she even offered, boldly, to go all the way with Yankl the butcher, if he wanted her to. To her surprise Yankl was horrified that she even knew of such things. He was shocked and disgusted at what she was willing to do. He gave her a little lecture on immorality, and warned her that she must never try it. She could catch all kinds of diseases doing that. It hurt him to hear her talking this way, just when she was at an age when a girl should be careful and keep herself clean and think of her future. He was so upset it was a little while before she could even soothe him into letting her do what he had trained her to do for her meat scraps. Without looking at her he made her say, first, that she hadn't really meant it, and that she didn't even really know what she was talking about. She had just been repeating what she heard some older kids saying. Only then, while she was parroting his words, did Hoda find that his dream was beginning to work for him again. Well, if that's what he wanted, okay by her. But things were never quite as satisfactory with Yankl after that, which was one more reason that Hoda knew she would have to try to work up a source of steadier income, so as not to have to rely on one person's whims for hers and her daddy's well-being.

It was beginning to puzzle Hoda more and more how unreliable people could turn out to be, people you knew, and thought they were your friends, and then it turned out that, like Uncle, for instance, in the first place, and now Yankl and Morgan, they didn't act like you thought they would at all. In the case of Morgan it wasn't that he'd done anything directly to Hoda. She wasn't surprised when he ran away from home. He'd been telling her for a long time that the minute he got hold of some dough he'd disappear, amscray, just like that. But she hadn't expected him to steal that dough, especially not from his own father. That was a really awful thing to do. Hoda couldn't imagine taking anything from her daddy. She knew Morgan was a wise guy and a show-off, and sometimes maybe he pinched things, like some of the other guys did, just to show they had the guts to do it, but to really steal, and from your own father; she never thought he would do a thing like that, and could hardly believe the other guys when they told her. And she didn't think it was funny, either, as they did. They thought it served his old man right for being too strict with Morgan, and making him stay in school, when he hated it. Maybe that was true, but Morgan had told her himself that his dad made him stay in school because he didn't want him to go bad the way his big brother Lambert had done, and get sent to prison; at least that was what his dad said, but Morgan figured his dad must think he was pretty bad already, because school was worse for him than any prison.

Morgan had often talked about his big brother Lam, and how smart he was, and how much time he'd served already, and how they didn't know where he was now and his dad said he didn't want to know, but Morgan would like to find him, and he bet he could, too, if he could get hold of a stake to get started with. Hoda warned him that Lambert might be in jail again, if he was still a crook, and Morgan got a little sore and said how did she know he was still a crook, and anyway even if he was it didn't mean they were going to catch him again.

Hoda said she hoped he had stopped being a crook, otherwise he'd get sent back to prison again all right, because that's what happened to crooks, and Morgan got even madder and said that's what happened only if they got caught, and if he ever turned crooked he'd make sure he wouldn't get caught, not alive, and if he went he'd make sure he took a few of "them" with him. Hoda knew that he was just boasting; all the guys talked like that. Nevertheless it was a really awful thing he'd done, to steal from his daddy, and if he could do something like that she didn't know any more what else he might be capable of doing. For all his big talk Morgan had never seemed like that. She bet he would feel lousy when he really realized what he'd done. He was probably feeling pretty awful right now, wherever he was, and wanting to come back and give the money back to his dad and apologize. Maybe he was just too scared to. But if he did maybe his dad would do the right thing too, and say, "All right Morgan, I didn't know you hated school so much. Maybe you'd better quit and get a job." That would make everything all right, and at first Hoda expected it to happen any day. But the guys didn't. They said he'd really taken off for good, and after a while passed, and he must have spent some of the money already, Hoda decided maybe he'd better not come home now, because his old man had told one of the boys that he'd put him in prison if he caught him, for going bad just like his brother. All the guys teased Hoda for a little while, because they thought she missed him. Maybe she did, a little, because he was the first one, and that was a lot of fun on the school steps, under their very noses. Those dumb teachers didn't know half of what went on. But Morgan shouldn't have done that to his dad. And anyway, he hadn't even said goodbye.

Thank goodness she and her daddy at least could be relied on to be good to each other and be what they knew they were and do what they expected of each other. Daddy too was very shocked when she told him about this boy she knew from school who'd stolen from his own father and run away from home. Of course you couldn't really blame him in a way, for running away at least, as she explained to Daddy, because his father had forced him to stay in school when he wasn't getting anything out of it. Morgan could never stand the teacher either, so you see she wasn't the only one. Maybe if his father had let him quit long ago this wouldn't have happened. She knew exactly how he felt about the school part of it; in fact, Daddy shouldn't be surprised if she stayed home from school a lot, to study by herself this winter.

There. It was out. She had worried about it, and yet now it had turned out to be surprisingly easy, thanks to Morgan. Just as long as she went on learning, Danile told his daughter fondly, and didn't get discouraged, and didn't take it into her head to run off with his little girl, who was the only fortune he had, he would be quite contented. They had a good laugh about that, and Hoda was relieved, because now, on days when she didn't have a cleaning job or anywhere else to go, and it was too cold just to walk around for hours, she could stay home without having to make up an excuse for why she wasn't going to school. She really felt sorry for Morgan, in a way, because it must be awful to have a father you couldn't get along with.

Not long afterwards, when the snow was already deep in the yard, and the peddlers and milkmen and breadmen had changed their wagons for sleds which packed hard, narrow paths over the groaning snow of the city streets, and Danile had shovelled a narrow path too, along a trench which Hoda had first scuffed out for him with her galoshes, from their door to the front gate, Hoda brought her friend Hymie home late one evening. She hadn't wanted to, but she couldn't avoid it; there was no place else to take him, and he had some money to burn. She couldn't afford to let him go somewhere else to burn it. She didn't know how they were going to manage it, but in the meantime she introduced him to her father, who was sitting and working by the stove, as a good friend, who even understood some Yiddish, if Daddy would talk slowly enough.

The first thing Daddy asked, in his gentle way, was how Hymie was enjoying his studies. And Hymie, who wanted to be a big shot gambler, was about to deny indignantly that he was still a schoolboy, when Hoda jumped in quickly and said that Hymie had been away from school for a long time, and now he had a problem, and she was going to help him. That's why she had brought him home. It was all true, wasn't it? Hoda never lied outright to Daddy if she could possibly avoid it. And later on, when the fiction had been fully established, she always denied to herself that she had been the first to state explicitly that she was giving private lessons to her visitors, even though it might have sounded as though that was what she had meant when she explained about Hymie. It was what Daddy thought she meant, and he was so pleased, she just let him go on thinking it. And he was so nice about it, gathering up his materials, though she told him it wasn't necessary, because they were going to work in her bedroom anyway, and insisting on removing himself and his work to his own room, while at the same time chuckling over her new vocation, and exhorting Hymie over and over again to "study, study," and then again "study," so that Hymie began to wonder whether he wasn't really as foolish as some people said he was, though he knew better than to say anything to Hoda about it. Crazy or not, he wasn't hard to get rid of at least; he even closed his door so as not to disturb them at their studies.

Hoda took Hymie into her bedroom, and as an extra precaution made him put her mattress on the floor, so no frivolous noises should carry by chance to the other bedroom. And she tried not to laugh out loud.

Afterwards, they sat and talked in the kitchen for awhile, and Hoda gave Hymie some tea, and took a cup in to Daddy too, and Daddy called out, "study, study," encouragingly to Hymie again from his bedroom. It made Hymie a little uncomfortable, because the word for "study" in Hebrew sounds like the word for "pig" in Yiddish, and he thought, *her old man really is cracked,* but didn't say anything, naturally, because of Hoda's temper. Then, when Hymie wanted her to go on the mattress again before they put it back on the bed, she said she had a better idea. Than what, for godsake? Some idea! Almost as crazy as her old man, but plenty smart, that Hoda. She said if he paid her a little more she'd throw in the straw bag her daddy had just finished making. When Hymie said he didn't want the bag, what would he need a woman's straw bag for? Hoda got huffy about it, because he'd come in her house and she'd made everything comfortable for him, and he had admired the bag, so why couldn't he buy it to give to his mother for a present, since he happened to have the money today and she bet his mother would like it.

All he'd said was, "that's a nice thing you're making," just to be polite to the old guy; he didn't want the damn thing. But he finally realized that if he wanted to get her on the mattress again he'd have to agree. "All right, all right," he'd shell out and take the bag too, though his old lady would think he'd gone nuts; he'd never brought her a present in his life. She'd probably get sore at him for not just giving her the money, instead.

When he left, with Danile's ringing encouragement of "pig! pig!" following him out of the house, so that he thought, uneasily, *Jeez, what a crackpot!* he had to stuff the bag into his coat, first, because he wasn't going to be seen carrying it, for godsake, in the middle of winter, too. That Hoda!

Danile couldn't get over what a doubly talented daughter he had, blossoming forth both as a teacher and as an irresistible saleswoman, but Hoda demurred modestly, and said that Hymie naturally wanted the bag for his mother once he'd seen her daddy's workmanship close up.

The fact that it was working out all right didn't prevent Hoda from feeling badly sometimes, particularly afterwards, when the guys she brought home had left, and she couldn't help remembering how nice Daddy always was about leaving the kitchen and closing himself up in his own chilly little bedroom while the guys all sprawled around and talked and joked and played cards while they waited their turns to go in her bedroom with her. She tried to make sure that he was comfortable, and didn't feel neglected. She always checked to see that the pipe in his room was open, so he would get as much heat as possible from the stove, and she made him put on a sweater, and brought him tea. And she told herself that he liked to work in his own room; he always did it at night, and anyway, it was only sometimes it happened, and other kids did it too; well, at least they brought home friends in the evenings and kibitzed around. But it was hard, for all her padding, to soften the knowledge that she was deceiving him, right to his poor blind face, and she had to develop a whole series of mental exercises to prevent the most miserable question from popping into her head before she fell asleep, but it slipped through sometimes anyway: *What if he ever found out?*

No he wouldn't. Daddy didn't know about such things. He'd never believe it. She'd kill anyone who told him. The guys wouldn't dare say anything, even though she could tell they thought it was pretty funny the way he kept calling out to them to study and cram. No, he wouldn't find out. Of course he wouldn't. Wouldn't what? What was it she'd just been thinking about? Something that made her feel awful. About Daddy? A bad thing. Not about Daddy if it was a bad thing. She couldn't remember, suddenly. It had just slipped away. But it would come back. And then maybe she would find it was a mistaken thought, and she would be able to think it into something good. Only she couldn't concentrate. It was gone. She couldn't remember. Let it go. Maybe it wasn't so bad if it went away just like that. Better it should forget itself, whatever it was, and let her begin to feel better.

Once, when she had a whole bunch of boys over, and they were making quite a bit of noise, she went in to speak to Daddy, and on an impulse, she told him that the boys weren't over to study this evening. They had just come over to have some fun, and they were playing games together. And Daddy had laughed and told her he'd thought as much, from the kinds of noises they were making. And why not? Scholars need to have fun, too, and he couldn't blame them for choosing their little teacher to have fun with. He couldn't help thinking how delighted her mother would have been had she lived to see her little girl blooming into a honeypot for all the bees. Hoda wasn't as relieved as she'd expected to be, for all that she'd told him a little more of the truth. But she was at least a little relieved, anyway. Daddy was glad she was popular. And just because she didn't feel sorry, like Daddy was, that her mother wasn't here to see her, didn't mean she was glad her mother was dead. She knew she could prove that to herself, and would, later on, when she had time.

Over against the bad feelings she could set the fact that some of the boys had brought friends, and one or two of them had regular jobs, and could come more often, and sometimes even treated a pal to a turn with Hoda. She could also usually manage, if she thought that someone had money in his pocket, to persuade him, if she was firm about it, and particularly if he was new, to pay the little extra and buy a bag or a basket, too. Once a guy was in the house, he didn't want to risk getting sent away with his load still on. He didn't have to know she couldn't afford to send him away, and she never actually said she would; but if he got worried it might happen, it usually worked. So Hoda was able, at last, to begin to reduce, appreciably, the stock of bags and baskets which were piled all over the living room, and in the summer kitchen, and which would otherwise soon have overflowed to the shed, where the winter cold would probably have ruined them. And she and her father were at least managing, like other living things that must survive on very little during the season of muffled life, to remain alive.

It was at this point that the woodyard delivered a cord of wood logs which neither of them had ordered, and the sawmen turned up, also unbidden, with their high-wailing power saw which, with short, anguished screams, sliced down the logs and scattered the snow with showers of golden sawdust. Then the men piled the stumps in a row beside the shed, grumblingly, because they had to go through deep drifts part of the way, where Hoda and Danile had had no reason to clear the snow. Hoda and Danile stood bundled up in their tattered winter coats, faces smarting and eyebrows frosted, and smelled the sawdust, sipping in short, quick sniffs which tried to prevent their noses from running, and listening to the eerie saw.

After they were all finished, Hoda did what her mamma had always done, she invited them in to have some tea and warm up, and Daddy talked to them in Ukrainian, and they felt better about having had to push through the deep snow because they saw that Daddy really was blind and he and Hoda lived alone together and hadn't made it hard for them on purpose, but just didn't clear enough of a path because they didn't know they were going to get more wood than what they had been able to stock up on credit before the snow had layered up so high.

For Danile and Hoda it was a moment of triumph, of sorts. Whether or not Uncle was conceding defeat, he had at least made a conciliatory gesture. "You see," said Danile gently, "he is not such a bad man, really. He doesn't want us to freeze."

Hoda was a little less sanguine. "He waited long enough," was her comment. But she was not disposed to be vindictive. Uncle's gift provided them with the unexpected luxury of knowing that they would be kept warm without worry for the rest of the winter, if the winter didn't last too long. This was more like things should be. If the worst can happen and your mother dies and all the good things you knew get spoiled, well, it's time for the best to start happening, too, though Hoda knew it wasn't so simple as it had seemed when she was a dumb kid. The Prince of Wales might actually be coming here, to her own city, and they even said he would drive through the streets so everyone could see him, but Hoda didn't really imagine that he was likely to catch a glimpse of her, much less get into the kind of conversation that she imagined herself having with him sometimes, and asking her to dance and discovering what a terrific dancer she was.

She sure was. Didn't she go to all the weddings in the neighbourhood? All that she got wind of, anyhow, and that were big enough for the dance to be given in a hall or a synagogue basement. A lot of them took place in the synagogue Daddy went to just down the street. If she possibly could, Hoda liked to get there on time for the ceremony. It was beautiful, all the nice clothes and the slow walking, and the singing prayers under the canopy, and the way the groom smashed the glass so decisively with his foot, and the bride's mother crying because her little girl was grown up and leaving her; Hoda always cried too, smitten by the pain there was in even the nicest things.

Sometimes, when she was lucky, she could even slip in and find a place for herself at the banquet table after the ceremony. If she hung around till everybody had a chance to get seated, and there were still some empty places set at the far end, and she just sat down as if she belonged, and her dress was clean and mended, even if it wasn't a party dress, and she looked nice, with a bow in her hair, or else that big cloth flower that her mother had treasured, the waiters and waitresses were usually so busy and in such a hurry that they just served her automatically. They didn't know she wasn't invited.

And the other guests were so busy eating and laughing and joking and judging the food and gossiping about everybody that Hoda found it easy to join in the conversation and laugh and joke too. Of course there were always one or two sour ones, who raised eyebrows and exchanged mutters and glances, particularly if she took several helpings. Sometimes one of them even said something mean, like "I didn't know you were connected. Which side?" in a sniffy tone of voice. But Hoda had an answer. She would reply with a cheeky grin, "Both. I'm a friend," which was perfectly true. You could be someone's friend even if they didn't even know you. Anyway, once you were in, nobody was likely to turn you away if you behaved all right, because it's a sin and a shame to turn someone away from a celebration. And rightly so; Hoda loved her weddings, particularly the dancing afterwards.

Sometimes she came to the dances with one or two of the guys, and they all made themselves at home and helped themselves at the refreshment table, where the father of the bride or another close relative presided, handing out the good things with a lavish hand, and calling out, "Everybody eat! drink! have a little schnapps!" until he himself could scarcely stand on his feet any longer, for the good example he was setting. Sometimes she hurried along by herself, late in the evening, pausing to be humbled, briefly, by the cool green, hot green, shifting green celebrant dance of the northern lights, in the depths of velvet blue synagogue sky. Nothing could keep her away from a wedding in those early years, whether there was a blizzard snowing over the whole world in great drifts of white, and she had to labour through thigh-deep mounds that grunted as she panted, and when she finally reached the hall she was all caked over, and had to shake herself off and stamp on the stairs before she could even go in, and then when she was in it took her half an hour to climb out of all the layers of woollen things that melted and got soggy as she undressed and made the little cloakroom smell even more rancid and doggy; or whether it was too hot a summer night for even Daddy to consider sleeping indoors, and he dragged his mattress onto the verandah because, he claimed, though he was wrong, that not even the mosquitoes could be very energetic tonight. Hoda could hear the music and see the yellow light of the synagogue hall pouring out the open windows and open doors, and people standing and sweating and fanning themselves, and a mother holding her baby so it could look through the door and down the stairs, and the baby blinking, stupefied, at the crazy whirl of dancing people, and Hoda, as she pushed by, asked the mother, "Who got married?" and the mother laughed and replied, "I don't know," and shrugged her shoulders after Hoda and jigged her baby up and down as though they were dancing too.

Hoda clomped down the stairs and surveyed the happy, red-faced, sweating crowd with a great, laughing, loving look, and plunged into their midst, dancing and swinging her elbows. It didn't matter that she didn't have a partner at first. There was dance enough in her for two. And a lot of the dances were horas and shers and other round dances and square, and they always needed extra people for sets when some old lady started clutching her chest or panting too hard to move. And people could feel in Hoda's happy, creamy face that this was what she was here for, big young kid, for the dancing, never getting tired though she puffed and gasped, always willing to come in again, for one more round and one round more. Hoda had heard somewhere that fat people are light-footed when it comes to dancing, and she was glad she had found out that she was one of that kind. She could feel herself rising and dropping and pivoting and cavorting, easily, lightly, gracefully. People even remarked on it sometimes, complimenting her on her ease of limb and tirelessness, and Hoda, without false modesty, agreed, which sometimes made them laugh a little. But she didn't care. She had always known, even when she was a little kid, that she really could dance if she wanted to, her own way, not hanging on to a silly chair and pointing her toesies, and she wanted to now and how!

People began to expect her at weddings, and if she arrived a little late some wag was likely to say to her, "Noo Hoda! You've turned up at last. I said to myself, 'So where's our Hoda? What kind of wedding will this be without Hoda? You might as well not hire musicians!'" Or someone would yell out a crack like, "You can start the celebration now. Hoda's here!" Hoda didn't mind. She would make some crack back and shout, "Let's go!" in her hoarse, resonant voice, and whirl into the dance. After a while to be expected is almost like being invited.

It was not only the dancing that drew her, eventually, to celebrations in the public halls. With the dancing came other things, came the opportunity to make eyes at her partners, make eyes like the heroines did in books, like that actress she saw on the screen in the moving picture palace that she and Pop the Polack sneaked into that time when the cashier had left, and they saw nearly the whole thing for free. Hoda could make big-eyes and narrow-eyes and up-and-down-eyes and sideways-eyes and one-brow-twitch-eyes and drop-eyes and flutter-lid-eyes and all kinds of other variations while she was dancing, so that her partner never knew what he was going to see the next time she faced him, as though her whole face was dancing too. She didn't say a word, except with her eyes, when he would begin to slip in special hand movements, touching and squeezing, getting in a quick feel and watching to see if she really meant what she was saying with her eyes. And soon he was finding it necessary, through newly discovered exigencies of the dance, to draw her close more frequently, push in when he should be backing out, and finally to grunt a short, urgent question in her ear, not realizing that his eyes had already been speaking, as eloquent as, if perhaps less versatile, than her own. Hoda responded with a little, low laugh from the glamorous depths of her dream, and, like the heroine of the silent film she had seen, managed, by making with her eyes and hands, though never losing time to the music, to ask her own mutely eloquent question, "How much?"

And even men who'd not intended to, who had reached a time in their lives when they only dreamed the opportunity might come their way again, ageing men, jumped and whacked their heels on the floor more smartly, inflamed by the movement and the heat and by her smell and her willingness, which, if conditional, was nevertheless somehow innocent, and gave them, too, the feeling of somehow innocence, even while they danced the fat girl harder, to make it understandable if wives should choose to wonder that they should want to slip out for a breath of air in the next break. When they left the hall they would cross to the woodyard where Hoda waited, or turn into the alley, or slip into the boiler room if it was cold out, or yes, unable to wait, would back her briefly against a wall or tree, and afterwards would pay her too, poor orphan, at times with an unexpected generosity born of schnapps and gratitude and the rare surprise of it all. And then they would limp back to the hall, to sit and mop their brows beside their wives who already sat spread-legged on straight chairs and hard benches around the walls of the room, and fanned themselves with handkerchiefs and now made mild fun of their exhausted spouses.

Soon after, Hoda would reappear; inexhaustible, dishevelled, Hoda would stand for a moment with her hands on her hips, her elbows out, her head on one side, and let her hips swing to the beat with ever widening gyrations, until, wound up again, she wound in again effortlessly among the dancers, to pursue again her pleasure and her luck.

Why shouldn't she dream of being the lucky one for a change? Dreaming is different from expecting. She'd get a place right at the front, at the edge of the road where the royal car was going to pass. When he came by she'd get a good look at him, and give him a chance to get a good look at her too. That was one thing about being fat, you showed up better in a crowd. After that it would be his move. She certainly wasn't going to throw herself at him, if he wasn't interested in her. Those ritzy royal people didn't like fatness. Or thought they didn't. Well, he had seen a lot of beautiful, skinny dames in his life already; they lay down at his feet wherever he went, it even said so in the Yiddish papers, though not in those words exactly. But he danced with them, and Hoda knew how guys could get when they were dancing. And no one ever heard of a girl saying no to a prince. But he hadn't picked one for steady yet, had he? He couldn't have found the absolutely right one. He was like Hoda, not going to settle for just anything. So it could turn out, though he didn't even know it himself yet, that the minute he saw her, the Prince might discover that the one he really wanted to love forever was a fat girl after all.

Even so it would be hard. There were powers that would do everything possible to discourage the match, though she, for one, was prepared to refuse all bribes. "We love each other," was her simple reply to all cajolings, to every attempt at threat and coercion. She loved the sound of it, the simple dignity, the immense promise, the foreverness, and sometimes said it aloud to herself in the bedroom. Only when Daddy wept because she was marrying a gentile, and his mother the Queen begged him to prevent the civil war that was threatening, did they give each other up a few times, and she promised to love him alone, forever, though they were to part, and he promised to be good to the Jews forever, though his heart was broken. But most of the time he got both his mother the Queen and his father the King to realize that she was best for him and was so nice the people wouldn't want to make civil war anymore when they got to know her, and she got Daddy to realize that she would be like Queen Esther and save the Jews her whole life long. It didn't really matter that she didn't believe any of it. All that was needed was for it to actually happen, for it to become absolutely true.

And if it had happened, would she really have liked him once she got to know him? Even if he was a prince, was he a nice person? Luckily, as she told herself later, she could take him or leave him. It was that cop who really griped her. Those damn cops, always bothering you for nothing, always interfering, always spoiling things. Just as the long, black motorcar had drawn close at last, just as she had really caught sight of him, just as she had surged forward, at the crest of the crowd, with her mouth opening to shout forth a great froth of joy, that cop came shoving along in front, bawling, "Back on the kerb! Keep to the kerb!" and planted himself, with his arms outspread and his big fat back square in front of her, shoving against her. At one instant the princely head had begun to turn toward her, and at the next, just as he was about to look into her eyes, the head and helmet of the cop shoved in between them, his back pushing her rudely, so that by the time she had jerked her face up over his shoulder the car had moved by and she was already out of the direct line of vision of His Royal

Highness. She screamed desperately, raucously, "I'm here! I'm here!" instead of the "Hooray! Hooray!" that the crowd was shouting in unison, and that she thought she was going to shout when she opened her mouth, but the royal head in the sedately moving vehicle showed no sign of having heard her separate voice, and continued to acknowledge graciously the general cry.

Of course she'd been stupid even to hope it could be otherwise, especially while the country was full of cops and teachers and capitalists. They always fixed things so people didn't get a chance. Why wasn't he out chasing crooks somewhere? Dumb cops. No wonder dumb Morgan knew he wasn't going to get caught by the cops, because they were even dumber than he was! All they knew how to do was stop you from trying to make a living and bully you around when you were just standing there waiting for the Prince of Wales. "Dumb cop!" Hoda yelled after the cop, who had moved on to shove other innocent people around. "Dumb cop!" she yelled truculently, complaining to the dissipating crowd, "He shoved right in front of me." But everyone else was talking about the Prince and how handsome he was and how he seemed so nice and how they'd seen him so close up and how they'd never forget it and how he made them feel proud to be in the Empire.

What did they know? What did they care about the Empire? If she were queen she'd improve everything for everyone, and see those cops got told off too, but a lot these people cared, even if it was for their own good. Not that she was sure she really wanted to be queen. Mr. Polonick used to say that royal families were useless, and just wasted the tax money anyway, though if she were queen she wouldn't be useless. Anyway, she would not have minded so much had His Royal Highness simply driven by without recognizing her. She wasn't dumb enough to think it could really happen that he would find her in all that crowd. But why should he be prevented from even having the chance to see her? Daddy said that all the billions of people in the whole world must feel just like she did sometimes; they must wonder why things go wrong, too. Did they all secretly think of marrying a prince or a princess? Did they all want to improve things? Then why did they let that cop shove her around?

She was still standing there, raging, when somebody came up behind her and cried, in a high, congested nasal voice, right into her ear, "Hi, Hoda! Isn't he wonderful?" She was tempted to snap out, "No he isn't!" But she was glad, afterwards, that she hadn't. It was only Seraphina, and she would have had to explain that she didn't really mean it; she was only mad at the cop, and she didn't feel like talking about it anyway. It was all silly kid stuff, standing on the kerb and screaming your head off. What for? What good did it do anybody?

But she didn't say anything when Seraphina went on parroting what everyone else was saying, about how handsome he was and how she'd never forget him, no, never never. Not that she even got a chance to say much; Seraphina was talking so much you'd think the nuns hadn't let her open her mouth for three years.

Hoda had heard from the boys that Seraphina was home from the nun's reform school, and that she was a changed girl. When the guys who used to hang around with her heard she was back, some of them went around to see her, kind of expecting her to be glad to see them after spending all that time in a convent with only other dames, and figuring she would be nice to them like before. But she wouldn't have anything to do with them. She had made new friends in the convent school, and now that she was out, she had, as Popowicki Polack described it darkly, "gone snob!"

Seraphina wasn't interested in the local boys anymore. She told them they were just kids, to their faces. She said she wasn't going to fuck for peanuts anymore. She had learned all about men in the girls' school, and from now on she was going to operate downtown where the big money was. She told the guys a whole lot of stuff about how a girl couldn't afford to waste her best years and good looks just giving it away for nothing. The guys were sore as hell. They said there ought to be a law against reform schools. Seraphina had been a nice kid before she got sent away. But it was funny, too, the way they had described it, imitating her high nasal voice and her silly giggle, especially when they came to the part about her good looks, because Seraphina, as Hoda remembered her, had always been pretty homely.

Hoda hadn't even thought of seeing her after the boys told her all that, even though she didn't have any girl friends to get together with now, except to talk for a few minutes if she ran into them outside, because most of her old friends were still just school kids, and she had nothing in common with them anymore, and wouldn't want to have much to do with them even if they didn't avoid her nowadays.

Seraphina, in spite of the way she was acting too good for the boys, wasn't at all stand-offish with Hoda. Hoda could hardly believe the change that had come over her. In just a couple of years she had grown from a skinny, sallow-faced, narrow-jawed, thin-nosed, dirty-looking girl, with stringy orange hair and plugged sinuses, who smelled funny when you came near her, to this gay, sophisticated vamp, hair chopped short and dressed just like a movie actress, who posed before Hoda now, pleased by the surprised look on Hoda's face, and cried out with the same whinnying, foolish, but good-natured laugh that Hoda remembered, "You like it?"

Hoda could not have told her whether she liked it or not; she had never seen anything precisely like it in real life before. She realized clearly, for the first time, that the backward, grubby Seraphina that she used to talk to because she felt sorry for her when the other girls called her a chippy and wouldn't talk to her, was really older than she had thought. Maybe she wasn't so dumb now that she was so grown up. Hoda was filled with a kind of startled respect. She had never seen so much stuff on anyone's face so close up. Seraphina had buried her natural pallor in white powder, on which two dramatic spots of orange rouge glowed with hectic improbability, where her cheeks were not likely to have bloomed on their own. She had painted heavy, black rings around her eyes, just like that movie actress Hoda had seen in the picture, only her short, colourless lashes couldn't droop down the way the screen star's did, and hardly managed to retain the tiny bubbles of black clinging to them. Her eyes inside the carbon rings looked pale and trapped, as if they didn't know what they were doing there. Her mouth was thickly plastered over with moist, black cherry lipstick, which ignored her thin lips to make an ambitious bow, with high points almost into the nose holes of her long, tapering nose. It looked kind of funny when Seraphina laughed, because when she drew back her lips the points of the bow looked as though they were picking her nose. Most impressive of all, Seraphina was wearing some kind of perfume. It was strong; it was sharp; close up it didn't entirely hide her natural smell and the two together could make you kind of choky if you stayed close too long, like a whiff of dog does sometimes, but from a short distance it was very good and rich-smelling, and Hoda maintained her distance, in spite of Seraphina's tendency to crowd, and breathed luxurious breaths. Perfume, to Hoda, was the height of elegance. Seraphina must have got hold of a lot of money somehow.

"So how you been, Hoda?" Seraphina paused long enough to ask but not long enough for Hoda to answer. "Boy, did I have a dirty weekend!" Seraphina giggled, rolled her eyes, and took Hoda under the arm, leaning on her intimately. She was scarcely a month out of reform school, but Hoda had a feeling that in relation to things hitherto unsuspected by herself, Seraphina was already a woman of the world.

"Didn't they want to make you a nun at the convent?" she asked, holding her head bent awkwardly sideways to try to get upwind of Seraphina's compounded scent.

"Me? A nun?" Seraphina whinnied delightedly. "Don't be silly! Can you see me, a nun?" Seraphina giggled. "It's unnatural!"

Hoda waited, politely, for an explanation. She had learned to be very careful when talking to goyem about their religions, in the hope that they would learn to be more delicate and stop making stupid remarks about her own. She was sick and tired of telling Pop the Polack to shut his goddam ignorant mouth. And the others were no better. She knew they did it sometimes just to tease her and see her get mad, but there were times when they talked, that she knew they weren't just being nice guys kidding around. They believed all those things that came out of their dumb faces, and they actually thought they were paying her a compliment when they said, "But you're all right, Hoda."

Seraphina still had that knack of making most of what she said sound as though she didn't know what it meant. But the things she said often made sense. You can't be a nun if you want to persist in the sinful ways of this world, Seraphina explained, in the tones of one who had learned a lesson by rote. Actually, she had thought at first that she might like to be a nun, because she liked praying, and had even prayed herself into a trance a few times. Sister had had high hopes for her. If she would only rid herself of sinful thoughts and sinful ways, or even if she would just try very hard to do so, God might help her and she might find her vocation. But sister thought she was being stubborn when she said she didn't have sinful thoughts; she didn't have many thoughts at all, only feelings. Sister kept saying she must try to think of something else when she got those feelings. But when she tried to think of something else she had to remind herself first of what it was that she had to think of something else instead of, and that was how she got more sinful thoughts in the convent than she ever did otherwise, and they gave her more sinful feelings. Sister said that was devil's work, leading her to hell, and the only thing for her to do when she had sinful feelings was to pray, and she used to pray so hard and fast to fight her sinful feelings that it was positively unnatural, and she used to wake up again absolutely exhausted. So she decided finally that she would just have to leave all the hard thinking and worrying about vocations to God, because what was the use of being dumb if you couldn't? And she got pally with some of the other girls, and they all agreed you might as well leave the hard things, like being good, to the sisters, because that was their job and they enjoyed it, and the girls all talked instead, every chance they got, about the fun they were going to have and the guys they were going to go with when they got out of there.

Hoda should have heard some of the stories those kids told! Seraphina had learned a lot, and in the end she and the sisters agreed that she didn't have the vocation, and she'd better learn a trade instead. Only she wasn't very good with her hands. So they released her finally because her ma needed her to help with the younger ones at home. She didn't like it much at home, either, and in a couple of months, when she wasn't jail bait any longer, she was going to leave home and live downtown. No more convent and no more looking after the brats, either. Seraphina was going to be a high stepper in town. Would Hoda believe it, she hadn't seen a guy close enough up to get a smell of for a couple of years, nearly three, except for maybe a priest or two, and they all smelled alike. There was even a sister sitting there when the doctor examined you; it was unnatural!

Seraphina had picked up that expression at the convent and she used it a lot, laying particular emphasis on the "nna" part of unnatural, perhaps because it bleated well through her nose. When Hoda admitted that no, she'd never gone downtown to look for pick-ups Seraphina said it was positively unnatural, and invited Hoda to come with her tonight. It would be a good time to go hunting, because a lot of rich Americans had come up to look at the Prince because they didn't have one of their own, and those Americans paid so much moolah, it was unnatural.

Hoda didn't much care for the idea of trying to pick up strange, grown men, in an area of town she didn't know well. What would they be like? Would she be able to talk to them? Seraphina was very confident about going into the big time. She seemed to know an awful lot of things. There were all kinds of things that puzzled Hoda, that she hadn't been able to ask anyone about since her mother had died. Maybe Seraphina knew. She sure knew stuff Hoda had never heard of. She could hardly believe that Hoda had never heard of jail bait, for instance. That was fucking under age. If they caught you, the guy got sent to jail, even if he paid you, and you could get sent to reform school, unless you started yelling it was rape, like that meant he forced you and you had nothing to do with it and they were sorry for you and let you go and told you to keep your legs crossed from now on.

Hoda didn't think it was worthwhile going downtown if that was going to happen to you. What if the cops caught her, and suppose she didn't remember to start hollering "rape" on time, or they didn't believe her, and they put her in a reform school, what would happen to Daddy? But Seraphina said they'd never catch her. "I'll lend you my makeup. They can't tell how old you are if you're wearing makeup." Seraphina really wanted her to come. She kept talking about the fun you could have, how sometimes the men took you out and bought you a meal in a restaurant, and let you order what you liked, and then they took you to a hotel, like in the movies on a honeymoon, and you drank whiskey together and really had a hot time. Seraphina knew a couple of dancehalls where you could pick up some really classy meatballs. You could make more in one night than Hoda could get off those punks she hung around with in a week.

Hoda was sorely tempted, but she decided she'd better not. She'd tasted whiskey at weddings and she didn't like it much. She really liked sweet wine better, and she didn't know how to act with strange men from downtown and rich Americans; she wouldn't know what to say to them. She'd like to see what the dancehalls were like, though. She didn't think she'd mind dancing with anybody, even if the steps were different from those she knew. She could do that all right.

"So come on!" Seraphina urged. "You don't have to do anything but dance if you don't want to!"

No, Hoda didn't think she'd better. What about those diseases Yankl the butcher had told her about? She had a feeling that downtown among total strangers and rich Americans was where you must catch them, especially if you went to hotels with them like Seraphina had done four or five times already. But Seraphina just laughed at her when she mentioned diseases, and said "I've never caught anything yet! Honestly Hoda, you're so fussy it's unnnatural!"

It was really tempting, just to try it once. All that money you could earn, that Seraphina boasted about, and not even have to make the bed afterwards. Tonight it was especially tempting, after her disappointment. Maybe that's why she had run into Seraphina, because she was meant to go downtown tonight. What if "he" were to manage to slip from the clutches of his rich, skinny, beautiful, dull gentile hostesses tonight, because he had a strong feeling that he must go out and search among the people of his Empire once again? It was all silly kid stuff and she didn't believe in it, but still, shouldn't she give him the chance? What if he was gone from his bed tonight, his place taken by his most trusty servant, his well-beloved figure disguised, perhaps as a rich American with natty light coloured clothes and a big roll of bills. He would scarcely speak for fear of betraying himself to others; but Hoda would know right away, and he would be glad. What a lot of crap!

"All right I'll come," said Hoda. "But I won't sleep in a hotel room all night." Maybe Seraphina's mother didn't mind much if Seraphina stayed away, because their house was so crowded anyway, but Hoda was not going to leave her daddy alone to worry all night. Even if she went to a hotel, just to see if it was really the way Seraphina described it, it would only be for a little while.

"Can I try your perfume, too?" she asked, when Seraphina had come over after supper and was smearing what felt like jam all over her face.

"Sure."

All made up and drenched in cologne, she looked at her face in the mirror, but couldn't recognize herself in the mask that stared back at her, until her eyes connected with the eyes, and the looking eyes said, *It's glamorous,* and the seeing eyes said, *Dumb cluck with dumb guk on your mug.* But the looking eyes said stubbornly, *But it is glamorous.*

It's uncomfortable, said the feeling skin, and twitched all over with a thousand little itches that wanted to be scratched.

"Don't smear it!" screamed Seraphina. "It's beautiful," she crowed.

It's just for tonight, like a disguise, Hoda assured her feeling skin and seeing eyes. *It is glamorous,* she let her looking eyes assert. It was somebody else, out there, helping her to hide, somebody who could make all kinds of faces she had never tried before, and when she made her familiar eyes into the mirror now, wow! they sure showed. Sexy. Glamorous. And safe too, older looking, at least seventeen and maybe even eighteen. No one would recognize she was jail bait.

She told Daddy she was going out with her girl friend tonight, and kissed him very lightly, so he wouldn't feel the makeup or smudge it.

"Do I smell nice, Daddy?"

"Yes," said Danile, trying not to sneeze. "Enjoy yourselves." He suppressed the urge to chuckle at the way she was suddenly fussing over herself, because he didn't want to risk hurting her feelings. When her pupils and boy friends were over she was his own little Hoda, noisy and natural and romping unselfconsciously about among them. But the minute two girls get together, a subtle change takes place. That's when the femininity begins to assert itself, and they begin to hatch their little plots to make captive, even more securely, by asphyxiating them if necessary, the same boys who already hang about them adoringly.

On the way downtown Hoda couldn't remember what the important word was, and had to ask Seraphina what that word was when you wanted to make people think a guy was forcing you. Seraphina trilled it loudly on the streetcar, so people looked around at them oddly, and Seraphina posed, pleased, and Hoda got a little self-conscious in her new face. But she repeated it over and over to herself, so she wouldn't forget it again if she needed it in a hurry: *"Rape . . . rape . . . rape . . . rape . . ."* No matter what happened, they mustn't take her away from Daddy. But when they got to the dancehall, and went downstairs into the dark, she forgot again. She stood for a little while near the wall, shy in this strange place, where all the lights were coloured, and wheeled around the room, passing, like waves, over the faces and ever-moving forms of the dancers. Beautiful. She'd never seen anything like it before. She waited, smiling hopefully and watching the different steps the dancers were taking, too shy at first to indulge her usual exuberance among these strangers. But Seraphina snapped her fingers and executed little steps by herself, and made nasal sounds with her big, painted-on cherry mouth, "Come on come on come on!" So pretty soon Hoda started doing it too, forgetting her false face and just letting all the little rolls and hitches go inside of her, swelling and rolling and rippling with the unselfconscious ease and rhythmic insistence of some ocean surface, and attracting, eventually, would-be navigators of crest and wave. Seraphina was dancing too, somewhere, in the undulating, rainbow-shotsilk darkness. Hoda remembered fleetingly, after a while, that there was some word she must be sure to remember, in case she needed it in an emergency, but she couldn't remember what it was, and after a while, the dancing and the newness and the excitement made her even forget to wonder what it could be.

It was easy, just like Seraphina said it would be, only, except for the dancing, she didn't enjoy it so much. The first guy who was willing to pay what Seraphina had told her to ask for, didn't take her to a hotel at all, but sneaked her out into the alley and part way up a fire escape. It was like what she was used to, only she didn't feel the same about it; she didn't feel she really knew what he was like, the way she felt when she did it even with total strangers, in her own part of town. He hardly said anything and she didn't really even know what he looked like. It wasn't as though they were having fun together at all, or sharing a good secret, or anything. The only compensation was that afterwards she could sneak back into the dancehall through the back way, without having to pay admission twice, so it was clear profit, anyway.

The next guy actually did take her up to his hotel room. It wasn't one of the two biggest hotels in town, whose names she'd heard of; it was just a messy little room in a hotel she never even knew existed, not far from the dance-hall. But there were certain unmistakable hotel luxuries, a carpet on the floor, and a sink right in the room with you. He really seemed to like her, and Hoda made a glamorous face at herself in the spattered mirror above the sink where he was putting water in his drink. He really tried to be nice. He had even stopped to buy a bottle of pop to put in her drink before they came up here. Then, while they were drinking and fooling around, he said, "Say, you're just a kid, ain't you?" and Hoda suddenly remembered the word, *'Rape! rape! rape!'* and stopped enjoying herself and got scared the cops were going to come in and catch her, and didn't enjoy her drink, though it was sweet, or anything afterwards, because she was listening so hard for sounds at the door. This one really liked her a lot, and wanted her to stay with him all night. He said he'd even get more pop for her to put in her drinks. He said "Let's tie one on, kid." But she said she was sorry, she had to get home because her daddy would be worried. So he asked her where she lived, so maybe he would come and see her sometime, but for some reason she herself didn't understand at first, she didn't want to tell him. He was too pushy, even after they'd done it. There was something scary about him, though he started out trying to be nice. Then he began to say funny things like how he could look after a kid like her, and see she got plenty of good contacts, and how she could make plenty of money with him to manage her. He knew a lot of guys who liked a fat young piece. But when she still wouldn't tell him where she lived he got kind of sore and said sourly, if she wanted to get on all right she should take his advice and not wear so much makeup. It ruined a guy's shirt so he couldn't wear it again tomorrow. And though he'd paid her in advance like Seraphina told her to make sure they did, he made it kind of hard for her to leave the hotel room till Hoda promised she'd come to the dancehall again tomorrow night. Like heck she would!

On her way out, when she got downstairs into the lobby, the man behind the counter beckoned her over. He said, "Hey kid, how about my cut?" He was very tough looking, and when Hoda said "Cut?" he said she'd better shell out some of what she'd made up there or he'd call the cops, because he was the hotel detective. Hoda got so scared she could hear her heart hammering, *'No – rape! no – rape! no - rape! no -rape!'* She looked around quickly and there was no one else in the creepy place and her throat was full of splinters of heart beat so she could hardly breathe, but at the same time when he mentioned cops and taking her money away from her another feeling surged up on top of her fear. So when he said again, roughly, "Come on kid, shell out!" and made a threatening gesture toward the telephone, without even thinking Hoda jumped and swung her fist over the counter, hitting his hand and knocking the telephone right off the desk. "Hey!" he yelled out, but while he was bending to pick it up off the floor, Hoda ran for the door. She turned, holding the door open, long enough to yell back at him. "If you want money, you can fuck for it yourself!" And she ran, ducking around a corner and into an alleyway when she saw two cops strolling along a block away, and waiting there fearfully, for a long time, before she worked up enough nerve to slip out and walk round to where she knew she could wait for a streetcar in comparative safety.

On the streetcar she sat with her hand protectively on the pocket in which she had pinned her change purse with the money, and thought about what a close shave it had been. Boy, it would be a long time before she tried to work downtown again. You might be able to make more dough but you ran a lot more risks and met a lot more creeps. Too bad the dance-hall wasn't closer to home, though. Maybe she could get some of her own guys to come with her sometime, when they had enough dough.

She wondered how Seraphina had made out. They had hoped to latch on to guys who would double date with them, but she guessed Seraphina had probably run into only lone wolves too, tonight, because she hadn't seen her at all after they both got to dancing. Well, at least she'd earned enough to pay Seraphina back for her carfare and admission ticket to the dance. And she still had enough left over to put her and Daddy ahead. Maybe she'd even keep something back from the household funds and begin to save for a small bottle of Seraphina's nice scent, which Seraphina said came all the way from Paris or Toronto, and you could get it at the fifteen-cent store.

As it turned out it hadn't been a very lucky night for Seraphina either. Hoda went over to her place late the next afternoon, to pay her back the money she owed her, and found poor Seraphina sick in bed, with her little brothers and sisters climbing all over her, though she kept shoving them off the bed and whining at them to scram because they were hurting her. Seraphina looked just awful. Her face was bruised all over, and her lip was split open and one of her front teeth was so loose, she could push it right up with her tongue. She whispered to Hoda not to say out loud what they'd been doing last night, because the excuse she gave her mother was that she had tripped and fallen down the streetcar steps, and that way her mother had only screamed at her for wearing those damn tight clothes like a chippy. She'd really be mad if she knew Seraphina had run into a crazy meatball last night. "He had a big wad of dough, and we went up to his hotel room, and he beat the shit out of me!" Seraphina whispered with difficulty, and with an expression of such idiotic surprise she almost looked pleased. "Look," she showed Hoda, under the covers, how her body was horribly bruised. Seraphina groaned, and sank back, screaming weakly at the kids who'd found their way back and were beginning to jump on the bed again.

Hoda whispered indignantly that it was just awful. He ought to be put in jail. But Seraphina laughed, unexpectedly, and gave her a very crafty look. "It's all right," she whispered slyly, "I charged him extra for it." She giggled weakly. "He paid me so much it's un-natural!"

Hoda was glad when she could decently put an end to her sick bed visit. It smelled just awful in Seraphina's house, of stale cooking and stale eau de cologne and the stale urine of a lot of careless people. Seraphina's mother came out of the kitchen before she left, and stood there growling hopelessly at her, in language Hoda didn't understand, and making accusing gestures toward Seraphina. Hoda shrugged her shoulders and made sympathetic noises. She realized now that Seraphina, good-natured girl that she was, in spite of all the things she did seem to know, was not the one who was likely to be able to answer the questions she'd been unable to ask anyone since her own mother had died. What Seraphina could teach her Hoda had not already learned, that she was not yet ready for what Seraphina called the big time, and she certainly wasn't sorry, if what had happened to them was any example of what went on downtown. Seraphina wouldn't understand it of course, but Hoda could see now why her mother used to say that these people had a long way to go to get civilized. Still, she wished there was someone she could talk to about the things that bothered her. More and more she missed having a real friend. Some things she just couldn't tell the guys, not simply because they didn't care. Some of them confided in her like real friends, and told her all kinds of things, even about the girls they really liked, as if she didn't have any feelings about being liked that way too. But her mamma had told her that she shouldn't talk to boys about things like what happened to a girl every month. It had to do with a woman's job in the world, and how she could have babies now, and her mamma had said that all she had to make sure of was that she kept herself clean so she wouldn't get sick or anything, and spoil her baby-making thing. Her ma had told her not to discuss these things with anyone because they were important, and sometimes ignorant people talked foolishly about it all and spoiled your feelings about it. And she had promised, too, that someday, when Hoda was a little older, she'd tell her more about it herself. There was nothing to be afraid of, Mamma had said, when Hoda was so scared the first time; Hoda came from a family of good, healthy baby-makers. Mamma said her own grandmother had been betrothed when she was eight years old, and had her first child at thirteen, and had countless more after that, though many of them died. But that was in the olden days, and nowadays there was no need to hurry these things. When the time came she would explain it all to Hoda. But instead of the time coming, all that other thing had happened and her mamma was dead.

Though there were some things that Hoda really wondered about, she understood very well, now, from her own experience what her mother meant when she talked of how people could spoil things, and she wasn't going to let them do that to something Mamma said was so important. Somehow she would find out what else there was to it, eventually. Only somehow, lately, she had been getting these awful fits of worry. What if something had gone wrong with her baby-making thing? What if it didn't get set and start working again and she lost the knack of making babies? Would she never be able to get married then, ever at all? What if her right guy came along and liked her like those guys liked some of the girls they cried on her shoulder about; how would she tell him that something was spoiled?

It wasn't that Hoda didn't know all about having babies. For crying out loud you'd have to have straw between your ears not to know. She didn't know exactly all the little details about what went on inside, but she knew if you kept on getting laid by the same guy he'd end up shooting all the different pieces in and you'd end up in trouble. That's why people who wanted to have kids got married, because one man's bits were more likely to fit each other and work out into an all-right complete baby. Hoda was pretty safe the way she operated because when you went with a lot of guys it was more like scrambling the parts of a whole bunch of jig-saw puzzles; you'd never be able to put together one right baby out of them, unless several guys happened to have parts that didn't fit in too badly together. But if you stayed with one guy only for time after time, and gave him enough chance to get all the parts in before the loose and extra bits got washed away every month, then you might just as well marry him and start ripping up the sheets to make diapers with.

She even thought of going to see a doctor, but not for long, not after what the doctor had done to her mother. All she had to do was complain to the doctor that she felt funny inside sometimes. That would be the end of her. Out with the big knife and into your gut. Oh no! She could just imagine herself lying covered over and still, on the living room floor, and Daddy sitting there and crying, and even just imagining it Hoda wept a little too. Anyway, she didn't need any doctor to tell her she'd been over-eating again, and that she would feel better if she lost weight. That's all he'd tell her. That's all anybody ever told her, as if she didn't know. Even the old ladies who knew her when Mamma was alive, who said they liked her, when they ran into her, told her in that blunt way that old people feel they can afford, as if only young people have to have respect, "Hodaleh, how are you? You're getting fat as a pregnant mare. Why don't you go on a diet? You'd look nice if you lost a few pounds, and then the good boys would chase after you, not just the discards." They were always making remarks like that, and if they hadn't been Mamma's friends so she had to be respectful, she'd have told them off long ago. Why should they call anybody a discard? Who gave them the right to discard somebody? She'd rather be a fat discard thank you very much, than somebody who went around discarding other people. If there was anything that burned her up it was when she saw in the synagogue how some of the men disregarded Daddy, which was the same thing as discarding him, as far as she could see, when they interrupted him in the middle of trying to say something, and they didn't even bother to listen, but talked right over him.

Sure, she knew Daddy told the same stories over and over again, and it was hard to stop him once the telling fit was on him, and sometimes it nearly drove her crazy too, but she understood what he was talking about and they never even tried to understand, and just made Daddy seem small and alone among them. They were the blind ones, though they didn't even know it, because they couldn't really see him, and the wonder of his life, and how he was chosen to save the town, and everything. And Hoda felt ashamed of herself for being embarrassed because he didn't even seem to know he was making it easy for people to ignore him. She was doubly enraged at these strangers for their disrespect, because she herself could hardly bear to listen to Daddy tell it all the way through any more, and when she saw he was going to begin to tell she began to cast about in her mind for something to distract him with, and sometimes she would make up any excuse she could think of on the spur of the moment to get out of the house, interrupting him too, and leaving him with the so familiar words in his mouth, while she rushed out to walk the streets by herself. Why? She might just as well have stayed and listened to Daddy, even if it meant she must hear the same old stories in the same old words yet again. Only she just couldn't bear it. Why? They were true, weren't they? every word. But oh Daddy, is it all you know? And especially, she couldn't bear it when she heard him begin with other people, and saw them glance at each other and set themselves to find a place to jump in and talk right over him, or just simply walk away, and leave him standing there, holding up his life that no one wanted to see.

She was bad, as bad as, worse than they were, because she knew better, and still could hardly bear to listen anymore. There was an awfulness in her, inside and out, she could feel it, though at first she didn't know what it was that was going on in there. Then one day it came into her head that maybe she was sick with the same thing Mamma had; maybe she had a big lump growing in there too. Sometimes she could actually feel it, if she lay still and put her hands up on her stomach, and pressed down with her fingers through the fat. There it was, she had hold of it, creepy death-making thing, pushing out, not caring a damn if it killed her dead. Naw, what was she scaring herself about? That was just a gas balloon, bubbling up inside and trying to work its way out; she could tell. How? Maybe Mamma thought it was gas too, at first. It's not gas, it's a lump. You're sick. You did a lot of things you're not supposed to, and Mamma knows, wherever she is, even if you fooled Daddy. Maybe you caught a disease. You'll die; there's rot in your stomach. You'll die like your mamma, screaming your head off. It'll hurt so much you'll go crazy screaming. I don't wanna go, Mamma! Not yet! Who'll take care of Daddy? I don't want to die, Mamma! Take it away! Don't let them give me a lump!

Noo, noo, don't be impatient. It'll go away. It'll pass. That's what Mamma used to say when she was sick. 'It'll pass, don't worry.' And it always passed when Mamma said so. Keep your mind off it. Hoda could keep her mind off it, if she tried. There was plenty to do. And see, it passed. She felt okay again. She didn't wake up feeling lousy any more.

But the fear of the lump didn't pass, the feeling that maybe she'd done something awful, and that lump was growing in her and spreading out and one day she would wake up screaming and screaming and screaming until they took her away. No she wouldn't. It was only the loneliness of not being able to talk to anyone about it that made her think horrid thoughts. It wasn't as if she was really even feeling sick or anything. She ate well enough; she couldn't be very sick if her appetite was that good. So she was fat, so what? She would continue to be fat if her appetite continued to be this good. For heaven's sake, she couldn't be healthier if she could dance the way she danced, after a day of cleaning somebody's house, and then bring someone home to the shack for what Seraphina had called "a little nightcap" afterwards, too.

The shack was working out fine, since she'd cleaned up a part of it, as a place to slip into from the back lane, especially with older customers, whose voices puzzled Daddy when she brought them home, since he had recognized one or two of them, and knew they couldn't possibly be students. So she had to pretend they'd come to buy baskets instead of what she'd really brought them home for, and instead of going in the bedroom with her they had to stay out in the kitchen and have tea and a chat with Daddy, and the expression on their faces when they found themselves trapped this way, and the frantic miming for her to do something about it, were really so funny that she had left one customer with Daddy once and locked herself in the toilet for a long time and had a fit of the giggles all by herself. Of course she had never intended to cheat them, and made sure she made it up to them later, but to avoid further awkwardness, nowadays she made use of the shack instead. Later on, when it got to be really cold again, she would have to figure out some other arrangements for the grown-ups. That was one of the reasons why she felt just sick, sometimes, because she was always having to think of more ways to keep on fooling Daddy, as if his blindness was never a final thing; she had to keep on blinding him over and over again. And it seemed somehow worse that it was always so easy. Whatever story she thought up, however flimsy she herself feared it to be, he found in it an interpretation which, if not precisely what she had intended, would lend itself to her convenience. He was so far from objecting, in fact, when she had announced, when the other kids were let out of school that summer, that she had completed her formal education and would not return to school in September, but was going to freelance in different jobs, that he commented approvingly on the forward march of modern times. In his day, in the old country, it was only learned old men who turned their homes into places of thought and study. Now, even a young girl, if she had the talent, and the brains, could do the same. It was as though there were something in Daddy that acquiesced in not knowing.

The worse she felt about it the more stubborn became her insistence that her clients buy baskets, because Daddy was really pleased with how well his business was going. And so was Hoda, too, with the increase in her earnings, which made it even more impossible to change the things that made her feel bad. Her venture downtown had taught her that she could charge a bit more than she had been doing, especially when she began to get grown men for customers, and then charge a little more on top of that for the bag or basket, if the customer hadn't bought one recently. And for the younger guys, she adjusted things according to a kind of instinct she had, about what they could afford at any given time. And when a bunch of them wanted to come on a gang shag, she gave them a lump sum bargain rate. It was, to use an expression that Yankl the butcher used to use when he wrapped her meat scraps, for "good will." That way a lot of young kids who couldn't afford it on their own got a chance, by clubbing together, and later on, when they did have something to spend, they knew where they could solo. In time Hoda was to become something of a legend in the district, as the girl who had broken in just about every mother's son of them.

Nor was the reputation which she was beginning to gain limited to activities in the strictly personal sphere. Hoda knew herself as a social being. She smarted not only from personal wrongs, but suffered also over the ills of society. With all that was happening in the world a person didn't have time and maybe didn't even have the right to spend all his time worrying about his personal affairs and feelings. Mr. Polonick had always said so, and she knew that was how Daddy felt, and she felt that way too. It wasn't only in Russia that things had got so bad they had to have a revolution to free the working classes from their slavery. The way the workers were being treated right here and now in this very city, no wonder they were out on strike. It was slavery, just like in old Russia; try to make people work without paying them enough to feed their families; try to force them to shut up. "Shut up and starve; you're only workers!" Well, we'll show you shut up. We'll shut you up too, all of you. We'll strike! See how you like it not to have the work rolling out and the money rolling in for a change! That was the way to do it. All the workers had to get together and to say NO! NO! NO! in one mighty voice, like they were doing right here and now, in this very city! Everybody was striking, everybody! Hoda got a feeling from people that she had never got before, a little bit like, only a lot better than it used to be in the marketplace. They were all striking out against injustice together. Hoda and Seraphina went all over to see, and Hoda talked to all kinds of strikers and they laughed and joked and Hoda was very excited, and encouraged everybody, and congratulated them because at last they had taken a stand, and when the workers at last stood up together and refused to work, the whole city stood still. Never was there such a ferment of still standingness. People stood and walked about on the streets, even on the streetcar tracks where now no cars ran. In front of closed shops people gathered and talked and asked what news and shrugged, because even the workers' paper wasn't coming out any more. If a rumble of wheels was heard down the way everybody ran to see who dared try to be a scab, and then they all laughed and joked with the breadman or milkman when they saw his permit sticker, and everybody was relieved, and then even the breadmen and milkmen stopped work. And then only the people wandered the streets and assured each other that they would hold firm, and wondered uneasily for how long that would have to be, and Hoda for one didn't care how long they would have to hold out as long as they won and taught those bosses a lesson!

But the bosses weren't going to give up their slave labour that easily. Hoda rushed to and fro with rumours of what they were planning. They had brought in blackleg cops! There was a big fight and Hoda missed it, between the strikers and the blacklegs. They had arrested a whole bunch of the good guys! All the strike leaders, but don't worry! The strikers were not afraid! It just made them mad! It made Hoda mad. Sure, the mayor and the council had stopped scratching their arses and now they were scratching the bosses arses! "Oh yes, we'll help you break the strike! We'll throw them in jail!" Well they could think again if they thought they were going to strangle the strike. In the synagogue even, the old men were horrified when Hoda brought the news of the arrests. Just like in old

Russia! And now the mayor had banned the big parade. They were going to bring in the mounties! But that wasn't going to stop the workers. They would parade anyway. "What do you have to do to win the right to live like a human being?" they asked each other, and Hoda asked too. Strike, yes, parade, yes, fight, even, if necessary, yes!

Hoda walked along the sidewalk, encouraging the men who marched up Main Street toward the City Hall. Let the mayor say "no no no" all he liked. Let him call in the mounties if he liked. They would stand firm! Pretty soon she was practically running, she was so eager to get there. Hoda had lost Seraphina somewhere in the crowd of men. Seraphina was all right in some ways, but she was too dumb to understand what the strike really meant to people, and was really more interested in picking up the odd little bit of business here and there, and Hoda suspected that she was not very high principled about whom she did it with, and would as easily take their filthy money from the bosses or blacklegs as comfort the strikers. She kept on nodding her head and saying "Nyes, nyes," when Hoda explained to her that that was scabbing, but Hoda had the feeling that she was wasting her breath.

Hoda was always to regret that she never reached the City Hall that day. People told her afterwards that everybody gathered there out front, all the workers from all over the city, and all they wanted was their rights, and what they got instead was those damn mounties charging them on their horses and smashing their heads with big clubs. But that didn't scare them. The workers fought back, and that was the thing Hoda wished she had seen, though she got her own in where she was, too, and she hoped at least one cop would never forget it. But what was the mayor doing all that time? You wouldn't believe it but he was standing on the City Hall steps, quacking away like a duck, while his cops were killing workers, and when even mounties charging on their horses couldn't make the workers go away the cops started shooting with guns, sure, they didn't care whom they killed, guys who'd fought in the war, too. But what did he care, standing there and reading from a piece of paper while the workers bled, siccing his cops on them in one breath and in another reading from his piece of paper that it was all their fault because they mustn't riot, mustn't strike, mustn't earn a living, mustn't feed their kids, mustn't demand their rights, mustn't even breathe or be human.

It's funny how you fall into things. Hoda hadn't even known she was a natural revolutionary till that day. Sure she was all for the strike and the workers, but she didn't really know what she could do till the day of the great parade when she saw the way the mounties were treating the strikers, and especially the way that cop was pushing Mr. Polonick around. It all happened so quickly she could hardly remember the sequence herself. First of all she was running along the sidewalk trying to keep up with the march of the men on the street. Then she recognized Mr. Polonick, who'd got unravelled from the marching workers and was running back and forth like a loose end beside them. She couldn't hear what he was saying but she could see from the way his arms were moving and the way he skipped around that he was talking to the strikers like he used to talk to the kids in class. And the strikers were marching quickly by and every now and then turning a tolerant head or waving an arm, unheeding but friendly, at him. What right did that mountie have to come riding straight up at him, crowding between him and the marchers, forcing him to skip and stumble toward the kerb? Damn cops! Damn bullies! And what right did he have to turn his horse around and come back toward where little Mr.

Polonick was straightening himself up again? And what right did he have (Hoda was running toward Mr. Polonick now) to lean down that way from his horse, holding that club of his up as though . . . "Oh no you won't!" Hoda grabbed up at the arm that held the club, jumping up at the mountie from the back and side so he didn't even see her coming, he was so anxious to take aim at Mr. Polonick. She felt the big arm jerk under her and she held on with both her own, sinking her teeth through the cloth that came handiest, into firm, living flesh. The cop gave a startled shout of pain and involuntarily loosed his hold on the reins. The horse jerked out from under him, and at the same time Hoda loosed the grip of her teeth and her arms and with one closed fist caught him on the side of the face as he fell. She heard the shouted "Hurray!" from the marching workers and the spectators as she stepped back, and saw that the cop was on his hands and knees and one of the people had rushed forward to kick his club out of his way. Hoda grinned round at the voiced approval of the world. "Good going! Did you see what she did? Pulled him right off his horse!" But she didn't have much time to savour her triumph.

"Run, Hoda!" Mr. Polonick was pulling her by the arm. "Run! They'll arrest you if they catch you!"

Hoda ran. Mr. Polonick ran with her. They twisted together down the side streets and alleys back toward home. Pretty soon Hoda had to slow down because her stomach was hurting from being bounced along, though she was holding it with her hands as she ran. Mr. Polonick had slowed down too. He thanked her. "You're a brave girl, Hoda," he said, after they had walked quietly down familiar streets again for a little while and seemed to have eluded all pursuit. "The rest of us talk a lot," he continued humbly, "but when we see the truncheon bearing down on us we're afraid. I was afraid. I thought, 'What am I doing here?' But you knew what you were doing there. You jumped right in, without talking, without arguing. You saw something was wrong and you had to act to set it right."

If they put her in jail what would happen to Daddy? "Don't tell my daddy, please. He doesn't know where I went."

Mr. Polonick said her daddy would be proud of her if he knew, but he promised. He made Hoda promise in turn that she would stay near home for the next few days and not let herself be seen too much in public till the strike was settled and the mounties were off the streets. Best she should not take chances in case this mountie or some of their spy scabs had got a description of her. Hoda promised. Then Mr. Polonick asked if maybe Hoda wouldn't come to a meeting sometime, when this was all over, of a group of young communists, his comrades. He wanted to introduce them to a brave girl, of the kind that had won their freedom from slavery for the Russian people. And he wanted the chance to thank her publicly for saving his life.

Hoda said yes, of course she'd come. She was a little dazzled by his talk. She hadn't even realized that she had saved his life. And she hardly ever got invited places, especially not this way, with a real "please come" and "it would be a great favour" in his voice, not like when a teacher speaks to a pupil, but like a grown-up speaks to a grown-up he respects and maybe even admires a little. They shook hands warmly when they parted, and Hoda almost regretted that she had decided it would be best not to worry Daddy, because she was really dying to tell him.

That was how she missed the big riot at the City Hall, and that was probably why in a part of her she never could bring herself to believe entirely that the great strike had really been broken in the end, because she had won her part of it, hadn't she? And she wasn't there to see the militia patrolling the streets, nor the workers starved into creeping, gradually, back to their jobs. For the next few days she kept her promise to Mr. Polonick and stayed in the house, not only because she didn't want to go to jail; as it happened she probably wouldn't have gone out even without Mr. Polonick's warning, because she must have twisted a muscle or something in her stomach when she yanked that cop off his horse and then had to run so hard. She felt a little sore inside, so she stayed home in bed and let Daddy pamper her.

When she emerged again she was surprised at how many people knew about how she had distinguished herself in the strike, and though sometimes it sounded as though they were mocking her a little when they talked of her brawny feat, she could feel the admiration in their voices too. Even Daddy found out about it. One day he came home from the synagogue and said, "Why didn't you tell me you fought with a cossack, Hodaleh? Is that why you haven't been feeling well? Did he hurt you? They say you jumped right on his horse and pulled him to the ground and gave him a thrashing. Did he really hurt you somewhere badly?"

Once he was finally reassured that she was unharmed, and she had given him her modest version of her adventure, he couldn't stop marvelling over it. "Your mother should have lived to see it. Maybe you take after her father, Shem Berl the soldier." But he made her promise, nevertheless, to stay away from arguments with cossacks in the future. For a girl once was enough.

As the months passed, Hoda extended and consolidated her various activities. She was neither slow nor lazy to turn her hand, or whatever else was necessary, to earn a few cents for herself and Daddy. Nor did she consider any labour beneath her, and one thing the women for whom she worked could not complain of: she was as cheerful about cleaning their toilets as their dishes. Unfortunately, it had already begun to be rumoured among them, that she would as willingly accommodate their husbands as take their household linens home to wash and iron, which mitigated, in some degree, her chances of popularity as a cleaning woman. More than one virtuous housewife, watching Hoda on her hands and knees, as she heaved her rump about on the floor, considered with distaste the possibility that her husband might choose to betray her, even briefly, with this rubbery mass, however young and willing she might be. No, not likely, even with his appetites. It would be indecent. But husbands are notoriously unable, even with years of training, to achieve the wifely ideal of fastidiousness, and few of the women for whom Hoda worked were willing, if they could possibly avoid it, to allow their men to confront the temptation of simple availability. The result was that Hoda often found herself being hurried and harangued, more and more impatiently, as the afternoon wore on, and sometimes hustled out of a house precipitantly, even before her job was quite done, by housewives who were, unknown to her, beginning to worry that their husbands would soon be home from work. Had she only known that the ladies were actually, in a sense, jealous of her, it would have gone far to ease her resentment over those dames who tried to get her to cram three hours' work into one, and shoved her out of the house at least an hour before her work was properly done, to do her out of that hour's wages. A fat lot they cared that she and Daddy couldn't afford to lose the money. If people hired you for a day they should let you work for the day. She couldn't afford to lose money that she'd counted on like that.

She couldn't afford to lose time, either. That's why she worried about getting sick. She couldn't afford to.be sick. And she wasn't going to let herself be, either. That's what she told herself when she got into those fits of feeling sure that there was something wrong with her insides, and that's how she usually talked herself out of them. So what, everybody gets constipated sometimes. But when she felt tired and nervous and funny for almost a whole week, and her stomach was all jumpy, and she stayed in evenings because she just couldn't bring herself to move from the house, and even let Daddy send away a couple of her pupils, because she just couldn't take them on now, she felt more and more certain that something awful was going to happen to her. And what she felt worst about, next to being afraid she was going to die and dying would hurt her something awful, and leave Daddy with no one to look after him, was the customers she was passing up, when she really couldn't afford to.

But she couldn't talk the pains out of coming back this time, though each time they left she prayed it would be for good. An unexpected rhythm of pain had somehow, at last, gradually emerged from the vague, amorphous discomforts that had been troubling her for months.

"I have a stomach ache," she told Daddy fearfully, now. "It keeps coming back."

And Daddy comforted her, with a formula that had become something of a joke between them, whatever little illness either of them had. If one complained, the other said solemnly, "I hear it's going round." That way you could reply with another little joke that made you feel better about how you felt. If Hoda said, for instance – because it was usually she who liked to trot out her ailments to have them minimized by Daddy – if she said, "Oi, I have a headache this morning," and

Daddy replied, "I hear it's going round," she would say, "No Daddy, it's jumping up and down," and they would both get a laugh out of it. Or, when she had been waking up feeling lousy that time a while ago, and she complained, "I have a stomach ache, Daddy," and Daddy had said, "I hear it's going round," she would say, "Listen harder Daddy, it's turning somersaults, too," and though she still felt rotten, she felt somehow better too, for being able to give a little laugh.

And so now too, she was comforted at first, because after all the pains weren't so bad, and not constant, and Daddy didn't seem to think it was anything to worry about, even though he had been there when Mamma was sick, and would have noticed if there was something really wrong. So this must be different.

Danile made her go to bed, and took his work into his own room, and shut the door and promised himself for the thousandth time not to sing and run the risk of waking her up, especially tonight, because the poor child obviously had some digestive upset, maybe a cold or something she'd eaten, that had held her down these past few days. She really had rather a delicate constitution. Everything seemed to go to her stomach, from fighting cossacks to any little cold. But she must have fallen very soundly asleep, because some time later, Danile, not quite as sanguine about her illness as he had appeared, came and stood outside her bedroom door and listened for any sound that might indicate that she was in discomfort. But all was still, and he returned to work, and to his unconscious melodies, for another hour or so, before he achieved the particular degree of tiredness which he knew would assure him his few hours of solid rest.

Hoda was ripped out of sleep by a pain sharper than any she had ever known before, and another and another, in a world that had shrunk, while she slept, to contain nothing but her body, awash on her bed, a world that was her body trying to turn itself inside out, struggling with a bowel movement that was the evacuation of continents. The ocean had already burst forth. Frightened, still asleep, she tried to raise herself up on the sopping bed, but the spasms claimed her, and she lay grunting hoarsely, not knowing whether she strained to help whatever it was that had torn loose inside of her to escape, or whether she was clutching, frantically, to retain her life. *"Daddy,"* she gasped out, her tongue strangely fuddled and thick, as in a dream when one tries to cry out for help, but can't. Her voice was constricted, shrunken to little, whimpering, pushing moans, conscripted to the general effort of straining on which her whole body concentrated. Daddy! she screamed soundlessly, inside herself, while from her mouth came wordless, unrecognizable grunts, animal sounds that strangled on themselves as she strained. She couldn't even try to call out to him again. All that was awake of her concentrated, savagely, frantically, on the lump that was tearing her insides apart. She didn't know what it was, and she knew it wasn't happening, but it was here, retribution. Was she screaming, or whispering, or making no sound at all? Over and over and over, *"Mamma Mamma Mamma."* Why did it hurt so? Poor Mamma! Poor Hoda! *Oh help me somebody! I'm dying. It's just awful. What is it? I'm sorry, Daddy; I'm sorry. Mummy; I didn't mean it. What did I do?* It didn't matter. Just push! *Help!* Tear loose the nightmare lump, shove it out into the oozing wet darkness. *Oh thank God it's only a dream. Shove. Sho-o-ove! I'm dying. I'm dy-i-ng! Oh I'm dying!* Was that Daddy who cried out, from the tranquility of his well-earned sleep, in answer to her own hoarse squawk, familiar words, muffled as in her own dream, "study, study!"

But I'm dying, Daddy. I'm dead. Hoda fell back, released suddenly into death, and lay there, until the very noisiness of her own panting disturbed her death. Perhaps it wasn't death but the long-awaited transformation then, and fat Hoda had dropped away from inside all at once, a ton and a half of guts, that had left only her true beautiful self, transfigured by this upheaval from within. When she woke up in the morning, the bed would be dry and clean, and all would be totally recovered from this strenuous dream. But there was something still going on down there, that wouldn't let her keep her eyes closed, something else beyond her own panting, a small rustling sound she imagined she heard from the mass of her own wet guts that she dreamed lay between her sprawled-apart legs. Vexed, she heaved herself up and peered in the dimness, at the warm, smelly dark mess that squirmed there. Squirmed?

Fearfully, Hoda nerved herself, laid hold of the sticky thing with one hand, poked with the forefinger of the other, shook the thing that took on a frighteningly familiar shape in miniature between her fingers, and poked again.

It squawked. The lump was alive.

SIX

There was no way for Hoda to know, nor would it have helped her much at that moment, to realize that in relation to the usual run of things she could consider herself lucky. It was an easy birth. It had happened very quickly, telescoped, as a dream is: the sudden, atrocious pain; the straining spasms, to which, half asleep, she had instinctively acquiesced, as to a dream; the bursting, tearing release; the relief of sheer exhaustion; all these were the mechanics of the event hard followed, however, by a realization which was not so easily to be borne.

So what if it was alive? It was only an awful dream anyway. But Hoda could not prevent herself from being dragged back into the dream. She drew back the hands that had touched the thing, drew in her legs, circling them widely around it, and dragged herself back to the head of the bed, where she crouched uncomfortably. Stop the dream! Get away! She tried to swing herself off the cot, and felt a sudden tug. It was coming after her! It was tied to her insides! If she moved any further it would unwind the rest of her guts, or else it would bounce down after her if she tried to run, and squawk, and wake Daddy. Daddy mustn't come! She swung her leg back carefully onto the cot. She bent forward, groping for the slimy cord which bound them together, grasped it with both hands, and tried to pull it apart. It wouldn't tear. She couldn't get a good grip. The thing squawked again. Frantic, Hoda hissed at it, "Shhhh!" If she didn't get rid of it the crazy dream would follow her forever! Crouching again, on the bed, she brought the cord to her teeth, tasted iron, slime, smelled her own insides, held her breath, and gnawed, chewing with little, desperate grunting sounds, and tasting a trickle of blood in the tube as she ground her teeth through it. It was leaking blood. It would bleed all over the place. But she couldn't keep it squeezed tight between her fingers this way forever. Make a knot. Clumsily, she knotted the small length of fleshy cord that protruded from the lump, knotted it once, twice, all the way, as often as she could, to hold the blood in, at least till she could get rid of the thing.

Meanwhile her own end of the cord took care of itself in another lurching, wrenching painful movement from within. Oh why doesn't it stop? Why don't I wake up and call Daddy? No! Daddy mustn't know. Something had gone wrong. Somehow they'd managed to shoot enough pieces in her to fit together. Hoda dragged herself off the bed and over to the light switch. She clicked it on, and blinking and holding her breath, she turned and looked at the godawful mess on the bed. It was so incredible it was comforting, as dreams sometimes are because they so obviously can't be true. She didn't believe in it but it made her do things, as dreams always do. It forced her to go near the thing again. She bent down to scrutinize it carefully. She tried to turn it over, but it screwed up its ugly face to yell, so she had to pick it up, fearfully, and hold it close against her chest, to stop it. It stopped. Her fingers continued to explore it carefully. She counted its fingers and its toes, made note of its ears, its penis. Nothing was missing, on the outside anyway, and the parts seemed to fit, in a funny way, though it wasn't pretty, and its stomach, with that silly extra, multi-knotted tail, stuck out almost as much as her own. Why was it so gummy? From her insides. And why were its eyes glued together like that? If it was blind people would know it belonged to her!

The thought filled her with panic. She wanted to throw it away somewhere, or hide it under the bed, or flush it down the toilet and forget it. But it was alive, and it would choke in there! What would happen if Daddy found out she had it, if people knew? Daddy would understand everything then. He would be ashamed. He'd never be able to face the voices in the synagogue again, or in the street, or all around him, voices that he would know at last were talking about her and what she had been doing and what had come to her. And he would have to believe them now. *Daddy, it's not true, it's not the real truth, Daddy, honest. It's something different.* How could she bear to face him, then, and be near him, and . . . *Do something. You can do something. You have to do something.* She was still holding the thing, against her breast. Her insides hurt something awful, and she couldn't help it, she just had to half sit, half lie back on the cot, trying to ease the raw hurt. She tried to force herself to think. The thing nestled comfortably and she was dimly aware that she held it comfortably too. She drifted off, half lying there. Suddenly, she snapped back, alert.

Clean up. Quickly. The voice that issued the order came from somewhere else, and she blinked rapidly around the room before she realized that the somewhere else was in her head too, high in a disassociated part of her brain. She struggled to her feet. What could she do, holding this? It was very quiet. Dead? A lurch of joy, a spasm of horror, then relief. It was asleep. She put the pillow on the floor, in a corner, and put the thing down on it.

While she worked her mind hammered, disjointed questions, incoherent accusations, denials, fragments of helpless prayer, prayer to Daddy, to Mommy, even to God himself, to please avert their faces and help her anyway, help her now! And somewhere, beyond the pleading and the ranting and the helpless incoherence, in another realm of thought a part of her calculated, daring to put a name to the thing for the first time, *a baby*. She mustn't have a baby. Not now. It wasn't time yet. The good things hadn't come yet! What would she do with a baby? Where could she put a baby? Where could she hide it? Nowhere. Give it away? How? No one must know. She was not its mother. Its fathers? Who? Ten maybe, more maybe. No mother. No father. Like an orphan . . . an orphan . . . an orphan . . .

Hoda knew, now, in that remote part of her mind, what to do. Later she was to marvel at the fitness, at the justice of it, and even to wonder, sometimes, whether it hadn't after all been meant to be that if she had to fall so hard, there should be at least this little cushion. God averts his face, and helps. Now, however, she thought only that she must hurry, hurry; it wasn't really happening but hurry anyway; it's so necessary to hurry, in dreams, so hard to hurry, in dreams, and so necessary and so hard to be careful, too, and hang on to the thread, and grasp details that suddenly loom up, disproportionately, absolutely important, so hard to emerge out of great gaps in consciousness, with an armful of foul linen, to find yourself standing under startlingly usual stars, on the summer kitchen steps, and wondering what you had intended to do, until you remember that for now you must hurry and hide the stuff in the shed.

The mattress too was soaked through, and hard to get a grip on. She struggled with it, till finally, bracing herself, she heaved it up and carried it, holding her breath, pausing every few steps of the way to stand and pant noiselessly, and squeeze her thighs tightly together to push her guts back up and prevent them from dropping out right on the kitchen floor. Finally, she succeeded in carrying it, too, into the shed. From the shed she brought the makeshift pallet she had stuffed herself, for business purposes, and remade her bed.

From the kitchen she brought a basin and the ever-ready kettle that stood warm on the edge of the wood stove. Carefully, she bathed the still sleeping thing. It made tiny little smacking sounds in its sleep, and dreams are so uncontrollable and ridiculous, she was almost enjoying herself, touching and laving its soft skin, but remembered in time that she couldn't be. She wrapped it in pieces of clean old sheeting, and laid it on the bed. Then she cleaned herself up as best she could, and out of more pieces of sheeting, tied a tight, wadded bandage around herself and under, to hold her guts and sop up anything else she might lose down there. Then she picked up the baby and sank down with it on the bed for a few moments, breathing heavily, her mind momentarily gone blank, watching it with eyes of incurious amazement as it lay asleep on her stomach. *Looks better now,* she thought.

Before it gets light. Before anyone can see you. Before it begins to cry again. She forced herself awake, and to her feet. *Pencil and paper.* Carefully, she printed the note, taking a long time because it was hard to think, and because notes are important if you can't put in some kind of strawberry or a family heirloom, for clues later on, when good things happen; so you have to make them pay attention somehow through the note. She tucked it in carefully among the baby's wrappings.

She put her coat on over her shoulders, and buttoned it at the neck, like a nurse's cape. That way if she met someone, they would maybe not notice what she was carrying inside. But she wouldn't meet anyone, not in the dark, not if she was careful.

Don't think. Go now.

Hoda slipped out the back door. She kept, as far as she could, to lanes and shadows, trying to tread noiselessly, like a courier de bois in the history books. The air was cool, the stars dimmer, more distant than they had been when she was dragging herself out with the mattress an aeon ago. Dawn hurried behind them, she knew, and hurried herself, fearful of discovery by light, but even while she hurried, she was dreamily aware that it was curiously real, the night she moved through, a meticulously authenticated dream, correct to the last detail in its self-deception, as though she was the only part of it that knew it wasn't real, or maybe she was the only part that wasn't real herself.

She climbed the steps and put the thing down on the porch of the old house, where anyone opening the door could not fail to see it. Then she grabbed the big, heavy knocker, and slammed it, again, again, again and it went "Bang! Bang! Bang! Bang!" on the door, crashing so loud she was suddenly pinpointed in the centre of all the noise in the universe, for everyone to see. She ran, thudded off the porch, scuttled, crouching, down the drive, and dived in behind some lilac bushes. She waited. No one came. She waited. Still no one came. A spasm of rage swept through Hoda. Who did they think they were? What did they get money for? It was all their fault! Why couldn't they answer the door? It could catch a cold out there, or a dog might get it. What were they supposed to be here for anyway? She couldn't wait all night. Soon Daddy would wake up and it would be their fault if he found out she was gone and she couldn't tell him why. Hoda felt like going back up there on that porch and banging and banging and banging until they had to come and when they came she wouldn't run away either; she'd stand there and give them a piece of her mind. She could almost hear herself yelling and yelling and yelling and yelling and if she started now she'd never be able to stop yelling again! And it would serve them right! Somebody had to let them know they weren't fit to take care of children.

Luckily for them, they opened the door at last, and Hoda saw a figure looking about, from around the edge of the door, and then the door swung wider, and the figure dropped down on its knee. She didn't stay to see any more, but slipped from bush to bush, the short distance to a break in the hedge near the gate, and sped a journey homeward which she could never afterwards even remember. Nor could she remember anything about getting undressed again, except that she strained and struggled to get her bedroom window open as far as she could, because the room still had that strong, iron smell. But as she began to fall asleep she realized that if Daddy noticed the smell he would probably think it was her woman's baby-making readiness thing, come on, and that would explain her stomach ache too, and for fear of embarrassing her he wouldn't even mention it, but be very gentle with her, like he always was, and everything would be the same as usual. Indeed, as she rustled about on the pallet, trying to get her sore insides more comfortable, her relief was so great despite her physical discomfort, she couldn't, for the life of her, remember why everything shouldn't be the same as usual on the morrow.

And Daddy was indeed very gentle with her during those few days when she hardly moved from the bed. She kept him close by her, and at first could hardly bear to have him leave her sight. For Danile it was like a touching return of the baby she had been. At first, worried, he wanted to call in a doctor, but she absolutely refused to hear of it, and when she insisted she knew what was the matter with her and it wasn't anything serious and she couldn't tell him but Mamma would have understood, and she just felt like resting, that's all, like Mamma used to say she should, Danile caught on, and sighed, as he often had when his wife was alive, over the problems of women and the mysteries of nature. It was curious that she was most like the child she had been once, now that she was most acutely in the grip of her womanhood. She listened now, as she had as a child, when he described to her again the special circumstances of their existence, and once or twice, he even detected, from the sound of her breathing, that she was weeping as he told her of their fate. Warm-hearted little girl. "Not to weep, child, we're in God's hands."

She wanted stories and still more stories. "No, not that one, Daddy, you've told me that one. Don't you know any others? Is there anything you haven't told me? Didn't anything happen when you went to the grocery? Tell me something new."

Her pettishness didn't disturb him; it was the peevishness of a sick child whose very boredom shows she is on the mend. So she was pampering herself, just a little, and demanding that he pamper her a little too. Why not? She was much better, he could tell. She even let him out of her sight long enough for him to run down to complete his minyan now. A couple of times they had had to get someone else to make up the tenth man at his synagogue, after they had sent someone to call him and Hoda had begged him to stay with her instead.

At first Hoda had simply wanted Daddy, wanted him to be there, blotting out everything that had happened with his presence. Then she had hoped, briefly, that by keeping him near her she might be able to prevent him from hearing about it. When she had awakened finally the evening after that dreadful night, after sleeping through the whole day, she hadn't been able to remember anything at all for a little while, and couldn't even remember what night it was, and then when she remembered she doubted whether it had really happened, and then when she felt her crudely stuffed pallet rustling beneath her she thought that anyway it was over with, and she could forget all about it. But her breasts and her insides and her tiredness wouldn't let her forget it, not entirely, and a little, nagging curiosity, not to know much, but just enough to put a period to her sentence, began to plague her. Did it still live? Was it blind? Had anybody guessed? Or had she dreamed it all and somehow exchanged the pallet for her mattress in her sleep? She had no stomach to sneak out to the shed at night and see. She was particularly nervous of the dark now, not afraid, just nervous, that's all, just because she was just nervous now anyhow. It would pass once she knew. She questioned Daddy closely, insistently, when he had been out for a moment, on a brief errand to the grocery. But Daddy had no news to tell her, so she had to let him go finally, and told him that she felt fine again now, and he needn't miss prayers at the synagogue any more. And to prove it she got up and got dressed and tried to prevent her steps from dragging as she fussed about the kitchen. If anything of importance had happened in the community the old men would not fail to know about it, and discuss it so Daddy would hear, and Hoda found some satisfaction in assuring herself that provided it had really happened, it was not the kind of occurrence that would easily be glossed over at large.

She was more right than she knew. What had not occurred to Hoda was that her father might have heard of the foundling that had been dumped on the porch of the Jewish Orphanage, even while he shopped for those few items at the grocery, and refrained from mentioning it to her out of a certain delicacy, which inclined him to protect his daughter from the sordid implications of the tale. No doubt she would hear about it in time, from her friends, and they would discuss it in the frank way of young people these days, and put their own constructions on it, for young people too must cope with real things as real things happen in this world. But it was not the kind of thing for a father to gossip about with his young daughter, particularly at such a sensitive age, and when she was under the weather, too. At the synagogue, however, Danile listened as avidly, and speculated as ardently as anyone else. Few who ventured out to breathe the public air that week failed to hear of the extraordinary case. The whole town was buzzing with it; at least the Jewish community perforce assumed that the rest of the city was buzzing too. It had been written up in both the English and the Yiddish newspapers, naturally in considerable detail, in the latter, and there was even a blurred, undistinguishable photograph of the rag-wrapped baby printed. The newspapers mentioned the note, too, which had been found among the rags, but did not print its contents, though the English papers were explicit in stating that the printed note gave no clue to the identity of the mother. A rumour circulated, and gained wide credence among Jews, that the Yiddish Press had been asked to suppress the contents of the note, by unspecified authorities vaguely described as "those above," with the result that, though never printed, and actually seen by very few, the words of the note were soon on every Jewish tongue. The possible implications of the curious screed excited much speculation, and continued to be discussed for weeks and even years after. No one who was old enough to take note of those rumours, in fact, has ever forgotten them, even to this day. And some, because of the added authority that time and faith add to speculation, and the further reduction of the possibility of checking primary sources that is assured by the passage of time, still hold, though vague as to all but the most rudimentary details, that the whole thing was not a rumour but a proven fact, and that the baby had even subsequently received a pension.

In her note, Hoda had pieced together, out of the confused shards of dream and desire and the longings of her shattered childhood, the following: TAKE GOOD CARE, A PRINCE IN DISGUISE CAN MAKE A PIECE OF PRINCE, TO SAVE THE JEWS. HE'S PAID FOR.

What could be more clear? Almost anything. Perhaps that was why the popular mind scorned the veils in which the subtleties of meaning were shrouded and comprehended directly the central core of the message, that somewhere, in secret, a Jewish woman had given birth to a son of a prince of the blood. Hadn't he been driven through the streets in his chariot, like princes of old, looking benignly from left to right, and raising every now and then an aristocratic finger? Who knows what might have caught his eye, as eyes of old have been caught, as King David's eye had been caught of yore? No wonder "they" wanted the note suppressed!

"Ha ha!" cried the old men, alert to insult. "They don't like it. They think we're not good enough for them!"

"Ha ha!" cried the old women, alert too. "But for him we are good enough!"

In vain doubting voices rose up, voices of those who considered it unlikely, and perhaps even undesirable, voices of those who pointed out that it was highly improbable, and probably impossible, scientifically speaking, and that, in fact, the note did not make much sense. These dissenters were swept aside by the enthusiasts, heady with royal dreams. Ardent men challenged doubters with the irrefutable fact that the Prince's visit was already legendary among gentiles all the way across the country. Our girls are less beautiful?

"Can you prove to me there's no baby and no note? All right then, I'll make it easier. Prove to me the note means something else! Aha! I got you, eh? How can you say to me impossible? He lifts a finger, so. A lackey comes running. 'I want this one, I want that one.' Hey presto! What do we see? A beautiful Jewish girl appears. They've done it before. They do it all the time! What do we know about royalty?"

"The swine!" some cried. And, "She shouldn't have gone. Her forebears would have rather thrown themselves into the fire."

And others, "Well, what's to be done? Perhaps it was meant we should have a prince."

Women seized on the event as an object lesson for their sons. "You don't appreciate our own girls; you run after theirs; but see, the stranger prince has taste!"

And idealists hoped for an enormous breakthrough in civil rights. Some even predicted that the numerous clauses, restricting Jewish admission to the medical college, would be the next to go.

The general stir had begun to abate by the time Hoda got to hear the story. She was already up and about the house, more to show Daddy she was well than because she felt she would ever want to rise and face people again. Some of the boys came over to pay her a simple social call, and remained to play cards on the kitchen table. Finding she hadn't even heard, they renewed their own interest in the telling, and Hoda listened, fascinated, to what the world had to say.

At first she could hardly believe that anyone could credit such stories, stories from which she had been entirely left out. She had difficulty, at one point, in controlling herself and preventing her tongue from suggesting tartly that rather than look for a rich American babe from Minneapolis or some place like that, who had sneaked the baby back over the border because she wanted the child to be a Canadian citizen so it would be eligible to take over the throne in time, they might think of a local girl, someone here in this very town, and maybe she didn't have to be rich, even, for a prince to fancy her. It was all so strange, especially when she thought that it was their own pieces they were talking about, and that, though she couldn't be absolutely one hundred percent sure that one of those unknowns hadn't been the prince in disguise, since she couldn't absolutely vouch for everyone she'd been with, his contribution, even if it was a royal one, could not have been very large. She wondered if it would give the boys any satisfaction to know that they were maybe all mixed up with royal blood in the foundling. They'd probably much rather knock up a princess for themselves.

Limpy Letz expanded Hymie's theory. "Sure, it could have happened out East somewhere, or even out West, though most likely you're right, and she came up across the border. They won't be able to trace it so easily. Why do you think it was wrapped in rags? The oldest trick in the world, to throw people off the scent. You can't trace rags so easily. How much do you want to bet they'll be getting some anonymous donations from out of town?"

Hoda had not imagined that she might ever want to bless Uncle Nate again, but she wanted to bless him now for making his donation in advance. Gradually, she allowed herself to join in the arguments and speculations, at first so as to avoid attracting attention by unwonted silence. But as the oddity of her position struck her, she began to enjoy herself, and found herself inventing more and more spectacular versions of what might have happened. It was almost as though another person came alive in her, who urged her on to grow more and more enthusiastic, become more and more daringly inventive in her hypotheses, suggest outrageous versions and defend them passionately, and be quick to point out the flaws in rival theories, until she almost began to believe in the reality of what she was suggesting, though the boys kept saying, "We're serious, Hoda, stop kidding around."

"Well, I don't see why not. Why couldn't she have come down from up North as easily as from East and West and South. You're prejudiced against our Eskimo Jews and our Indian Jews. She probably came down the river in her kayak in the dead of night, and had it right there in the boat in her big fur pants, by the light of the silvery moon."

Involuntarily, Hoda shuddered, and glanced round fearfully, but no one was looking at her oddly. Kidding around, that's what she was doing. She was joking about it, as though she were really having fun. How could she be? It was only another kind of pretence; she couldn't really be enjoying herself; she must be acting, like in the stories, while inside her heart was breaking; it must be, even though half the time she didn't know how she felt, or if she had any feelings at all. She just knew that there were some things she had to do, and one of them was to out-talk any possibility of suspicion, and maybe that was why she was kidding around, because it diverted suspicion if she didn't seem to have anything serious on her mind. And if she made up all kinds of other things that probably could not have happened, what had really happened began to feel somehow as unlikely as any of them. Maybe they wouldn't even believe her if she came out with it and said, 'It's mine, it's mine, it's mine!' *Forget it. Don't try it.*

She wished they would stop talking about it. She wanted to stop thinking about it, to forget the bare and lonely secret that was waiting to spring out. If they kept talking something would happen, a sign would appear on her, she wouldn't be able to help it, and they'd all know. They'd look at her and understand. That's it! They'd see she was thinner, and they'd realize why. She slumped against the table and at the same time tried to blow out her stomach from within. But she hadn't got much thinner. And anyway, they never really looked at her that closely. She was fat, and fat was fat and people figured what's a thimbleful one way or another. It was true; the realization was like another giving way of something inside of her, the sinking feeling when props shift and life sags into another position and you see things in a way you'd never looked at them before, and you can't stand them anymore; yes, it was true. They never really looked at her. She wasn't real life to them, most of the time. What did they care about her, really? Like even now, when they knew she hadn't been feeling so hot, they were putting out feelers, hinting around, letting her know that they had the dough if she had the go. That's all they came for, and then they went away again to live their real lives somewhere else.

Look at them sitting there, talking, arguing, making themselves at home, and none of them knew how she felt. Inwardly, she raged at them. Who did they think they were? Who did they think she was? She'd like to tell them something, all right. But what? What was she hating them for? She was never dumb enough to think that one of them might be the one, though maybe she had hoped a little sometimes, at least that one of them might really like her, even in secret, the other way too. She was always watching for signs, and responded hopefully when she thought she'd seen one, but nothing ever came of it. So what? They were mostly no-goods anyway, even though they were nice enough guys. And if she had the go she'd take their dough, why not? She would, just as soon as she found out what had gone wrong, and was feeling a little better down there. Hymie was hinting again, not pushing, just feeling around with his hand under the table. It just didn't seem worthwhile to show her anger, or even to feel it much anymore.

"Sorry, Hi," she said, trying to sound lazy and casual, "it's my time of month. Next week." There. She'd mentioned it straight out to a guy, in front of three of them, in spite of what Mamma had said. She felt badly, as if she'd given away a secret, and a little embarrassed, because it was so personal and important, but she had to do it. Mamma didn't understand. She had to. She'd done it on purpose. It was her alibi, in case anyone wondered why she'd been in bed. It had just happened to be a bad month.

Hymie looked a little embarrassed too, and said "That's okay," in a chastened way. Afterwards he wished he'd had the wit to say, "That's okay, I don't mind, if you don't," because he wanted to try it when a girl was that way sometime, but catching him off guard, like that, for godsake, she had made him feel like she was his big sister or something.

See, Hymie was really all right. They were really all right guys. The main thing was that they should never suspect, that no one should ever suspect. She must never, never do anything to enable people to make the connection. Nothing should ever be allowed to slip out; she must never even walk past the orphanage again, in case someone, who maybe hadn't been sleeping well that night, had happened to be looking out the window, and now was just waiting to see her and recognize her and yell out, if she came by again. Well she wouldn't. It was all over with, her part of it, just as if it had never happened. Really, you could almost say it never had. An accident can happen to anybody, but it can be all right again. Even if you get hurt, it can heal up and leave no sign that it ever was. The baby was going to be taken care of, and it was even pretty lucky in a way; it had started right off being famous. Limpy said people were even calling it "the little prince," and were kind of proud of it. Well, they should be. If they only knew who he really was, and understood who they were, she and Daddy, well . . . maybe they would some day.

Someday maybe, when things had got better, and she was married, and rich, she would drive in at those orphanage gates in a big, black limousine, with a chauffeur, and the kids would line the hedges and stand looking at her. And she would get out of the car, with the chauffeur holding the door open, and somebody would come running out of the orphanage door, rubbing his hands and bowing, the same somebody maybe who took so long to open the door that night, but who hurried now, all right. She would climb the porch steps slowly, with dignified wavings up and down of the big ostrich feather in her hat, and everyone would breathe deeply her perfume and stand there holding their breaths and waiting for her to speak. And very quietly and politely she would say, "I've come for my baby."

It was simple and beautifully said, and everyone was deeply touched, particularly Hoda. The furor that followed her announcement she rather hurried over, because she really couldn't imagine the thing as anything but that tiny, gukky little red object that she had washed and wrapped, and when she tried to blow him up to a young boy in her mind it didn't work, with his frog's legs and his scrunched-up face. At most, she managed, with difficulty, to labour into being a very misty, fuzzy picture of a boy of indeterminate age, suspiciously like an old picture she had once seen of the young prince. But in truth she couldn't really be bothered with that kind of soupy stuff anymore, about princes and all that. It was just something she'd thought of putting in the note to make sure they took good care of the baby, since she couldn't make them do it by telling them directly that it was entitled to Uncle's big donation. And she could not either, somehow, right now put much heart into the fantasy of when she would be rich and would come to the orphanage to claim her own, and how it would be a great honour for them. It was a too far away thing, a duty she had still to come to, that had still to ripen for a long, long time before it would take-on the taste of pleasure.

She was subject, particularly at first, to sudden, devastating fits of comprehension of what had happened to her, storms of feeling which she could not contain, and which she allowed herself the small luxury of releasing in showers and squalls for Daddy to mop up with comforting words and tender attentions. But Daddy's tenderness and love, though willingly enough accepted, were proferred in innocence, and Hoda at one and the same time felt both guilt at her own unworthiness and, what increased the guilt, something which was close to contempt for his inviolate ignorance. When Daddy said to her, "Hodaleh, Hodaleh, surely it can't be that bad, to drown the whole world like in the time of Noah's Ark again?" she thought to herself, "That's what you think. A lot you know," and was guilty. Nevertheless she let him cuddle her and took comfort in it.

One thing Hoda knew she had to do. She had to make sure it didn't happen again. Between Seraphina and the public library, she soon found enough information to restore some of her old confidence, though much of what she learned was a great surprise, and for days, whenever she thought of it, she would exclaim inwardly, *'So that's how it works! Well how was I to know?'* From some of the books she pored through, she learned enough, even, to enable her to quickly gain the ascendancy over Seraphina in point of knowledge, for Seraphina's was a crudely functional, though essentially accurate, grasp of the facts of life. Seraphina followed Hoda's learned explanations with gratifying, high-pitched, nasal exclamations of "Nyyyo! You donnn't say!" as Hoda's words negotiated, unimpeded, the sparsely populated world between her ears. But from Seraphina she did learn a maxim, which she henceforth adopted, and insisted that the guys act accordingly. "I'll play," she told them, "if you'll play safe." And she got Hymie to pick up a whole bunch of safes for her at the drugstore, and she checked each one for leaks, and when someone didn't come prepared, she sold him one, at a moderate profit, and she and Hymie even talked of finding out where they could get them wholesale and going into business. Hymie had all kinds of good ideas like that. He wasn't going to be a poor bum all his life. "Sure," Hoda liked to rib him, "you're going to be a rich bum." But he could take a joke, and maybe he was a slob but he wasn't such a stupid slob.

"Yeh," Hymie said, kidding her back; "there're only two kinds of bum to be, a rich bum and a fat juicy bum."

That Hymie, he wasn't going to stand still and let himself get kicked around in this life, not if he could help it. And neither was Hoda, *"that's for sure"* she vowed. She was her own recovered self again, and more, yes, Hoda knew she was a great deal more, though the cocoon that she had outgrown was not made up of many layers of fat, as she had once dreamed. She had not emerged a butterfly; well, she had not started out as a worm, either. Butterflies are lovely, but who knows what they feel like inside? Maybe it's better to see one than be one. Could a butterfly know what Hoda knew? Maybe it wouldn't want to, either, but Hoda couldn't help feeling, not glad that it had happened, no, never that, but glad that she knew, somehow, almost glad, anyway. Daddy always said it was good to know things, but did Daddy mean it was good to know the things you want to know? No, that was a mean thought against Daddy. Didn't he know more than enough about what he would never have chosen to know, how to be blind and at the mercy of all? But did he find it good to know that, too? It didn't make Hoda feel better to know what she knew; it made her feel awful when she let herself think of it, but at the same time she felt as though there was somehow more of her, on the inside, and that she was a different shape in her head from what she had been before. And now that she knew a thing or two she figured she could get along all right, and she addressed herself with determination to blocking whatever other nasty kicks should come flying her and her daddy's way, yes, and making welcome whatever nice surprises came along too.

Hoda went back to her two full-time occupations, blocking life's kicks and trying to catch a glimpse of life's butterflies. As time passed and public interest in the unresolved mystery of the foundling waned, and the public tongue sought fresher delicacies with which to titivate the public palate, Hoda began, more and more, to achieve her wished-for day-by-day forgetfulness, until finally she had no longer to consciously prevent herself from thinking of it all the time. The times grew fewer and eventually very far between, when something, she didn't know what, triggered off a thought of that nightmare night, and with it came a rushing flood of feeling that she could not control nor escape, and she felt awful, just awful, and wanted to die. But she was learning to make very little noise when she was in pain. She went on living.

And so did Pipick, whose life she had innocently set in motion. Though his origins had aroused so much speculation, the baby himself, since he could not answer the questions he raised, was not the subject of as much concrete as theoretical interest. Most people were content to have paused before the orphanage gates and to have caught sight of the wickerwork carriage being wheeled, at an erratic pace, around the orphanage grounds, by, of all people, the wife of the Director of the Home. Normally, it would have been only the fitting thing for no one less than the wife of the Director to take personal charge of a foundling of this degree of notoriety. But how could this woman he trusted with a baby? Not that anyone had anything against her, poor unfortunate, but see, even from this far away you could tell she was jerking the carriage around like a mad woman. She would crash it into a tree! Someone should speak to him!

But in spite of the fact that there was not a man among his board members who did not consider himself capable of wiping the floor with Samuel Limprig, B.A. (U.S.A.) Director; speak to him about his wife was something that even the toughest among them, and among them were some of the toughest men in the community, had never yet been able to bring themselves to do, nor would they, even though more than once during this busy time, board members had paused on the steps of the institution and watched, frowningly, the jerky progress, not so much of the carriage, as of the spastic limbs of the director's lady, as she moved slowly and with an intense caution that was completely belied by the anarchic twitchings of her body. The board met with unaccustomed, and Limprig felt, though he knew better than to point it out, unnecessary, frequency during that first period of excitement. Every time one of these imperious men, or his imperious wife, had a new idea about the baby, he demanded a meeting to discuss it. They were activists, his board members. They did not believe in simply standing by and holding some prince's baby and looking foolish. So they called meetings and called each other foolish instead. There was simply too much excitement about and they were too closely involved, to want to sit at home.

Of all the boards of charitable institutions in the community, at this point, the Orphanage Board, though most of its members sat on other boards as well, felt itself to be the strongest and the most successful, as the campaign which had led to the purchase of the children's home itself gave evidence. Of its members, each one was proud of its strength and felt himself to be a potent contributory muscle. Each separate member knew exactly how the institution should be run. Limprig B.A. or no B.A., and each was capable of shouting down not only Limprig, but the entire rest of the board, on any point about which he felt called upon to express himself with feeling. Each man understood this about the others, which made for a kind of wary mutual respect. Limprig himself had quickly learned, in matters of policy, not to take any sharply defined stand with his Board, for fear of bringing down a categorical and arbitrary opposition from some totally unexpected source, for his board members sometimes played policy, not in any subtle, diplomatic, effeminate manner, but as some who indulge in beer parlor sports like Indian wrestling, for no other reason than to satisfy a kind of aggressive high spirits, and because there happens to be room on the table for two elbows. He knew also that his board members, once they had exercised the right to the occasional ukase, were usually content to go home and let him get on with his job. It was a task for which he was well equipped, both as to the running of the institution and the placating of his employers, with whom he was never too assured, to whom he never stated his logical conclusions, though he might lead them on to stumble over his conclusions by themselves, as it were, and be properly impressed by their acuity when they did. No wonder his board was inclined to congratulate itself on its choice of Limprig for Director. Oh, he had his shortcomings, and his wife might be reckoned among them, but the board members could not blame themselves here. They had known nothing about her; how could they? Do you ask a man you're interviewing, "Is your wife sound of mind and limb?" Whose business was it to ask such a thing? And she had certainly not, since they had come here, caused any difficulty. On the whole, she tended, rather, to keep herself out of sight! Not until the arrival of the foundling, in fact, had she given any cause for what might remotely be called complaint. Never mind Limprig's wife. She simply existed. Never mind also how he had put his credentials up on a brass plate outside his office door, like a doctor; some thought it gave tone to the place, while other plain people felt it was a bit too much in the ostentatious American style; never mind, though some did wonder whose money paid for that plate. A man who didn't make any more than the salary they were paying him, oh he didn't starve, mind you; it was not by any means a small salary, though it was only a salary, for all his American education, was entitled to his little brass plate. It was the paradox of the learned, as so often noted by men who live in the world of affairs. They study, they study, and what do they learn from it? Enough to get a salary determined by men in the real world, and a little brass plate to soothe their vanity.

This touch of contempt they felt, enabled his board members to allow themselves to respect and even, in some areas, to defer, though only half aware of it themselves, to their Director, without feeling any threat to their own preeminence. And they had the satisfaction of knowing that in bringing someone in from the outside who was less green, less freshly from the old country than even they themselves, who had fairly recently ripened to the desirable and negotiable shade of gold to which all aspire and few attain, they had not only impressed the town with the importance of the job to be done, but they had imported a worthy addition to the community, for Limprig, though brought up and educated in America, was not one of the alienated. His Yiddish and Hebrew background was sound, and he could as well bandy words, when necessary, with the Bundists and the Zionists as with the Orthodox and the gentile city fathers, with whom his job also brought him occasionally into contact.

Perhaps it was his very lack of airs, other than the original assertion of the brass plate, which enabled Limprig to succeed, fairly quickly, in reconciling those few members of the intelligentsia, who felt that the directorship might just as well have gone to someone local, who was familiar with and loyal to the community. It was noted that he elbowed no one, and seemed to prefer, except for the occasional cultural exercises in which he was asked to take part, to lead a very quiet life within the walls of the institution. In public, he seldom appeared with his wife, though she sat and watched when the orphanage children gave a concert or had a party or showed how well they could conduct a service on the High Holidays.

On the occasions when they did appear together he was observed to be meticulously devoted.

Poor man. There had been considerable gossip and speculation about the Limprigs, on their arrival in the city a few years before. The case of the foundling provided a new reason to open old doors and try to peer into what must be the dark areas of these private lives. Why had he married her, a man of such intelligence, such education? He had been heard to say once, apropos of something or other, half apologetically, "My wife has been ill." When had she become ill, and how? What had caused her movements to become so crippled it hurt you to see her? Many explanations had appeared, as from nowhere: that she had fallen down a flight of stairs, and he had come home from work and found her there, that she had had a small something amiss in her somewhere, and he had allowed the doctors to butcher her up, that this had happened when she was pregnant and he had allowed the doctors to use some new fangled method which had crippled her and lost the child, that it was hereditary and she had married him anyway, without telling him, that it had simply happened, and he was so devoted to her because it had been a love match. According to the mood of the teller, and the need variously to assign praise or blame, to one or the other, or to feel a little tug at the heart-strings, the various theories had somehow evolved. Who knows? And how come, when you think of it, a B.A. (U.S.A.!) should choose to come up here and work for a parochial institution where he had to bury himself in snowdrifts for seven months a year, when he could get just as good a job in a climate where humans live, not fools like us? Go ask him. Somebody had, as a matter of fact, asked him why he had chosen to work up here, in what to a metropolitan American like him must be the rear view of nowhere. Limprig had answered him, apparently a straightforward, satisfying answer, though not a particularly memorable one, since the man who had taken it on himself to ask, upon being asked, in turn, afterwards, what account Limprig had given of himself, couldn't honestly remember anything but the most general reasons, like for instance that he liked Canada and enjoyed the climate. It was the kind of answer that you only got suspicious of afterwards. Liked the climate! You could have made that one up yourself!

The fact that the director's wife was the only one seen outside of the building with the baby, helped to preserve its privacy at least, since many who would otherwise not have hesitated to walk over and peer into the carriage, for the satisfaction of taking note of certain resemblances, kept their distance, out of a revulsion for the person of Mrs. Limprig which bordered on fear, the irrational fear of her bizarre movements and the oddness of her stance, even in repose, which, try though they might to assure themselves she probably couldn't help, they nevertheless suspected must, in some profound, unacknowledged way, be her own fault.

In the first week or so, several romantically inspired citizens did step forward and offer to take charge of the upbringing of the foundling. But there was a good deal of yes and no-ing over these proposed festerings out, and some questioning of motives, and even some examination of these proposals in terms of moral trust; the responsibility having been placed in collective hands, perhaps the community should continue to direct the child's upbringing, for which, in the future, some recognition would surely come to the Institution. Perhaps even a certain possessiveness played a part in the hesitation of the board, which, with Uncle Nate recently elected and cautiously learning the ropes among them, voted to a man to give the situation more time to clarify itself. The one woman who presented herself with an offer to care for the child, for no other reason than that she had plenty of milk and plenty of children and one more wouldn't hurt, poor little creature of disgrace, was held to be unsuitable because, besides being poor, she did not show an adequate appreciation of the possible complexities of the situation. Limprig, who was among those who did not readily credit the theory of royal origins, and saw in the note the signs of acute distress of a woman probably temporarily unbalanced by fear and shame, was inclined to favour the candidacy of the somewhat simple minded mother, and diffidently put forward some small arguments in her favour. He was eloquently silenced by the gruff, heartfelt outburst of the town's leading garment maker, a man with three successful sweatshops to his credit. "Limprig, you're talking from your B.A., not your heart."

It was admitted, however, that as usual there was something sound in Limprig's reasoning, at least to a point, and the board voted to hire the poor woman, who could do with the few extra cents, as a wet nurse to provide for at least a part of the boy's nutritional needs. No matter who the child was, the community had no intention of scanting its responsibilities.

So it was that, what with rumination, consultation, and the occasional pithy altercation, some months were allowed to pass, during which time the half-expected missive from the mysterious mother who was presumed to have left the child, did not materialize. No note, no cheque. What then had the note meant? Now that the excitement had died down, and more heads cooled, more people began to consider other possibilities. As the most glamorous possibility lost its categorical force, so too did potential foster parents lose their enthusiasm. It was, after all, a great responsibility to take on.

While these problems were being debated on the administrative level, others were being pursued in the religious sphere, though decisions here had of necessity to be reached more quickly. Chief among them was the urgent question, was the boy to be circumcised as a child of the Jewish faith? The theological considerations behind this apparently simple question were of a complexity far too intricate for even an attempt to be made to trace them here in full. Suffice to say that the first requirement, that the mother of the child must be a Jew, under the circumstances might logically be assumed to have been met. Further, what little information was at hand implied that the father was not a Jew, so that, though the child would also appear to have been born out of wedlock, and was therefore presumably a bastard, he was nevertheless not the worst type of bastard, and could, according to Maimonedes, be admitted unreservedly as a member of the Hebrew faith. Had there been any reason to suspect that the putative father was a Jew, who had, knowing better, sinned against his covenant, the judgment on the child would have been far more severe, as a child of disgrace. But since the gentile knows no better, his responsibility is less, and why should mother and child be doubly penalized for what his lawless appetites have no doubt forced on them? So the child, though a bastard, was declared no momzer, and as close to the seventh day of his birth as could be ascertained, he underwent the small operation which ushered him formally into the ranks of the responsible. He acquitted himself like a man. He squawked.

The assembled company of some of the town's finest, saluted him approvingly, drank wine and ate chick peas, and remarked that the birth of Moses had also been a very mysterious event. At another ceremony the child was, in fact, given the formal name of David Ben Zion, David Son of Zion, to signify his acceptance by a community which had royal names of its own to bestow. But the curious, knotted little tail which had been hanging from his navel when he was found, and which, though since dried away, had left an odd little lump, had already won him another name, the one by which, to the mortification of his boyhood, he would henceforth be known. Because of his odd little navel, they nicknamed him Pipick.

SEVEN

It would be unfair to suggest that during the years that followed, Hoda tried to erase all memory of her black night and of the existence of a living issue. True, other pains and other pleasures dulled the intensity of recall; gradually a shadow formed over the area in her memory, a shadow that gained in opacity with time, so that, like the craters of the moon, from a distance the dark spot seemed more like a smudge on an unbroken surface than like the pit into which she knew she could fall if she allowed herself to venture too close. But she could not pretend the smudge wasn't there. What had happened had happened, and Hoda was not capable of forgetting entirely. But she allowed herself to temporize with memory, promising herself, as time passed, that one day, as soon as she had a chance, tomorrow, maybe, or the day after, she would sit down and try to figure out what meaning that distant night and the living souvenir which it was sometimes so difficult to believe really existed, had in her life. She still walked blocks out of her way when the occasion arose, rather than pass anywhere near the Orphanage, which was for her the geographic incarnation of the shadow pit in her mind which she dared not approach too closely. With time, the shadowed area did appear to shrink, for Hoda had many other things to think about. Those few forbidden blocks around the Orphanage also shrank, as Hoda grew more familiar with the wide expanse of the city which existed beyond the bounds which had had meaning for her in childhood. But she could not simply forget, and though she now had a proper contempt for silly, impractical, childish fantasies, Hoda still believed that in the endless folds of time that were yet to unwrinkle before her, were hidden all the correct solutions to all her problems, and she promised herself that she would make good all her errors, the minute the proper shape of her destiny was revealed to her.

Meanwhile she continued to do her best, and became, in time, well enough known for it in the district to have earned for herself a fairly regular flow of clientele and a certain degree of notoriety among decent folk. Of the latter Hoda was to some extent aware, and when it was, occasionally, underlined for her attention, she expressed a large, contemptuous willingness to be tolerant of public opinion if the public would, on its side, keep its opinion to itself and not bother her and her daddy with it. Among themselves, if people wanted to talk about her, let them. Her touchy spot was, of course, her daddy. For herself Hoda didn't give a damn what any bunch of old busybodies thought. What did they know about her life? And what did they care, either, about the important things? But close to the surface of her defiance was always the fear that someday, someone would bludgeon his or her way through her father's innocence. It would take a bludgeon, it seemed to her sometimes, to break its way through that amazingly tough shell of softness, in which the most obvious revelation of the truth lost its shape and disappeared. But someday, nevertheless, it might happen, perhaps in the jigsaw way she used to think babies were put together in the dark. Danile would submit to endless violations in his darkness, but one day a final clue would be left that would, though he struggled against it, force the fullness of knowledge on him, and even to Danile the blind, the ugly truth would be born. Oddly enough it was only in relation to her father that Hoda saw it as an ugly truth. For the rest, as she did not tire of asserting, when she discussed it with her friends, she didn't give a damn what they thought; they were all hypocrites anyway.

The reputation which she had among some, for being a little bit crazy in the head, just like her old man, was gained at least in part by the lengths to which she would go to maintain a decorous attitude among her clientele when her father was anywhere in the vicinity. Hoda insisted that there was to be no rough and tumble loud-mouth swearing in Danile's hearing, though he understood little enough English. If the boys wanted they could go out in the back lane behind the shed and roll the smut around. But the green young lads for whom it was a daring adventure to be awaiting their turns to shag the district whore found it difficult to conduct themselves as though they were sitting in a dentist's anteroom. They were keyed up; the quarters and nickels and dimes had been scraped together with some difficulty. These were festive moments, and the especially exciting quality of their joint venture in exploration of the sink of flesh was heightened by the peculiarities of this particular whore and her father. For Danile still called encouragement from the other room, and his interpolations of "Study, study, pig, pig!" were apt to send the novices, who had been warned to expect this, into fits of laughter. But if they became too rambunctious while they awaited their turns in the kitchen, Hoda's voice would be raised in threatening warning from the bedroom. Whereupon her father, as though to temper the sternness of Hoda's words, would raise his voice again and shout even more encouragingly from his room for them to apply themselves, for study is sweet; knowledge is good.

The younger boys looked forward to this as part of the entertainment of a visit to Hoda. They knew, of course, that there was a point beyond which it was dangerous to go in revealing their enjoyment of the fringe benefits of her favours. It was dangerous to laugh too loudly, dangerous to comment or make snide remarks, dangerous to try to tease forth a display. Nevertheless they half hoped that one of them, though each prayed it wouldn't be him, might accidentally cut across Hoda's sensibilities and raise her ire, the result of which was reputed to be almost as much fun as the moment of intimacy with her masses of playful flesh. On one memorable hot summer's evening, when Hoda had, on request and out of sheer good nature, taken two of them into the shed with her at once, the rest of them had wandered out into the front yard, where, totally ignoring the fact that Danile was sitting on the front steps quietly weaving his basket, they discussed noisily what was likely to be going on in the shed. One joker in particular kept loudly calling obscene encouragement back to his buddies. His raillery was cut short very suddenly, when the shed door flew violently open, and Hoda lumbered out, stark naked, and came raging toward him in an avalanche of flapping pink flesh. The boy, quailing before the fury of her expression, took to his heels, and luckily for him, was able to make it out the gate before her. Legend has it that she chased him halfway down the block, hurling imprecations all the way. But legend exaggerates. She stopped short at the gate, and in a whirl of arms and belly and breasts strode back to confront the other two gaping offenders with an absolute decree that they too would have to get the hell out if they did not learn how to behave themselves decently. And to her father, whose grasp of English smut was still thankfully negligible, she explained briefly, as he had raised his head enquiringly from his work, that she had chased the boy home because he lacked respect. Glaring another warning at the two chastened adolescents, she strode back to the shed to complete her business, while the boy who had been banished made his way cautiously back along the fence to the gate, where he discussed with his friends, in tones that fluctuated between laughter and chagrin, whether he dared enter again, since after all he had chipped in too, and he ought to get his money's worth.

People tend to get the stories confused. Hoda did actually chase someone out the gate and down the street, but that was on another occasion, and then she was fully and decently dressed. This time she wasn't chasing a customer, either. It happened as a result of her habit of putting pressure on her clients, to make them buy her daddy's handiwork. Originally this had been a very useful and reasonably profitable way to prevent the house from being entirely overrun by the products of Daddy's indefatigable industry. And it enabled her customers too to balance whatever uneasy feelings they might have had about having digressed to indulge in a little vice, with a pretty counterweight of virtue, in the form of a totally unexpected and apparently gratuitous bonus of affection for their wives. But once the professional nature of Hoda's activities had become common knowledge, the women began to ask themselves what their men had been doing in that place where baskets also happened to be for sale. The possession of one of Danile's pretty, sturdy bags or baskets gradually became, perhaps unfairly, tantamount to an open admission that a husband or a son had strayed. The feline, "What a pretty straw bag! Is it new? Did your husband buy you a gift?" was more than once to needle an aching, humiliated heart, and receive reply from behind a tight-lipped smile, "No, I've had it for a long time. I bought it myself as a matter of fact from that poor foolish blind man. I feel so sorry for him. He can't help it if his daughter's a whore." And the deft attacker would counter with some delicately ironic comment on what a tragedy it was to be blind. During those transitional days when Hoda's function was first becoming widely recognized in the district, more than one guilty husband was to curse the expansive moment when he had submitted to the temptation to give his wife some pleasure too.

At first Hoda was disturbed to find the bags she had sold the evening before were being abandoned in the yard and along the back lane the morning after. She cursed her customers for the insult to her father's craft, and cursing, gathered the pretty straw and wicker things up again, hating the meanness and obtuseness of people who could take something so nice and throw it away just like that. Not until some time had passed and her customers had even come out and openly offered to pay her the extra money, as long as she didn't try to make them take home the baskets, did she realize fully that her major area of sales was really drying up. So she settled for a token basket-selling transaction, which at least maintained her income, and once again began to cudgel her brains for ways to reduce their stockpile.

But she was still able, once in a while, to really sell a basket to an innocent customer. It was the morning after a brief visit from one such customer, a new friend, that the occasion of the great chase took place. Daddy, thank God! was still at morning prayers in the synagogue and Hoda was making his bed, when she heard the woman screaming outside. The voice drew rapidly nearer till she had no difficulty in making out the Yiddish words, "Where's the whore? Where is she, the whore?" Hoda went to the window. Neighbours across the way had already opened their front doors and were peering down the street. The vocalist, still shouting in a high-pitched, overwrought voice, appeared, waving a wicker basket and banging it against the fence. She must have begun her shouting a good way down the street, because there were people already following her. "Where is she, the husband eater?" she screamed, and planted herself before their gate, a wizening, overworked woman, whom Hoda knew only by sight as someone who lived around here somewhere. The stranger announced loudly now that she had come to have it out with the strumpet, that she meant to shame her before the whole neighbourhood, the fat cat who lay and lapped cream while decent women slaved themselves into the grave, and for what? So their husbands should sneak money from the till and go swim in polluted beds. "A present he had to bring me? I gave him a present! I'll give her a present too! Where is she the whore, the Delilah, the outcast? I'll make her such a scandal she'll be ashamed to show her face before people again! I'll tell that old blind fool such a story his fingers will curl up and he'll never be able to weave rubbish again! Come out! Where are you hiding, you prostitute you!"

At first Hoda could hardly believe that the stranger was actually calling her. She went to the door fully intending to go out like anybody else and see what the name-calling was all about. But when the woman remained by the gate and continued to shout she realized, uneasily, that the dame was actually after her. Hoda was astonished, and listened unbelievingly. She had never given much thought to the wives and girl friends of her customers before, except, occasionally, when she developed a crush on one of her clients, and wondered wistfully what it was like to really exist for a man. She had never imagined that she would be blamed and screamed at, in front of the whole street, by someone she'd never even said a word to before in her life. Surely how that old lady reconciled herself to what her husband did had nothing to do with Hoda.

But what if Daddy were to hear her screaming, and in Yiddish, so he could make no mistake about what he was hearing? There were all kinds of people outside there already. Soon someone would let them know in the synagogue that something was happening so close by and then they might all hurry their prayers and come rushing out to see. They mustn't! What right did she have to yell and scream about her daddy and his baskets anyway? Who did she think she was, to come and try to spoil things? What did she know about Hoda and about Danile and about anything? Hoda didn't even know who her husband was, but if he wanted to come and be her customer she wasn't going to stop him either, for someone who yelled and screamed in front of the whole block, and called her names and insulted her daddy!

Gone was that first impulse to lock the door and hide behind it until the stranger had gone away. Hoda would meet fire with fire! She flung open the door and went storming down the steps and thundering up the path. "Who you calling names?" she bellowed. "I'll show you to smash my daddy's baskets!" For in truth, the basket the woman held was beginning to jar loose, from being repeatedly slammed with force against the fencepost. Hoda did not pause as she raved, but charged like a youthful amazon at first blooding. "Call me names, I'll break your neck! Nobody calls me names!" She thudded to a halt just inside the gate, eyes smouldering sparks, fists clenched, towering over the little, old-looking lady, who had taken a few hasty steps back from the fence at her turbulent approach. For a moment they were both silent, confronting each other, and Hoda was dismayed to be standing here thus, threatening a little old lady who was half her size, whose face was shaking and who kept blinking her eyes. Why didn't she just go away, quickly, before Daddy came? And the rest of them too, the damn nosey-parker busybodies whom she could see out of the corners of her eyes, grinning and enjoying themselves because somebody was miserable.

But her antagonist was not to be robbed of her moment. "You see, you see?" she turned to the spectators. "You see the shameless whore, she has the nerve to face me! I'm not afraid of you fat cow, you sleep with every filth; you stay away from my husband, you hear?"

"Who you calling cow?" bellowed Hoda, and wrenching open the gate, threw her weight forward threateningly, as though she were about to charge, but paused long enough to give her opponent the opportunity to turn and run before she actually took after her. The idea of bumping the old lady and maybe even accidentally knocking her down appalled Hoda, no less than the idea of suffering physical violence at her hands appalled the little grocerywoman, in whose dream of a dramatic confrontation in which she could publicly pour out on the whore some of the bitterness of her own heart, the idea of physical indignity had never occurred. With some trepidation she realized that the whore might have other ideas, and she was torn between the desire to make public capital of this additional affront, and real uneasiness about her own physical safety. She was not an unimaginative little thing, and already, as she retreated hastily down the street, hurling insults over her shoulder, she could see herself crawling, all bleeding and broken up the steps of the grocery and collapsing before her stricken, weeping husband, with a final, "Look, see what your whore has done to me!"

As for Hoda, all she wanted was to get the old lady and the spectators far away from the house before the end of prayers brought Daddy home. So she pursued with threats, "You call me names I'll kill you, you hear?" all the way down the next two blocks and round the corner and up the street and across the road and down another narrow street, while the woman ran terrified ahead of her, but not too terrified to call to left and right to the heads poking out of doors and windows, "You hear her? You hear her? She wants to kill me! Be my witness! You're my witness!" all the while she ran, with Hoda heftily clopping along behind her, bawling to left and right, obligingly loudly, to make sure they heard her, if that's the way the old lady wanted it, "I'll kill her all right! She comes near my house and calls me names again I'll kill her all right!"

Hoda had already had to slow down considerably, to let the panting old lady catch her breath, and she felt a real pang of pity when she saw the woman clutch her breast. Soon, she was simply trotting along at the shoulder of her antagonist, every now and then letting out a token bellow as the gasping woman found breath for a half-hearted curse, and once, when her enemy stumbled, Hoda automatically reached out and steadied her on her feet. The woman betrayed, for her part muttered an automatic "thank you," and only half-heartedly shook off her helping hand, as they slowly continued the motions of the chase.

When they reached the grocery store, the husband over whom all the public fuss had been made made the mistake of poking his head out the screen door, as his wife panted labori-ously up the steps, still clutching the somewhat beat-up basket. Hoda, who had come to a halt on the street on the far side of the ditch, recognized her client, and without thinking, said "Oh, hi! Do you live here?"

The grocer stood paralysed while his wife fished for enough air to scream, "You hear that? She knows him! She *KNOWS* him! The whore knows him!" Winded, stricken anew, the grocer's wife gasped out brokenly, "You see . . . I've brought her to you . . . Don't say I'm not a good wife! . . . I've brought you my shame!" And she flung off his proffered supporting arm so violently that his funny bone cracked painfully against the door jamb. He was whimpering his anguish when, an instant later, she sagged, crying out, as his knees buckled under the unexpected load of her, "Look! Look at your disgrace! Don't worry about me! Go to her! Go to your shame!"

Hoda was tired of being insulted. She was sorry for the old lady to be so upset, but what a lot of fuss she was making. If she always carried on that way no wonder the poor old guy sneaked off sometimes to find a quiet nooky. The street before her house was probably clear by now, and with luck she would be back home as though nothing had happened before Daddy got back. If only no one would say anything to him. Why did people always have to spoil things and try to make you feel dirty? Hoda didn't see why that woman had to keep calling her all those names over and over again. Just because that was how she was making a living now didn't mean that was all she was ever going to be. Did that old dame think that all Hoda wanted to do for the rest of her life was pump old cripplecocks like her husband? Well, she had another think coming. Hoda and her friends had all kinds of ideas they were working on. Someday she'd show them all. And even then, when she was right up there and didn't have to do it for a living anymore, she wasn't going to quit just because others wanted her to anyway, only if she felt like it. If she felt like doing some charity work, on the side, she'd do it, like for that poor old guy for instance. With a wife like that he deserved a break sometimes. How was she so much better than Hoda anyway?

The grocerywoman was still raving at her shrivelling old man when Hoda turned away. "Any time you got half a buck!" Hoda called back to him encouragingly, and swung off down the street. For all she cared he could have stayed home in the first place. Who needs bad feelings?

She need not have worried, in any event, that someone might tell Danile about her morning's encounter. Those who had already tried, in what were considered the early, retrievable steps of her downfall, to warn him of the dangerous course his child was steering, had found him apparently incapable of conceiving her fall, since the days were filled for him with living proof of her goodness and devotion. And even the hardiest old dame, determined that truth must out everywhere and in every instance, so that her life was littered with the unmarked graves of those who had died of truth, liberally administered, found herself hesitating, nevertheless, before the prospect of coming out and telling Danile, to his masked yet vulnerable face, "See here, your daughter's a whore." To justify itself, such a statement must somehow be made to fit into the category of good advice, and it was a little late to say, "Tell her it's not nice," and "no nice boy will marry her"; and anyway, Hoda herself had been told these things to no avail. On the other hand it could be, and often was, said in her favour, that whore or no she was still a good daughter and took care of her father as well as any virgin might. Anyway, he probably knew, though he wouldn't admit it openly. You cannot tell with these quiet, foolish ones how much they really do know. Silence is the wisdom of fools, no less than of the wise.

A curious divergence of opinion had grown up, over the years, regarding Danile, among his cronies at the synagogue. Some continued to hold that though he was not an utter simpleton, he was simple nevertheless, restricted in his capacity to absorb the facts of existence. Others suggested that the man was perhaps not so simple, that he was not necessarily restricted by nature, but that his blindness made him more delicately selective of those, among the superabundant facts of existence, that were truly significant to man and God. They came close to hinting that there was something perhaps of holiness about him. It had more than once been noted that the questions which he propounded, granted that he was not much help with the answers, but then neither were the wisest, sometimes, were not the questions of a fool. To this there were some, with battered heads dragging graveward, who replied as though they were already tasting dust, that only the greatest fools go on formulating clever, unanswerable questions, making leaking vessels to hold their ignorance. A well-turned question is the highest art of fools, and Danile was a master of the aesthetics of ignorance, and hence, certainly, a fool. The largest group of old men, however, less patient or more practical or less flexible, brushed aside the webmakers and their reasonings and held categorically that the man was an utter idiot, and getting to be even more so of late; witness his maddening habit of telling you the story of his life, over and over again, in the same words, every chance he got, and as if he was proud of it, yet! He was a good enough natured idiot and all that, but say what you liked, when Danile approached, conversation stopped. Whatever you were talking about had to wait; the moment he found an opening, and he could catch you pausing to try to sneak a breath in halfway through a word, he jumped right in, relevant or not, and there you found yourself, ready to exhale, your son's latest business coup still half-bottled up inside of you, and Danile was already babbling about his graveyard and his wedding and God's grace in giving him a daughter who could spread her legs and let in the whole wide world.

But irascible though they could be sometimes, even the most irritable of the old men would not go so far as to say that last within hearing of Danile himself. To shame a man so would be a greater sin than whoring. There should be some parity of epithet possible in an argument. There is no glory in stripping a man naked and defenceless before men, no victory in the one truth to which there is no reply. Besides, the old men liked Hoda. She had grown up around the synagogue, had cadged snuff to sneeze when she was still practically a baby, and now that she was grown did not forget the fact that they existed, as some of their own grandchildren, who were preparing to enter more elevated professions, preferred to do. She still hung around and chatted and joked sometimes when she came to pick up her dad. And though most of the hard-core, day-by-day worshippers were regrettably beyond the point, had they so desired it, of being able to make use of her professional ministrations, they still relished the chance to be seen in animated conversation with her, braving alike the arched enquiring brows of friends and the ironic, twitch-mouthed glance of wife, if she happened to be present, to taste for a few instants of the same bittersweet public illusion that women know when they grow publicly younger year by year.

No, Daddy didn't know; that was one thing she could be sure of, she who knew her daddy better than anybody. He probably didn't even know such things went on, outside of the Bible. She remembered how once, after she had been telling Daddy, to ease her conscience, how some of the boys who came to see her really weren't students of hers, but were really kind of boy friends. Danile had told her all about how when he was a young boy he used to stand outside their hut in the old country and listen for the voices and the steps of the girls as they passed, and sometimes he would even bring himself to call out "hello" to them, and sometimes they would answer him, and he would be happy all day after that. It flashed through her mind, *did even Daddy think those other thoughts too?* But he went on to tell how there was one particular girl he used to think about a lot, because her voice was so nice when she said "hello," and he carried the feeling of her voice around with him and imagined how beautiful and perfect she must be, and how loving in every way, though she never said anything more to him than "hello" sometimes, yet he always recognized her voice from far away and those were the times when he worked up his courage to say "hello" and to wait and hope that she would say "hello" too, this time.

"And did she, usually?" Hoda asked.

"Sometimes," said Danile.

"I'll bet she really loved you too, only she was shy, and maybe she was afraid to show the other girls how much she liked you," said Hoda.

"No," said Danile.

"I would have said 'hello' every time, Daddy. I wouldn't ever have passed by without saying hello."

"I know," said Danile gently. "You'll always say hello."

It wasn't what he said so much as the way he said it that made her feel, for a moment, desolate, when she really should be feeling glad, shouldn't she? What was it that lurked behind even the nicest words that you could say to each other? What gave you that uneasy feeling that your tongue was turning around and without even knowing it was making a joke on itself? Word to word, sentence to sentence, whether you knew them to be false or felt them to be true, spun out across an abyss, with you swinging helplessly from them, blindly spinning and patching and crisscrossing the net that was to catch and hold the shape of the darkness in which your life was forming, but instead was itself contained by the chasm. And sometimes, as she scuttled about, weaving her thread and trying to attach an end of it somewhere where it would hold and be secure, Hoda felt a sudden rushing of wind, and didn't know where her words had gone and where her net was going, where her threads connected and what the meaning was of webs that were attached to her own. What did Daddy think? What did he feel? What did he know? Could it be that Mr. Polonick was right when he said to her that time, "What makes you think your father doesn't know about you, Hoda? Do you think he would tell you if he knew?" He shouldn't have said that. It was a thick black thread that didn't belong, and she didn't know where it led, but she kept running into it; what if Daddy did know? Why didn't he say anything then? Was he so ashamed? Or didn't he have the words to tax her with? And if he spoke what would she say in reply? She was really glad he didn't speak, wasn't she? It was all right by her if he didn't try to interfere. Why did it upset her so to think of it, to wonder whether he knew? But she didn't really believe he knew. Mostly, from the way Daddy talked, it was as though he had spun his last new thread, and somehow thought he had completed his net to hold his life in, and just kept running back and forth and to and fro over the parts of the pattern he remembered, and what Hoda did to earn their living was a part of the dark abyss which he swung through but could not know. Let it be so.

That Mr. Polonick, why did he have to say things like that just because he wanted to win his argument and get his way? Why wasn't he content just to make his revolution and save the world and leave her in peace? Why did he have to mix in her private affairs too? He was always telling her how bad it was, what she was doing, but could he give her an alternative for right here and now? She kept telling him she wasn't going to be doing this for a living all her life. Just as soon as she had enough money to try to do something else with, of course she would quit. Did he think it was always such a pleasure, having to, whether you felt like it or not? She herself had thought it would be at first, but you learn different. Did he think she liked being pointed at and called names? Not that she cared, but still, what did he want her to do? She was hardly managing to keep them going as it was. But at least they were independent. They didn't need any uncle to boss them around. Hoda always brought in her uncle when she talked to Mr. Polonick, on purpose to sidetrack him away from the lectures on her personal morals. She liked to hear again how she and Daddy were victims of capitalist brutalization and greed, how in a world where money was god even family feeling was destroyed and only money and power counted, and a man like Uncle would not think twice about abandoning his own relatives to poverty and starvation.

"Yeh," Hoda agreed, "Uncle's a rat."

But Danile usually had something to say in defence of Uncle, if the subject came up when Mr. Polonick was paying them a social visit, as he often did nowadays; and then, oddly enough, Mr. Polonick taxed him with clinging to outmoded bourgeois values and loyalties. Since the time when Hoda had, he was convinced, saved his life, they had become close friends, and Mr. Polonick often dropped in to talk or called to take her to meetings. Hoda had mixed feelings for this man who claimed he owed his life to her. It was all very well for him to be grateful but he didn't have to act as though she owed it to him to let him save her in return. She knew that it was all for her own good that he kept at her that way; "Where are you going, Hoda? For heaven's sake, comrade, do you know where you're going?" They called each other "comrade," and Hoda liked that, but why did he have to keep asking her things like that? He was old already and he lived alone and he wasn't married or anything, not anything at all as far as she knew. Sometimes she felt like asking him in her turn, "Well, where aren't you going, comrade Mr. Polonick?" But she had too much respect; she was younger after all, and anyway she didn't want to hurt his feelings. But she wished he wouldn't ask her questions like that. They made her uneasy. She didn't even know where she'd been yet, and she knew that someday she would have to maybe sit down and think about it, if somehow something else didn't turn up that would illuminate the way as she wanted to know it, in a total vision, where she had been and where she was going and how to make everything all right. He needn't think that she wasn't concerned enough about it without his prodding. But punitive though his gratitude seemed to be at times, she was glad he was their friend, especially for Daddy's sake. At least he listened to what Daddy had to say and showed respect, even if he didn't agree and called Daddy a victim of outmoded ideas that prevented him from rising up and breaking all his mental chains.

Hoda enjoyed going to meetings, and she particularly liked it when she got something to do afterwards, like passing out leaflets. She didn't mind helping out, and she liked the conversations and arguments she got into with people, when she pointed out how wrong they were, though they would never admit it. The comrades were a good bunch of guys and at least they were trying to do something for the good of the world, not just hanging around and gambling and dreaming about the breaks like Hymie and Limpy Letz and Popowicki. A person should think of someone else besides himself. And some of them were more practical idealists than Mr. Polonick, more like Hoda herself, who readily admitted what Mr. Polonick deplored, that she didn't have what he called a militant mind yet. It was true. One or two of the comrades had become her customers and they sometimes even joked about the revolution together. It was a good thing Mr. Polonick wasn't there to hear them then.

"When the revolution comes, first thing I'm going to do is liberate you, Hoda, free you from this capitalist treadmill. No more slave labour. No more tied to the buck. Free love for all. I'm only pretending to go along with the system now because I know you're a worker just like I am. But after the revolution we're going to put the fun and freedom back in fucking!"

"What will I do for a living, comrade?"

"You'll get an honest job, that's what you'll do. No more of this hideous degradation. You'll hold your head high, that's what you'll do. And when you fornicate it will be only for pleasure, with dignity, for fulfillment of the highest functions of womanhood. Your days will be spent in building the public paradise and your nights will be spent in building the private paradise!"

"I spend all that time building paradise, who's going to live in it? All this free love they're passing around, I'll be too tired to enjoy it after a hard day's work."

"We fight and die for them and all they can do is grumble. My God, you're beginning to sound like my old lady."

"Comes the revolution maybe your old lady won't have to work so hard and won't be tired," Hoda suggested. "You'll stay home in your own paradise."

"With my wife? For this I manned the barricades and stormed the City Hall? Long live the ongoing revolution! Karl Marx was right. The dialectic is the thing." All it meant was that after the revolution he wasn't going to put all his eggs in one basket either, if he could help it.

Mr. Polonick was for a different kind of revolution, more of a close-legged kind of affair, with everybody drinking from his own private cup, like Lenin said. Hoda didn't follow the intricacies of argument of some of the lectures she attended, but she could see from the different characters and the different attitudes of the different revolutionaries why it was going to have to be a perpetual revolution, whether it was a peaceful one, as Mr. Polonick and Hoda herself would prefer, or, as some more fiery comrades advocated, a radical, violent affair. She, for one, couldn't see any way out of it. Take, for instance, in her own work, a man like Mr. Polonick; she could feel how deeply he was the way he was, and feeling it she could understand it. How much difference would the revolution really make to him personally, in his private life? If, for instance, he were to make himself come to Hoda one evening with even a buck-fifty in his hand she would be so embarrassed she would almost die, simply from knowing how he felt. And she didn't see how, after the revolution, it would be any different for him if he came, as would be his right, without any money at all. Even if he got his own private cup after the revolution, how would he feel and how would he make her feel? He'd probably still rather stay thirsty, and go on dreaming revolutions. That didn't mean that the revolution wasn't going to be good in other ways of course, but just that it wouldn't fix everything all at once. For sure Hoda could see that this revolution was going to be a very very long-drawn-out affair, but ever since she had struck her first blow she had figured well, so what? At least it was time somebody got started on it. As the comrades said, there was a lot to be done! Even if Hoda hadn't thought that the revolution was a pretty good idea all in all, she would have gone to the meetings and helped anyway, partly because of Mr. Polonick. She felt a certain responsibility for him. He was not a very practical kind of person. There was nothing wrong with his ideas except that often they didn't match how things really worked. He always looked straight ahead and never saw anything coming at him from left or right. Hoda was a lot younger but she knew that the world was somehow too complicated for him, maybe a little like it was for Daddy, only in a different way. But she couldn't explain it to him because it would hurt him, and he was getting hurt all the time anyway. It was odd about a beautiful soul like Mr. Polonick; though he was aching all the time, not only for himself but for the whole world, he could hurt you too, without even feeling the pain he was inflicting, like when he planted that barb about maybe Daddy knowing all the time what she was doing. He didn't have to say it. Even if it were true, and how would he know anyway, did he have to say it, and complicate for her the familiar dearness of her daddy's face with hints of the vast, unfamiliar world that lay behind it? Mr. Polonick was right, all of her daddy's familiarly threaded, expected, redundant flow of words that made her so impatient sometimes might really be intended to conceal rather than reveal. Conceal what? From whom?

Oh, Polonick didn't know what he was talking about. Why couldn't he just relax and learn to get some fun out of life? He couldn't seem to bring himself to stop worrying about the world for even a minute, for fear, maybe, that he would lose count of all that was wrong and have to start counting all over again. Sometimes Hoda was invited to a party at the home of one of the comrades, and everybody had fun. It wasn't as though they were forgetting the revolution or anything, just enjoying life in the meantime; but Mr. Polonick wouldn't dance or kibitz. He just sat there smiling nervously and looking on, and the first chance he got he would try to corner somebody and start an ardent conversation about glum things that really counted.

Daddy, on the other hand, could really enjoy himself, just like a little kid. When Seraphina and her pimp came driving up that time in his elegant automobile and took them for a ride, her daddy climbed into the rumble seat like a young boy, with hardly any help from Hoda, even though he'd never even seen such a thing and had only heard it described, and couldn't even see where he was climbing. He felt very quickly all over and around with his hands and settled himself, chuckling away and looking about him for all the world as though he could see, while Hoda described what was happening when Seraphina's pimp was cranking up the engine.

Not long after she had passed the jail-bait age, Seraphina had done exactly as she had said she would. She had taken her jars of makeup and her big blue bottle of eau de cologne, and her set of lacy underwear, which she kept hidden away from her brothers and sisters and sometimes used to bring to Hoda's to change into when she was going on the prowl, and had gone to work for this guy she had met downtown who was really big business, and now she was a regular woman-about-town, and even had her turn to be taken around in his automobile. Hoda had a suspicion that she herself was being taken for the joyride because Seraphina's business agent, "Call me less Les, more more, hotcha baby" wanted to look her over, since for a couple of years now Serry had been urging her to come on up and Hoda just hadn't bothered. He looked a little surprised when Hoda said Daddy would love to come too, and threw a quick frown at Seraphina, but then he said all right, he supposed Daddy could sit in the rumble. Hoda figured what the hell, let Daddy have some fun too, and she climbed in back with him, though it was a tight squeeze, and Les muttered something about the rear axle. They might not get a chance to go for a ride in an automobile again for a long time. It was nice of Seraphina. And it was fun, too. Daddy sat beaming at the breezes that whipped his face as the car went rushing along. Pretty soon he unclasped his fingers from the side grip and held them up in the air for Hoda to see that he wasn't even holding on, and she laughed too and enjoyed the way the wind was blowing about her thick mop of sandy hair. Seraphina was really doing all right for herself, in some ways. Hoda knew that the guy knocked her around occasionally, which she herself would not have been able to tolerate, but Seraphina, though she complained, stayed with him because she was convinced she really had the whip hand, though he might sometimes do the whipping.

"I told him, 'You lay a hand on me once too often and I know where to go! I'll go live in a house!" And she did know, too. Seraphina really knew her way around. "When I tell him that, he treats me with so much respect, it's unnatural!" Seraphina giggled. "You have to know how to handle them, Hoda."

Les drove them all the way out to the Municipal Park, where he drew up at the pavilion and got out, and Hoda and Seraphina got out too, while Daddy waited in the rumble, and Les linked his arms in both of the girls,' and led them into the high-raftered building and bought them both ice cream cones like a regular sport, and an extra one for Hoda to take back to her daddy. While they were on their way back to the car he suggested that since she and Serry were such good friends, maybe Hoda would like to come in and do business with them. Serry was doing all right and he had plenty more contracts he could cut her in on. But Hoda, busy licking the drippings and barely catching the piled-high ice cream as it settled and overflowed the cones, explained between licks that she had her daddy to look after, and didn't want to tie herself up with anyone else at the moment. Then, laughing, she rushed ahead to get his ice cream to her father while there was still some left.

"She's too fat anyway," Les muttered sourly to Seraphina. But there was an unmistakable vitality about her, that should go if you sold her right. Later on they parked in front of the house for a few moments, where all the nosey neighbours, Hoda hoped, were looking, and when Daddy had gone in, Les offered her a modified "commission basis" kind of arrangement in case sometimes a special job came up for someone her type. Not unflattered, Hoda said "maybe sometime, if it pays enough," because after all it had been pretty nice of him to drive them around and buy them ice cream when they didn't even expect it. And it wouldn't hurt to keep the door open, though she knew that as long as she could manage it she'd rather freelance. It was good for a guy like that to think she was doing all right and could afford to be independent. Then if he did occasionally offer her a job it might be worthwhile.

Even if they hadn't had so much fun, she and Daddy, riding in the rumble and eating ice cream, the drive would have been worthwhile for one thing alone. On the way back, Hoda suddenly yelled out loud, "Broom Shop, Institute for the Blind! Daddy, did you see that?" And for the rest of the trip they speculated about the place, where Hoda was sure she had seen handicraft for sale in the windows. A couple of days later Hoda, with an armful of some of Daddy's nicest bags and baskets found her way, after a lengthy streetcar ride, back to the broom shop, and from there to an office where she and a lady discussed her father's case and the lady commented on the beauty of the baskets and said of course she would put them up for sale. She even thanked Hoda for coming forward and bringing Danile to her attention. Then she asked if they needed any help, she and Daddy, and Hoda found herself replying, with modest pride, that they didn't really need anything at all, that she managed to bring in a little money at her job, and that it would be enough help for them if the Society would put some of Danile's baskets on sale.

When she thought of it afterwards Hoda was surprised at the way she had waved aside the offer of assistance. There had scarcely been a moment since her mother died when they hadn't needed help, and now it was offered finally, and just for the pleasure of making the gesture, she had refused it. Why hadn't she at least waited to find out what they were willing to do? But she wasn't sorry. Such a nice woman that was, so friendly and polite, Hoda simply had to stay equals with her.

Satisfying as the interview with the lady from the Blind Institute had been, it was even more gratifying to tell Daddy all about it afterwards. She did not even try to keep count of the exact number of times she repeated to him what the lady had said, especially the compliments that were paid his work. And each time she saw the struggle against too immodest an expression of pleasure in his face, which finally gave way to a great wide beam which seemed to illuminate the room, as he repeated in a slightly tremulous voice, "So the government likes my work?"

It was inevitable that they should speak of Uncle, now, and celebrate that day, years before, when they had rejected his offer to put them in institutions, and he had left them with the direst prophecies. How far away that was. Now they heard of Uncle mainly through the Yiddish papers, where they read, and Danile didn't begrudge it him, though Hoda sometimes grumbled, of his success as a figure in the social and philanthropic world; for as the years went by he had become a member of the board of this and an organizer of that. After each new triumph of his, something would arrive for them too, so that Hoda could pretty accurately prophesy when she saw his picture staring out at her from the paper, with that "yes, it's me" expression all those pictures wore, or read an item which referred to him, that within the next few days she would find some household bill had already been paid, perhaps the rent for a few months, or an unexpected order of groceries would be delivered to their door. Conscience money, Hoda called it, but Danile said no, Uncle simply wanted his family to share his happy moments. Hoda argued that it was a kind of blackmail, to force people to wish you well, even when you had been mean to them. Danile said that since he wished Uncle well anyway, with or without bribes, Uncle's gifts became, willy nilly, gestures of pure generosity, which someday he still hoped to be able to reciprocate, though he hoped Uncle would never have need of his help.

And Uncle's gifts did come in handy. Sometimes, in fact, when things were really tight, she would leaf through the Yiddish paper and say to herself, "What's the matter with Uncle? If he doesn't do something to get himself in the paper soon we're really in trouble. Come on Uncle, attend a banquet, get on a committee. For crying out loud, you want us to starve this winter? You'll be sorry when that gets in the paper!" Of course she wouldn't speak so in front of Danile, who became upset when she was too rude about the old man. Hoda knew that it bothered Danile that Uncle had made no attempt to re-establish personal contact. Whenever the subject came up he always repeated the same saying, "My mother always used to say, 'sometimes it's better to be friends from a distance.'"

For her daddy's sake more than for her own, since she could find her own friends, it rankled with Hoda. Someday she too would like to be in a position to reciprocate Uncle's gifts, for her own satisfaction, to let him know they were evens and equals and quits, if he didn't want to be real friends.

Danile wished that he could somehow let Uncle Nate know about their small triumph. In spite of their differences he was sure that Uncle would be pleased that he didn't have to be ashamed of his poor relations. They weren't such shnorrers after all, as the government could tell him.

"Why don't we just send him a present?" said Hoda, without thinking of what she was saying, though she knew the minute the words had formed that it was a brilliant idea. Why not do exactly what Uncle did when some happy development made him feel expansive? Hoda selected from among the finest and largest of the baskets she had in stock, what they finally agreed was the best, and though Danile found some small faults to deplore, she overrode his suggestion that he set to work right now and create a special basket which would be the ultimate in basketry, for Uncle's gift. She wrapped it very carefully. On a white piece of cardboard she printed in her fine print,

Dear Uncle Nate and Auntie Gusia,
My father and I would like you to have this gift. Daddy's bags & baskets are now also prominently displayed at the Broom Shop of the National Institute for the Blind. We hope that you will use it and tear it in good health.

Hoda did not imagine that with this gesture they would achieve the longed-for parity, but it was a step in the desired direction, an announcement of intention. Let Uncle know.

While the enthusiasm was still on her, she set forth to deliver the gift. It took all the enthusiasm she could muster for the project, to provide the push which would carry Hoda within sight of Uncle's house, for Uncle lived not far from the orphanage, within that shadowed area into which she had not dared to venture since her terrible night. Still she set out, and such is the peculiarity of the human imagination, that the instant she crossed some demarcation line of the mind, she felt as though the atmosphere in which she moved had changed entirely, and she was oppressed by a sensation of heaviness and a feeling of unreality. And yet she did not even have to catch a glimpse of the Children's Home on her way to Uncle's. When she was about a block away from Uncle's house she found the messenger she wanted, for she had no intention of delivering their parcel like a little messenger girl herself, and frightening Auntie Gusia into thinking that maybe she wanted to be invited in. A little boy was dawdling along the walk, his schoolbag strapped over his shoulder.

"Hey kid," Hoda called out to him, "little boy, you want to make two cents?"

The little fellow came forward, and the sane, familiar contact with another human, eagerly responding to her call, lifted her sense of oppression momentarily.

"You look like a smart kid," she said. "I want you to deliver a parcel for me. It's not heavy, see? It just looks big. I'll point out the house, and you deliver it to the lady who answers the door. Don't leave it on the steps; wait till they open the door. I'll watch you from here. I'll give you a penny now, and when you're finished come back here and I'll give you the other penny, okay?"

"I know how," he said gruffly, shoving the penny deep in his pocket. He trotted off, with the parcel lightly floating in his arms and the first penny he had ever earned weighing down his pocket. Halfway to the house he lost the feel of the penny. He paused to jiggle his thigh against his pants. He stopped, gripped the basket for a precarious instant in one hand as the other snaked down to make sure the copper was still there.

Scratch your arse later, Hoda implored silently. *Get a move on, kid, and let me get out of here.* There was nothing to be afraid of she knew. But how do you argue with dread?

The child came racing back down the street for his other penny. "I know how deliveries work," he said, trying to hold her attention.

"You're a smart fellow. Next time I need a delivery boy I'll call you," said the fat lady, already half turned away. She threw a funny look down his street and moved very quickly, almost running, away.

"Tomorrow?" he called hopefully, but she didn't hear. Pipick watched her. So that's how things worked. You could just happen to be coming home late from school and a stranger saw that you were a smart boy and you got lucky, all of a sudden, just like that. Other times you could wish and wish and wish, all for nothing. She was going to call him again, and he'd look for her too, when he came home from school every day. He moved homeward, stopping every few steps to pull his coppers out of his pocket and examine them. Maybe she'd give him other things, too, all kinds of things. You could deliver things a lot faster if you had an automobile, like Mr. Limprig. He examined his grandfather's face on the pennies. Our father who lives in heaven and our grandfather who lives in Windsor castle. Sometimes he thought it was his own special grandfather, really, but then they laughed and he knew it was just teasing. Relations and locations and belonging and how things worked were a perpetual puzzle to Pipick. Why did Mr. Limprig prefer to take the girls for car rides when they paid no attention and didn't learn anything, no matter how far he drove, and how long they stayed away to charge up his battery? And then they wasted time getting sick so he had to stop for a long time to make them feel better like that, the way Shirley had showed him afterwards, behind the outbuildings.

"I promised not to tell," Shirley explained, guiding his hand. "I didn't promise not to show."

It was only that stuff again. "When you were driving, or parked?" he asked suspiciously. Shirley was vague about whether they'd been driving or parked, and thought maybe it was both. "Then who shifted gears?" Pipick had a brief flash of hope. Maybe Mr. Limprig could use someone who would honk the horn and shift gears for him. He had a momentary vision of himself, not taking any room at all, hardly, between them, leaning forward from the edge of the seat, and shifting gears and honking the horn and maybe even helping steer while Mr. Limprig's hand was busy. It was one of those perfect solutions which Pipick knew, even at the instant when he conceived it, was somehow not likely to come to pass.

"And he said I should never let any boy do it to me," Shirley said, "and I won't."

"All right," said Pipick.

"Next time," she added.

At the wheel, Pipick took the curve into the orphanage drive with masterly skill. "Bravo, Prince!" his grandfather cried, as he flipped over and over in the air and landed face up in Pipick's palm. "Heads I am, tails I am too." Pipick paused to scrutinize the library window recess, and waved at his friend who waited for him, so well hidden behind the drape that only he who knew she watched for him could tell she was there. He ran to show Mrs. Limprig his earnings. She at least was on his side where car rides were concerned. When he had stood beside her in the recess and watched Mr. Limprig drive by with Shirley smirking beside him, Pipick could feel that his monster friend felt as badly as he did.

All that evening Danile drifted about in a daydream in which Uncle came in person to compliment and to thank them. Hoda, having returned safely from the area of almost superstitious fear, suffered a curious reaction. Several hours after her return she suddenly broke out in a sweat, her heart palpitated violently, and she experienced sensations of acute panic, which were all the more frightening because they were accompanied by the almost irresistible urge to go running out of the house and down the street in the direction of the orphanage. In order to try to resist the impulse, which at moments came over her so strongly that she nearly screamed out against it, she told Daddy that she was tired, and that if anybody called on her to tell them please to call again tomorrow, and shutting herself in her room she undressed and climbed into her bed in the darkness, and lay there trembling and sweating and gritting her teeth against the almost uncontrollable impulses which assaulted her in unremitting waves, to go jumping out of bed and running off into the darkness, naked as she was. When she awoke the next morning the sheets were still damp and she was still desperately clinging to the pillow around which she had wrapped herself, but the fear and the crazy impulses, at least, were gone.

EIGHT

So uncles do relent. But they don't necessarily consult your convenience in their timing. Don't expect them to come rushing over to acknowledge your gift right away, for instance, as Daddy did, day by day and hour by hour for weeks. Just forget about him and one day there is a knock on your door and there he stands in his opulence, muttering about the state of the front steps, and Hoda must usher him in to where three of her students lounge. Regretfully, Hoda shoos the boys out. "Take a break, kids. Take a rain check; come back later." There is a disgruntled mutter, which she quells with furious eyes. "I said later." An afternoon's business lost. So what? All the more reason to be gracious to Uncle, who doesn't know he's costing her.

Or does he? "Tell them I won't stay long." Uncle calls over his shoulder. He has surprised himself by embracing Danile, who has come forward with a little cry, arms outstretched, to his voice. For a moment, remembering that Danile is blind, and the outstretched arms were not necessarily an invitation, Uncle feels a fool. But Danile is weeping. Uncle is reassured, and leads him, unnecessarily, but with a strong, affectionate grip, to a chair. In their subsequent conversation he touches Danile occasionally, pats his knee, seizes his arm, and finds himself surprisingly gratified in his own gestures. Hoda stands watchful, her eyes following Uncle's eyes, which rove ceaselessly but avoid her own.

All right if he knows. So what? Let him open his mouth, just once. But Uncle sat. Uncle drank tea. Let him look then, he would find nothing remiss, scarcely a speck of dust, only two cups and saucers piled neatly in the sink. These Hoda hastily rinsed out, relaxing as she finished, mistress of her mansion.

Uncle didn't stay long that first time, but he stayed a lot longer than he'd intended when he decided, "What the hell, I'm in the district. Why not?" Thoughts of his cast-off kin had been nibbling at the edges of his mind lately, and though it wasn't a firmly premeditated visit, he'd happened to bring along a copy of the English paper, in case they hadn't seen it, with his picture and the notice in which he was listed as one of the organizing life members of the new Jewish Country Club.

"They didn't want to sell it to us," he growled, "the best golf course in the province; it hurts them Jews should enjoy it. But we matched them, green for green." Uncle expanded under Danile's admiration and Hoda's enthusiastic appreciation, the way things should be, not like with his wife. To her credit Hoda refrained from picking an argument, though she wanted to ask him whether any poor Jews would ever get a stroke at his green. That was conversation for Mr. Polonick. For Daddy's sake, she was discreet. Of course they already knew about the country club. Uncle had been prominently featured in the Yiddish paper, and in fact she'd already had the conversation about it with Mr. Polonick, but some things bear repeating, especially if you can add something from the personal angle, like the fact that the picture in the papers must have been taken at least twenty years ago.

He stayed, but not long enough to take supper, though Hoda pressed him and he was astonished to discover that she knew the old country style of fixing offal fit for a king. His wife, to keep up with her daughters-in-law, and at his own command, had moved with the culinary times; what the hell, he could afford it. But Uncle felt a pang of nostalgia as Hoda reeled off the half-forgotten names of delicacies sacred to the unrecognized deprivations of childhood, when to have any-thing to eat at all had been a blessing. He actually promised to stop for a meal sometime, and in parting, he took one of Danile's hands warmly in both of his, slipped into it a handful of small bills and loose change he'd pulled uncounted from his pocket, and squeezed Danile's fingers somewhat painfully around them. He departed through blurred eyes, his mind already shaping the inchoate feelings which would inevitably surface when, inevitably, he would drop a hint to his wife that he had seen his kin, and she would try to spoil it for him. *"They're mine, dammit, I don't give a goddam what you say, they're mine!"* There was unexpected pain in it, but it was true. They were his in a way his sons no longer were. Sons! To get a few appreciative words out of them you had to buy them a golf course. Who else needed a golf course? Oh, he was proud enough of his educated children. They were the ornaments of his golf course, but the golf course was in itself an ornament, not central to his existence. What was central to it Uncle no longer knew, perhaps only the inner end of the lopsided ball of twine into which his years had wound. But he knew that there were hot spots in his world, places where thread ground against thread for whatever reason, producing his multiple irritations, his occasional tenderness, and whatever other discomforts kept the whole rolling from its invisible source.

There is a time for buying golf courses and a time for talking with your own. *"I've earned it,"* growled Uncle with the baffled greed of one whose primary dreams have come true and been found wanting, and who is reduced to riffling through his long cast-off pile of auxiliary gratifications. *"I've earned I should be able to sit and talk a few minutes with my own. So what if she is what she is? So she makes more sense with her arse than my own son makes with his whole life!"* Here Uncle sobered. It would be dangerously close to bait Gusia with her best beloved youngest. The last time he had come down hard on that one Gusia had unexpectedly rolled eyes upward, turned a hideous grey, and pitched forward at his feet. What had followed had been a further shock; the doctors, the consultations, the diagnoses, the confrontation with his sons, the embarrassment of his reluctance to explain exactly what had happened, the mixture of guilt and relief and irritation when Gusia too maintained her silence. Uncle's mind slid hastily away from the trump card of Gusia's mortality. *"They're mine"*; he clung stubbornly to what he knew.

Uncle Nate came again to see them, not very often, but often enough to establish a pattern of expectation and, in Danile, a pleasant source of anticipation between times. Hoda anticipated too, but with far more jumbled feelings. Whether it was something her friends had said, or some whiff of possibility she had picked up herself during that short hour, or something she merely fancied during those fits of craziness that came upon her, Hoda looked forward to Uncle's visits with a kind of erotic dread. He knew, it was obvious he knew. Then why did he come? What did he really want? He talked to her all right; she was included in his conversation, but he scarcely looked at her, except only sideways when he thought she wasn't looking. What did it mean? What should she do if he did something? Where would they hide from Daddy? How could he? Oh, it was wrong of Uncle just to come and sit and not look straight at her so she didn't know what to think, and had to hold herself in readiness, and didn't want, and didn't know what she would do, and kept imagining what he would look like and feel like growling his wrinkled hardness into her in shuddering spite of herself. Had it already happened and is that why she could feel it so strongly, and was she so confused because she was trying so hard to prevent herself from remembering that it happened every time he came? It must have happened. If she just let herself she would remember the details, their every movement, Uncle and Hoda writhing together, though she knew, she simply knew that it had not, that it could not have happened, that it just wasn't so.

It wasn't so, and at some time during each subsequent visit she would realize that it wasn't going to happen this time either, and in her relief would go almost crazy with affection for him, begging him to stay longer and rushing about, concocting delicacies for him and once or twice even bringing him practically to the point of tears, what with the pressure of her warmth and the memories he and the tremulous Danile were conjuring up between them of the saintly sister it seemed to him she more and more, in certain ways, resembled.

Let people talk. When the time came you could buy a girl like this a husband and set them up in a little business and they'd prosper, sure they'd prosper, you could see by the way she went about selling that straw junk he wove, a real little hustler. What was talk compared to the feeling you got when you were in a place, when you felt at home with people? Even that crap he wove endlessly, while his sightless eyes were raised raptly to your face, sure it wasn't worth much on the market, but you had to marvel at the way his fingers worked, all by themselves. It reminded Uncle of a concert his effete younger son had taken him and Gusia to once, white-tie stuff, a pianist sitting there so close they could almost reach up and touch him from where they sat in the best seats in the house. The music had made Nate sleepy, but that guy's fingers! And they paid off, those fingers, they raked it in! He had been impressed to hear how well they paid. Not so his nephew's labours, of course. Well, shlimazel was shlimazel, but there were times when Nate was almost hypnotized by the silent music of those performing fingers. His own hands had been so filled with little excrescences during his childhood and youth that all he had ever wanted to do was keep them hidden away. He still had to remind himself sometimes, even now, that he could put his hands on the table with any man, and snap his fingers, win or lose. But the sight of his nephew's hands relaxed him. He could sit watching, silently, with only a grunt now and then, during the length of an entire cigar, while Danile worked, his smiling face somewhat mitigated in its blank intensity by the curling smoke. Why couldn't he relax like this in his own goddam golf club?

Hoda eventually achieved an equilibrium in her feelings toward Uncle. What she dreaded simply never happened, and crazy though she sometimes felt herself to be, and out of control of anything that might happen to her, she was still capable of bringing her weight down on the side of her good luck. She neutralized the obsession finally by having a screaming fit at Hymie and Limpy Letz when they ventured to tease her once too often about what she could get out of the old man if she played her cards right. Ultimately, she even forgot, except in the vaguest way, as one sometimes remembers an irrelevance, that she had ever had dirty thoughts about him. Uncle's visits had become far too important for her to let any craziness interfere with what she might learn from him.

"Show how she goes again, Uncle. How can anybody be that way?" Hoda laughed, Hoda bellowed while Uncle obligingly did another takeoff on the spastic Mrs. Limprig, shaking and twitching in every part separately as he jerked about the room. Danile sat quietly, turning his head this way and that to follow the sounds of Uncle's movements, and smiling his uncomprehending appreciation of their mirth. There was discovery in it for Uncle, when he relaxed with his niece, shucking off what he considered his white-tie personality, and playing the card, telling stories, doing takeoffs, acting out how he felt about the world of people. "You're so funny, Uncle," Hoda guffawed. "You're such a clown! You should have been a comedian!"

Her lips felt all stretched out of shape and tired, but she didn't want to stop laughing because then he'd stop doing the orphanage people. You had to encourage Uncle all the time, show him you appreciated, or he'd try something else, and then she'd have to spend a lot of time being fascinated while he talked about all kinds of other things and imitated people she wasn't personally concerned with at all. Even when his attitude was kind of mean, and the imitations themselves clumsy and made him look silly, and had nothing to do with anybody she was secretly connected to, she had to encourage him.

"You're a genius, Uncle. Oh you give me a pain in the side. Don't stop! It's from laughing."

"I always wanted," gasped Uncle, puffing and wiping his perspiring face. "I always felt I had it in me. But what can you do? They crowd around you all your life, 'Am am am, hum hum!" Uncle acted out the hands that clutched him all over, the hungry mouths demanding "I want, I want," the multiple responsibilities that had crowded him into the upholstered corner of his life.

Persistently, adroitly, Hoda went after details, any and all details; like some nocturnal animal gathering scraps to weave a nest she wheedled the clues which kept her secretly in touch with her other world, and with the strange, glamorous special ones who inhabited the forbidden region. There must be something in what Daddy said after all, that nothing is accidental. It couldn't be an accident that Daddy had an uncle so conveniently placed to her need. When she felt one of those panic fits coming on she could say to herself, over and over again, *Uncle's coming soon, Uncle's coming soon, Uncle's coming,* and hold it at bay so that it didn't slop over uncontrollably into her real life, at least during working hours, when she could least afford it. Sometimes she could even stave it off altogether, with the repeated promise that Uncle was coming soon with news.

Uncle seldom mentioned the foundling, though, having dismissed all that princely crap from the start. "What kind of prince?" Like Limprig, Uncle saw no royalty in the woodpile. His brief speculations on the subject were enough to make Hoda uneasy, so close did they skim the truth. "A snotty little kid like any snotty little kid gets dumped in a home," and Uncle did an imitation of a snotty little kid with this tongue snaking up to his nostril. Hoda's hilarity was out of all proportion. She actually shed tears. Henceforth, when she dared, she'd ask, "How's the snotty little dumpling, Uncle?" But he usually didn't know what she was talking about, and when she did make the question more explicit he generally shrugged it off irritably. Sometimes, Uncle realized, this niece of his was a bit of a cow; childish still, with no conception of the appropriate concerns of a board member.

In a way Hoda was relieved to be able to circle around her subject without getting to know much about him directly. It was not that she didn't care, but she could not afford to get too interested at this time. Although she had no intention of abandoning her responsibilities, she could not let herself get caught up and sucked into something that might tempt her to give herself away. For the time being she had enough to cope with in her real life. As she often quipped to the boys, "I may be screwing my arse off but I keep my head screwed on tight." Wasn't her friendship with Uncle Nate plenty proof of that?

Nate, of course, could not know that he was being manipulated by this big, clumsy-looking girl. She never asked for money, did she? Sometimes he tried, half deliberately, to give them the impression that if they wanted or needed any-thing, they had but to ask; he was curious to see their greed. The lack of response in terms he could understand puzzled him. They admired; they oh-ed and ah-ed his financial exploits as they did his social successes. But they never asked for anything, and God knows, looking around him, Uncle could see that it was not because they were not in need. Nate had in mind that someday he would have to do something solid about their situation. He would have to think through what would be best. He still remembered another time when he had tried to help, and he honestly preferred gratitude as a response to his magnanimity. So far, this time, though they had not shown any excess of greed, they had not turned down his bounty either. Hoda's hearty, matter-of-fact "thank you, Uncle Nate," and Danile's profuse Yiddish and Hebrew quo-tations, which, with the heavenly energy generated by his own generosity, cranked him up the celestial barber chair toward beatification, did not pretend false pride. Still, Gusia could in no way be justified in her conviction that they were trying to bleed him. On the contrary, Hoda even sometimes said, "You didn't have to, Uncle," like the summer when he had a whole season's ice delivered to their icebox, twice weekly. "But it sure is nice," she added as she served him up a big glassful of iced tea, with mint from their own garden, as she called the surrounding jungle.

Better than anything, she listened to him. Nate could not imagine saying to either of his manicured daughters-in-law some of the things he could just naturally talk about with Hoda. Why, they would lock him away if they ever saw him doing his takeoffs. All of them together, with Gusia in the lead, would have him carted off to the little red brick house if he ever did go crazy enough to act his real natural self with them. What a thing to have to say about your whole life! Who was crazy in this world?

"So what happened?" Hoda prodded.

"You can imagine," said Uncle, "a bunch of kids asleep in a dormitory, and one of them wakes up and there's this weird shadow jumping around on the walls in the moonlight. You're half asleep and there's this apparition, jerking around, bending over the beds . . ."

"Scared 'em?" said Hoda.

"Shitless!" said Uncle. "Time the Duchess gets there it's bedlam, and nobody with the sense to turn on the light." Uncle made the gesture of the sensible widow Tize flicking on the light switch, then sprang round with unselfconscious agility to crouch, like a trapped animal, Mrs. Limprig trying to disappear into the far wall of the dorm.

Something funny happened to Hoda then. In the middle of her laughter she was jerked through her own skin and found herself, suddenly illuminated, clawing the wall in the roomful of screaming children.

"But why?" Hoda cried out, shuddering, for Mrs. Limprig had crackled through her like a crazing of the flesh.

"Why? Why?" said Nate. "I just told you." He tapped his head. Mrs. Limprig had come to cover the kids who threw off their blankets in the night, particularly one kid, the foundling, whom Uncle had last seen skipping along beside her, while she moved in what could have been a crazy imitation of the skipping child. Uncle had shown how they looked, acting first one then the other, back and forth in an orchestration of jerks and twitches.

But Hoda didn't mean that when she cried out "Why?" She cried out against expanding suddenly into another's world, experiencing another's flesh, another's senses, comprehending another's anguish; why should she have to know that? Why should she have to know Mrs. Limprig as she had never known anything before? All she had wanted was to keep in touch. *I know, I know, I know.* The very words expanded, vibrated with inexpressible meanings and dimensions of pain and exhilaration.

It was gone almost immediately, her revelation, and Hoda, who had cried out against it, wanted it back, the sudden enlargement, the unbidden, anguished thrill, the knowing that was not just trimmed to your head but flowed through your whole being.

She was afraid that Uncle would recognize some change in her voice when she said, with another's lingering despair, "So you told her to stay away from the dorms."

But Uncle was having too much fun to notice the collision and absorption and sundering of worlds. "Not me, Limprig himself told her. Listen, they have a hard enough time keeping help in that place. If we start dragging them out of bed in the middle of the night they'll all quit. The Duchess will go crazy. We'll have to stick a broom up her arse . . ." Uncle roared out at his own vision of the immaculate house-keeper with cleaning implements in every available member and orifice, doing the job alone, and repeating endlessly her high purpose as she waggled her brooms fore and aft, the stir-ring little slogan born of an innocent reverence for the past, which she brought forth at every opportunity. "This was once a Stately Home, and if we all pull together, it will always be a Stately Home."

Uncle Nate got particular enjoyment out of kidding around about that Mrs. Tize, whose English accent in fact intimidated him. A Jewish woman, penniless, you could say an immigrant like himself, why should she look so antiseptic and sound so la-de-da?

Even Director Limprig, B.A., came in for his share of Uncle's mockery. Well, he was a mark, for heaven's sake, a man who couldn't even talk to a woman without snaking his eyes down to his fly every few seconds, as if he was terrified some-thing would jump out and go "cuckoo!" at her. And Nate would pungently speculate on Limprig's possible relationship with Mrs. Tize, since it was unimaginable that he could get his wife to hold still long enough to . . . and what the hell, any normal, healthy male. . . . Of course the Duchess would probably subject that cuckoo of his to all sorts of hygienic rites; he could imagine. . . . Uncle just barely remembered in time that he was too much of a gentleman to discuss these with a woman, even his whore of a niece, though she could probably tell him a thing or two. Reminded, Nate clamped his lips together and glared reproachfully at Hoda.

He sure had his moods. Once, when Uncle had been holding forth on Mrs. Tize and her superiority and standards of cleanliness that made it so difficult to keep help at the orphanage, Hoda, in an unguarded moment, had suggested impulsively, "I could work for her." Uncle had gone coldly still, except for the perceptible quivering of his self-esteem around the edges. "My niece?" was all he said finally, after an impressively extended pause, during which he wondered savagely what the hell he was doing here. And indeed, that time he left shortly after, and stayed away so long that Hoda was beginning to fear they had lost him again. Though she was amused by a scale of preference which would rather accept her on her back than on her knees, she trod carefully indeed around Uncle's dignity when he finally honoured them with his company again.

Hoda's experience of Mrs. Limprig opened her up to the possibility of further inner expansion into other worlds. If that could happen between you and somebody you'd never even seen, what of the people with whom you were in actual fleshly contact, could you enter them too, and at will? Could a human being bear the pain of so much growth and such fierce illumination? Is that what God was? Poor God! Imagine comprehending everything, totally, constantly, in that way, the pain of it, and the thrill of power in it! Words and their threaded links were merely a pretty game you played compared to real knowing. And yet that was how you spent your whole life, diddling with the trinkets and sniffing around the edges of what really was.

It would be nice to be able to talk to somebody about what had happened to her, but she could see where it would only get her into trouble with Mr. Polonick, the most likely person, if she tried to speculate with him about her revelation. He would probably accuse her of being faithless to her atheism, or something, and badger her to admit that what she had felt could have meant this and that, anything but what it was, and think he was flattering her, as he sometimes did, to soften his criticism, by telling her all about her sympathetic and hyperactive imagination. Before she knew it, his reasonings would be standing triumphant over the corpse of her real experience. No thanks.

She knew what she knew, and it was not the last time she was to experience those sudden spasms of comprehension of simultaneous worlds. Sometimes it was a total stranger, glimpsed in the street, knowing what it felt like to be in his body, comprehending in a flash the cast of his being. Sometimes it was more detailed, and she had to experience the complexity of a particular experience in another's life, and for an instant she was caught in an excruciating resonance. Maybe that was what made it so hard to bear, all the vibrations and the echoes of being one and more than one. *Why me?* she would protest, and almost immediately would begin to wonder how to do it again.

Could you train yourself, if you tried hard enough, to go in and out of people at will? What if she practiced with her customers, really concentrated. If you could time it right, could you manage to jump into him just as he was jumping into you, and feel exactly what it felt like to be him pumping it into you? She'd often thought it would be nice to feel what they were feeling too. If you could get it to work then you really would find out what it was like to go fuck yourself.

The thought broke her concentration at a crucial moment, and provoked a gust of hilarity right into the face of a customer's passion. Fut! Everything got spoiled for him and Hoda felt just awful, and tried to make him stay and try again and was so nice to him, but everything she did just seemed to make him more dejected, and she couldn't blame him. No guy likes to get laughed at just when he's giving you his present. A person had to be so careful, even though she might have the highest aims. After that she didn't try it often with the guys. She had a living to make, and she couldn't risk driving away her customers, even for the sake of science. Only sometimes when she felt a particular attraction, she would try to concentrate on becoming what was behind his eyes, because it must be such an extraordinary thing to become the one you loved loving you. Of course for it to be really right he should be trying for the same thing, shouldn't he? In which case he would be two people, himself and you, and you would be two people, yourself and him, so you would both be four people, who were really only one person, since each was the other. Boy, could you get all mixed up, just thinking around, but Hoda enjoyed it. There was no end to it. You could spend your whole life just thinking around, if you had to, though it was not like knowing, and anyway, who had the time to think much or to know much for that matter, the way things kept happening and changing the whole basis of your thoughts, just when you thought everything was more or less in its place for the time being.

Poor Uncle, he might be rich and a capitalist exploiter, but sometimes he did try to help people, in his own way, and he really wanted theirs to be the best-run orphanage in Canada. He was so upset. Who would have guessed that such an educated man as Mr. Limprig would turn out like that, and be so stupid as to let himself get caught at it, too? Little girls yet. Immoral. Criminal, шмок! Such fine tits as Mrs. Tize's, just hanging around, and a man chooses to ruin a perfect set-up, which he ran like clockwork, "like clockwork," Uncle mourned. That a man should have no discretion! It wasn't as though all the kids were total orphans, or even real orphans at all. Some were sent in from the country just to be near Jewish schools and high schools. They had parents who cared about them. It was bound to leak out. The little girl who had leaked had managed to bring together her separated parents by telling her mother how nice Mr. Limprig was to her sometimes. Now her parents, instead of hating each other, hated the orphanage because it was unfit to bring up their children.

And how come the Duchess had known nothing? She probably couldn't believe it of a man who kept his fingernails so clean. Uncle couldn't resist mocking Mrs. Tize, as though it was somehow her fault that she was interested in the wrong kind of dirt. Mrs. Tize, when confronted with the story, had been staggered. A perfect gentleman, always such a perfect gentleman in all the years they'd worked together.

"Sure, because you're not seven years old, he's a perfect gentleman."

"Oh that poowa child," Mrs. Tize had wept. "I don't understand," Uncle mimicked her, "I just don't understand."

"Who understands?" Uncle wanted to know. "When you have to start worrying about understanding it's too late already."

Hoda had listened to Uncle at first with a detached attitude to all the fuss. She was, if anything, slightly amused. It was hard not to suspect that what Uncle hated most was the inconvenience. And after all, Limprig had not actually harmed the kids. Where would she and Daddy be if Yankl hadn't helped them out that first while? She'd probably be a graduate of Limprig's finger instead of Yankl's short arm. Hoda swallowed a giggle. Still, it was interesting to hear how horrified everyone was and how the father had threatened to kill Mr. Limprig and how hard it was to get him to agree it would be better all round to hush it up. And in spite of Uncle's scorn she was a little moved by the way Mrs. Tize had wept in English. But it was not until Daddy hesitantly began to question Uncle in Ukrainian, and Uncle answered, groping for words, and Daddy got so upset, and was so disgusted, and cried out in Yiddish against human baseness, that something came to life in her, shards of an irrevocable Hoda buried all these years in her own flesh, searing through her to a lost wholeness. This time the instant of illumination was like an electrocution. The fat, hungry little girl pushing open the door of the butcher shop, the bell tinkling above, warmth rushing over her, and clean meat smell; her moccasins scuffing through the sawdust, feet drawing lines as she approached, heavy-footed with dread that he might send her away empty-handed, not knowing yet and knowing all. Her nose dripped, and Hoda tried to draw the sleeve of her coat in such a way across her face that the butcher wouldn't realize she was wiping her snot, and send her away in disgust. Yankl, behind the counter, talking, talking, beckoning; the pile of scraps beside the chopping board; Hoda obediently taking her glove off, the wincing of the soft, elastic skin and Yankl snatching it away with a grunt as it wilted prematurely between her cold, red fingers. Yankl's voice commanding "Wait," as he turned away, and "Blow on your fingers, suck them, suck them," and all the other words that helped him to get it ready again while she obeyed, sucking her fingers and hoping maybe it would be the whole pile of meat and bones for her and Daddy. "Now!" the soft, elastic film of skin working over the hard, slightly granular tube to its rubbery knob and back to the hair that always got left in her hand, back and forth, "Hard, *hard*. FASTER!" The spasm, the sudden, disturbing limpness, jerked quickly away, and Yankl, still talking, wrapping the scraps and hurrying her out of there. Fat little Hoda in eternal triumph anyway, hurrying home, and fat big Hoda, comprehending, in infinite grief.

"What are you crying about?" repeated Uncle impatiently. "I told you I fixed everything."

It had simply never occurred to her before. *He could have given me the scraps. You don't do that to children.* Hoda suddenly stopped crying, raised swollen eyes to Uncle, uttered, with difficulty, the panic question, "Did he touch the boys?"

Uncle was again irritatingly reminded of the limitations of this niece of his. He had come with the generous impulse to share a diplomatic triumph, and instead of the admiration he expected, Hoda managed to make him remember uneasily that the board had sworn itself to secrecy. "Not enough the girls?" growled Uncle.

"Yeh," said Hoda bitterly, "yeh," but was relieved, too, that the future was still intact, or at least unknown.

It was true, curiously enough, that during the Limprig investigation, it was Uncle Nate, least subtle of men, who distinguished himself above all the other members of the board. He had, during the past number of years in which he had been invited to sit on more than one board and partake of numerous counsels, gained enormously in his confidence in himself as a man fitted to sit among the worthiest. He had risen to such a height among the beautiful that he no longer felt it necessary to be perpetually concerned about whatever enemies might wish him ill. Freed of such petty hostilities he could turn his mind to problems and assess them with clarity and a certain admirable rude justice.

Having dissuaded the child's father from calling in the police, they were left with the question, what to do with Limprig? The man's behaviour from the beginning, when the chairman of the board brought him unexpectedly face to face with his accuser, with a gruff, "Let's settle this here and now," had been most frustrating. He had retained, in face of the child's father, an admirable imperturbality of surface, over flesh which had turned to jelly. Of his inner state, only a faintly glossy sheen on the skin of his face gave indication, and the curious softness of his voice, when the chairman stated the charge in an embarrassed way and urged him strongly to deny the absurdity, and Limprig murmured in response, "The child exaggerates." The chairman was at first puzzled, then put off, and finally dismayed by the curious offhand quality of Limprig's reiterated demurring murmur, which had almost an air of modesty to it, in his soft, melancholy, albeit a trifle nervous tones. "The child exaggerates. No really, the child exaggerates." This was hardly the thundering disclaimer required. But it puzzled the angry father sufficiently to keep him silent and uneasy. He was a simple working man, not used to these educated perverts. If the man was innocent why wasn't he shouting? On the other hand, what if he was so innocent he didn't need to shout? Could the child, after all, have been lying to them? How come, when they never paid much attention to her chatter anyway, they were suddenly listening so hard to this? It had better be true, it had just better be true, or they would be sorry, they would, wife and daughter both.

Escaping, Limprig went directly to his suite, locked himself in, and stood with his back against the door. Naomi Limprig, who had been preparing to go out and take her station at the library window, for the children would soon be coming home from school, took one look at his face. "What is it, Shmuel?" she asked, with difficulty, but she already knew. She turned and shuffled back into the bedroom and lay down on the bed. Pretty soon he would come in, and sit on the bed, and whether or not she pretended to be asleep, he would explain and explain and explain. Selfish Naomi, she would not even listen, no, not any more. Now all she would hear was the roaring sound in her ears of her own small world tumbling over and over as it fell.

Almost immediately, the board received a note from Limprig, very well if somewhat ambiguously expressed, in which he referred to the exaggerations of children, the loss of confidence of the board, and the impossibility of functioning in such a situation. He ended by tendering his resignation, in order, he explained, to avoid further embarrassment and above all, any damage to the institution which he loved so well and could assure them he had served as faithfully as was in his power these past fifteen years.

If the man did not choose to defend himself there must be at least something in the accusation. What did he mean by "exaggeration"? "Not with a whole hand?" as Uncle quipped. Or had a fatherly caress on the part of a lonely man become exaggerated in the telling? "God knows," one of the old guard became quite emotional on Limprig's behalf, "it's not difficult sometimes to misconstrue a fatherly caress."

It was at this point, when the baffled board members were grumbling back and forth at each other, because the man himself was putting them in a position where they had to accept his resignation and disrupt a setup which had been their pride for years, that Uncle Nate offered to talk to Limprig and see what he could do toward clarifying the situation. Limprig was summoned to his own office, and with the rest of the board waiting in the library, and the intervening doors carefully closed, he was interviewed by Uncle Nate.

"See here, Limprig," said Uncle bluntly. "I don't know if you were fiddling with the kids here or not. Never mind!" He held up his hand and waved away Limprig's nervous gesture. "I don't care, one little girl, two; you've felt one, you've felt them all, if you're going to get yourself caught, if not today, tomorrow. You go in for that kind of thing you might as well have a party."

"No," Limprig began. "No honestly, I just . . ." and he made a despairing little gesture with his hand.

"Limprig, I say, put down the finger! I don't want to know how!" Even Uncle was a little embarrassed by the helpless little gesture. "We know," he added hastily, "you're a good man. Like I say we've never had any complaints; till now we've been satisfied. I for one feel it would be a shame to lose a man like you. When I know you're in charge I don't have to worry my head the place isn't being run right, see?"

Limprig nodded, accepted, perforce, the right of the board to select this most uncouth of its members to treat with him.

"But we can't have any scandal," Nate continued reasonably. "We can't have fathers in here all the time threatening to call the police because you . . ." Here Uncle couldn't resist the desire to repeat Limprig's repellent but fascinating little gesture.

Limprig, who had not at all intended for his gesture to be illustrative, uttered a curious little moan, and looked away. "I've resigned," he said desperately. "You have my letter of resignation."

"Yes," said Uncle. "I know. And I don't mind telling you between you and me it won't be so easy to replace you. Listen, Limprig, we're civilized people here. How many good administrators have we got? I myself don't believe in wasting a good man. You've got a little problem, the way I look at it, it doesn't have to mean the end of the world. Put you where your problem doesn't interfere and you'll still be a good administrator, right? Well then, I'll tell you what. I've got a little proposition I want to make to you. Maybe you noticed last month my picture in the Yiddish paper? Happens they just elected me chairman of the board at the Old Folks' Home. You know we've got a building program going on. They said 'Nate, at this time we need you!' Oh it's coming to me that chairman's seat. I've worked. Plenty of time, plenty of money I spent."

"Congratulations," murmured Limprig faintly.

"Thanks. I suppose you're surprised I should be talking to you before the rest of them? I'll tell you straight. It happens, we need a good man to put the Old Folks' Home in order, a man like you in fact. So how about it? Resign here, okay, like you did, but make it like a transfer to our place. That way, people won't wonder why all of a sudden you're resigning and running away someplace. We won't have any scandal. You'll still have a job, and if you want to tickle an old lady sometimes, there it won't be a sin, it'll be a good deed, a real mitzvah. So what do you say, Limprig, how about it? I'm chairman. My word goes. If I want you, you're in. Believe me, you'll solve all your problems. When you walk through these doors to face the boys, you'll be a man with a job." For all his grossness, Uncle knew where some of the finer nerve endings are located. Shortly afterwards, Limprig's hesitations swept aside, the two of them passed through the file room, and with a gesture, Uncle Nate flung open the library door. "Gentlemen," he announced, with a flourish of his cigar, " I want you to meet the new Director of the Old Folks' Home."

There were enough members of the board capable of a humorous appreciation of the admirable symmetry of Uncle's solution to congratulate him on being sly enough to turn their loss into a gain for the Old Folks' Home. Only a few were heard to mutter that Uncle might just as easily have presented his proposal to the board, which would have given its blessing perforce, instead of turning the occasion into a dramatic little coup. But they were unfair to suggest the old thief had set up his "steal" because he didn't know any but the crooked way of doing things, even when there was no need. Uncle wasn't even thinking of pulling a fast one. He acted in response to an inner sense of dramatic fitness in setting up his little scene. And what, after all, had anybody to complain about? Surprise dispelled their embarrassment in confronting Limprig face to face, most of them for the first time since the problem arose, and now instead of dwelling on what they would all rather forget, they were able, thanks to Uncle, to enter, with Limprig, into a calm discussion of the details of his relinquishment of office, and arrange for all to be carried out in satisfactory order. "Like they told me," Nate could not resist adding the imaginary compliment the board should have paid him, when he was telling his story to Hoda and her father, "Nate," they said, "You're a Solomon. A Solomon," Nate repeated, moved, and gazed with visionary intensity at the tip of his cigar.

But people don't appreciate. Nate was to discover very shortly once again that the world is unworthy of its Solomons. On the morning of the day that the Limprigs were to move to their new residence, Naomi Limprig, neatly dressed and wearing her mother's pearls, was found hanging in the file room, the same closet through which Uncle Nate had led her husband from despair to a new life. Uncle was not even the first to be called to the scene. He was on time, however, summoned by the murmuring undertow which drags people to the scene of disaster, to elbow his way through the little crowd and stride up the drive, the only board member to actually see the suffering in that grotesque, frozen face and be enveloped by the nimbus of horror which temporarily changed even him. Standing there, hanging on to the newel post, after the policeman had taken him firmly by the elbow and led him, still identifying himself, but now apologetically, from the library into which he had burst in the pride of his self-importance, Uncle wondered, though with uncommon diffidence, how he could best assert himself in this situation. Looking up, he caught a glimpse of Limprig, just turning back from the top of the stairs, and realized the man must have been on his way down, and had turned back in order to avoid him. For once the impulse shrivelled in Nate, to summon him peremptorily down. He was too stunned by the intensity, the savagery of grief in the face that had been quickly wrenched from his view.

Nor could Uncle take better hold when he found his way finally to the cot in the sick bay where Mrs. Tize half-sat, half-lay across the sedated but still restless child who clung to her, while she tried to soothe him with stilted words of unaccustomed tenderness. Uncle wanted to let her know that he too had seen, that he too needed comforting. But Mrs. Tize knew her place. Still stroking the muttering child, she gave a terse, low-voiced report, while Uncle listened with head thrust forward, because her accent seemed to have become more pronounced, and rested his eyes on her left breast, which lay like a cat on the counterpane.

Thus Uncle learned that Mrs. Limprig must have taken a long time to expire, and that she must still have been twitching when the little boy who came to the library to greet her every morning heard the thumping of her foot against the library wall, and opened the closet door. Summoned by his screams, Mrs. Tize had arrived to find an insane tug-of-war going on between Pipick who was hanging onto her legs and trying to pull Naomi Limprig down to the ground, and

Limprig, just arrived, who was trying to raise and support the body. Ruth Tize had wrestled the child away and dragged him out, still screaming "Mamma," though she tried to muffle his screams against her breast. Remembering, she wept, and her very sobs had an aristocratic, hard-to-come-by sound to Nate. In his masculine innocence responding sexually to her distress, he asked with gruff tenderness what he could do to help, to which Mrs. Tize, somewhat removed from the impulse which responds to disaster with the urge to new life, and resenting, too, momentarily, the proprietary interest of the gods in human sorrow, replied somewhat tartly, "Oh, call a board meeting."

"Poo wa lie dee, poowaladdee," he thought he heard her whispering to herself as he left.

"They're all crazy," he told Gusia plaintively afterwards, and not until she had replied, with her infallible instinct for saying what he did not want to hear, "So who told you to get mixed up with them in the first place?" was the knot inside of him released and swept away in a cleansing rage. But there are residues of feeling that simply cannot be yelled away, meaningless details that reverberate unphrasable questions. Uncle took his uneasiness to his poor relations, and tried to unburden himself of what he had seen. But as soon as Hoda realized that he was actually going to imitate the face of the strangled Mrs. Limprig, she jumped up and turned away from him, yelling, "I'm not looking! I'm not going to look! Uncle, I'm not looking!" And Nate was left hanging his tongue out and goggling his eyes in the face of a blind man. And not only that, the stupid cow refused to turn around again until he had assured her at least ten times that he wasn't doing it any more. Uncle was frustrated. He had been upstaged every time he put his foot on the boards lately. He sulked, but Hoda was too distracted to notice. She was terrified that he might yet spring Mrs. Limprig's death mask on her, and if that happened she didn't know what would come bursting over her. Was the punishment for wanting to know too much that you got your wish? Something reckless and crazy in her kept rearing up and saying, *All right, show me uncle, show me!* But she bit her tongue back and watched, ready to whirl away the minute he should try it again.

Uncle sought Danile's sympathetic ear, to which he found himself confiding even his disappointment in Limprig, who had turned his face from him, "As if I was an enemy. Did I do him any harm?"

"Oh, no!" cried Danile, and he described for Uncle how a man in the bitterness of his grief will turn inward and eat his own entrails.

Uncle was soothed, not so much by the sense of Danile's words, for he scarcely listened, as by the ardent sympathy in the sound of them. It occurred to him that he had always had bad luck with cripples, particularly female cripples. But he refrained from voicing this complaint, and instead came to the decision, even as he was sitting there, that he would forbear from recrimination, and would let Limprig know, at the appropriate time, that his job at the Old Folks' Home was still waiting for him whenever he was ready to take up his duties. He interrupted Danile to tell him this, and sat back, much comforted by his own magnanimity, nodding agreement as his nephew praised his compassion and applauded his wisdom.

After that Uncle seemed to lose much of his interest in the affairs of the orphanage. He was not impressed by the new Director, for all that he was a local man and a family man and his life was an open book. It was not a very well-kept book, was Uncle's point, but normality was the cry among board members now, and Mr. Popoff's promise, that moving his large family right into the orphanage would have the natural effect of turning the whole home into one big, happy family, swept aside Uncle's objections that in past community service Popoff had proved himself to be but an indifferent administrator. Uncle gave way with unwonted mildness when he was overridden, and turned his attention elsewhere. Henceforth he contented himself with only token attendance at board meetings, where he nevertheless made something of a nuisance of himself by grunting irrepressibly at each new proof that he had been right about Popoff from the start, sighing heavily through the Director's prolix and circumlocutory reports, rumbling ominously to indicate disapproval of some proposed decision, and groaning outright at times for no immediately traceable reason. All of this made some of the members quite uneasy, but when he was asked to give an opinion, Uncle now invariably replied, "I'm not talking," or alternately, "I'm quiet, I'm still."

Hoda no longer tried to coax Uncle Nate to elaborate imitations. She would not again try to affiliate herself intensely and secretly with the orphanage staff. You didn't know what you were hooking yourself onto. She felt at one and the same time that she had had some kind of narrow escape, and that she had failed once again in some unspecified area that she could not bring herself to try to examine. One thing was sure, Mrs. Limprig's way was out; a fat lot of good you would ever be able to be to the boy someday if, when he needed you, you were hanging there. No, Hoda would continue to keep tabs, but from a distance, and await her time. She found some comfort in the new theory of the happy Popoff family, despite Uncle's patent lack of enthusiasm. All

CRACKPOT

she wanted, after all, for the time being, was that the kid should be brought up in a happy family.

Uncle, who missed the old enthusiasm over his imitations, and put himself out now to bring forth the hearty guffaw, nevertheless held his ground when she argued the merits of the Popoff method with him. "Limprig was a better director than Popoff with his hands tied behind his back," he insisted. "Maybe we should have kept them tied there," he added, and won his laugh from Hoda.

Of course she continued to look forward to his visits, but the prospect of a visit from Uncle Nate was no longer able to fortify her, even temporarily, against her own craziness. She was still periodically assaulted by the urge to flight, which she resisted only by wrapping herself around her pillow and lying there, haunted by the spectre of herself running, sucked by invisible forces through the dark streets. Some time was to pass yet before she learned to deal with the fits of craziness in their own language.

NINE

You'd think that in all the years since she'd been making her visits to the City Hall, Hoda would have lost the feeling of uneasiness with which she approached the place each time. Not so. Even though she joked with her customers about it, and reassured them often enough about what she called "my connections at City Hall," because it was good policy to let them know they were safe with her, and even though she brazened it out by being her most aggressively rambunctious self while she was visiting her "connections," her stomach didn't stop turning over and over until she was safely out of there again.

Maybe that was why she always walked, even in winter, though it was quite far, not only because she saved carfare but because by walking she could get some of the pleasures of delay out of all the familiar sights and feelings and pauses along the way, and almost forget where she was going. The very normality of the scenes she passed might lead, by sympathetic magic, to the right kind of conclusion to her errand. In spite of her discomfort, she went more often than she intended to, more often, certainly, than they wanted her up there, as they made clear. Well, that was just too bad, whatever they thought. She was a citizen and she had her rights and they ought to be glad she had a sense of responsibility. Did they think she enjoyed coming and seeing their supercilious faces and being treated at fingertips' end like an overfull specimen bottle? She came because she had to, because sometimes she awoke in fear that something had gone wrong, and when she felt like that she didn't care any more that she would have to face that "Oh my Lord look who's here again" expression on their faces. She had never liked their attitude, and she still didn't like their attitude, but she could cope with it all right. Just let them tend to their part of the business, and let everything be all right this once more; that's what she was thinking all the time inside of herself, even when, in the early days, she was putting on the noisy routine that she had discovered would embarrass them into seeing to her business promptly instead of keeping her waiting for hours as they used to do at first, though she always got there early and sometimes even arrived before they'd opened up.

It was two or three miles up Main Street before you reached the City Hall. On the way she could see what shops had been forced to close down since last time, and peer in on their dirty, empty insides, and try to remember what they'd been like just a little while before. And she could stop and discuss the depression with old acquaintances in the Farmer's Market, where the peddlers and farmers were just beginning to unload. Sometimes, on an impulse, because of that sixth sense she had developed for business, she'd detour behind the Farmer's Market past some of the wholesalers, where the wagons were loading, and if she was lucky she'd maybe do some business with the energetic young teamsters. A couple of times, in one place, she had been briefly with the big boss

317

himself, though the honour didn't really impress Hoda, since he didn't pay any more, or in any other way distinguish himself from anyone else by showing special interest in her. She just didn't have Hymie's luck.

What with her detours and stops to chat, by the time she moved beyond the market area into the Main Street again, the merchants were arriving and opening up the little dry goods and dresswear and secondhand shops, and the chip and vinegar stands were open for people to grab an early cup of coffee. Hoda scrutinized carefully, with as much fascination as she had felt for the stuff in the fifteen-cent store windows when she was a kid, the elegant items that were laid out one almost on top of the other behind the metal screens of the pawnshop windows, good-quality stuff, really cheap if you could afford it, and really classy if you could use it; jewellery and watches and all those musical instruments that Hoda felt she could have learned to play when she was a kid, that Ma and Pa used to talk of getting her someday when they could afford one, like a violin, so she would have been a great musician. If it happened to be spring she looked out for the crude glamour of a new fly-by-night gypsy fortune-teller's window, mysterious signs boldly drawn, significant objects, discreet and faintly sinister folds of dark curtain. It was pretty cheesy when you stopped to look at it close up, like at the circus, but still they might know something. Funny how you never hear people wishing fortune-tellers good luck, though they go to them greedy for good fortune. Sometimes she thought of doing a little fortune-telling herself as a sideline, to liven up her business. After the main course maybe: "Say, mister, while you're here, how would you like me to tell your fortune?" No, not unless she could learn to be more careful when she opened her mouth. You learned a lot about guys in her business, but not much that they wanted you to tell them about afterwards. "I see a big future for you mister, six-eight-ten inches maybe." What else, for Hoda?

Past the big railway hotel she trudged, where strangers and the rich hid behind long windows with thick, velvet curtains. That was where she'd thought that guy would take her, long long ago, that first time she'd come up town, that first time she'd discovered these other sleazy places were hotels too. Past the beer parlors, where, even at this time of morning, the half-breeds lounged patiently, waiting for opening time to cut the glare of their days. Hoda always hurried past the half-breeds, afraid because she knew that if she let herself she would know what they were like inside too. And in the face of knowing what sense did even Mr. Polonick make when he said, "Well Hoda, that's progress. At least we'd cure them of T.B. and educate them to join hands with all the other oppressed, and take them off the reservations, and they'd become free men just like anyone else." It irritated him when Hoda replied, "You mean we'll cure them of being Indians one way or another." And he'd explain once more how you can't fight the future. You musn't stand in the way of progress. Why not? What is this progress anyway? A word, that's all, a word for what happens, and a word for what should happen, and a word for what doesn't happen as well. If you stand in its way maybe that's progress too. But it was not much fun teasing Mr. Polonick anymore. He never had had much sense of humour anyway, and as he grew older and all the bad things that he predicted would happen to the world if people didn't wake up, actually happened, he grew more irritable. Once Hoda had said to him, "Maybe dumb fascists and those crazy German Nazis think that's progress too, to run around killing people like us? Maybe they think you can't stop progress too?" Well, she wouldn't try that again, not with poor old Polonick. He nearly had a fit. You couldn't really blame him. God himself must be a pretty dyspeptic kind of a guy by now. But she still didn't like what happened to the Indians and the half-breeds, Polonick and progress notwithstanding. Nevertheless she hurried past them. Can you reply "I feel something special for you," when someone calls out "fuck fuck jig jig" as you go by? From her they didn't want something special.

Grim reflections were followed by considerations more tender, as Hoda passed three movie houses, one after the other, slowing down to go over, frame by frame, the stills of six not quite current movies. One day when she had some spare cash she was going to blow herself to an orgy, double feature in one, spill out on the sidewalk and blink her way into the next door double feature, and after that stagger into the next, and when she emerged finally it would be dark out except for the lights outside the movies, and maybe if it was Saturday, the strings of lights all lit up across Main Street. She'd stand there on the sidewalk, saturated, groggy, and someone would come up to her very naturally and say, "Hello big and beautiful."

What then? She was getting sick and tired of stale old dreams. Maybe on the other hand three double features in a row would cure her of them once and for all, and she'd come out saying "phoney, phoney, phoney baloney" and that would be it. For all the toughness she had developed over the years, and the real disenchantment with all kinds of dreams that had once seemed endlessly exciting and always possible, Hoda still surrendered herself at the movies, sat alone in the darkness with her eyes glued to the magic light and shadows of "if only," yearned and suffered and thrilled as the "why not" romance moved inevitably to the point where she knew, with an exquisite sense of illumination, ever new, that now . . . now

. . . they're going to . . . and for real, not for money, and forever and ever and ever more. And it was always like it was going to be the first time for them, and the first time always, even when you could see they'd been around, and it returned to her, too, a first-time feeling that made first times possible again for a little while. She knew it was all a cheat and false and that wasn't how things happened even as she surrendered herself, and yet she fell, each time. Maybe that was why she still had kind of a soft spot for the little boys who came to her in groups; *"God, they get younger every year!"* She got a kick out of them: the ones that thought they were so experienced, maybe they'd been two, three times already, showing off how well they knew the ropes with her to the tyros, who tried to pretend they knew the ropes too. Hoda went along with it all. A lot depended on how you treated them. Hell, the first few times should be a memory. Even when you fizzed out, right away you would want to start again, and you knew you could never go stale, not for long. You knew a lot of things then that you didn't know any more. Hoda could still remember her first few times, how they had felt, anyway, though some of the details were a little muddled up in her mind.

But she didn't really delude herself that even three double features would keep her groggy enough long enough to believe that anyone who approached her in this area of town meant anything but simple business, and not very good business either, judging by the types who hung around. Even if someone offered her a turn in the big hotel, behind the velvet curtains, would she go? The cops bear down on you for hustling in a place like that unless you can afford to go dressed really classy, or so Hoda had heard. She had never had any kind of run-in with the cops in the course of her business career, and didn't intend to begin now. Leave the big hotels to the rich amateurs. Hoda had never got over her mistrust of the downtown trade, where a girl really needed protection, and even so, with all her protection, look what had happened to Seraphina. That's just it, what had happened to Seraphina? Nobody knew. Seraphina, and her pimp too, the flashy Les, had simply dropped out of sight a couple of years ago. Her mother didn't know where she was, and was pretty rude about it when Hoda came, with the friendliest intentions, to enquire. And nobody else seemed to know or care either. Maybe Les had got restless and taken his girls, like he had always promised he would, out east and into the real big time. Or maybe he was serving time, and the girls were scattered. But where? Hoda hoped that Seraphina really had made it out east in the big time, like Hymie had. But she doubted. Serry would have sent a card, at least. One time she ran into one of Serry's reform school pals, who told her that last she had heard, Serry wasn't even with Les any more. Someone had seen Les and asked after her and Les had said he couldn't afford to support a sick pig, coughing and puking blood all over his customers. Put that together with what Seraphina had told her towards the end, that Les was bribing her with little extras to take on specialty tricks and let them beat her up, and Hoda didn't like it at all. She told Seraphina she was crazy to do it, but Serry had laughed a funny, frightened laugh, and said what could you do if those were all the customers he got for you nowadays, and maybe all you were good for anymore like he said, and a girl had to eat, and you know what a temper Les had; if you're going to get beaten up anyway it might as well be on a full stomach. It's unnatural to puke on an empty one; the doctors don't like it.

Hoda had got mad and stormed at her and tush tushed the way she was running herself down, "You don't need him! Why don't you leave him and go to a house like you always said?"

But Serry, poor dimwit though she was, explained that Les was her only security, and nowadays she didn't seem to look so good to the brothel keepers either. Anyway, she didn't mind the beatings so much; they always stopped sometimes and then you felt better, and besides, she couldn't run out on poor Les. "I'd worry how he was getting on. You get set in your ways, Hoda."

Well, Seraphina might, but Hoda wouldn't; that she promised herself. Nobody was going to call her a sick pig and abandon her. Where? Hoda had written a letter to the T.B. Sanatarium and called up the contagious diseases and chronic sickness hospitals in town, but they didn't have any Seraphina, so all she could do now was hope that her old friend might just turn up again like she always had. As for Les, she hoped he was doing time, that's what she hoped. Even if a guy was a pimp he should have a sense of responsibility. But when she caught herself thinking something like that, say about somebody like Les, Hoda laughed at herself, because actually, she did know better, though it still griped her, the way things were, the way people were, the way everything was.

Look, even the way the City Hall was; should things be like that right in the very centre of the city where you belonged? Concerned as Hoda was with very personal things on the one hand, and with large, universal political and humanitarian problems on the other, she always felt when she thought of the City Hall that this should be the place where everybody would feel the same concern for everybody else. But instead, it was from the top of the stone staircases out front of the City Hall that the mayor had read the Riot Act and given the order for the militia to charge on the workers in the general strike. And it was here that she herself came, fearfully, to perform her regular personal errand, and got a sinking feeling every time she caught sight of things she really liked to see, like the old trees, the landscaped lawn, and the pretty flower beds. She stood and looked at the large statue of the heroic soldier going out to get shot, and she knew that though she felt ever so close to them and sorry for them and everything, she would get little sympathy herself even from the old soldier bums and cripples who hung around here, if she were so far to forget herself as to ask for it, that is. What did she expect? If you're going to peddle your arse you can expect to get sold sometimes, so why should they sympathize? And yet she sympathized with them, didn't she, with all these listless figures of crippled and jobless old soldiers and down and outs who leaned against the City Hall fence and watched the pigeons and hardly ever looked up at the fine old dark metallic figure in full battle dress and pigeon shit, that stood for what they themselves had been like before gunshot and gas and government had brought them back to hang about the City Hall and the welfare offices because there was nothing else for them to do, good old soldiers who knew better than to disobey the green and white wooden signs that said, "Please don't walk on the grass." They'd peddled their arses too, hadn't they? and cheap. And had they known any more what it was all about than Hoda had, when she had thrown all her innocent goodwill into pleasing and being pleased? Oh, Hoda was not afraid to say what she thought about it all, and she said it, too, inside, when she was waiting her turn. That was probably another reason why they rushed her out so fast, which was all right by her, better than being kept waiting all day, like they'd probably start doing to her again if she gave them half a chance.

Not that Hoda minded the City Hall itself. In a way she liked being somehow connected to a nice, big, ugly old building, and this one was maybe as big as a palace, the crazy, haunted kind you sometimes saw in pictures, gloomy but impressive, the way those broad, double-armed stairways led up to the front entrance, and all those bumps and protrusions and separate cockeyed little constructions rising up and up all over the place, with hundreds of little windows set into masses of stale old genital-coloured brick. Once you got in there you were lost right from the start, unless you happened to be familiar with all the little crooked byways of government. That much Hoda knew from experience. She didn't often look in at that entrance nowadays, only sometimes when they wanted to warm up after a rally, maybe she and one of the comrades would slip in for a few minutes and pretend they were tourists. She was now far from the naive young girl who had first climbed up the staircase and tugged open the massive door and wandered about among unfamiliar musty smells and huge, dark paintings, and broad stairways.

At first she had thought that people just didn't know, and you had to persist until you got hold of maybe the mayor himself, who must be the only one who knew anything around here. And since she was still pretty young at the time, she had felt called on to explain her perfectly simple errand confidentially to each one she asked, repeating painstakingly over and over again that she had been told that if you went to the City Hall, they would give you a free check-up to see if you had caught a dose or anything. All she wanted was to find the doctor. They sent her from office to office, and after a while people were popping in and out of office doors, and she was sure she heard giggling, and she was getting hot and sweaty, and she began to understand that they weren't being as nice and polite as they sounded. She didn't want to begin to cry in front of them, so she yelled out her errand into the next deceptively polite face, and he scuttled back into his office, and then the guard came and directed her curtly out the front entrance again and right around back to a mean little door that led into a cellar, and had a sign over it that said "Public Health." Here at least you'd think the people knew what they were being paid for, and would treat you like any other patient. Well they didn't. They acted as if she was something at the other end of a long stick. They kept her waiting for hours, and were a lot more polite to people who came in after her, and didn't keep them waiting nearly as long either. Sometimes they even made her come back again in the afternoon, and kept her waiting then too.

Sure, and Mr. Polonick agreed with her; that's how they treat you when you're a charity patient. They wouldn't keep a society lady waiting if she was afraid she had a social disease, but someone who had to earn her living and didn't really want to spread anything bad around, like Hoda, her time could be wasted. Hoda bitterly resented their attitude, but at first she didn't know what to do about it. If she made a fuss like she felt like doing, they might call in a cop or guard and start investigating and who knows what trouble they could get her into, if they wanted to, those cops.

Remember what Mr. Polonick says, she reminded herself. *They may be doctors and nurses and educated goyem, but they're still public servants, and you're the public, and they're at your service. Treat them nicely, even if they have no manners, like you'd treat any other servant.* So she did; she ignored their frigid manners and their cold faces, and she chatted and joked at them, and during the time she spent in the waiting room, she entertained herself, and whoever else happened to be waiting, with conversation and jokes, and in general tried to cheer up the drab little anteroom. Sometimes it got pretty busy, and she met all kinds of interesting people. It turned out this place wasn't only for checking against the dose; it was for pre-maritals, and vaccinations of all kinds, and other odds and ends of public medical service. Sometimes when a good-natured bunch happened to get together in there they had a very good time. Hoda, once she got going, could keep them in stitches for hours. The audience in the waiting room was usually fun to kibitz with, because they were all a little anxious about one thing or another, whether they were worried they might have got the clap, or thought they might be a little preg-nant, or simply didn't look forward to having needles stuck in them. So they laughed with a nervous readiness, an almost pathetic willingness to have their jitters turned to hilarity. Hoda actually began to enjoy these visits to the Public Health, at least the chatty waiting part.

Then she realized that they were suddenly rushing her through practically the minute she arrived, taking her first, interrupting her conversations just as they got started, pushing her tests through the lab, dismissing her before she hardly had a chance to open an acquaintanceship with anyone. It dawned on her then that there was something the staff didn't like about her conversation. The minute they heard her voice, they couldn't get her out quickly enough. That's when she really began to enjoy the game. "Hi there!" she'd call out innocently to a young couple who sat facing her on the opposite bench, that you could see from miles away were green little pre-maritals, probably waiting to get vaccinated for their honey-moon trip. "You two been playing around?" Or else she'd fix the young man with a bright grey eye and say tenderly, all the while sloshing her yellowed retort gently to and fro. "Don't I know you from some place?" Other times she teased and joked suggestively with the young louts who sat sheepishly clutching their own specimen bottles. She developed, over the years, a kind of sophistication, a public attitude, a way of outfacing whoever faced her. Deliberately, she would introduce the questions, "What do you do for a living?" so that she could work round to telling them, in her turn, still sloshing her specimen innocently, "Me? Oh, I make ends meet," and her wicked chuckle would bust out of her and she could just feel the doctor and nurse squirming in the examination room, and imagine them muttering, "For God's sake get her out of here!" Or she would say brightly, when she saw the expression on the doctor's face when she appeared again, "Just keeping clean like you want me to, Doc." And she was amused because, rush though they might, it still took them a little time to process her business, and it eased her own nervousness to know they didn't have things all their own way.

All that had been in the early years. Now Hoda had been coming so long that she even had, as she jokingly put it, seniority over the doctor. Several young men and women had taken their turns in looking after her urine. She had even picked up the odd bit of biographical information about some of them, past and present, and could tell you where this one now had his private practice, or what hospital that other one worked at, and how his nurse had followed him there soon after, though his wife probably didn't know it. She was free with these little bits of information, like a kindly hostess putting her company at ease. Sometimes a young staff member, hearing from Hoda's lips some item of private information about a predecessor, cringed to think that somehow the odd little intimate fact about himself might find its way out of that great mouth and strip the cool white coat away from between himself and his patients. And regrettably, it happened occasionally that a patient was jabbed with unnecessary force, as a direct result of the fact that Hoda's voice was coming through loud and clear in the examining room, and the patient went off convinced that the Public Health had the heaviest-handed doctors because, as the fat girl said, the city didn't care about you if you couldn't afford to pay.

As time passed, though Hoda still loved a cheerful bit of a chat and a kibitz with strangers that she met there, her conversation began to reflect the increase of restless bafflement that she felt about everything. The sentences she puzzled together lost some of their youthful clarity and certainty, and gained a little more of the disturbing resonance of ambiguity, took on, in fact, something of a rudely philosophical cast. Oh, she still joked, but her jokes had an acidic, even faintly seditious tone that sometimes made her audience a little uneasy. She would get started on the condition of the water fountain, for instance, out front there, with the pigeons and the lounging bums, and how she wouldn't take a drink out of it if you paid her. What did the mayor think, she wanted to catch a social disease or something? But then, after a brief guffaw, she would go on more moodily, to the dirt and the spit, and remark on how people could hardly wait to get to the City Hall to clear the disgust from their throats. What could those strangers think when they came to town, all those visitors they had the "Welcome Visitors" sign up front for, whoever they were; for her part Hoda never saw anyone but down and outs and the occasional farmer bringing his wife to show her things weren't so good in the city either.

And Hoda would ramble on about things she had half-mulled over in her head, making sure she interspersed her comments with jokes, so her fellow patients wouldn't begin to get

restless and turn on their haunches away from her. But sometimes she gave way to the pressure of her thoughts, and went
off, after a light-hearted beginning, into long, discursive mono-
logues, noting the restiveness of her captive audience after a
while, but unable to stop herself just yet from trying to hunt
down and capture the truth towards which her unwinding
words seemed to beckon, perennially teasing her to the perennially incomplete revelation of words, and yet more words.

"Have you ever noticed that motto up front? I mean
what's written up on that big fancy shield, right in the centre of
the building, up over the front doors. You know, like, our city
motto. You don't even know your own city motto? What kind
of citizen are you? I know it all right. I ought to. It says,
'Commerce, Prudence, Industry.' That's my motto too, in fact.
I figure if it's good enough for my home town, it's good enough
for me. Commerce? Any time you like. Prudence? What do
you think I'm doing here with the bottle? Industry? Hell, I ain't
had no complaints yet. I figure I'm a model citizen. What I
want to know is where does it get me? Ten-twelve years ago,
believe it or not, I was sitting here just like this, holding my
sample and waiting for the doctor to tell me what a beautiful
specimen I got. And here I am still sitting with the bottle.
Instead of those pictures they have on that shield up there, that
nobody looks at anyway, you know, the sheaf of wheat and the
buffalo and stuff, they should pay me to go sit up there, just
like I am now, or maybe in my bareskin, on a bench, holding
the bottle in my lap. People would look then all right. Yeh.

"Mind you sometimes it pays off. I know a guy it paid
off for, in a big way, too. He went into foreign commerce.
There's money in that, if you've got the right product. Of
course he started small. He was only a driver when he got into
the business. Would you believe it, he actually asked my advice

whether he should go into it or not? You'd be surprised how many people tell me their troubles, ask my advice. But my friend Hymie, he's a millionaire today because he didn't take my advice." Hoda chuckled. She always got a laugh out of remembering how she had advised Hymie to stay away from the booze pipeline people.

"You see what happened, in those days, not so long ago either, just yesterday in fact, when the Americans weren't supposed to be able to get hold of any liquor, my friend was sniffing around for contacts, because he wanted to build up a really classy floating crap game here in town, with good bootleg stuff to bring in the big money types. First thing he knows he gets offered a job, hauling the whiskey around. 'Should I take it, Hoda?' he asks me. 'It's good money.' 'What's so good about it?' I says. 'Gambling's one thing,' I tell him. 'You can run a pretty clean game. But bootlegging? It isn't honest! Crooks and murderers and racketeers,' I says. I don't mean the friendly-house kind of bootlegging we got here," Hoda caught herself up quickly. "If the government's crazy you can't blame anyone for doing a little under the counter finagling. I don't ask where every drink somebody offers me came from myself, and I don't think anyone has the right to tell me I should drink or I shouldn't, either, or where I can and where I can't." Hoda smiled genially at her audience. In a place like this you never knew, you could be talking to bootleggers, and she wasn't out to hurt any feelings.

"But peddling booze to the Americans, international commerce, stuff like that, you know yourself who gets into that. You see it in the movies. Crooks and murderers and racketeers. 'That's no job for a nice Jewish boy,' I says to him. 'And besides, it's too risky. In those rackets it's the small fry always get caught. The big shots grease their way out of trouble. You want your mother to have to live through it, all the neighbours should know she has a son sitting in jail?'

"So he says, 'Listen, she complains anyway because I just sit around without a job. At least if I'm in jail I don't have to listen to her. Anyway, I don't have to be a racketeer or a murderer. It's just a job to me, a job with a few risks, so what? Instead of just sitting on my arse I'll risk it for a change, and if I lose I'll sit on it again and let the government take care of me."

Hoda beamed around at the uneasy faces of her captive audience. She loved it when she came to the fairy-tale part of Hymie's story. Who would have thought that it would happen to Hymie, after all, Hymie whose imagination had never dared soar beyond the vision of himself as the brains of a thriving floating crap and poker game, with three or four handpicked alternate locations, a smoothly organized pickup system, a cheap source of good bootleg booze, to attract the better clientele, and Hoda, all girded about in spangles, to give the deal class and provide the sundries. But who got the glass slipper after all? Those early dreams must look like pretty penny-ante stuff to him now.

"That's what he used to say me. 'It's my arse I'm risking, Hoda!'" She liked to repeat her more pungent bits of dialogue, particularly when she encountered faces like these. "Well, when a guy says that, what can you answer? 'All right, it's your arse, risk it then!' And he did, see? And everybody's kissing it now. You know how come? One of his boss's daughters happened to notice him. I don't know, maybe he was lifting a case or something; he's a big, healthy-looking boy. Anyway, whatever she saw, she liked it. And he had enough prudence, for a change, not to knock her up before her daddy proposed to him. These big-time bootleggers are fussy about how you fool around with their kids. And now Hymie's moved down East, and he's gone into industry, and he's a millionaire today. How do you like that?"

Hoda didn't expect an answer to her strictly rhetorical question, but went on triumphantly to the moral of her story. "So don't you ever be ashamed of your city motto, is all I can say. You take those three words, plus a little bit of this and a little bit of that, and you can end up where you won't ever have to worry about commerce, prudence and industry again, because when you're up there that high, anything you do or don't do is all right by everyone all over. And I'm the dumb bunny who tried to tell him it wasn't honest!" Again she chuckled, solo laughter, shaking her head at her own stupidity. "Honest! Come to think of it, maybe they should change our motto up there altogether. Instead of those three words and those pictures, they should have a picture of a big, naked arse, and underneath it just two words, 'RISK IT!'" Hoda laughed so hard even those of her fellow patients who were profoundly shocked, particularly the two schoolteachers at whom she had, by some perverse intuition, aimed most of her monologue, and who had not expected to encounter anything like this when they came to get vaccinated before their holiday trips abroad, couldn't help the momentary flutter of guilty smiles that were not smiles really, but, the involuntary expression of their astonishment. At times one's own dear familiar country can suddenly seem so foreign.

"Honest, that's really what happened," Hoda assured them earnestly. "You don't have to believe me, but if I named names you'd believe me all right." After she told the story in a place like this, she worried a little that the goyem might think that all Jews were bootleggers and millionaires. Well, to hell with them. They could see she was poor and honest, couldn't they? And anyway, whatever you said they'd think what they wanted to. Maybe Hymie was a bootlegger, but those hadn't been Jews who'd stolen all those millions that were supposed to go into building the Parliament Buildings downtown when she was a kid; they were big-shot gentiles, practising their own variety of commerce, prudence and industry. Let anyone make a crack and Hoda knew what to come back with all right, for all the good it did.

Whatever her visit to the Public Health had been like, whether she had been able to work up an interesting conversation, or had got a few laughs, or had delivered herself of a stimulating monologue, or had just sat alone and stared at the rough, broad dark floorboards, it was always good to get out of there, safe again, at least for another little while. In a mood to give thanks, she usually walked over to the square behind City Hall, to see if there were any comrades she knew around, busy educating the people, so she could maybe cheer them on and help humanity along a little. Not all the comrades enjoyed having her assistance, unfortunately. Some were even quite rude when she offered them encouragement. "But I'm on your side," she would find herself protesting. "It's my revolution too."

Well, it's a free country, and they couldn't stop her, when they acted that way, from gathering a little group of people around herself and starting her own separate public discussion. What if she sometimes got off the subject? It could be just as important to give people the feeling of how you felt, and get the feeling of how they felt, as it was to stand up there telling them how they ought to think. If some of those big-talking comrades would stop talking and listen sometimes and try to understand how their audience really felt, they wouldn't always be so sure of themselves. Every person you talked to hauled out his own favourite strands and snippets of experience, even where they weren't even relevant, and was passionately faithful to whatever his own personal blend of knowledge and misinformation was, that felt to him like the truth. You could be wrong in your arguments, and so could they, but it was only what you felt that you admitted, and if you felt right, no matter how dearly somebody else thought he was proving you wrong, you weren't going to give up the argument that made you feel right. Hoda often admitted to herself afterwards that she didn't know what she was talking about half the time, but she knew about how she felt, and about how people felt, never mind the comrades and their militant-mindedness. They could be as logical as they liked, they wouldn't get anywhere until they could capture people's militant feelingness. But they wouldn't listen to her, even when she tried to tell them.

Sometimes, when her little discussion group degenerated, when that thing happened to her audience – she was never quite sure what it was but she always knew it was happening – when they started throwing mocking comments at her and baiting her about personal things, and egging her on, she knew she had lost them but she had to go on, trying to retrieve the good feeling of friendly contact, even in disagreement. When that happened she was almost glad that they were baiting her again because it was a reminder that this too was what people could be like, not just cheerful fellow-patients in a waiting room, or reasonable citizens solving world problems together; this was how they could turn, as easily as they could turn into the angels the comrades assured them they would become if they changed the world and everybody got the chance to be good. What if you gave them angel food and they still preferred to turn on you this way when they got the chance? So much which she had once thought was unreal and would change because it was a transient distortion in a life which simply hadn't managed to get into perfect focus yet, she had begun at last to fear was not distortion at all, but the clear reflection of a natural and ineradicable ugliness. What could a person do?

A person could do her best, as Hoda was willing to tell anyone who was willing to listen. Like she and her daddy had done. Look how a blind man's labour had enabled them to turn the inside of a shack into such a pretty home. Daddy's hands had begun to slow down some lately, but still they had made enough pretty things to last for ages. She was gratified, often, when she caught the look of surprise in the eyes of a new customer as he gazed around at all those colours, and the clean, delicate buff-yellow of the natural straw in between. "You like the decor?" she would ask.

Large straw mats covered the coarse floorboards, on top of which a straw runner ran from front door to summer kitchen door; that one had to be replaced after winter, because the snow from her customers' boots soaked it through and started it rotting. But they had plenty more. There were straw mats on the table and on the dressers in their bedrooms, and the orange crates near the windows had straw mats on them, on which sat wicker baskets with Hoda's plants in them. There were straw mats tacked to the front wall, to help keep out the weather where the verandah had collapsed and ripped away some of their meagre insulation, and to hide the stains of damp coming through. There was even a straw mat on the tank behind the toilet seat, where Hoda kept some of her toiletries. It was lovely.

If only the verandah hadn't collapsed that way; after all those years of listing a little more each year, it had suddenly buckled, pulling away from the body of the house, and sagging so badly that it was impossible to approach the front door without running the danger of collapsing the whole, delicately balanced structure. Hoda had then hung up a large sign: DANGER. PLEASE USE BACK DOOR. VERANDAH UNDER REPAIR. The last sentence of the sign was for the benefit of city government spies. The fear which had hung over her for years, that some city spy would come along and condemn the old house, had increased tenfold since the visible collapse of the front facade. That's what they did when they got the chance, chased you out of your own home. That was one of the reasons why she hadn't applied for government relief when everybody was out of work and she was feeling the pinch too, in her meagre income, because she was afraid the relief spies would come and investigate and report the condition of the house and force them out. Where would they then be able to afford to live, except in somebody's house, some other working class family, the two of them together in one room? How would she conduct her business then? If they thought they were going to force her back to alleys and backyards like when she was a kid they were mistaken, not after she had fixed everything up so comfortably; she was too old for that kind of kid stuff. And how many of her customers could afford to take her to a hotel? Anyway, once you began in those hotels, the pimps started sniffing around you, and everybody else wanted payoffs too, all the lousy middlemen. She didn't want to stand around all night either, in all weathers, on street corners, to try to keep her customers circulating. This way she was known; her place was all set up, it was kind of a landmark, even. There might be a big turnover in her business, but the new ones always found out where to come. She had a good reputation. And the old ones, when they wanted to return, could always find out; "Fat Hoda, is she still there in the old place?" She got a lot of nice surprises from old friends she hadn't seen for years that way, some of them visiting from out of town, some of them just getting nostalgic for old times, who were glad to know that things were still the same.

But if the place was condemned and they were forced to move out, what then? All the good will she had built up, all the friendly atmosphere, all the good company she could offer, the privacy, the relatively spacious accommodation for lounging around and waiting in, the unhurried graciousness of her approach, everything that gave her work a solid foundation would be gone. And then where would they be? No, she'd have to get someone to clear away the verandah altogether, chop it up for firewood, and just have a couple of steps up to the front door. She would pile dirt up against the bottom of the front wall to keep out that damn draught that was bothering Daddy so much lately. In the summer maybe she'd plant flowers or something all around there, so it wouldn't be so obvious where the verandah had been ripped away.

There was always some new problem to worry about. You just managed to get one thing straightened away and something else turned up. If only it added up to something, but days and years were all that she had thus far been able to add up, to a sum which still surprised her. Who could believe she was suddenly a grown woman already? How to cope with the fact that she was no longer a child? How responsible was she for her childhood when she was so different now? Seraphina used to have a joke she was always repeating, "One thing, Hoda, we sure won't die not knowing." Hoda had laughed heartily at that, but now she had begun to wonder whether she wouldn't rather not have known some things, at that price. What price? Actually, she had avoided presentation of the bill, hadn't she? She had left no return address. Was that the price, that she was forever more to be haunted by the feeling that there was still a debt outstanding?

Perhaps because it had happened so many years ago, and there was a thick, though transparent film of anaesthetizing time over the rawness of the events, Hoda thought often, not so much of what had happened, but of what her duties and her responsibilities should be now, toward the issue of that distant past. When you're grown up enough in time you should be grown up enough to know. But Hoda didn't know, couldn't think straight, was subject to strange gusts and fits of emotion when she tried to think it through, and was reduced, each time, to a placatory gesture, to fill in the meantime. Thus she pacified herself, and tried to overrule the persistent suspicion that in fact some situations are irremediable. Perhaps she was not quite old enough yet, but she was still not completely able to accept the idea, particularly in relation to herself, that there were some things that she might not ever be able to make good.

Often she thought of meeting the boy, of seeing him for the first time, of arranging it, perhaps, so that someone might point him out in the street. Then she might make his acquaintance, as it were, accidentally, and become his friend, and give him things, and take him places, and become a kind of fairy godmother to him. There must be an awful lot of things you could do for a kid like that. There were an awful lot of things she had wanted when she was an adolescent. Sometimes she dreamed it through to the point where she actually told him who she was, or he guessed even, because there was that natural thing between them, that chord that twanged the minute they saw each other; and they both cried an awful lot, Hoda especially, thinking about all those years she had missed and how crazy she was about this kid. What the hell, she wanted to be crazy about him! Sure, and then she'd bring him home, and somehow maybe she'd even be able to explain him to Danile, though she couldn't think how, and then what? How would she be able to explain herself to him? She was not ashamed, usually. She had done the best she knew how. Maybe she shouldn't have; well, fat lot of good it did to think that now. Before you knew what it was all about, there you were, enmeshed in your life. But you couldn't explain that to a kid, and you couldn't bring him home to it, for fear that maybe, the way he'd grown up, this kind of mother might seem worse than no mother at all. There was nothing wrong with being a whore and being handy when they wanted you; for your allotted moments you were most precious, like a secret idol in a religious rite, yeh, a private ritual men performed to insure their public well being. That was Hoda all right, one of those big, fat idols, all smiles and warm tummy rolls. But afterwards? Everybody knows that idols aren't real. And the trouble was, a kid, who was brought up to think what everybody else thought, he might hate to discover he was the son of a prostitute, especially after wondering all his life, and maybe being filled with a lot of crap about being the son of a prince, which was really her own fault too.

Even Hoda herself didn't particularly like that word "prostitute." She much preferred something like the name Limpy Letz had once coined for her, when they had been discussing how slow business was, and he had suggested that she put up a sign outside, "SEXUAL WORKER. REASONABLE RATES." That was an honest name, clear and simple, with no built-in contempt. Mr. Polonick had no right to think she was trying to make fun of the revolution when she told him. She was a worker all right. Why is one kind better than another? Sometimes she suspected there was something profoundly

snobbish and intolerant about him. And if Polonick was falli-
ble, what of an ignorant young boy who knew nothing of the
world? He had probably dreamed of an altogether different
kind of mother. No, getting in touch with him just like that
was out. The only way she could approach the kid was if she
gave up her profession, if she changed her life entirely, if she
got married, for instance.

Ha ha ha. Who would have her? She was practically an
old maid already anyway, and though she had never entirely
given up the habit of hoping, she knew better. And even if
someone turned up who actually wanted her, what kind of guy
would he be, someone who wanted everybody's warmed-over
leftovers? She might joke about how old spaghetti that's aged
in its sauce for a while is five times as good as the freshly
cooked stuff, and a lot of her friends might agree with her, otherwise why would they come so often? But they nearly all
wanted their own personal plateful, that they kept tucked
away at home, to be fresh at the start.

What would happen if she did get married and suddenly
sprang a grown son on her husband? If she was going to give
the kid a home at last it was going to be a decent home. She
wasn't going to let any step-father mistreat her kid, that's for
sure. Twist and turn though she might, Hoda couldn't find a
foolproof solution that would be good and let her be good at
the same time. She only got herself upset and sometimes was
even unnecessarily irritable with Daddy as a result, and ended
up by bringing on one of those attacks, those fearful impulses
of flight towards her past that she was so afraid she would one
night give way to, and run raving through the streets. At ordinary times, when she was in control of herself, she knew very
well that the last thing in the world she wanted to do was go
near the orphanage. Sometimes, when she read in the Yiddish

paper that a fund-raising tea or an open house was being held there, and everyone was invited to come, she would have a momentary vision of herself with a whole crowd of tea-drinking ladies chatting amiably all around her, chatting and chatting, and Hoda too opening her mouth. But all that came out was scream after scream after scream. What would happen if she actually went, if she actually sat among the teacups and suddenly, into the warmth and the cosiness and the good feeling toward orphans that they were all brewing and sipping together she cried out that she was the one, that she was the mother who had abandoned the son! What would happen? Would they go on drinking and chatting and offering tea? No, that was more like every day, when you screamed silently and unheard among them. What then? Would they support her tenderly, on either side, and lead her, weeping, with soothing utterance to comfort her groans, cringing and ashamed and in hope, to some glad confrontation she could hardly visualize? Or would they, after small reflection, unsurprised, lead her to where the accounts were, day by day, of what it had cost them these many years, all her fears neatly added up in dollars and cents. No, not neatly; she knew that much about the way the place was run nowadays.

If it were only a question of money, what need was there for her to reveal herself and put herself at their mercy? On those nights, when no customers had come, and she had been maybe rude to Daddy over something, she couldn't even remember what; afterwards, all kinds of tags and fragments of thought would begin to jostle each other in her mind. And by now she could recognize when it was beginning to come over her, that let-go-inside feeling that was a prelude to panic fear, that humming in her nerves, the building up of the desire to run madly through forbidden streets.

She had a crazy fantasy that kept tempting her. Suppose she were to re-enact all her movements of that long-ago night? Only backwards. Suppose she were to leave the house, walking backwards, in the night; suppose she hurried backwards through the lanes and alleys and along the hedges and fences and across the lamplight islands of momentary yellow in the dark, moving jerkily and hastily backwards as though drawn against her will, retracing inside-out her steps of long ago. She might be able, that way, somehow to erase her earlier path, negating what had been, nullifying the past, rolling it up out of existence and finding at last that it had never been. Of course she didn't believe such nonsense. But if it brought relief you didn't have to worry about believing it. What did it matter, when her stripped-down nerves began to vibrate and hum and shrill and in a minute, any minute now she would no longer be capable of caring what she believed? What was believing anyway? At last, to ease the storming of her nerves, she worked out a formula for flight. She found a reason to retrace her steps, with all secrecy, in the night.

That first time she actually did try to fulfill the fantasy, waiting till she was absolutely sure Daddy must be asleep, and inching backwards, because she wasn't sure whether she was allowed, by the formula, to glance behind, feeling her way along the wall, out of her bedroom, back along to the summer kitchen door, groping it open behind her, backing out of the summer kitchen, dropping down because she was afraid she might slip and fall and make a noise, on all fours crawling ignominiously backward down the summer kitchen steps, rising and edging around by the side of the house, and having come round front, standing at last on the path, facing the house, and moving back along the long walk toward the gate with something of more confidence in her retrograde steps, but as she moved, seeing suddenly the dead, still, darkened house looming up in front of her out of the night like some not quite substantial apparition, seeing it from without herself, all cock-eyed, all unreal, like some grotesque vision of her own existence, severed from herself, and for one endless moment, while she hesitated in her backward movement, unable to tell for certain whether she was still inside there or standing out here staring at a separate existence that she could not comprehend and that did not comprehend her either. She, who had experienced at times an electrifying sense of the unity of beings, now felt the jagged chill of dislocation, of separation even of herself from herself.

It was fear that in the end made her give up the attempt to move backwards along her earlier route, rational fear, fear of falling, of being seen and carted off to the loony bin, and underlying the rational fear, the fear of moving back even further out of herself, out of her world, out of her mind, into a world of gesture, of a gestural code that suggested itself but did not explain itself any more than what she knew as her rational world was ultimately explicable to her.

Backwards wouldn't help, she told herself suddenly, sharply, and realized that she had been standing and staring at the house for ages. Backwards! What was the matter with her, was she crazy or something? She had actually got down on her hands and knees and crawled backwards down the back steps! What a nut! It wasn't even really backwards anyway, if you were going to be accurate about it. To roll it all back you'd have to start out at the orphanage, in the night, and pick up a baby off the porch, and move back down the steps with the bundle in your arms, and all along the haunted streets, and up the back steps, and put it down, and out to the shed, and pick up the filthy pallet, and backwards up the steps again, and put it on the bed, and then how did it go? What were the exact steps?

You'd have to get them all in the exact order, inside out, and spread your legs, and even your gasping and groaning would have to roll themselves up inside out, and the thing would have to shove its way back up, and anyway, could you roll up just that fragment without having to roll up also everything that had happened to you and to him and to everyone since that time? And even if you could possibly do all that, would that eradicate it? Or would it be like in the movies, all neatly packaged up and ready to play itself again, after the projectionist has, just for fun, shown you the film running backwards while he's rewinding it. No, backwards wouldn't help, but a forward gesture, no matter how little it really meant, at last brought temporary ease. That was why she became so anxious always to have a little money put by, so that she should not be caught without a means to relieve herself, on those occasions when she could no longer fight down her impulse to flight. At such times, instead of clinging to her pillow as before, she arose from her bed, dressed, prepared the envelope, slipped once again out of the house, and sped forward in fear through the eerie night, along the dreaded route, to make the secret, propitiatory gesture which brought relief.

As a result of Hoda's occasional night-time errands, many years after the foundling was deposited on the orphanage porch, many silent years after, mysterious envelopes, addressed simply to "The Director," began to appear, at irregular intervals, in the orphanage mail box. Each envelope contained some cash, and a note wrapped around it, on which was printed neatly, FOR THE PRINCE. The sum was never large enough to rekindle the kind of excited speculation that had first been rife regarding the boy's parentage, but the note and the gesture were enough to arouse old curiosities somewhat, and remind his guardians of the puzzle of his identity.

TEN

Not long after his Bar Mitzvah, old man Popoff called David into the office, and after a lot of crapple crapple crapple about now he was a man and capable of understanding, he showed him the envelopes with the money and the notes, FOR THE PRINCE, all identical, and printed nicer than he could have done, but telling him nothing. He stared dumbly at them for a long time, while Ralphie's old man crappled on like he was reading a book, about rational appraisal indicating, and paltry sums. He resented that about paltry sums, because they didn't look so paltry to him, and they were his, and why should they run down what was his? Old Popoff was in no hurry to hand him over his paltry sums, but put them back in their envelopes with their notes and put the elastic band back around them and they disappeared somewhere in that junk heap that was his desk. You could tell Tizey never got a look into this room. She'd go off her chump.

Popoff was sure that he, David, agreed that they should put the money aside till such time as something really important came along to spend it on. He himself was in favour of buying tools with it, when David was ready to learn a trade. David agreed with nothing, but said nothing. He wasn't going to let anybody know what he felt or how he felt, which wasn't very hard because he felt nothing at all, except that when Popoff went on and on, his voice, filled with sympathy, crawled over David's skin like worms, and he wanted to yell at him to shut up, goddam, shut up! when he didn't even dislike the old guy. He just wanted to get out of there, that's all. Wherever he was, he always wanted to get out of there fast. Something might be happening, somewhere, something that might be very important to him, if he was there. You never know. That was practically his motto, "You never know."

He wasn't interested in the money, anyway, not at first. He had his paper route. And his life outside. Mostly he only slept and ate here, and things were the way he wanted them, for now. No one dared call him Pipick anymore, except Tizey, when she forgot, and Tizey didn't matter. Sometimes inside of himself he thought *Pipick,* or *Prince Pipick,* when he was feeling particularly like an arsehole. But to the guys he was David, and sometimes the Prince. Why not? And the small fry called him King David. Okay; he was the oldest of the real orphans, and the only really mysterious one. And he looked after them when he was around, like, he knew what they felt like.

Mr. Limprig had always called him David, and still did. He was surprised anew each time went to see him, what a little, scrunchled-up old man the Director was growing into. David was way taller than him already, even before he was thirteen. He never stayed long; they didn't have much to say to each other. But Mr. Limprig always asked him, "Is there anything I can do for you?" before he left. And David always said, "No. Is there anything I can do for you?" Mr. Limprig glanced him a funny, open look for an instant, and shook his head. Afterwards, it always seemed to Pipick that it was that glance he had come for.

One day, when he'd just come out of Mr. Limprig's office, an old man grabbed him by the arm and asked him in Yiddish, "Boy, how old are you?" And when David replied, the old man said, "You want to do a good deed? Go with this man to his synagogue. They're short a tenth man; somebody died; it'll be a double mitzvah if you go."

Afterwards, the old men had made much of him, and asked him questions about himself, and had oho-ed and aha-ed when he'd told them who he was and where he lived, and they had recalled in detail and with a great deal of incidental argument all kinds of things about him that he himself had known only in the vaguest way, because the stories and rumours he had heard had always been vague, and filtered through the minds of children. Sometimes Tizey said something when she was in a good mood, about what he had been like when he was a baby, but she refused to discuss what she called "all the other silly gossip." She always said, whenever he pestered her, that he should be glad that he was sound of limb and healthy and that he should look after the good inheritance of mind and body that had been bequeathed him, crapple crapple.

But when the old men talked he realized how famous he had been, and when they ended by inviting him to be their spare man, the pisher at their minyan, he accepted. From then on he hung around the synagogue a lot, helping out and celebrating with them on Holy Days and ushering in the Bride of the Sabbath with herring and wine, and trying always to be on hand at prayers, in case one of the congregation, as so often happened, should have an urge to make water, and by absenting himself to pish, should short-hand the minyan. Of course, the more refined among the old men didn't use the expression "pisher," and were a bit apologetic when the others did, but David could take a joke.

For quite a while he was remarkably diligent in his voluntary duty, though the Old House was not the closest synagogue to the orphanage, and afterwards he had to rush to deliver his papers. But the old men praised him extravagantly, and he went about with the rare happiness of being conscious of his own virtue and conscious that others were conscious of it too.

The congregation was much impressed by the piety and sense of responsibility of the foundling son, and dredged up instances from the Holy Works of like special cases who had been mysteriously introduced among the people, to perform eventually feats especially assigned from heaven. Word got around to some of the other synagogues in the neighbourhood that the Old House was particularly lucky in having rather a remarkable pisher nowadays, that very selfsame little foundling who had once turned the whole town upside down, now grown a very pious Jew. Naturally, the case was somewhat exaggerated at times, and one version even had it that the boy showed a wisdom, and a grasp of the Holy Works far beyond his years, had discovered a Vocation for the rabbinate, and was beyond doubt on his way to becoming somebody extraordinary. Nor did those who began to come to see for themselves, visitors from other synagogues, who saw that the young boy stood innocuously praying like everyone else, do anything to diminish these rumours. They returned home to their own synagogues shaking their heads and prophesying, "This will be a Gaon, a wise man to teach wise men, a blessed genius!"

Danile heard the reports of one or two friends who could hardly praise highly enough, and his imagination, ever on the alert for the extraordinary sign from above, was much exercised by this unusual boy. He was particularly keen that his friends should describe the appearance of the young man in detail, and was the first in his synagogue to put forward the daring hypothesis that somewhere in the world the Almighty must be preparing a champion, destined, the sooner the better, to engage and vanquish this new fiend of Europe, this German Hitler, who was threatening to destroy the Jews. The threat was old; we had survived it before, but the danger was ever new, for we were never prepared for the fact that these barbarians meant what they said. The Books showed that Jews had always fumbled, and vacillated, and were weak of spirit, and that their hero must struggle through error and hardship and death with his people, and teach them to re-dedicate themselves to life. Danile never had the actual temerity to say it, but he wondered, yearningly, who this young stranger could really be. He would have liked very much to share the honour of saying his prayers in the company of the young man, but he did not know the way to the Old House, and was loath to put anyone to the trouble of leading him. He waited wistfully for someone to offer to take him to a service with the prodigy, particularly since he had been active and daring in their speculations together, and though he even brought himself to hint, sighingly, that he would like to hear the boy just once, the others did not seem to catch on. It was not their fault, really. If he had asked right out someone no doubt would have taken him, but since he himself was a faithful member of the minyans of his synagogue, and had even been known to crawl out of a sick bed to make up the number, for Danile had begun to suffer from chest infections, particularly in the winter time, not surprisingly in that draughty shack, it did not easily occur to them that he might be spared for once to go elsewhere.

But the Almighty sees where men are blind. It so came about that one of Danile's fellow congregants was actually present at the Old House, when a man came hurriedly up from yet another little synagogue. They were short a man, he explained. Could they borrow the pisher? Since, what with the addition of one or two guests who had come precisely to pray with the pisher, the Old House congregation had well over their minimum complement, they could not very well refuse, and David went off with the suppliant, leaving several disgruntled visitors who thus lost the opportunity to pray with him, and could not follow him because such a mass discourtesy might leave the Old House short again.

There followed a small epidemic of "borrowing the pisher," and David, never quite catching on to how it came about that he was always being rushed off to another synagogue, developed, in a short time, a wide acquaintance with the synagogues in the neighbourhood, and with any number of friendly elders, before the men of the Old House caught on to what was happening. Meanwhile David tried to recruit another spare man or two from among his friends, to come to the rescue of these dying congregations. But the boys, especially Ralphie Popoff, Scion of Happy Family and supposed Best Friend, razzed him mercilessly about his newly revealed piety, and he hated himself for giving away what he hadn't even realized should have been a secret, and even worse, for trying to appease their laughter. "There's nothing wrong with doing them a favour."

Why couldn't he simply say, "I BELIEVE, SO fuck off you slobs!" Because he didn't know what he believed, when it came to that. He just enjoyed. By this time the hard-core congregation of his home base had worked out a simple method to resist piracy. The minute a hurried stranger appeared, as many men as necessary of the home congregation detached them-selves from the group, and hastened, each with his own way of making obvious his sudden, desperate need, bent double or scissor footed, out of the Temple of Prayer. Their fellows were thus able to point out perfectly truthfully, that they too were short-handed.

But David's enthusiasm had begun to flag. He had to admit that there was logic on Ralphie's side. Right after prayers, even on Saturday, he scooted out to deliver his papers. That made him a Hypocrite, as Ralphie kept telling him gleefully. For a time he thought he might improve his spiritual position by making one of the congregation in body, but refusing to pray. But when he tried to keep quiet someone would nudge him, and motion to someone else standing by. "Louder, he wants to hear how the younger generation can pray." So David figured finally, what the hell, if it pleased them. Anyway, he didn't care if he was a Hypocrite. He couldn't really believe that God was such a sorehead. But it made it easier, later on, when he began to hang around and think more about hard loving the dames, and how to get money, and what was it all about anyway, for him to skip services, first of all on Saturdays, and then, if he was going to skip the holiest day of the week, well, it wasn't such a big thing to stay away more and more.

Luckily for Danile, though, during that period before the congregation of the Old House set into effect their counter pisher poacher plan, he got his wished-for opportunity to pray in company with the young man. He was profoundly moved by the experience, and repeated more than once, both to himself between prayers, and later on to his friends, "We will hear more of him. Yes, we will hear more of him."

He was full of the young stranger when he came home for breakfast, and described in detail to the half-listening Hoda the quality of his voice in prayer, a certain youthful musicality of enunciation, yet with definite timbre, which marked him indubitably as one who was born to pronounce the Holy Words. "We are far too prone," opined Danile, "as we grow older, to hear or to imagine evil sounds all around us, sounds hard to distinguish, indefinite, indefinable, hemming us in and arousing in us a terrible fear." He, Danile, had himself often been subject to such fear, a terror that welled up in him, from nothing, of nothing but the sounds of the world around him, teasing him horribly. Of course this was foolishness, and he wouldn't dream of even mentioning this childishness to Hoda, but for the fact that through all of these indefinite and unaccountable imaginings, these untonguable questionings that are roused up in us by the noises of life, The One Above sends down to us every now and then, to reassure us, one pure note.

"You should have been there, Hodaleh. You know how sometimes you grumble and I say to you, 'Surely the world can't be that bad,' and you say, 'Yes it can, Papa, it is.' You would have felt your answer this morning. We will hear of him again. There was not a man in the congregation who didn't agree. Suddenly, we were short of a minyan, Saturday morning, too, when our synagogue is never short. Somebody ran to beg their pisher, you should excuse the expression; that's what they call him. And when he arrived our men suddenly began to appear, from nowhere, and some of their wives, too, chattering in the woman's section, more than one usually hears. I didn't know they were planning this. There was such a crowd, almost like for a visiting cantor from Europe. But he didn't pay any attention; he just went quietly about his prayers. The only thing was, he left right after he was through, before anyone could stop him. I would have liked to exchange a few words with him."

"With whom?" said Hoda. "What sounds?" Her wandering attention had been caught by something he had said about sounds that bothered him. Did he mean in the house? Was he talking about her and her clients? Long usage had dulled her concern about the possibility of Daddy finding out what she did for a living. It somehow didn't seem so important after all these years that it had been going on. It seemed incredible that after all these years Daddy would suddenly know, and it would still be important to him. If you hadn't seen someone for a long time, and you suddenly found out he'd died fifteen years ago, did you feel the same grief you'd have felt if he had just died in your arms? She was a grown woman now and had been making a living this way for half her lifetime. No, the climate of feeling had changed in that time; or was it simply that her own feelings had changed, had dulled, somehow? Though the gestures of filial piety had not diminished they had become, with the passage of time, more perfunctory. She said "yes Pa," and "no Pa," ungrudgingly, but half the time she did not hear what he was saying, perhaps because she felt as though she knew already what he was likely to say on just about any occasion. Sometimes she felt a little guilty for taking him so for granted that it might seem almost as though she were dismissing his importance. But maybe, as she told herself when she woke up guiltily, on occasion, from her reverie, and found she hadn't heard a thing he was saying, maybe it was just that he was so much a part of her that she didn't have to pay so much attention; he was like her thoughts that went on by themselves and she hardly knew she was thinking them either. She felt better to think that; she didn't really have to listen all the time to what she had heard before; all she had to do was suit her response to the tone of his voice, and he was contented.

Why was it that the more you knew a person the less you thought about him and even, in a way, the less you thought of him? *Oh that's just his old immigration story again,* you thought to yourself, or even, *Oh, that's just his chest rattling again. I'll have to give him steam tonight.* Not like that first time he had got bronchitis and you had stayed up with him for nights and cried over his every breath. She could remember, dimly, a time when every word that Daddy spoke had been suffused with wonder for her. But that was when everything had been filled with promise, even, for godsake, the Prince of Wales! Oddly enough she had just been thinking of the Prince of Wales, wondering whether he had made anything of his life, wondering whether he had any regrets. She hadn't thought about him for years, not really thought, that is. But now, for some reason it had come into her mind that he too hadn't married, and was still hanging around. He went here; he went there. Was he still looking? She wondered what kind of things had happened, or for that matter hadn't happened, to him as well. She wondered whether for him too there might not be some area of princely secrecy and sorrow, whether princes, too, can be short-weighted by life. She no longer imagined that she would have been able to converse with him very freely even had life somehow managed to throw them together. No doubt he was a victim of his class and his education, as the comrades suggested, and it would show in his politics. Maybe he was even practically a reactionary. Nobody ever tried to swing a truncheon at him for just wanting his rights as a human being. And yet, he too must have missed things. She pitied these princes in a way. Was the passing of possibilities so enormous, equally enormously painful to them? Was he too even now thinking, *What have I done with my life?*

What did Daddy mean when he talked about sounds? No, it was just about some kid going to be a cantor or something. It was a good thing Daddy had the synagogue affairs to concern himself with. It was nice when a kid had a special talent, and could become a great cantor, say. "Ya Daddy, I'm sorry I didn't hear him too," she hazarded, with obliging mendacity, because there was nothing she'd rather do these mornings than stay in bed and catch up on her rest, especially if she'd had a busy night. It was a nuisance dragging her mattress off and on the bed all night. But she still insisted on performing that noise-reducing ritual with her customers, though now she pretended to them it was because the coils underneath were so bad she was afraid of falling through or else, if something snapped, of somehow being skewered fore and aft simultaneously. When she explained it that way it put them in a good mood.

For a long time the thought that someone out there was interested in him, was maybe even watching him when he wasn't aware of it, had made David feel all twisty inside. Sometimes, when he was outside just walking in the street, he'd stop and whirl around very suddenly, darting his eyes quickly every which way round; maybe he'd catch someone at it. The way people looked at him he could tell they thought he was crazy, flashing around that way suddenly, but he just had to do it. Sometimes he thought he had caught the person and he tried to hold her, appealing, willing her to admit it was she. But nothing ever happened. She just looked away, and maybe glanced quickly back once or twice, and then kept on looking away, and even when he walked after her a little way, she just walked faster, and once a lady turned around and said in an excited voice, "If you don't stop following me!" Then the time came when he began to think more and more about the money, and what you could do with it, and how to get hold of it.

Mrs. Tize, of course, recognized the signs very early. They were so physical. Normally, when the time came, she sent the boys straight to Popoff, as she had had to do even in the case of his own eldest, the goat-like Ralphie, when she caught him pawing one of the kitchen help in the pantry. David too, when she saw that the age of heightened prurience was upon him, got the mandatory heart-to-heart from Popoff. He had also, because he was in some sense special to her, the privilege of Mrs. Tize's lecture, which was normally reserved for the girls, and heard all about the dangers of interfering with oneself or with anyone else, to his initial puzzlement, because he didn't know how it was possible to interfere with oneself, and as for anyone else, Tizey knew he minded his own business. It was only when she got to the birds and the bees that he realized what she was trying to tell him, and, young rascal that he was becoming, proceeded to goad her to a fury with his teasing.

He was the only one in the place who could tease her openly that way, and get away with it. Mrs. Tize felt, if uncomfortably, a special responsibility for the boy. For it was she who had dragged him from the closet on that unforgivable morning, she who had wrestled with him, holding him firmly to her with superior, adult strength, while she shouted orders, distractedly, to the other children to stay away and be off to school. It was she who had felt her breasts crushed by the storming, squirming, clattering-hearted little boy, and had weathered the battle through, thankfully, to his final exhausted whimpers. Though she had never really had the time or the introspective inclination to think about it very much, somewhere in her blood and bones Mrs. Tize had felt and recognized, during their struggle, the intensity of the little boy's grief. It had left her with that uneasy feeling of particular responsibility for him, which she might have found irksome, considering all she had to do around the place, had the youngster, as he subsequently developed, not been a quiet, and until recently, withdrawn and largely undemanding boy. Mrs. Tize had little time for the whining and dependant type of child, and sent those gladly off to the Director, who so widely advertised himself in the community as the father of them all.

She was careful not to allow her partiality to become too obvious; in fact, if anything, she was more of a nag with him than with the others, treating him frequently to impassioned lectures which, when he was feeling particularly cheerful, he repeated with her, word for word, only getting just a little bit ahead of her with each word, so that in the end he had her racing through her own words to keep up with him, to the amusement of those foolish girls in the kitchen. Tizey's passion for cleanliness and hygiene had long ago crystallized into set-pieces of oratory, into which she poured a good part of her emotional being. And once she was launched on one of her favourite little appeals it was impossible for her to stop herself in mid-career. She was like a toboggan going down an icy slope. It was maddening to have him racing, like her shadow, just that little bit ahead of her. Exasperating boy!

But though he teased her, David protected her too. Ralphie would have loved it, but he never told him of the lecture he had received on interference, that classy English version of jerking yourself off.

He didn't tell Ralphie either, or anyone else, for that matter, how she had hung on to him once, when he had run crazy and wanted to break his goddam neck, and how she had squeezed and gripped him up against her great big tits. If Tizey knew how he remembered her that time, Chrise, she'd stick a toilet brush down his throat and scrub him inside and out. That was love; that time was love, the real McCoy, wrestling with her, all those tits, hundreds of them, all over him, pressing up against him and rubbing him all over while he fought and screamed and yelled and hurt and hurt and hurt. Funny how only long afterwards did he remember and cling to the memory of how those breasts had rubbed into him and soothed his hurt. That was love all right, that and not all those little green shoots of tenderness his heart had been putting out all his life, those delicate little tendrils of love that kept starting out in spite of himself, only to get chopped or crushed or ripped away, or were just left to wave around in the empty air till they turned all brown and curled up and folded into themselves with a dry little aching sigh, and flaked away. But she had stayed with him that time, old Tizey, had hung on to him, no matter what he did, that time when was so crazy with what he had seen that he didn't even know what he was doing anymore. She stayed with him and hung onto him even though he was fighting her so hard and even trying to hurt her too, maybe. She had hung on till he was so exhausted he couldn't struggle anymore, and he just gave up, and ended by hanging on himself, clinging to her, and even when he stopped fighting she still held on to him, just pressing him against her and rocking him a little; that was what he remembered most; he could still feel her all the way down, and she held his face against her soft breasts and wouldn't even let him look up, not that he wanted to, not that he wanted to see anything any more; she held him and held him and held him in a dream of her holding him forevermore.

If only she knew how much he thought of that now, that hanging on, her straining with him, those warm, giving tits moving all over him as she struggled; if only she knew how often she *interfered* with him, old Tizey, Chrise, she'd take gas!

Trouble was, he couldn't blame her. It wasn't nice; like with your own mother. It wasn't healthy. Like Ralphie said, if you don't get rid of your load it goes bad inside you; the poisons go right to your head and you start thinking of all kinds of funny things, like ramming Mrs. Tize yourself and giving her what she needed. Maybe that was how it was with Mr. Limprig. Ralphie had decided long ago it wasn't going to be that way with him. He had begun by blackmailing the older guys to stand him to free rides or he'd tell his old man. Then he went on to introduce the younger guys to nooky for what he called the modest fee of his company. You had to be a real little bastard, not just a born bastard, to work the angles like Ralphie. But he wouldn't give Ralphie the satisfaction of knowing he needed an introduction. He'd work his own angle.

A guy had a right to spend his own money any way he damn well pleased, didn't he? He could just imagine telling that to old man Popoff.

"Yes David, and might I ask what you're thinking of doing with all that money? I am, in a sense, your guardian; not that I want to pry, but perhaps I can give you the benefit of my own experience in discussing your purchase. Remember, money spent cannot be retrieved. What is it you think you want the money for, David?"

"I want to fuck my goddam head off!"

His own money, his own business, his own life, and he sure wasn't a thief to be taking what was his. He wasn't even worried about being caught anyway, as he kneeled there. All he was worried about, listening in the murky office, were the funny knocking sounds he was expecting, in spite of himself, from behind the closet door. He was crazy to think his money would still be here in the desk. He was crazy in the head. With his luck, the money was back there behind the door, in the big black safe with the gold mermaid, and hanging up behind the door, guarding it, a funny, sour smell, a dress he'd taken hold of, movement, limp and heavy at the same time, swaying under his hand.

Mamma!

Crisp to his fingers, cutting memory, forestalling flight, a fat little package, real. Unafraid now, with cash-cold nerves, he slipped open the envelopes, one by one, abstracted the notes and bills, folded up empty sheets, inserted them, wound the elastic band around the thick-as-before package and thrust it deep into the drawer where he had found it. That much belonged to them. He had taken his own from the now ghost-less room, and considered calmly that it might be years before Popoff noticed. And if he noticed, so what? Cocky now, let him prove something. What right had Popoff to leave his money lying around where any randy old thief could lay his mitts on it anyway?

Ralphie was right. Just knowing that he could have it whenever he wanted it, just being able to slide his hand along the crude money belt he now wore next to his skin, just touching it made him feel healthier than he'd ever felt before, so healthy he could even put it off, bide his time, wait for exactly the right moment, the particular evening when Ralphie and the other guys were ho-oh-yo humming about their loads like a chorus of Volga boatmen.

"Be my guests." David, cool.

Ralph the spokesman, puzzled: "Since when?" screwing up his eyes at David.

"Not funny," Spook the pessimist.

From Gordie the Fortz, dumb Gordie, eyes shining, mouth open but afraid to express hope, too loyal to express doubt, a long, low enquiring fart.

"Well," David suave, shrugging, "if you gentlemen won't join me, will you excuse me?"

"Where'll you get the jack?" This from Ralphie, sudden.

Negligent, a flash of green. He would have gone alone this first time had he known the ropes. But he did not want to make a fool of himself.

"Your Royal Highness!" Ralphie's reaction was worth it. "Gentlemen, make way for a Prince of a fellow! Henceforth, we will guard your bawdy with our very lives. Yessir your Majesty, we are your soldiers upright, hard and true. For your sake we will plunge into battle, this very evening, and to a man we'll fall, and even as we die we'll gasp, 'The King is dead! Vive le roi!' Forward, gentlemen, I say! Hardon ahead!"

If they had been able to they'd have carried him into that chippy's house on their shoulders. And the way he felt he would have dived down into her from way up there, voom! and disappeared right up to his happy, wiggling toes.

Ralphie led them through the back lane to the rear entrance, pointing out the shed she called her summer residence. "See," for Pipick's benefit, "the kitchen blind's up and the light's on. That means she's free. She'll pull the blind down till we're finished. Sometimes if you come and she's got the blind down you might as well forget it for awhile."

"I like a well-organized whore," remarked the young Prince approvingly, and didn't even have to watch for the effect of his words. He could feel them looking at him respectfully. Inside of himself he could feel himself looking at himself respectfully too. Like the hero of a goddam book. Prince David Pipick Ben Zion MacFuck, the fastest trigger in the West!

Unfortunately, it turned out to be true.

ELEVEN

To put it at least partly in Hoda's vernacular, the poor kid got so hot with trying to grab her all over all at once, he came at her in such a rush, once they'd got the mattress on the floor and she'd slipped out of her loose kimono that had come open anyway when she bent over with the mattress, that she hardly had a chance to lie down when he was already on her, and so uncontrollably excited with it all, that he'd barely crossed the threshold when he tripped his load. Nothing unusual. To her. How could she know the desolation, after all that dreaming, all that planning, all those risks, to have scarcely had the chance to begin to savour heaven, and to suffer such a rude and sudden, such an ignominious loss of his voom voom? She had tried, actually, to ease him into it, recognizing a novice simply from the look of him, and a special occasion from the fact that his friends, and particularly the greedy little Ralphie, allowed him to go first while she was still fresh, and that with such elaborate expression of respect. She had talked to him soothingly, in a voice which he found surprisingly pleasant to listen to, deep and strong and chuckly. But her flesh told against her efforts to calm him. She was fat, all right, all massive and floppy under that loose kimono; he couldn't stop looking. When they put the mattress on the floor, just like he had heard they always did, he tried to carry it from the bed by himself, to prevent himself from reaching out and grabbing with both hands, too soon, though he was entitled to, because he was paying for it and could do anything he wanted, but it wouldn't have been nice when she maybe wasn't ready yet, and he wanted her to like him, a little.

"Easy, easy," murmured Hoda in his ear, but he couldn't help it. All that butter flesh; he had barely time to gasp out, dutiful, chivalric, desperate, "I love you!" and it was gone, his voom voom burst away from him. Gone! But he didn't want to go yet! He wanted to lie there, rubbing and nuzzling and listening to her comforting him, and believing her words when she said it sometimes happened that way, believing her so long as she let him lie there.

Hoda murmured on, automatically, stroking the head on her breast, letting him cuddle awhile, recognizing his disappointment, and his fear that she would send him out too soon so that the other boys might catch on to what had happened, and recognizing, also, perhaps something of other unfulfilled needs, in the way he was still clinging to her and rocking desperately in her arms, remembering too, the "I love you!" that had broken from him, and thinking of how these kids said the oddest things. What private dreams burst out of them at times! She was genuinely touched by them, the young ones especially, the novices, like this one. One thing, however, she had learned long since; she couldn't afford to let herself get too sympathetic, couldn't let him nurse his disappointment for too long at her bosom, not more than his money's worth, anyway. Her other customers were waiting. And so, per force, the boy had finally to take his badly bruised self-esteem with him from the room in which she still lay on the mattress he had so chivalrously tried to arrange all by himself, and little Ralphie Pan had come skipping in immediately after, with all his bag of tricks, to have his quota of fun.

Cringing inwardly, David maintained his superior little smile in face of the questioning smiles of his friends, and even summoned up enough art to raise an ironic eyebrow in the direction of the little room into which Ralph the Flash had disappeared. Then, with the air of one who had private thoughts, no doubt of pleasures recently experienced, to consider, he seated himself and looked around him, avoiding conversation. He noticed, for the first time, the woven straw walls, with the large damp stains on them, and scuffed at the woven straw carpet underfoot. Funny place. It reminded him of something, at first he couldn't think what. Then he remembered. "I'll huff and I'll puff and I'll blow your house down." What made him think of it was the sound of coughing from behind another door. That must be the blind old coot who was supposed to yell things at the guys in Yiddish. But he wasn't yelling now. He sounded as though he had a bad cold. Savagely, David wished he would yell anyway, or start choking or something, so they could interrupt and call her away and spoil things for Ralphie. He was immediately ashamed of himself for thinking that. But why the hell were they making so much noise? She hadn't laughed that way when he was with her. Nor had she said anything like what he heard now, distinctly, "You stop that!" and she burst out giggling again, in her deep, nice, low, chuckly voice. Why was he so mad? You weren't supposed to be furious with jealousy over a whore. It wasn't her. It was Ralphie enjoying himself like that, and her giggling and letting him, and Ralphie still doing things and spending so much time, while she had sent him out practically right away. Who was paying anyway? He knew he was being a poor sport, and told himself to stop being silly. But he had had hardly any time, and because he had gone off so quickly didn't mean that he wanted to quit already. She needn't think that he was just a one-shot deadhead. Why the hell didn't Ralphie get out and give the other guys a chance? Shnorrer. Did he think they had all night? That was an idea. All night. Fix Ralphie. Fix the chippy. Fix himself up most of all. How could a guy do anything when they were all waiting outside and she just wanted to hustle him out so she could take the other guys? He didn't have a chance, especially if he had never done it before and was a little nervous right from the start. That wasn't the way he was, and he could prove it to her.

When the others were through, and had given the final hikings and hitchings up to their trousers, preparatory to leaving, which are roughly equivalent to the movement of hand or cuff or napkin across the mouth when other appetites have been satisfactorily sated, King David remained, casually seated, one leg balancing easily across the knee of the other. "You guys go ahead," said the Prince. "I'm staying a while." It was gratifying, the surprise, particularly in Ralphie's eyes, and the envious, respectful grins that followed. He could tell from the shrewd, speculative calculation in his good buddy's look that Ralphie was wondering whether he could cut himself in on this. But the intention died on contact with David's cold stare, a look that said simply, "Try it and I'll kick your head in."

The whore waited till the others were gone before she said quietly, "You know it'll cost you more to solo."

"I've got more," he said sullenly, and turning away from her he fiddled, tugging up his shirt and fooling with his hand in his belt. "How much for all night?" he asked, over his shoulder.

"Nobody stays all night," said Hoda. "I got responsibilities. Anyway, don't you have to get home too? Won't your folks worry about you?" All she needed was that the cops should come round to her place looking for somebody's kid they sent out an alarm for. Oh sure, at this stage of her life that was all she had to get mixed up in. No, about this Hoda was very firm. Not all night, but, as she pointed out, they had plenty of time. While Pipick was still turned away, fiddling with his money belt, she went into the other room where the intermittent coughing was coming from, and murmured in there, her voice making to and fro with the voice of the cougher. By the time she re-emerged he had her sum counted out. "All right," she said. "Make yourself at home. Only you'll have to wait a minute. I've got to make my father some tea. Do you want a cup of tea?"

"No," said Pipick. "No thank you." But when she was pouring, and glanced at him enquiringly, gesturing with the tea pot, he took one anyway.

"Lemon?" she said. "Sugar?" just as though he was her guest.

"Thanks," he said, "thanks," and hesitated.

"Go on, take as much sugar as you want," she said, divining. She poured a cup for herself and took one into the other room, from which he could hear her voice, alternately urging and soothing. Pipick blew and drank. Hoda came and sat down to her cup of tea. "He gets this bronchitis," she explained, and Pipick had the feeling of being in someone else's life, like, not only visiting a whore, and that he had to show he knew it, somehow. "Uhh huh," he said.

"Yeh," she continued, "sometimes he worries me."

"Uh huh," said Pipick. He was beginning to get nervous, but he didn't want her to know he didn't know how to make what was going to happen next happen next.

"Say, do you want a cookie?" asked Hoda. She reached back from where she was sitting, to the little cupboard beside the stove and dipped her hand into a box, pulling out a handful, and offered him her hand. "I'm a good cookie-maker. No?" She proceeded very quickly to chew down her whole handful, while Pipick watched her mouth, to prevent himself from dropping his eyes any further down to where her robe had come apart when she had reached back for the cookies.

"All right," said Hoda, still chewing, as she rose. "Come on?"

Pipick jumped up and followed her into the little room.

"Close the door," she said. "Relax," she said. "You got to learn to take it easy."

Pipick felt quick anger rising in him. Did she think he didn't know how?

"It's your money," she went on, as though again divining his reaction. "I want you to get the most out of it. Trouble is, with these one-two-three in-and-out deals, you don't have much chance to develop your style. You know, guys have said to me, 'Hoda, I never knew what it could be like really till I did my first solo with you.' Guys I knew well. Trouble was they could never afford anything but a shag before. One-two-three-in-out. It's the capitalist system. You don't have any money, you've even got to fuck on the fly. You got a little money, you got time to develop a little style, to find out how you really like it, to get the taste, like. This lousy way of life we got here, it cripples people. Would you believe it, I got some customers who don't even know any better? They think that's the only way, like they was going to the toilet or something.

They come in, flip open the fly, whang whang, in-out, pay the shot, and they're gone again. They probably wouldn't recognize me if they saw me in the street, unless they happened to have a hard-on. Cripples. They've been stunted, see, by the system, from childhood, poor guys."

Pipick was surprised at how talkative and friendly she was. If you wanted a girl to do it for free, you had to do a lot of talking, more than he'd ever been able to manage so far. But when you paid them, they sure got talkative; it saved a lot of trouble trying to think of something to say. And it was interesting. He didn't know much about politics and what the system could do to a guy's sex life. But he wasn't surprised. They were all a rotten lot, directors and boards of governors and no doubt prime ministers as well.

"I've been thinking about it for a long time, you know," said Hoda. "You have to. If it's your profession, what you do all the time for a living, you should think about it, think what it means. You're spending your life; it shouldn't just be all wasted. Why do you think it's called making love? When something's not there you've got to make it, see? Why do you want to make it? Because it's not there, and you need it, see? So what the hell good is it to come rushing in and out, just like that, whang whang? I figured it out, once. Guys do that, one, maybe because they can't afford to solo, like kids, see? Or else they do it because they don't want to make love, really. They just want to forget that feeling they got that maybe it would be nice to make love. They want to kill love instead of making love. If they kill it they think they won't need it anymore. I don't know, that's what I think anyway. Me, in the long run I don't care. I see so many, what do I care if they want or not? Sometimes the ones who want to make love are a bigger pain than the quickies. They try to pretend they're doing a lot more than just making a little love. They try to pretend they know how to make more than just a little love at a time. It's a lie. Nobody knows that; well, God, maybe. Sometimes all the love you get even though you're making like crazy is just a shiverful, a flash of feeling between you. You know that radium stuff that you hear so much about? How hard it is to get it, and how little of it you get in all them rocks up North? But look how worthwhile it is. With that little bit you can see right through everything. Sometimes I think, what's going to happen when I get up there and the Almighty says to me, 'All right, Hoda, what have you been doing all these years?' And I'll say, 'Well, Lord, I made a little love.' And he'll say, 'Not bad, Hoda. I ain't done much more myself." Hoda laughed and laughed again. David laughed too, though he was a little shocked at the way she thought she was buddy buddy with God, considering.

"So why don't you take all your clothes off?" continued Hoda amiably. "You might as well be comfortable. What's your name, kid?"

Pipick hesitated.

"I mean not your whole name, just a name to call you by. It's more personal, like. Don't worry, I don't want to know your secrets."

"David," he said, and hesitated still. "My clothes, like," he said.

"Sure," she said genially, "you work better without them. Who needs 'em? What's the matter, you ain't shy, are you? Listen, believe me, I've seen everything you've got. There ain't nothing you can show me I haven't seen before, believe you me. You wouldn't believe some of the things I've seen. What the hell, it's just people."

Pipick still hesitated. First of all there was his navel. She thought she had seen a lot, but he couldn't believe she had ever seen anything like it before, for a big guy like him to have a belly button that stuck out of him instead of being neatly tucked away in a little trough like most guys had. Even the skinny ones, who had bump-outs, never had anything as silly-looking as his. And then there was his money belt. He wasn't going to take that off, not with any whore. How did he know what she had put in the tea? Suddenly he'd find himself getting sleepy, and when he woke up she'd hustle him out, and next time he took a look all his money would be gone. And what could he do about it? Complain to old Popoff? Sure. *Look, my money that I pinched from your desk, that whore took it away from me.* But he had such a great yearning to roll all of his naked flesh around on all of her naked flesh, and to really make love like she was talking about, not like the other guys did with her. Not like Ralphie, for instance; that was something that Ralphie didn't know anything about, with his showing off, and making her giggle, and boasting. Ralphie was a whang whang, not a lovemaker. To make love you took your clothes off and stayed. He hadn't expected her to be so talkative and friendly. Maybe she really liked him.

"Want some help?" said Hoda. She could see the kid was beginning to relax. But he didn't want her to help him undress. He was turned away from her, fiddling about with his belt. "Look, put everything on the chair over there," she said, cheerfully, easing herself down on the mattress. "Don't worry, I won't touch your stuff. I make an honest living."

Pipick was ashamed. "I know," he said, not looking at her. How did she know what he was thinking? He felt as though he had been caught having a dirty thought. She probably thought he was a cheap little punk who counted his pennies and was always afraid he wasn't getting his money's worth. That's what it must have seemed like to her when he had clung to her before and she had had to tell him when it was time for him to get out and give the others a chance. What did she know about him? She thought he was just like all the other cheap Charleys she knew. Pipick slipped his money belt down and stepped out of it. Hiding his movements with his back he quickly stuffed it deep into a pocket of his pants.

"You're a well-built kid," Hoda said affectionately, to his back. Pipick felt her words flow over and define every part of him. He straightened and pulled his shoulders back, tensing his muscles. Yeh, but wait till she saw his navel. He turned, holding his hands across his belly, trying to make the gesture seem natural.

"Peek-a-boo," said Hoda. "Don't be shy. It's too big to hide," and she laughed.

After an instant Pipick realized she wasn't talking about his belly button, and he laughed too, with pleasure. He wanted to say something clever, like "You ain't seen the half of it," or "It feels better than it looks," but he couldn't bring himself to, yet. He hardly knew her, and after what had happened already, he didn't want to boast too fast. Afterwards he could say all those smart things, when he had made her giggle. He still didn't uncover his belly button, but continued, as though absently fingering it, to keep it covered with his hand as he eased himself, with great self control, down beside her.

"You see," said Hoda, stroking his chest gently, "people don't touch each other enough. They grab or they pull or they shove, but they don't really touch. That's no way to make love." That meant that he could touch her too, freely, not just because he had paid, but because they were making love. Right now. This putting his hand out was making love. A part of him could already hear himself saying, " *We made love,*" not just *"we fucked"* or *"we screwed,"* but "WE MADE LOVE." And he would add, looking at the other guys, smiling gently, *"practically all night. You should try it sometime if you can manage it."* They probably wouldn't even understand what he meant. But they'd know they were missing something, all right.

At the same time he hoped this making love part wouldn't be too long-drawn-out before they got to the fucking and screwing, because all this touching and feeling and running around of hands, wow! phew! whow! delicious as it was, was putting his voom voom in jeopardy again. Even while he was feeling her, holy cow! everywhere, all over! he was aware of the enormous effort of control; he mustn't let himself like it too much, not yet, not yet; there was a certain pleasure in straining against too much joy, too soon. The things you could do! But she had better let him get on her soon! He wanted to say it again, that thing he hoped she hadn't heard him say last time. And he had to struggle to control that, too, from bursting out of him, *"I love you!"* Hell, that was no thing to say to a whore! But he had to say it to somebody. Maybe she wouldn't even hear. She hadn't made fun before, had she?

Hoda had moved her expertly negligent hands down around from his chest and back, while he buried his own working hands and nuzzling face in her generous immensities. "Hey," she said suddenly, "what's this?"

From where he was burrowing he heard her amused voice with a sudden, cold shock. In his mind he had been saying, *"I love you I love you I love you,"* and she had been wrapping herself helplessly around him, moaning her acquiescent moans, urging him to hurry, before she died of a love no one had ever made her feel before. Into all of this her cool, amused, conversational voice, her finger diddling with his belly button, and unmistakably, an undertone of laughter. Weren't they making love then, like she said? Shouldn't she be as hot as he was, not caring about

373

anything, not noticing anything? And there she had to go and find that goddam pipick, and her voice, funfull and ordinary, as if all of that love-making she'd been talking about was just another lie, like the ones people were always making up, all your life, promising and leaving you, talking and talking. Goddam her, she hadn't even let him shoot his load this time! Suddenly her voice had cut in, and she was making fun with her goddam finger. Making love! Sure! They'll pretend all right, until they find out you're a freak. Then they don't even have to pretend anymore. They just laugh their heads off.

He jerked roughly away from under hand.

"Hey, what's the matter? Did I hurt you?" Hoda was concerned. "Hey, is it a hernia or something? I didn't mean to be rough. I never noticed it before I touched it. It's sensitive, hey?"

Sure, now that she'd fixed him, she could make a fuss, pretend she gave a hoot. Did she think he gave a good goddamn about the concern in her voice? Fat lot she cared, fat slob. If he was a freak she could damn well give him his money back. She said she'd seen all kinds, hadn't she? Was he that much worse that the touch of it threw her right out of making love? Making love! Making up love, you mean!

"Hey, are you all right?" said Hoda. "Don't you feel well, kid?"

"I'm not a kid," said David, vehemently.

"All right, you don't have to yell," she said. "You'll wake my father."

"I don't care about your goddam father," he muttered, under his breath.

"What?" said Hoda. "What did you say? Say, what's got into you all of a sudden? We were doing all right. Just because I touched your pipick, why should you get so upset?"

"I hate it," said Pipick. "Like I'm a goddam freak."

"Go on," said Hoda. "What kind of freak? Just because of that? Well for godsake!" She laughed genially. "If you're a goddam freak with just that little bit of extra flesh, what am I? I got an extra ton!"

"That's different," said Pipick. "That doesn't matter. Everybody laughs."

"And you think they don't laugh at me? They've been laughing at me all my life. Do you think I don't know it? 'Let's go see fat crazy Hoda tonight!' Isn't that what you kids said?"

"I'm not a kid," repeated Pipick sullenly, not anxious to have the topic shifted from his grievance to hers, and a little ashamed, because she was right. But she needn't think he was just like the other boys either. What did she know about him anyway?

"I never called you crazy," he growled.

"Well, let's forget it then. You'll sure call me fat, anyway. How do you like that? We were beginning to have fun and all over a little piece of skin we're in an argument. I don't care about your pipick. You can take your hand away. I think it's kind of cute, but I won't touch it any more if you don't want. Look at that, all the time we're wasting over nothing."

"It's not nothing," said Pipick, his resentment finding a grievance to hang on to. The way he felt now he didn't know if he'd ever be able to have a hard-on again. She could damn well coax him, after what she'd done. She didn't have to pretend it was nothing that bothered him. She didn't have to think he was nobody. What was nothing about making a guy swallow his load? "I've had it all my life, ever since they found me. For all I know it might be hereditary; they have bleeding sickness in royal families; maybe they have it done that way so their kids shouldn't bleed to death."

"Sure," said Hoda patiently, responding to the tone rather than the sense of his words. "It's not such an unusual thing, I'm sure." Funny kid; now what the hell had royal families and bleeding sickness to do with his navel? It was better not go get too involved with them. Some of the kids she met nowadays really were mixed up in their minds. "Come on now," she lay back invitingly.

She didn't give a damn, he could tell her by voice. She wasn't interested in him at all. He could see that now, for all her talk of making love. She thought he was just another kid, with a funny freak of a navel. She had probably even forgotten his name that he'd told her, the way she kept calling him "kid" as though he was just anybody and nobody. Making love! Even a goddam low whore couldn't touch him without laughing.

"I don't care even if my father was a prince!" he burst out. "I wish they'd left me out and never found me till I was dead! I wish my goddam belly button had bust open out of all those knots and let me bleed to death! I didn't want to be alive! I didn't ask for any goddam life!" Let her know, this damn chippy, who it was who wished he were dead; let her know it wasn't just any kid who sat beside her clutching his pain, a dying prince maybe but a maybe prince who didn't give a damn if she felt sorry for him or not, only when you pretend you give enough of a damn to ask a guy his name you should damn well call him by name! He was ashamed and angry even as he uttered his outburst because she'd made him show off with all that silly Prince shit nobody believed anyway. And she didn't even answer. She didn't even bother to answer him, and suddenly Pipick in his rage realized he had a bigger hardon than he'd ever had in his life before; he was one big hardon, from top to bottom of him; every single inch of him was one big FUCK YOU! and to hell with the lovemaking! He turned on her, swooping furiously, and swooping, met her as she was rising, with equal suddenness and violence of movement. They collided, and Pipick grabbed, fiercely happy at the resistance, ferociously determined to wrestle her down. But he was not, in spite of her bulk, as quick as she, or perhaps his desperation was not as great. Hoda heaved like an erupting mountain under his assault, struggled one arm loose, and fetched him a wallop that sent him thumping off the mattress and smack up against the wall. At the crashing noise he made against the wall, she paused abstractedly a moment for a sound from the other room. Then, with enormous reluctance, she turned her furious eyes to where he lay sprawled, staring up at her through eyes from which tears had sprung, tears of astonishment and outrage at the unexpected savagery of her rebuff. Hoda struggled against the feeling of dislocation. What? What? What? All her life she had spent bottled up in this room, and she would never escape it, and every now and then someone picked up the bottle and shook it and shook it and she was flung to and fro, drowning and gasping and clutching at her life. Maybe if she reached over and turned out the little lamp that she always joked with her customers about, it would disappear, she would disappear, he would disappear. What was he doing here anyway? As though she hadn't seen him before she realized that this was a little boy cowering before her, a big, little boy, with tears clinging to his face. *Go home to your mother, little boy.* She shuddered. Without having forgot a word she had the feeling that her memory had completely left her. "I'm sorry. Did I hurt you?" she said stupidly. He didn't reply but his eyes filmed over, and he dropped his head with a sudden, stubborn movement.

"You shouldn't tell lies like that," she said. "I can't stand lies," she continued, lying, because she really didn't care about lying, if it was necessary, though in a way she wasn't lying, because she didn't like it much when lies were necessary. Lies were something she wanted to think about. Really, she had always wanted to think out seriously how she felt about lies, sometime when she had enough time. "You shouldn't tell lies," she repeated, with the feeling that she was talking aimlessly, while her mind stumbled back and forth over the fragments of the evening, and tried to comprehend some enormous connection with the rest of her life. "Why should you pretend you're something when you're not?" she challenged him fiercely. "Why do you have to be ashamed if your father is a grocer or a peddler, or whatever he is? What kind of talk is that anyway, about princes and dying?" She gave him no chance to reply. "I can't stand liars," she repeated doggedly, and concentrated, for an instant, on pulling on her kimono as quickly as she could and wrapping it carefully, tightly, around her, even turning the lapel and collar up. "You're talking crazy," she resumed accusingly. "Maybe you should go home to your ma and pa till you feel better." She watched, with frantic hope, for the effect of her words. Some of these kids had the craziest imaginations, but when you caught them out and didn't take any crap, when they went too far, that is, they realized something or other, and then they stopped and things got back the way they were.

"I am not any goddam liar," growled Pipick, "and I haven't got any goddam ma and pa," he added, almost spitting the words out. "I'm an orphan. I'm a goddam bastard prince." He drew back, as he said it; the way she was looking at him, the way she was crouched over him, tigerishly, she seemed like she was getting ready to take another poke at him. What was the matter with her? All right, if she wanted to play rough, he could play rough too. He'd show her what kind of "kid" he was, freak or no. He'd show her he never came to any goddam chippy to get smacked around. Almost he wished she would try it again, just once. He wouldn't just lie back like any little gentleman. He'd take her all right. Oh then he'd take his money's worth! She might be big and fat but he was all muscle. She'd said so herself. Maybe she wanted it that way. Some of them liked to get knocked around, didn't they? Was she waiting for him to take a poke at her? Was she showing him another kind of lovemaking? She said she'd make his time worth it. Maybe this was part of the show. Maybe it wasn't. It was more like she didn't like him. She couldn't stand him, he could see it. Why didn't she like him? What did he do wrong? Could it be because of his navel? But Mrs. Tize always used to say he was silly to be self-conscious just because they teased him. It showed how much someone had cared about him; they'd knotted it so carefully so many times. And it really wasn't so much; if he'd been a skinny little guy no one would have really noticed it, because nobody expected skinny little guys to have room to tuck their navels in. Anyway, what right did someone have to hate you on account of your navel? So who cared if she hated him? Why should he care? What did he care how she felt? She was crazy, like the guys always said. Only they said it as though it was some kind of joke. Nobody ever told him she could look at you out of glaring wide grey eyes full of hate for you that way. Why didn't anybody like him? To Pipick's horror, he felt his eyes fill with tears again as he blurted once more at her unbelieving face, "I am not a liar."

"Why should I care if you lie?" said Hoda, suddenly reasonable. "Go on, say what you like. It's no skin off my . . ." He was just a little boy. The whole bunch of them were just little boys. Kids. She was twice his age. At least. She was old enough . . . old enough to feel the clutch of cold panic in her heart. How was she to have known? How should she know who he was? Look how tight shut she was holding her kimono now, with both hands. Where the hell was that cord? She tore her eyes away from where they kept trying to slither down to his navel to tie a memory to, and sent them darting around for the kimono belt. They felt funny in her head, her eyes, as though they had been frozen open wider than she could bear.

"Where the hell?" she muttered.

"I can prove it," said Pipick, taking advantage of the fact that she had raised herself onto her knees and was looking around for something, to pull himself up quickly, standing towering over her now, with his back against the wall. Crazy old dame, on hands and knees now, crawling around and muttering. Now she was trying to disentangle her kimono cord from the bedsprings.

Pipick cat-footed swiftly to the chair, and felt in his pants pocket, fumbling around. "I can prove it!" He turned to her again.

"What can you prove?" she raged now from her knees, knotting the kimono cord tight, with angry movements, again and again as she spoke. "Who cares what you can prove? Why should I care what you can prove?"

"You called me a liar! Nobody calls me a liar!" snarled Pipick, almost beside himself with fury. "I don't know why you're against me, but you're not going to call me a liar and get away with it! Oh no! Oh no!"

"Why did I call you a liar?" said Hoda distractedly. "I'm sorry. I don't feel good. When I don't feel good I say funny things. I don't even know you. What's this thing?"

Hoda moved her face from side to side, as though with distaste, before the slips of paper he was shoving in front of her eyes. "What is it?"

"See what they say? FOR THE PRINCE! That's me, see? They were sent to me! At the Home where they left me! I don't care if you don't believe them, but I'm not a liar!"

"I don't feel good," said Hoda. "I just don't feel good."

"Just because you don't feel good doesn't mean you have to call me a liar. You think I feel good, somebody laughs at me, and then for nothing she hands me a chop on the kisser, and keeps yelling at me I'm a liar I'm a liar?"

"I'm sorry," whispered Hoda. "I'm sorry. I just lost my temper. Honest, I got an awful temper. Ask anybody. I thought you were making fun of me, trying to pull a fast one, like I was dumb or something, talking about being a prince and all that."

"I thought you liked me," said Pipick bitterly. "We were making love, like you said, not like the other guys."

"No," said Hoda. "I mean yes but," she amended quickly, watching him now, "why should a kid like you, a nice clean kid, come to a . . . come to someone like me? I suddenly thought, 'He shouldn't be here. This kid's not like the rest of them.' That's why I got mad. I thought a kid like this is lying when he comes to a place like this, like he's lying to himself, I mean, because he's pretending he's an ordinary cheap punk who can go to an ordinary prostitute like everyone else. Sure, I know what I am. And I know class when I see it. I could tell even by the way you acted that something inside of you was against it all the time, because deep down you knew there was something better in store for you in life." It came pouring out of her, a passion of argument, logical, earnest, desperate, and made more effective by the fact that she was still kneeling on the mattress, her robe tightly bound about her massiveness, her face distraught, contrite, and he was standing above her and looking down as though she were pleading before him on her knees.

This was better. It was as one whole, long, obscure thread in his life had always led him to believe things should be. He believed her.

"It's all right," said Pipick earnestly. If she really meant she was sorry he wouldn't hold it against her. "I'm not a snob." All he wanted was his money's worth. He didn't want her to feel bad. Maybe he'd been too touchy.

"You see," said Hoda, encouraged, "I'm way too old for you . . . David." She said the name tentatively. "I'm old enough to be your mother." She forced it to come out. She forced herself to say it.

David laughed. "Don't worry." He knew the answer to that. "I like older women."

"No but you see," Hoda said quickly, "it's the way I'd feel. I'd feel silly, doing it with you, honest, I'd feel kind of, you know, like your mother or something. I don't know, it just wouldn't be right with someone like you, like too good for me."

"Listen," said David, proud but just in his ascendancy. "One thing's for sure. I don't want to insult you, but you don't look like my mother to me and you won't feel like my mother to me, so just let's forget about my mother. And even if I believed in all that prince crap, you'd still be good enough for me. You can't help it if you're . . . the way you are. And I don't mind, as long as you're nice to me."

There was a plea in his voice, and a counter plea in hers that she could hardly expect him to understand. "But your mother wouldn't like it if you . . ."

"Aw, forget my mother!" He couldn't keep the sharpness from his voice. "How do you know what she would like? You want to know the truth? I don't give a good goddam what my mother would like and what she wouldn't like. If she wanted to have a say in my life she shouldn't have left me bawling out there like some kind of baby cat nobody wants."

"You weren't bawling," said Hoda, and added quickly, "were you?"

"Aw shit," said Pipick, "I feel like I've been bawling all my life."

"You had a rotten time," said Hoda, "all this time."

It wasn't even said like a question. She said it as though she understood it, somehow. It was tempting, the way she sounded; he was tempted to tell her. But not now, he didn't want to talk now. If he started he would talk and talk. There was something better than talking, and that was what he wanted first and most. She wasn't going to talk to him into forgetting that. If she still liked him and wanted to talk to him afterwards, all right.

"I'm sorry you had such a rotten time," she said quickly, to keep the conversation going, but he didn't answer. He was looking at her in that familiar, puppy dog begging way they got sometimes when they couldn't afford it, the kind of helpless way she used to fall for sometimes when she was a kid, and think maybe if she let them have a free one they'd really like her better afterwards. Till she caught on. If only she could get him interested in something else. It wasn't right he should be looking at her that way. Why was everything so dense in this room? Why did every instant weigh so heavily, demanding something of her always, no moment willing to let her pause to draw breath to think what it all meant, what to do, how to fend him off, how not to hurt him, no moment bringing her a thought, telling her what was right, telling her how to help him, how to save herself. Stop! Yell borrows! Hold off the game a while and let the players rest and breathe freely and think of strategy. But there were no borrows for grown-ups; there was no moment of grace. All of her moments were crushed into this one horribly hard-to-breathe-in moment.

Tell him! Tell him now! Tell him? After the contempt he hadn't been able to hide when she had tried to hint? Tell him, sure; give him something to be proud of. How to make happy a miserable little boy. Oh sure, tell him, *"Say, you know what? I just remembered. I AM your . . ."* Sure, go on, tell him, after what's happened already too, what happened earlier on tonight, before you knew, that you keep trying to forget. *Well that wasn't my fault; I didn't know. I couldn't help it. Fine, so tell him now, apologize, say "oops, you know what? Sorry!" Go on, make him happy. Take him into your confidence.*

Never.

"What's the matter?" he asked impatiently. She had recoiled from him and seemed to be listening for something, with a curious, distant, pained expression on her face.

"Nothing," she said, stalling. "I thought I . . . I want to be your friend," she added humbly, vaguely, by way of explanation, while a part of her seemed to look back over the whole vista of her life that had been till now, and knew, with surprise, that even until this moment, though she had suffered some, she had been innocent. For some reason it was that lady in the Bible that Hoda remembered now, and suddenly understood what had really happened to her. She had always felt sorry for that one, who, just for looking back, had been turned into a pillar of salt. Now she saw that when Lot's wife looked back she simply became what she had been, concentrated essence, pillar of tears. Most of the time you trail your life behind you in a constant dribble of leaking time, and if you don't look back, except maybe a glance sometimes, you hardly know it's there. But comes a time, unexpected and unwanted, to you of all people, when you, of all people, must look. At least Lot's wife had had fair warning, but warning or no she wouldn't have been able to help it, Hoda knew, when the time came for her to learn at last what it was to shoulder the burden of her life. Lucky Lot's wife, nevertheless, to be forever what she knew forever and not be called upon still for more. What was it she herself had to do? She tried to come back to the practical facts. No kid needs a whore that much. He wouldn't die without it. It only seems desperate to a man at the time. Afterwards, he laughs. And what are you giving the kid if you do? A bad and expensive habit.

I can't afford to support him in whores, she thought crazily.

She gave a funny little laugh that made Pipick shudder, involuntarily. Boy, she sure was nuts, the way she kept on changing all the time, and listening as if somebody else was in the room and talking to her, and making funny sounds. He sure had never imagined that you had to go through all this when you did your first solo with a whore. For two pins he'd get his clothes on and go home. But then he'd have to ask for his money back, and he was too embarrassed. No wonder everyone always said that about how impossible women were to get along with. Here he had to pay for this, too. Imagine what it would be like with someone you wanted to get it from for free? And yet he had the feeling now that somehow he was handling himself all right. If he just waited, he had the feeling she would come round. Somehow he was going to do all right. Somehow, by saying that about how she wanted to be his friend she was letting him know that he was the man all right. He knew, somehow, that she didn't say that to many other guys. She didn't have to, did she? Unless they impressed her that they weren't just ordinary guys. Now if only she'd let him put the final stamp on it for her, slip it to her signed, sealed and delivered. If only she'd let him he knew he'd be a different man from the kid he'd been just a few moments ago. He felt different already, somehow. Something had happened; he'd let her know something about who he was, not just all that royalty crap, that wasn't it, but somehow he felt she understood more how he was, and what he was as himself, a kid who could hold his own. Now was the time. Pipick dropped to his knees beside her on the mattress.

"Listen," said Hoda quickly, "don't you have a girl friend? You know, a nice kid your own age?"

"Oh Chrise! No!" he almost exploded. "I ain't got nobody!" He put his hand out to touch the lapel of her robe. Hoda moved back quickly.

"Listen, I'll bet there's somebody crazy about you, who'd really love to have you all to herself; you probably never even noticed her and all she wants is for you to look at her. What do you want stale old sold meat for? I'm just an ugly old whore, and when I think of that cute little girl who's crazy about you I don't want to spoil you for her." Why couldn't she just send him away? Just say "Go, I'm sorry, I just can't now." So it'll hurt his feelings. He'll get over it.

"Nobody's crazy about me," said Pipick angrily. Was she going to begin all over again? What did a guy have to do? "Nobody knows I'm alive. You said you want to be my friend. Why don't you like me then? Why can't I touch you any more?"

It was the tone of his voice that chilled her, that went through her with the certainty that he believed every word he was saying.

"Of course somebody loves you," she said. "Don't talk silly. Naturally people love you. I . . . I liked you a lot, right from the start."

"If you like me," said Pipick stubbornly, trying to pull her kimono apart at her breasts, "you show me."

"Me I'm nothing," said Hoda, trying not to sound her panic. "I just want to help you, I mean not just like this. I really want to help you like a friend. Tell me how I can help you. I don't want to . . . to . . ."

"To what, you don't want to?" Pipick's face was very close to hers, and he was whispering, though she felt as though he was shouting in her ears. "Everybody wants to help except they don't want to help with what you want. Everybody's nice only 'don't come near me, no no, Princey, nicey nicey, only don't come near me!' Prince! Prince! Do you know what kind of a nickname that is? It's the name of a dog! 'Nicey nicey Prince. Now go way, and keep your dirty paws off me.' They call me Prince and they still laugh at me like when I was Pipick. What's the matter with me, hey? I'm some kind of freak, just because I'm nobody, from nowhere, with a screwy belly-button, and even my names get tossed to me, like some kind of bones, and if I growl enough they toss me the bone I like better. 'Nicey nicey, don't bark now.' So why don't you tell me, 'You're a freak; I don't want to fuck you!' No one wants to fuck a freak, even if he pays you! Why don't you tell me, like that, straight out, see? But don't yes-no, yes-no me; don't tell me how much you like me when you'd rather go hang yourself than come near me!" Almost, he was crying; only the fact that he had got hold of the cord at her waist and was trying to fumble the knots open prevented him from crying. As it was he could hiss, with tears in his voice as he tugged, "Goddam, you got yourself tied up so tight here I can't even get it open. 'Help me,' she says, she says she wants to help me! You want to help me? What can you do for me? What the fuck do you think you can do for me?"

There was never enough time to think things through, to consider what was right, to figure out what was best. Always there was time enough only for regrets. Always she had wanted to do what was right. At first she had thought that what felt good was what must be right. Well, how was she to know? And how was she to know now that what felt just awful, what aroused in her a revulsion of loathing at the very thought, was wrong? If it wasn't right when it felt right, was it wrong because it felt wrong? Oh she knew it was wrong all right, in all her flesh, wrong for her. It wasn't that it had happened once already. When they did it by accident, before she knew, that was nothing, just a dirty trick. But knowing, if she chose to do it again, it was for a reason, and because she was a person, and she had a debt, an enormous, inerasable debt, and because it was the only thing she could think of that she could do, that maybe she was fit to do for him.

One last try she made, feebly. "I don't feel good," she said.

"You'll feel better when I'm through with you," he promised urgently, pitifully cocky.

Pipick was still tugging at the cord which she had nervously knotted again and again. "Tear it darling," said Hoda through gritted teeth. Pipick's heart sprang with his muscles, and the cord sprang open. "You see," said Hoda gently, "you don't really need my help. You can do pretty well on your own." She touched his arm. "You want to know why I've been stalling you so long?" Hoda laughed, falsely, but how was he to know? "Because I wanted it to last longer. See how many times you've had to control it already? Someday you'll be so good you'll make them squeal whenever you feel like it. You know what a friend of mine once told me his father always said? I always remember what. Pop the Polack told me about his old man. The old man used to say, 'Dogs, when you beat them and women, when you please them, should squeal." Hoda laughed, and so did Pipick, extravagantly.

Then she used all her art to make of her ordeal a memorable moment for him. One small concession she tried to reserve for herself, when she suggested that they might turn out the little lamp and enjoy themselves better in the dark. He remembered, however, what she had said that first time, joking in her lazy, chuckly voice. That was what had got him so excited it was probably the reason why he blew off so fast. Hoda had spread herself out before him like the whole world in miniature, and said, and it was the last thing he heard before his voom voom left him, "I keep it on because I like to see what I'm doing." Triumphant, he repeated her words now at her defeat, denying her even the darkness in his innocence. When it came down to it, though, what she suffered most acutely, was the sudden fear lest she should, by some grotesque accident, enjoy him. But in the end she knew, in a curious, distant way, that if God so willed, it was within the range of her sense of humour to bear that too. Into how many pieces does one break and still bother to count the pieces? Enough that he was fragile and she held him tenderly, and tried in the only way she knew how to make up for all the harm she had done.

Afterwards he talked a lot. He'd never talked as much to anyone in his life before as he talked now, lying close beside her, feeling her along the length of him. It worried him a little that he was talking so much. He found himself telling her things he'd never even wanted to tell anyone before. But then he figured, what did it matter if he told someone like her anyway? And she listened as if she really was interested in everything he said, and made sounds as if she really understood. She even groaned, once or twice, deep down in her chest, he could feel the vibration, when he told about something, he didn't know why he happened to think of it, that had been particularly hurtful to him. She sure was a good listener, and he told her so, when he was getting dressed, and was a little embarrassed because she kept on telling him what a good lover he was and how he was far too good for her, and he wanted to tell her something nice, too. She kept on repeating that she didn't want to take his money any more and that with what he had he could get any girl he wanted, if he set his mind to it, for free. She said he was the kind of kid who was too fine to have a business arrangement with. She really wanted to be friends with him, and he could come to see her any time he wanted, not for fucking, like, but for friendship. She'd like to help a kid like him make something of himself. She bet her father would like him, too, and her father was a terrific judge of character, even though he'd been blind ever since he was a kid. Why didn't Pipick come for a meal sometime? She was a terrific cook. The hope even flashed into his mind, from the way she was talking, that she might be willing to give it to him for free when he ran out of money. But right now David, Prince Pipick, hero, conqueror, lover, putting on his clothes, could still afford to smile down at her benignly, with proud mien and glistening eyes, and assure her earnestly, "That's okay, I've still got some dough. I can still afford to set you up a few more times at least. I know you've got to make a living."

One thing still disturbed him, and now he had enough nerve to ask. "I didn't make you laugh, though, the way you did with Ralphie." Maybe she was just trying to be kind to him after all, and throw in a little flattery to make up his money's worth.

"Ralphie?" Hoda's head was so full of cutting fragments that she had, for the moment, no notion of what he was talking about. "Who's Ralphie?"

"Ralphie," said Pipick, surprised. "You know, small Ralphie, the one I came with, runty Ralphie the rounder."

"Oh, that one," said Hoda. "I don't know why you run around with boys like that. He's not your type. He's the kind of kid gets others in trouble and gets away with it himself." She could not resist the urge to try to teach him, while she had him this moment, to warn him, to try to get him to see a million things clear that she had learned about.

Pipick was quickly impatient. Who'd she think she was, his goddam mother giving him be-careful advice? Or was she trying to shift the subject and make him forget he hadn't done so well as she pretended? What did she think, he wanted some damn whore to lie to him? "Yah," he said pointedly, "but you sure giggled a lot when he was with you."

"I giggled?" she made an effort at recall. "Oh, I giggled all right, the little brat! He makes me giggle on purpose, and one of these days I'm going to toss him out on his arse, that's what I'm going to do. You see this little runt, he found out I got a couple of ticklish spots. Don't tell him I told you, eh? I play along; I figure a little guy like him has to impress the other guys one way or another. But he should know when to stop. Sometimes when he comes in he starts teasing me, you know, just pretends he's going to start to tickle, kind of fooling. He doesn't actually tickle, just pretends he's going to. He knows I'd bust him one if he really tried it. I can't stand being tickled there, and even if you pretend I break out with this silly giggling. It's embarrassing. But little Ralphie, I think he works himself up that way, and like I said, it makes a big impression on his pals, so I let him. But don't tell the kid I told you, eh? He's an old customer and he brings them in."

Inside of her Hoda felt as though she didn't ever want to see any of those kids again, not that way, not to come near her. Why was she saying these placatory things, then, as though everything was still the same? "You should get yourself some friends more your type. It's not going to do you any good hanging around wasting your money on whores. Hell, the way that Ralphie carries on, I've seen the type, he'll end up a pimp, I'm telling you. That kind of kid lets himself get carried away working the angles; I can't stand pimps, and he's just the type to end up a nooky bookie living off somebody else's arse. Mind you I like the kid. But I look around and I see all these kids, the world's still in a mess, everybody's suffering, everything's all fouled up, and all a kid like that thinks of is his own cushy tushy. Sure I'm a communist, and I'll let the whole world know it. I'm with them one hundred percent, if only they'd lay off free enterprise. I don't mean the big capitalist bloodsuckers, but small little businesses like mine, where you give value for money. I wouldn't care so much about that either, if it was for the good of everybody, only I have responsibilities."

In the end, he had a hard time getting away. Every time he made to go she seemed to think of something to ask, or something to suggest or advise. Pipick had been through a lot this evening and he was getting very tired. He began to suspect something of the drawbacks in pleasing a woman too well. But he was generous in response to her gratitude, and even tolerated her solicitude over his open shirt buttons; in her way she was just like Mrs. Tize; it amused him how much all these older dames were alike, even though Mrs. Tize was a lot older, even. But there was something more about the way this one was acting towards him now, something much more, and whichever way he looked at it he could think of only one explanation, and no matter how often he rejected it he had to come back to it again in the end. *She's nuts about me.*

He could hardly believe it, but look how she was acting. Well, he wasn't going to worry about it now. All he wanted now was to hit the old sack. And when the guys came to wake him in the morning he'd shake them off and they'd have to leave him to sleep in. He could already hear them; *"Okay boy, okay Prince Charming, okay Golden Boy, okay, okay!"* He gloated in advance at the envy in their voices as they faded from the dorm. *"Lucky bastard!"* And they were right, goddamit; for once they were absolutely right!

Finally, Hoda realized that she was holding him not simply for tenderness and the hunger to be with him yet awhile longer, but because she was afraid to be left alone. She forced herself to loose her grip. She allowed him, finally, to swagger off into the pallid end of night. And she lay down alone. And she touched, that night, the outermost boundary of aloneness that can be reached by a human being who is yet denied that privilege of loss of responsibility in suffering, which is the gift of madness. For though her mind stumbled and floundered helplessly amid the painful fragments and the bizarre ironies of her life, and she felt that truly she must be going mad, she arose that morning, without having experienced the intercession of sleep, and brought Daddy his ginger and honey mixture that was the best thing to take for his chest, and fussed over him, and felt for the first time in what seemed like a long time, an acute and tender awareness of his existence.

TWELVE

The trouble is, though you've had enough and more than enough, time won't stop of its own accord; it won't hold still or even pause a moment to ease you in the travel sickness of your life. So with Hoda, morning came again, and noon and night, and ebb and slack and flood, and sun and clouds and moon, and Hoda thanked God for ginger and honey to ease what she didn't know how to cure. It would be an exaggeration to say that she contemplated suicide. It passed through her mind, but as a self-indulgence not relevant to the terms of her existence. Sure, knock herself off and who would look after Daddy? Who would help the boy, in whatever other way that is, that he might need her help? It was all very well to think about death and how nice it would be to be out of things, finished, through, away. And she did think of it now, thought of it often, thought of how everything dies, thought of all that had died around her in her lifetime already, and all that would continue to die. But when it came to the actual details of how she might take steps to end her life, to crush that existence which had been so proudly presented to her; no, she thought of Daddy and she couldn't see how dying would make anything better at all. Even if you were stripped down to the core, you must wrap yourself around your life and just hang on. And if she had no core? What if she was like the layer-locked onion, and had no core, only function? Very well then, Hoda too would continue to function, as best she could. Lucky onion that is not required to know itself and weep as well.

Oh, she wept. She couldn't stop herself, night after night, and sometimes, to Daddy's distress, for no apparent reason, she burst out in broad daylight, without warning, even to herself, and was unable to stop, unable to bear his blind words of comfort, shaking him off, turning away. And one day he said to her, hesitantly, "Hodaleh, if it's someone who's hurting you, don't worry. Your time will come. Your destined one will come. Believe me, I know. Who should know as well as I? He'll come."

He was so serious. He really meant it! *Oh sure he'll come, Daddy! They'll all come! In a glass slipper they'll come, up your elbow, in your armpit; blow your nose and they'll think you're making room.*

"Who needs him?" That much burst out of her. "Who wants him? I wish they'd all leave me alone!" Which was a laugh, considering, and she gave a little laugh in spite of herself.

"You'll see," Daddy repeated softly, "you'll see."

"It's too late, Pa. I should have written to the Prince of Wales a long time ago and told him he was making a terrible mistake. If he was going to marry a commoner and disappoint his whole Empire he should have looked a little harder and really done the job. To give up my Em-pieah,'" she mimicked, "'foh-wah the woman I love.'" Oh sure she was jealous that she would never know such love; no one would ever give up a seat on a bus for Hoda, let alone an Em-pie-ah. But was that a job for a grown man, to sit and admire some dame all day long? There were a few more important things that needed doing in this world. What about this Hitler? And that Mussolini? Shouldn't somebody up there be doing something, somehow, and soon? She didn't believe that was all there was to it anyway, this great love stuff. Who knew what really went on among the Highnesses?

"We yearn for the Leviathan," remarked her father thoughtfully, "but in our great hunger we'll even worship shmaltz herring from afar."

"What?" said Hoda. "What are you talking about, Pa?"

"You and the Prince of Wales," said Danile apologetically, "and it made me think . . ."

She couldn't help laughing, through wet eyes. You sometimes forgot how funny Daddy could be, if you really listened to him.

Pleased, Danile laughed too, adding that of course he intended no disrespect to shmaltz herring.

"I think they call them kippers." Hoda couldn't remember when she had last heard him laugh that way, like a little boy.

At some point, she hadn't even noticed when, Danile had stopped even trying to tell her the old stories, so effectively had she learned to cut them off over the years. And she realized now, with fear, that she was in danger of forgetting how they went, not their general outlines, of course, but the sequence, the rhythm of them, the inside secrets, the series of surprises and revelations by which they evolved, and the way they held you with wonder and the feeling that they were true, and the truth had a terrible tenderness in it as though it were holding in fierce but incredibly compassionate hands all the aching fragments of all the aching lives, not because it was going to heal them, because perhaps even those cupped hands were powerless to do so much, and the tears you wanted to weep had nothing to do with feeling better afterwards, but to reveal them to you, so that knowing nothing really, you could still for a moment know a compassion and a dignity beyond your pain. Perhaps in the old stories she would find some surcease from the wringing of hands, and from the need she had to throw out fruitless challenges to her fate, when, feeling all wrenched apart and broken into a thousand thousand pieces, she would demand with bitter, logical rigour, *If I'm broken, why hasn't all feeling leaked away? If I'm broken at least let me be empty.* Was that too much to ask, that she become as empty as the silence seemed to be, to which she addressed herself? Apparently. All right then, if she must continue to feel, she would demand something from those feelings too, that they be true for instance, that they correspond to what was, what really was in her life.

That was why she had been afraid, at first, to ask Daddy to repeat the old stories to her, because she remembered her own unadmitted disbelief that had inspired the boredom with which she had eventually silenced him. And she remembered, with an absolute memory, her childhood intuition that her mother, too, had somehow refused to share the spirit of the stories, though she had never denied their factual truth. What if they too should arouse in her this savage disdain that most of the movies she saw nowadays, and the magazines she read and the way people talked about life, too, now inspired in her? She would have to control herself then, and prevent herself from giving way to the urge to mock him. Why did she want to hear them again anyway? Didn't a part of her want to destroy them, too, once and for all? That was something the

nicey stories never told you about, how with pain and tenderness and all those other goody nicey things went a savage
desire to destroy what you loved, and a terrible fear that
somehow you would succeed, or even that you would discover
that you had already done so. Didn't she really hate those
stories? Hadn't they betrayed her again and again in her life,
and made her the butt of laughter and contempt?

It was with great fear, as of a terrible, impending loss,
that she began once again to coax her father to tell her all
about themselves. And it was a hesitant Danile who fumbled
forth his treasures, rusty, not from neglect, for they had never
ceased to be the central subjects of his rumination, but because
he had been telling them to himself so soundlessly for so long
that it was something of an effort to give them vocal weight
again. And also, the load in his chest was particularly heavy
this winter, and it was often easier not to try to speak at all; but
he was eager to please her and to share once more the great
moments of his life. Hoda listened intently, and his words
took on a curious resonance inside of her. She interrupted
sometimes; sometimes she nodded "oh yes," as though impatiently, because the sequence of words itself was connected
now to feelings of impatience, but she no longer tried to stop
him, and listened instead with extraordinary attention, as
though trying to draw his words more completely into herself
by this means.

If she had hoped to hear those stories once again as a
child hears, she was disappointed. But she was not aware of
such a hope, nor of the disappointment of being barred from
a return to innocence. She simply felt the old stories, felt her
emptiness filled with resonance, transformed to resonance.
She saw the old stories, saw through the old stories, saw
beyond the old stories to what the man her father was and

what the woman her mother must have been; she heard the stories and knew them all, and gathered them back into herself and knew herself as well, not as she had once known herself, in a sudden, comprehensive flash of revelation, a simultaneity of multiple Hodas, but as she flowed in the sequence of her days. And when she returned to the contemplation of her immediate existence, that restless human impulse which will not hold still any more than time holds still, conceived for her the notion that somehow the boy, protected though he must be from personal knowledge, must learn what was important in the stories still. It was all very confused in her head, but she knew it had to be possible somehow to change things between herself and the boy, lest she herself, for all the tenacious way she was gripping her sanity between her teeth, should let go suddenly, unable to bear any longer the foul taste of her life. That was her greatest fear, that she might become like one of those mad ones in the stories, who wander the streets, objects of stones and hoots and barking dogs, or get locked behind big red brick walls to scream their lives away. What of Daddy then? And the boy? What if she went mad and it all came streaming out of her, the whole unbelievable story, and she went on and on, puking it out in the neutral zone of madness and leaving them to drown in the filth? *Oh no!* she thought. *Oh no! You don't catch me going bugs!* And she guarded herself against the living presence of madness, and to her burden was added the task of evaluating each impulse, monitoring every word, assessing all laughter, lest among them be the giveaway traitor that would release the chaos within.

Somehow she must convince the boy, somehow persuade him, turn him from a client to a friend. She did not delude herself that this would change what had already happened, but it might enable her to pass on to him something that was precious of themselves at least. Even if he never did know how or why it had come about, maybe she could still achieve a proper, loving friendship with him in which she could work for him as she did for Daddy, and teach him their stories, and protect him and help him avoid all those traps that she knew were waiting for him in life. Oh they were waiting for him all right, traps that a kid like him was incapable of conceiving even, for all he thought he was so grown-up a young man who visited a whore already. She could tell, from the way he acted with her, something of the danger he was in. She had good and sufficient proof, in terms she understood only too well, of the kind of boy he was.

Every now and then, in Hoda's business, she met a guy who got his fun mainly out of trying to please her. It was so rare as to be practically a perversion; no, much more rare, more like a miracle. Hitherto it had been a prized experience, one of those occasional surprises that toned up her faith in human nature, which normally did not get too much encouragement where she lay. She could just about count off the guys it had happened with on one hand, give or take a finger. They had generally become friends of hers, almost like lovers, more personal and indeed more passionate friends than was usual in the business way. And once or twice she had even let herself dream foolish dreams about them. But now, dammit, as if things weren't bad enough, just her luck, her own kid had to go and turn out to be that way. She had to become an actress on the mattress for him. And she had to be so careful. It was so easy to shake his confidence, to make him doubt.

"You're a nice boy," she kept telling him, after those tender and loathsome encounters, avoiding his warm and gratified eyes, afraid that even into this innocent phrase her voice had loaded uncontainable secrets that would somehow seep into his understanding and blight him too, forever. Astonishingly, he did not appear to understand anything beyond the words and their encouragement. She was relieved, but upset, too, that it must still go on. "I like you anyway," she persisted. "I'd rather just be your friend. Honest David, you should be saving your money for school books and stuff for next year. This kind of thing can wait. Listen, I know guys, they started out too young and went at it too strong; by the time they were thirty-four – five years old, they were all shot, not a bang left in them. They come around to see me now like to show me their souvenirs. We have tea and they tell me what they used to be like. Save it, kid, don't waste it. Someday you'll really want it for someone special." But no matter how earnestly she tried to dissuade him, the boy was disinclined to turn aside and ascend to higher things in her company. It had become a part of the game for him, this having to talk her into it anew each time, and in fact gave him the habit of persistence over reluctance which was to stand him in very good stead with women later on.

"Don't worry about me. I'll have plenty left," he replied confidently.

"It's not good for you," she nagged. "You start with your mind on whores and it's bad for your studies and you'll go from bad to worse. Before you know it you'll end up with your whole life wasted, like me."

"Your life's not wasted," he replied gallantly. "You're the best thing that's happened to me," he added, and was immediately sorry he'd said it. You never knew how she'd take it. Sometimes she got too serious, and he didn't quite know where she was trying to lead him.

"A young kid like you fooling around like this. It's not the real thing anyway. The real thing a kid like you shouldn't have to pay for."

Again he knew he shouldn't say it, but he couldn't resist. "You can give it to me for free if you like," suggested David, daringly.

"Like a pimp?" said Hoda sharply. "Or you want we should get engaged, maybe?" she added quickly, because she knew that in the mythology of adolescent boys, older women were always desperate to get married, and would snatch from any cradle. She had long ago learned to bear the appalled faces, and even to be amused, eventually, when she teasingly hinted to her younger clients that she was like other girls and might even want to get married too.

"I'm too young to marry," protested David, a little frightened. Was she serious? Was she practically proposing to him or something? Why did she keep on telling him how much she liked him? "I just said that because you said that," he added lamely. He didn't want to hurt her feelings. Did she realize how young he was? He couldn't even get a licence. He'd have to lie about his age! How did he get himself into this? "I can't get engaged. I don't even have a trade yet or anything."

"A kid like you should go to college," said Hoda. Well, why not? He was a smart boy, that much she could tell. The things he had told her about, that he'd built, she'd never heard his buddy Ralphie talk about figuring out complicated things like that, though he was always boasting how smart he was. "If you want, maybe I could try to help you go to university," she suggested, tentatively, off-hand like. "Only you'd have to help by saving your money and giving up screwing around, with professionals, anyway," she added.

"Okay," said David cheerfully, relieved, and having got used, by now, to her zany suggestions. "When I'm through high school in a couple of years, if I get that far, we'll draw up a contract. Let's not talk now, hey?"

"No, I'm serious," said Hoda, shoving his hand away. "I really think you're wasting your time. What do you mean 'if I get that far?' You've got to get that far. You're not going to get anywhere without an education, you can take it from me."

"Look, remember what you said that time, when I came with the guys the first time, and we were kibitzing around and you said 'To err is human, to recline divine?' So how about it now, divine? Recline!"

Just her luck he had a sense of humour, too. It ran in the family. Hoda had more than once these days to groan inwardly over the little homilies with which she had been wont to put new customers in the mood.

Well, what should she have done? What think? What feel? Should she have quit working? Closed shop? Turned away her customers? Crossed her legs and looked virtuous? And sent her Daddy after all this time to the Old Folks' Home, maybe, and stood in line for relief tickets like everyone else, and not done anything for the boy at all? Hell with all that. In the end she didn't even turn away his friends or the other young kids who came, though she had lost her taste for young boys. It revolted her, in fact, to lie with them now. But revulsion is not a valid economic consideration. And besides, when David began to turn up less frequently because he was running out of money, and he had to begin to space his treats, she could keep in touch through the other kids, by introducing him as it were casually into her conversations with them.

Too soon it happened, actually, that his money began to run out, when she had not even had a chance properly to begin to do him any good, in any of the other ways, the real ways that counted, that is. Already he was drifting beyond her reach. What of her long-range plan to get him and Daddy to know each other eventually, a knowing which would lead perhaps to a loving, three-way friendship? It became something of an obsession with her, this vision of a healing, three-way friendship, and perhaps she behaved rather foolishly as a result, in trying to maintain a contact with him through his friends. The boys couldn't fail to notice her interest. She tried to control herself, and not ask the same boy too often, or seem too interested in the reply. And yet when his pals didn't turn up for awhile she couldn't seem to prevent herself from asking even stranger kids, and when she got any little scrap of information, she forgot her determination not to seem too interested, and pressed eagerly for more, so that inevitably the word got around among the boys that the fat old chippy had the hots for the royal orphan. The guys razzed the pants off David. Ralphie insisted that the reason Hoda was so nuts about the Prince was that he had something special in those pants of his, something he took such good care of, he'd never even let anyone get a look at it. Why else, come to think of it, had he always refused to take a shower with the other guys? Obviously he was shy of revealing to them some exceptional endowment, and that what other than a princely weapon, an instrument so magnificent, so superbly potent that it had aroused even in the redoubtable Hoda some special responsive fire? They even coined a new nickname for him, Super-Crotch. And Ralphie introduced him to some of the older girls he knew as "My famous young Chinese friend, the Mandarin Won Lon Kok."

It was embarrassing and silly but not ultimately unpleasant, for it gradually filtered through to David that the nice girls weren't shunning him because of those stories. Quite adequately furnished by nature, he had never aspired to the stunning measurements which rumour bestowed upon him, but he was canny enough henceforth to keep his privates, which now proved the unexpected beneficiaries of his lifelong embarrassment over his belly button, even more carefully private. Cocky young lover that he had become under Hoda's reluctant tutelage, and always willing to be put to the test of performance, he was nevertheless, like any young prince, not beyond the temptation to pretend as well to some more special attributes of the divine. Though it bothered him.

All right, if that's what they wanted. But why did there have to be so much bullshit? Often he had the feeling that he was somebody temporary, an all made up kind of guy, and other people were doing the making up most of the time. People were always hanging things on you. It was as if they really wanted and needed somebody to hang all kinds of scraps of thoughts and ideas and hopes onto, things they wanted for themselves, and sometimes things they didn't want for themselves, their nightmares, so they hung you with them, like when those dumb yoks had got hold of him that time and nearly beat the shit out of him, for nothing, like, just because he was a Jew and the guys called him Prince and King David sometimes. So they cornered him and tried to get him to say there was only one Prince of the Jews, and that was King Jesus, and when he told them that was a matter of opinion, like you're supposed to when it's no use arguing, they tried to force him, all of them against one, and guys having to push each other aside to get a poke at him. To hell with them. If it was his last chance in the world, and they were nailing him to one of their bloody crosses, he wouldn't say it. Maybe he didn't know who he was but he knew he didn't want to be one of them, picking on someone who couldn't lick all of them at once, though he'd offered to take them on, even two at a time, and afterwards when he was crying with rage and frustration because they were holding his arms, and they grabbed even the leg he was trying to kick out with, they called him a crybaby and a chicken Jew who couldn't take his punishment. There was something phoney about those goyem. He hoped he didn't have any of their lousiness in him, prince or no. That was where Ralphie was smart. He said he'd have said right away there was only one king of the Jews, like they wanted him to. Why should he let the dumb yoks beat him up for nothing? What the hell, there were at least two Jews who'd know the truth, himself and Jesus Christ. Well, maybe Ralphie was right; maybe he would have got a few less lumps that way, but David was not so sure. He had the feeling that when they wanted to give you lumps they'd give you lumps no matter what, because wanting to give the lumps was the real thing, and the rest was all made up stuff anyway.

That was one thing about someone like Hoda; at least with her there was no pretense. But was that entirely true? Didn't he feel even with Hoda sometimes, that she too was in some way making him up, that there was something disproportionate and unreal in her interest in him? Was he really that good? Was he really that interesting? Or was it all that made-up stuff about him that she was really interested in, all that maybe and mystery that would attract an ignorant whore who probably read love books? Made-up stuff attracted more made-up stuff, and he began to wonder whether it would matter to anybody if the real person disappeared altogether, for all they knew him, or cared, or for that matter if he never even emerged, but remained smothered under everybody's make-believe, including his own. They seemed to like the idea that he was some kind of super-crotch a lot better than they would ever like knowing that he was a real guy dying to please them.

Maybe out in the world it was different. Sometimes he could hardly wait to shake this town. There were advantages to being an orphan, advantages Ralphie didn't have. You might be alone but you were free. And he intended to stay that way. Hoda would get over him if he simply stayed away. He didn't like to hurt anybody; he couldn't help it if she was nuts about him, but he wished she'd stop sending those crazy messages the guys kept passing on to him. He had always dreamed that somebody would be crazy about him someday, but not someone like her, for crying out loud, not that way, not in clean love, though he had a good feeling for her still, remembering how relaxed and open he had felt when he used to lie so close up against her on the narrow mattress, and talk. She'd given him his money's worth, and a lot more. It wasn't his fault if he didn't want all the rest she offered. Why should he want to come and have supper with her and her dad, like she was always asking him to do? He didn't want to hurt her feelings but there were at least a hundred and one other things he could think of he'd rather do in his spare time. It disturbed him, though, to realize that she kept asking because she must like him a lot, and he couldn't feel the same kind of liking for her. Why couldn't there be an open-feeling leak between people, so that when you liked someone a lot your feeling would be caught by them, like a germ, and they would have to feel it back? And the same if they liked you, though he couldn't make himself feel enthusiastic about catching Hoda's love germ, no matter how fair an exchange it might be. They'd look so silly, the two of them together the way she seemed to want it, like maybe even going to the movies together and being seen by someone he knew, and maybe she would even insist on clinging to his arm! Not that he cared; he could go around with anyone he damn well pleased. What did they know about her anyway, or the things she had told him about her family? Crazy things, some of them, all about graveyards and stuff, but they hadn't seen her cry as he had that time when she told him about how her mother died; it was embarrassing, she had looked like such a great big fat little girl all of a sudden and Pipick had felt pain in his chest just looking at her face gone young and hearing her voice cracking its knuckles painfully. He had been so strongly tempted then to tell her what he'd never told anyone before, how the one he had loved as his mother had died too, so horribly, and left him alone. But he hadn't said it. He was afraid he might cry too, and he didn't want her to see how hard it could make him want to cry, still.

But it would look silly if he started going around with her; it would, that's all. The guys would really enjoy it. It griped them that he held out for the privacy of the occasional solo trip nowadays and bowed out of the gang banging, even that time Gordie offered to stand treat. Stripped of the showing off and pretence that was mandatory in front of the other boys, the truth was that he liked paying court to girls, and it didn't matter that his reputed score far outstripped his actual success, just as his reputed size outstripped what was necessary for efficiency and possibly even comfort. He just liked fooling around with girls, that's all.

The boys were not slow to pass on to Hoda the stories of David's feats as a young gallant. When she heard of her favourite's success, and the alacrity with which he took advantage of whatever opportunities presented themselves to him, for the boys found it paid to please her, and often brought highly embellished accounts, Hoda was inclined to suspect that he must be the true son of her old friend Hymie the millionaire after all, who had also known how to befriend opportunity. She could not refrain from passing back, through his friends, snippets of good advice to her son, like that for heaven's sake he should always test his safes, and not get any poor kid into trouble, and that the minute he noticed any-thing funny he should go to the Outpatients and Venereal at the City Hall and have himself seen to for free, and be sure to tell the girl to do so too, if he knew which one it was, and stay away from her till she did.

She found out other things about him from the boys too, tag ends of information that she cherished and spent hours speculating over, his aristocratic habits for instance, delicacies of behaviour that she could not credit to Hymie, say, or Morgan, whom she had also suspected of being the boy's father, after David confessed to her how he had stolen his own money in order to be able to come to her. Hadn't Morgan stolen from his father too? Was stealing from your guardian something a kid inherited? But no, it seemed to her that Morgan had disappeared much too long before the child was born. From whom had he inherited those really nice impulses? She was inclined to credit her own side of the family with these fastidious traits, particularly Daddy, and Mamma had been very gentle and refined too, even though she had had to climb on walls to earn a living. Yes, the boy was decidedly like her family. He had a nice nature, that was for sure, though her own effective contact with it turned out to be all too brief.

Against the disappointment of her hopes of a healing, three-way friendship, she allowed herself to set at least the relief from her physical ordeal, when he stopped coming. She contented herself with fishing for news of him, and trimming each item to fit her growing catalogue of his virtues. See, he had worked the whole summer as a Newsie's helper on the moonlight train to the beach. That showed he wasn't lazy. Generous he definitely was, even according to Ralphie, and quick to squander his money on chips and hot dogs and ice cream cones for his girl friends, of whom he had an enviable number, enough, at any rate, to have dulled his taste for professionals, one of whom, and Ralphie was not above teasing her rather maliciously, had managed to scare him off by going serious on him and nearly ruining his reputation.

Hoda accepted the rebuke with unwonted docility, and determined to withdraw even further into the shadows. Ralphie too came much less frequently now that he had entered the University, and had begun to devote himself to emancipating the college girls from the miserable restrictions of their bourgeois backgrounds. Ralphie described his educational campaigns, and the gratitude of his converts, with characteristic fervour. He also let her know that he had introduced their mutual old friend, young master Mandarin Won Lon Kok to some of his college girl friends, and the young prince had proved himself as fascinating to older women as ever. Though she listened to Ralphie's boasts with the qualifying ear of long experience, she was secretly delighted to hear that her son was moving in educated circles. She was not foolish enough to imagine that educated women were magically different from any other; yet she began to cherish the hope that contact with women of parts, whether carnal or otherwise, might stimulate in him the desire for higher education. It was pleasant to dream along these lines, and to plot how she might manage, unknown to himself, to help further his long and expensive course of studies, in medicine perhaps. It would be ideal for David to become a doctor because then Daddy could become his patient, and he could take care of Daddy's bronchial attacks, and they could get to know each other, and he would become fond of Daddy, and eventually they would all three become good friends, though she wouldn't even expect to mix in the kind of circles where he would spend most of his time. Perhaps she might even manage to steer him on to becoming Uncle's doctor, and taking care of his strokes, if Uncle could hold out long enough. For not long after Auntie Gusia had dropped dead suddenly, Uncle had begun to have those strokes that people said came from trying to hold in his temper now that she wasn't there to yell at any more. Hoda and Daddy went regularly to the nursing home where Uncle's kids had finally sent him, an elegant institution on the other side of town. Here Uncle was a pioneer, the first and thus far only Jew enrolled in the home for rich, elderly and decrepit gentiles. Uncle's kids were much too high-class to send their father to the Jewish Home for the Aged. Unfortunately, Uncle's strokes had completely wiped out the English language from his mind, with the exception of a few coarse expressions, which he used freely and indiscriminately during his better moments now, to express to all about him his loneliness and his rage. But more often, when Hoda and Danile were there, he wept, and once or twice he begged them pathetically to take him home.

Though Hoda was spoiling to give her rich cousins a piece of her mind, she never managed to encounter any of them during her visits to the nursing home. She thought of phoning them up, but she was afraid, the way she felt, she'd antagonize them so much, they'd end up telling the gentiles not to let her and Daddy visit any more. The rich can do such things. So she and Daddy came as often as they could and Daddy sat and held Uncle's hand, and Hoda dreamed of a son who would pass a healing hand over Uncle's fuddled brain and bring him back at least to die where he belonged.

For quite a time now she had been putting aside every cent she could in a yellow cocoa tin on which she had printed the label "Medicine" and which she kept on top of her dresser. When the box was filled she took a walk to the bank and had the coins changed for paper money, and tucked the bills away at the back of the middle drawer of her dresser, in an old chocolate box with a picture of a gypsy with a rose hanging from her mouth on its cover, souvenir of a gift that a customer had brought her once, in a fit of drunken gallantry. On the white inner floor of the box she had printed large, "BIG MEDICINE," a designation which elicited anew a chuckle every time she opened the box to tuck in another bill and glanced underneath the little pile. It was summer again, and though she knew she had a long way still to save, the little pile had already thickened comfortingly, when she heard of the big blow-up which abruptly ended her dream career as a fairy godmother. And even then she heard only by accident, so determined had she become not to make a nuisance of herself by pursuing her enquiries into David's daily life and annoying him as she had done previously.

This summer, once Daddy had managed to catch his breath at last, Hoda insisted on a new regime. Every afternoon she took him to the park to sit in the sun and dry out his lungs in preparation for the winter to come. She had of late become very interested in medical things and had realized for the first time that if you really thought about it, a lot of medicine was just sheer common sense. She brought along a huge picnic lunch, and she and Daddy sat and sunned themselves, and then Hoda searched among the trash bins and the bushes and usually found enough empty soft drink bottles to take across to the grocery and cash them in and get a couple of fresh cold drinks to help the food go down.

On the way back with the drinks one day she happened to run into Gordie the Fortz. Eagerly, she spread herself across the path in front of him, though it was obvious from the way he kept glancing around so uneasily that he was not happy to be detained thus publicly by Hoda. Hoda didn't want to make him uncomfortable; she had nothing against him. She had heard from Ralphie months ago all about Gordie's good luck in finding himself a sweet and loving little girl he was crazy about, who was not only pretty, but blessed as well with a chronic catarrhal condition which had also affected her hearing somewhat, so that neither hearing nor smelling his effluvia, she could the more unconditionally adore him. Hoda certainly did not want to disturb a romance so clearly arranged in heaven, but so much time had passed, by then, since she had seen or heard of her David, or of Ralphie for that matter, that she couldn't help detaining the good natured Gordie to ask hopefully after the rest of the gang.

Gordie was in the grip of that tender euphoria in which even the most apparently earthly clod apprehends, perhaps for the first and last time in his life, that he is fit for a far more rarefied sphere than that which he normally inhabits. He was like a coarse, vigorous flower at precisely that moment in the morning before it has been called on to weather the rigours it was created for, of wilting sun and blazing light, and hiss of rains that will nevertheless never manage to wash away the heavy dust which will have tattooed itself irremoveably deep into its petals by late afternoon. There it stands, sun-drawn petals uplifted, deceptively delicate in the morning light, that bloom which will spend all the week of its life asserting grimily, 'I am I,' still instinct now with another intuition, *I am not only I.' Love had awakened in Gordie a hitherto dormant, now vibrant respect for all womanhood, and his present embarrassment with Hoda was at least partly due to the fact that even she, though she represented only the very crudest aspect of the function of the female divine, even she shared some of the glow. He'd given up whores, as far as he knew, forever. And now he was reluctant to discuss, even with her, in any detail, the affairs of his friends who were still involved in such crudities.

Hoda was not unused to the prudery of young boys in love, having been more than once suddenly forbidden to utter, from her profaning lips, even the name of a newly beloved one, though it had hitherto been bandied about quite casually. But once Gordie, not realizing that what was already past history to him was shocking news to her, had spoken of Ralphie's trouble and David's flight, she would not allow him to pass, but stood there, not much taller than he was, but towering, somehow, blocking the path, leaning toward him imploringly, wheedling in her resonant, husky voice, "What do you mean he pissed off? When did he piss off? Where did he go? How come I never heard? What kind of trouble?"

Perhaps Gordie recognized, through the haze of his own preoccupation, that a species of love was operative here too. Certainly he realized that he would not get by until she was satisfied. So he told her how it all began when Ralphie went and blew that exam. Ralphie the genius committed the one unforgivable error, and brought sin and evil into his daddy's world. He embarrassed his old man by not bringing home all the prizes in the pot for once in his whole life, and all of a sudden his father knew there was a sinful, evil influence at work somewhere, somebody BAD, and somehow, before long, he knew his name was David.

"David? Sinful? What do you mean, sinful? What do you mean, evil?" roared Hoda so suddenly and stridently that she startled even herself, and so alarmed Gordie that he made a nervous movement toward her, ducking his head as though he were going to try to sneak through under her armpit and run away. All he needed was his Fanny should come running. But

Hoda grabbed him by the arm as he tried to shrug his way past her. "What about David, I mean?" she asked in gentler tones, wheedlingly. "What did he do? Why did he have to run away? What's all this sinful evil crap? Come on. I just hate to see a nice kid like that get into trouble. They're always picking on orphans."

"He scrammed, that's all. Nobody knows why, exactly. He just took off. The funny thing is, he never actually had much to do with the operation. You know how he was kind of a snob about that kind of thing. I don't blame him now so much, though he used to get on a guy's nerves sometimes. He just liked to hunt by himself, like, sweep them away on his charger; it was easy for him, with that big lance he's got. You ought to know."

"Yeh yeh," said Hoda. "So what happened? Why should he take off before school's over? He did all right in school."

"Oh sure, lucky stiff, I could never get exempted from my finals."

"Exempted?" crowed Hoda. "I never knew he was exempted. So what they got against him? They don't like it when an orphan kid turns out to be smarter than them, eh?"

"I told you, Ralphie flunked an exam, see?"

"Sure, now I get it, the Director's son. And that don't look so good, so what do you do about it? You kick the poor orphan in the arse, that's what you do you capitalist bastards!" Hoda was yelling now. She had Gordie by the sleeve and she was shaking him to and fro. "That's what happened, eh? And all you guys just stand around and let them do it. That's what always happens. The workers just stand around and let each other get beat up."

"Naw Hoda, hey come on, let go! Hey come on lay off! Listen, you want me to tell you or don't you?" With difficulty,

Gordie struggled free of her grip. "Nobody got beat up. I wasn't even there. What's eating you, Hoda? I told you, Ralphie flunked an exam, see? No scholarships for Ralphie for the first time since they invented scholarships. So his old man wants to know why? And he takes a good close look at Ralphie's marks and he sees that Ralphie may have flunked only one, but he's been slipping all the way down the line. So his daddy wants to know WHY? So Ralphie tries to double lip him that it's all his extra curricular activities. He's a Big Time Operator on campus. They can hardly carry on the college without him. You know how Ralphie talks. It's just he's too kind and good and responsible when they need him, so he works side by side with the Chancellor and the Senate, and the result is he neglects his studies and ends up in this terrible horrible disgrace. For the first time in his life he has flunked a subject. A thousand thousand apologies. Henceforth Ralphie will work, Ralphie will sweat, Ralphie will raise himself up again to be Number One Genius on campus."

"Yeh yeh," Hoda interrupted impatiently. "I know Ralphie. So what happened to David?"

"It's all tied up," complained Gordie. What was she pumping him for, and yelling at him, and making him keep his Fanny waiting, if she didn't even want to listen? "For the first time in his life Ralphie didn't manage to con his old man. Don't ask me how come. Maybe he lost his nerve. Ralphie isn't used to flunking exams. Me, if I didn't think my pa was going to like my report card, I used to sign it myself. He's got enough troubles. But Ralphie never flunked before. The old man started digging, and he found out that Ralphie and a couple of the other guys had set themselves up a little apartment downtown, with a built-in housekeeper. Well, you know the guys. And they're sharing everything co-op. They're a syndicate, see?

And any other guys who want to use what's handy have to pay cash on the line. The way it worked out, it cost the syndicate practically nothing; they got theirs for free, and when the operation really got going, they even started to show a profit.

"Pretty soon they're running parties and charging a house fee. I wouldn't bring my woman to that kind of party, but you know these college types. And Ralphie's the chief cashier. So that's where he's been all those late nights his dad thought he was studying with his friends."

"David," said Hoda sternly. "What about David?" And she shifted her weight and seemed to distribute herself more solidly across his path.

"Yah, well, the thing about David was that Ralphie talked him into lending the syndicate money a couple of times, like in the summer when he was working on the trains and had some ready cash, he loaned Ralphie some dough to help tide over the girl's rent till the operation got back into kick again. When old man Popoff started digging around, and he found out King David helped finance the operation, and then you know, he heard about his reputation, like how the guys called him Super-Crotch for a joke, and he realized how all this terrible horrible dirty stuff had been going on right under his snoot all this time, right away he decided that must be who was leading his boy astray. All the guys knew it was a lot of crap, but old man Popoff, he got some kind of whole posse worked up, and they were meeting and yelling how to save our fucking kids. Then, when the Prince peed off like he was saying 'I am the guilty one,' the old guys could relax and lean off, because now the evil influence was gone, see?"

Hoda saw.

"And then, when old Popoff discovered some stuff missing from his office too, that only David could have taken because it had to do with him, you couldn't convince him his runaway wasn't rotten through and through, and good riddance to bad rubbish, and that's what keeps him from running a perfect orphanage, orphans."

When it came to concrete details about the disappearance of the boy, Gordie had few. David has just taken off, that's all, disappeared, beat it, flit, scrammed, amscrayed. When Hoda raged about his interrupted schooling Gordie, who was not particularly interested in schooling himself, simply shrugged. But what of his plans to go to college? Gordie had never heard David talk of going to the university. As far as he knew the Prince had always planned to pull out of here one day. He had been hoping to get onto the transcontinentals as a newsie this summer. Davy'd always had his sights beyond the skyline.

Knowing Ralph, Hoda summoned patience and waited, but though he eventually did turn up and talked a good deal about his own misadventures, swearing ardently that no matter what happened, he would not ever make the mistake of flunking an exam again, he was, if anything, somewhat evasive when she questioned him about David, and when pressed, claimed that the kid had been planning to make tracks for a long time. Anyway, he'd probably turn up again someday when the heat was off.

Why don't I hate him? Hoda wondered, as she submitted numbly to this cocky little fellow who had so casually used and now dismissed his friend. *Because it would be a relief to hate him, instead,* she answered herself coldly. And anyway, what would be the point in driving Ralphie away, who might be her one thread of contact in the future, in case her son should return? But she knew, even though for a long time she left the chocolate box with its hopeful message and little cache of bills almost superstitiously alone, she knew with a great weariness of spirit, as she had known from that moment when she stood, hot and sweaty in the midsummer sunlight, facing Gordie the Fortz unbelievingly on the cinder walk of the park, and heard him blurt out that her David had run away, and felt the chill from the two pop bottles that she held in her hand snake suddenly up her arm and into her heart, that she had lost him forever.

David had no such grim feelings about his departure or the events which had brought it about. Oh he was sore all right, because it was all wrong. One minute he was everybody's best buddy, and then all of a sudden he was the wrongie of all the ages. But he was not, deep down, profoundly surprised. He had been quick to sense the point at which old Popoff's rage and offended pride were beginning to crystallize around him. Once it began to happen it went on happening, and it was no use just standing around and wondering over and over again, *why me for crying out loud?* Somehow, he didn't know exactly how, and he didn't want to think too much about it, Popoff had found out all kinds of things about him, though what they had to do with the fact that Ralphie had flunked his exam he wasn't even going to try to figure out. There was the old guy gone berserk, knocking on all the doors in the district, yelling for all the parents of all the girls to lock up their daughters against the wicked schoolboy seducer in their midst. Worse than that even, he was leading the innocent sons of Orphanage Directors astray. And somehow Ralphie wasn't managing to make things clearer to his dad. It was while he was trying to figure out how he was supposed to act till it all blew over that the little envelopes, emptied so long ago that he had almost forgotten about them, had come to David's mind. Rooting about as he was doing now, old Popoff would not fail to uncover his one area of genuine guilt. He was a thief; well, a burglar anyway. Who knew what the old man would make of that discovery? One thing was sure, he was not going to wait around to find out.

What if they sent out an alarm? What if they pursued him? Capture the evil schoolboy! Bring him back in chains! Lock him up! Bring him out on public display twice a day and let the world examine his fabulous genitals. The rise and fall of Super-Crotch. Hanging on underneath, while the train roared along, holding tight for his life for mile after mile of grit-eyed cinder mouthful, while the noisy stinky metal worm to whose belly he clung zoomed him along an endless, rushing tunnel of wood corrugated steel gutline, there was plenty of time, if not to think, for random thoughts to chug their endless train through his head. Worm within worm within worm, worming along. In the long hours and days he was to spend hugging the boxcars above and below, or huddling within, he let his thoughts, undirected, exhaust their interest in the life he had escaped. Afterwards, reborn again, the first of many times, into the world, he carried with him only one faint regret, that he hadn't said goodbye to Tizey or to Mr. Limprig. He wished he'd thought of leaving Tizey a note at least. He did not, after all, want her, too, to think of him as an ungrateful lout. He promised himself to write them both just as soon as the heat was off and he had some good news for them.

But in those first aimless years the definitive good news never quite arrived. Should he say, "I am sitting here in the park doing nothing; there is nothing to do?" Or should he say, "You will be happy to know that I sit every day in the public library and read until they send us away at closing time. It is warm in here." Or should he write, "Spring. It's time to move on. Maybe if I head West again . . ."

Later on, when he was overseas, it seemed foolish to write at such a time, though sometimes he longed to reach out to someone. But it would be like asking someone to worry about you, to let them know after all this time that you were a soldier, and fighting, and perhaps afraid. After all, what did he have to say to them, even now? Time and distance having put them into perspective, he could allow himself to doubt, without feeling much pain anymore, whether they had ever greatly cared. The fact that he himself cared, a little, had little to do with them. Someday, perhaps, when the war was over, he would return. He would satisfy their curiosity, however mild, to see him a grown man. And he would try to find his bearings, one last time, in a childhood which, concrete enough in its details, remained disturbingly unsubstantial in its essence. It was not that he had much hope of discovering who he was at this late stage; rather, that he had left without in some way affirming who he was. It seemed to him that even if he returned simply to say goodbye it would be an affirmation of his existence as a self-created person. Yes, some day he would return to say goodbye. If he lived so long.

THIRTEEN

Hoda kept the home fires burning. Business was good, but the fervour with which she threw open her vital commodity to the boys in khaki and the boys in blue transcended mere cupidity. Here at last was the larger struggle, the just cause in the interests of which a person was entitled, nay, required to cast self aside. Here was a use even for that great, hollow space inside of her that other people thought was packed so tight with guts and grease and mindless chuckle. Hoda became the regimental drum, and the lonely, frightened, cocky young fellows, with small amounts of money to spend, usually for the first time in their lives, found their way unerringly, when they were in need of particular comfort, from their dreary barracks to the welcome of the tumbledown hutch of Mamma Hoda, as she had come to be known. Good old Mamma Hoda. All night long they banged, and all night long she boomed, the large resonance of her response warming and reassuring them wonderfully, and reconciling her briefly to her own emptiness.

"Bundle for Britain," she cheered her clients on. "Fornicate for freedom," she invited one and all. "Let my end justify your means," she counselled, though she felt a little guilty about using that last one; she had heard ends and means discussed so seriously and often by the comrades and Mr. Polonick, rest in peace. But there was a war on, and the boys had to get some fun out of life, didn't they, before we sent them off "to feed the guns" as Mr. Polonick used to say? "It's all in your point of view," she advised. "Don't think how I lower your morals; think how I raise your morale. An army travels on its stomach, all right," she quipped indefatigably. "And here's a stomach that can testify for the air force too," she would affirm, slapping her great pot.

She had always enjoyed fooling around with sayings and slogans; you could camouflage enormous distances with words. In fact, if you fooled around with them long enough, you got so you couldn't believe a thing they said. And actions, too, could fool you into thinking they had more meaning than they ever could have. In the enthusiasm, for instance, of the early months of her war effort, Hoda even nourished the peculiar notion that no one she had ever held in her arms was going to die of this war. No one, she was determined; everyone who had ever lain in her arms belonged in her circle of safety. And to keep its magic tight she would not except even the bastards who'd made fun of her afterwards. That was democracy. The sons of bitches got away every time. But what did it matter, as long as the ones who counted could benefit? Perhaps it would turn out that she had done her boy some good after all; perhaps she had unknowingly rendered him safe, wherever he was now. But her private wish circle did not retain its magic for long. The boys who were sent overseas began to die, and the news of their dying cut great gaps in her ring of hope. Not for the first time, she was forced to jettison a wishful expectation. It always surprised her anew afterwards that she could ever have been so dumb as to hope to impose her desires, no matter how strong, or how right, on a life that paid no attention.

All right, so she couldn't help what life did, but she could still stick by her own principles, couldn't she? And she would, too, as long as she knew what her principles happened to be on any particular occasion. When it came to big Dick she knew all right what her principles were, Polack or Ukrainian or whatever he was, that much she knew, even though he personally maybe didn't mean any harm, and even though no one else had ever proposed to her before and no one else would, probably, ever again. Still, she was so sure of her principles with him that she even lost her temper over it. Not that he wasn't a nice enough guy, as guys went, as far as she knew him that is, and she knew one end of him pretty well, since he had been coming, as he himself reminded her, "long time."

Long time or no, he sure didn't know anything about what she was like if he thought he could come tromping in, through all the blood of all the Jews that all the Germans and Poles and Ukrainians and Rumanians and Hungarians and Lats and Lits and louts all over the world were spilling, and ask her, just like that, to marry him.

"What do you mean get married?" Coming, as it did, just prior to the consummation of a long-established ritual, Hoda, supine on her mattress, did not understand at first that she was finally receiving the proposal of marriage about which she had long since ceased to dream.

Kneeling in his socks beside her, not with any premeditated romantic intention, but because that was the point he happened to have reached before he could bring himself to express what was on his mind, the bashful Pole repeated his proposal. "We get married, I go war, you get allowance. After, we buy house, maybe; maybe you buy house," he amended, with melancholy respect for fate.

"Married!" In spite of her feeling of outrage Hoda did not fail to notice that he wasn't thinking sensibly of gaining a draft exemption, but, like the big dumb banana he was, only of that little bit of extra allowance that his wife would be warming while he was in the trenches. She didn't like at all the idea of these nice healthy young boys and men going out into all that killing, and she couldn't blame them even when they chose to be zombies. She certainly wasn't one of those who refused to comfort the zombies who hesitated to sign on for overseas duty. And she could even understand those who panicked at the idea of the uniform altogether. At the same time she felt strongly that somebody had to fight this war; somebody had to stop the Hun and make him run, or we would all be lost utterly. It was just so complicated, a person didn't know how to reconcile all her feelings. Perhaps that was why she was touched and exasperated by big Dick too, even at the same time as she was mad as hell.

"Is that what you're going to fight for? So you can save enough money for a measly house? What are you, a mercenary or something? Is that all this war means to you?" she demanded truculently. "Is that why you want a wife?"

Big Dick explained as well as he knew how; "Is war. We marry. I go."

"Is war you go. Is kill you go. Is slaughter Jews you go. This side, that side, whatever side you're standing on, you go. Over there you'd be telling your whore of a wife to save your allowance while you go kill Jews and over here you think you can tell me to save your allowance too. It's all one to you. Well let me tell you something, it's not all one to me! What do you know about getting married? You think that just because we lie around here f-f-for crying out loud, that's not married! First you have to be a human being, and some things you do and some you don't do! And if you're going to kill me off over there you're sure as hell not going to marry me here!"

Dick could not quite make out what had sprung her ire. He knew that Hoda had sometimes rather a touchy temper, but they had always got on well, and he could not understand what he had said to start her yelling this way. "I don't care you Jewish," he assured her gallantly. "We like. I come many times."

"You don't care if I'm Jewish. You hear that? He doesn't care I'm Jewish! What do I care if you care if I'm Jewish? I care, you hear? It's whether I care that counts. Big favour he does me, he don't care. Big deal we like each other. So what? So what's that got to do with it? Like! Like! So you like, big thing, thank you very much! And what if I don't give a damn if you like me or not? What if I don't want to be your big favour, the one you like, your goody goody Jewgirl while you're hating and killing all the others? And if not you," Hoda swept aside his gesture of protest, "someone just like you. Don't tell me no! If we were over there you'd be just like the rest, so if I can't trust you there I'm not going to trust you here either, that's for sure. Go marry him yet! Sure, marry him! No sirree mister, you can be sure of that! With me your relationship is going to be strictly platonic!" Hoda threw herself back on the mattress from which she had risen in the ardour of her rage, and flung her legs apart. Fiercely, she squinted upwards, her mouth set, silently daring him to reopen the subject.

Dashed, not having quite comprehended her hail of words, but understanding, as he could not fail to do, that he had been emphatically rebuffed, her lover, humbled, risked only a sigh as he prepared to settle for that part of her which was not rejecting him. How did a man get a woman to like him well enough? Nor was his perplexity eased when Hoda, once her fit of temper had passed, aware that acceptable or no, for better or worse, she had actually at last received a proposal of marriage, and no one could now take away from her this technical victory in the history of her life, took pains, in spite of her unreasonable feeling of disappointment, to be exceptionally kind to him. Not that she intended her subsequent kindness to be taken as encouragement for him to try again, no, certainly not, nor did he misinterpret it so, which just went to show that it was a good thing she had rejected him so summarily in the first place, since obviously he didn't like her well enough to try again. Whether he ever found a woman to share his allowance and buy his house before he went over, as Mr. Polonick used to say, "to feed the cannon," Hoda was never to know, but though he had meant little enough to her, she was not soon to forget him, nor easily to shake off a certain melancholy of remembrance, over the high cost of principles, perhaps, or perhaps simply over the fragility of romance.

Later on, though, she was glad that she hadn't made the terrible mistake that so many other girls had made, of rushing off impetuously and getting married to some unsuitable stranger. She could have ruined her life entirely. Yes, she was glad afterwards that she had waited and done her bit and kept her nose clean. Oh sure, she had had to wait a good long time, but in the end it was worth it, wasn't it? And there was plenty to do during those years of waiting. Nor did she stint of herself. Sometimes she was tired, or wasn't feeling too well, and really would rather have rested a few hours. "This old war horse is going to need either a new mattress or a new spine soon," she joked with the boys. And the boys swore, each time, that court martial or no, the next time, the very next time, they would dare the danger of getting shot at dawn to snitch her a new mattress from stores. Oh the ride she promised them then! But though the question was often joked about in barracks, and some of her regulars actually had some half-arsed intentions, somehow they never got quite drunk enough, and the liberation for active duty of Hoda's top priority mattress remained among the uncommitted heroic actions of the war at home. Still she carried on, and no matter how tired or out of sorts, when her old buddy Limpy Letz sent along a message, for instance, that he had organized a little party, just a small stag with modest stakes and a little bit of booze, she never failed to reply that she was ready to help the boys relax, no matter what time the game broke up, win or lose. And win or lose, Limpy's treat, she sweetened the end of the evening for them.

It was this initially loose arrangement with Limpy, as a matter of fact, that grew finally into a relationship which, by the end of the war, had entirely changed the focus of her career. When he expanded his premises by taking over the storefront which had operated as a cover for his backroom operation, Limpy at long last began to approximate, in a small way, the prosperity of which he and Hymie the lucky bastard, and Hoda too, had dreamed in those early years. But it was not because of sentiment or nostalgia that Hoda, before long, was securely installed as the sweetheart of Limpy's delicatessen and kibitzarnia. She was useful. Her great girth bedizened in spangles, her hearty laugh booming out, she nightly strutted and shook, now and then executing a dance step to take someone's mind off a bad hand, here and there patting a head encouragingly, queening it over the tables, setting the right tone for easy spending and demonstrating capabilities altogether more complex than those which she had hitherto had the opportunity to exercise in the course of her career. More and more Limpy grew to rely on her. Almost without realizing it at first, she began, less and less, to rely on the old means of earning her income. On mornings when there were no funerals to go to she still rolled out of bed pretty late, but afternoons now found her generally in the delicatessen, and if she happened to have stayed late at the cemetery on funeral days, though he thought she was nuts, it never worried Limpy, because he knew that on those days, when she did come in, she'd make it up to him by relieving him a little later on at the cash, or by serving at the tables or behind the counter, if necessary, when the girl wanted to get off early, or even, by getting down on her hands and knees and giving the place a good scrub down.

Often Hoda brought Daddy along, and Danile enjoyed himself, sitting and chatting to the old men who played chess in the back room during the afternoons, or else simply drinking tea and waiting in one of the rear booths till she came to join him when things were slack. Limpy didn't mind having Danile around. "With your pa here I don't need a little bell on the door up front," he used to say in his wisecracking way. That was because Danile's hearing was still so acute. When the street door opened Danile always raised his head hopefully and called out "hello," just as he used to do when Hoda's clients came to the house, and woe to them if they didn't reply politely. Even now, in the delicatessen or the kibitzarnia, when somebody walked in and Daddy said "hello" in his bright way, and the person didn't answer, if Hoda was around she would call out, "My father said hello." She seldom had to repeat "My father said hello," more than twice, before even the least friendly disposed stranger felt somehow compelled to grunt an "hello" in reply.

On the whole, however, in these days of the common cause and everyone all pulling together, there were few unfriendly people around the place, especially not with Hoda there to cheer everyone up. And she was pretty nearly always there. Sometimes she didn't even go home for supper, but would fix a snack for herself and Daddy in the delicatessen, and carry right on getting things ready during the slack period after supper. But usually she'd take Daddy home and give him real food, and then return to work again later in the evening when things were already beginning to get going in the kibitzarnia. Originally she had presided only on weekend nights, but as business boomed, pretty soon she and Limpy were wrangling, in a good-natured way, about when she was going to have at least one night off in the week, because she didn't want, not at first anyway, to give up her freelance business entirely. Eventually, however, it was Hoda who persuaded Limpy that it would pay them to keep those two young chippies on call on a commission basis, because her own time was really becoming more and more valuable at the management end.

Even the simple gestures of living seemed to flow more smoothly now that she had moved up into administration. True, everybody complained of rationing and of shortages, and Hoda complained patriotically, like everybody else, though most of the things that were short she was getting more of than she'd ever been able to afford in her whole life before, thanks to Limpy's connections. She complained more out of sympathy than out of need, because it was good for morale to let people complain a bit, and even to complain with them, because you were all pulling together, until you remembered how little you really had to complain about, any of you, compared to those poor people overseas, and felt ashamed, and re-dedicated yourselves together to the greater cause. Complaining cleared all kinds of impurities out of your system and left you fresh, and all the better disposed to work your arse off in your particular branch of the war effort, especially if Limpy's connections in the black market could dress you suitably for the job.

"That's show biz," as Hoda got into the habit of saying to the two young chippies when she reminisced with them and gave them pointers on how to get ahead in the entertainment world as she had done. She reasoned, not entirely inaccurately, that they could not help but be impressed. With the blessing of Limpy, who hoped thereby to counteract what he called her morbid streak, which threatened sometimes to spread out beyond those peculiar practices to which she had thus far kept it confined, she allowed herself to indulge a late-blossoming urge to elegance. Though new clothing materials were almost non-existent nowadays, she was nevertheless able to blaze forth in dresses which for sheer yardage and swoopage and colour once moved Limpy to leap from his chair and cry out as she swept, all adazzle, into the back room, "Gentlemen, here come the Northern Lights! All of them!" And the whole room burst into a spontaneous ovation, like fans did for movie stars or radio comedians or royalty. Hoda, good sport that she was, acknowledged their greetings with a deep flourishing curtsy, which set her bracelets and bangles a-tinkling, and brought Limpy hobbling hastily forward lest she should be unable to heave herself aright again, and all the stars of the northern lights come tumbling and crashing down right here in the otherwise dimlit room and hold up the game. But Hoda, for all her clumsy-looking weight, had remained agile, and the upward sweep of her right hand as she completed her elaborate respect caught Limpy a fair friendly chop in the kisser, and sent him staggering back to a fresh gust of applause from the assembled guests. That Hoda!

At first Limpy's wife had complained when she heard he'd taken the notorious whore into the business. "All right," he'd said. "I'll kick her out. You don't want my business to embarrass you in front of your friends, fair enough. So you want to come and be my hostess instead? Sure, come and we'll put a bangle on your business and let you shake it for the boys so your business can embarrass me in front of my friends for a change. Come on, I'll pay you just like I pay her. I told you, to run a classy game I need a hostess who knows the ropes. The money I bring home, that doesn't embarrass you before your friends, does it? No, sure not! If you think you can bring the guys in and keep them coming like Hoda, you're welcome any time you like to come and try."

It was a genuine fact. That Hoda had the makings of a first-rate business woman. Too bad she was also a little nuts in the head, but that was all right. If you knew how, and Limpy had long years of experience, you could handle her. Mind you, you couldn't tell her anything, not that one. Just you watch out, for instance, if she got the idea you were trying to interfere in her life! So you just had to let it go, whatever she did, just turn a blind eye, like her old man. If she wanted to come by the store early in the morning, sometimes two, three mornings a week, all soberly dressed, like a potato sack just rolled in off the farm, to tell him she might be a little late in to work that afternoon, all right, let her go, let her be late. Who knew what possessed her that she couldn't let a funeral go by without running to take part? The same Hoda who would later on be laughing and kibitzing the night away, to get hold of her in the morning, first you had to find out who died lately, and where was the funeral being held. Like the time he'd lost his keys and couldn't open up the business, so he chased all the way down to her place and she was gone already! Where to? Old Danile didn't know, only that she'd be gone for a good couple of hours. In that case Limpy could take an educated guess. If she didn't tell her old man, it was something unpleasant. When an old acquaintance or crony of Danile's grew ill or died nowadays, Hoda tried to keep it from his as long as possible, answering with soothing evasions when Danile chanced to ask. Limpy thought she was being stupid to try to hide these things from the old man. In the first place he was bound to hear sometime. In the synagogue or at the grocery or wherever, people did mention the dead sometimes; they didn't just disappear like stones in water, did they? And anyway, it was the facts of life. Sure, maybe it would upset him, because it happened so often to people he knew; he was an old guy already, naturally people he knew were dying off. But you couldn't fool him it wasn't happening, could you? At least if he knew, he knew. What does a guy feel like, especially an old blind guy like that, when people keep on disappearing, voices he knows just fade out, and no one wants to tell him what's happening to them, only the world gets emptier and emptier of people he can name. What did Hoda think, he didn't feel creepy about it sometimes? But go talk to Hoda, like talking to the wall, only with her you had to be careful. The wall could fall on you.

Sure enough, he'd been right in his guess about where she was that time. He had had to ride all the way out to hell and gone where the graveyard was, at the end of the streetcar line, and to drag his feet through the gumbo field, weaving between gravestones to try to get some protection against the miserable wind, sinking ankle-deep every step, with mud suck sucking under him, and finally there she was, turning damp, reproachful eyes on him because he was cursing at an internment. Not that anyone else could hear, but you get Hoda at a funeral and you'd think she was the rabbi's other wife. Why the hell shouldn't he curse blue? She didn't even have the bloody key with her. Said she never brought her bag when she knew she'd be going to the eulogy in the synagogue; she just took her carfare and her handkerchiefs in her pocket. Her bag was at home, keys and all! That Hoda! She was irritated with him too yet, for taking her away from the funeral before it was time to throw her handful of earth. What a character!

Time was when she had danced at every wedding. Limpy could still remember those days. Now she followed the funerals. What gets into a person? It was true they didn't have weddings nowadays like they used to have, but there had been no spectacular improvement in funerals as far as he could see, and for Limpy's money, a second-class wedding was still better than a first-class funeral, even in these decadent days. But Hoda went her own way. Somehow, wherever and whenever a funeral was to be held, she got wind of it, and came and hung around in the yard, or sometimes even came right into the house and mingled with the other mourners, and marched with them after the coffin, and boldly asked from car to car for a lift out to the graveyard, and usually got one, eventually, from someone who still knew it was a sin to refuse.

Nor did she maintain a decent silence, always, but sometimes she bawled and sobbed the entire route, and was so clearly moved by this death as to put even the next of kin to shame. Her presence caused a certain amount of irritation and even embarrassment at times. Particularly when the corpse was male, and Hoda happened to let herself slip too fervently into the swing of mourning, people would begin to wonder, and considerate friends of the bereaved, happening to notice her among the mourners, often went to a good deal of trouble to manoeuvre the widow about so that she should not become aware of Hoda's ambiguous presence. But Hoda's interest in most of the funerals she attended was not, strictly speaking, a personal one. Sometimes, in the midst of her tears, she would turn to ask an adjacent mourner, "Who was it?" As often as not, if she didn't happen to know who had died, she even forgot to disturb the purity of her mourning by asking, and weeks later, in her wanderings about the graveyard, might stop to read the little note on a comparatively freshly turned plot and be surprised that someone else she had known or heard of was also gone.

There was really no mystery about her passion for funerals, as she would gladly have explained to people if they had bothered to ask her, instead of making snide remarks. She came to funerals because she was drawn to funerals, had been drawn to them ever since that day when she had followed, with a few remaining comrades, the sparse funeral cortege of Mr. Polonick. Some of the comrades were by this time away in the army, "feeding the cannons," as Mr. Polonick, bless him, used to say, and some were in detention camps, put away with the rotten Nazis by the dumb government, as they probably would have put Mr. Polonick away too, if he hadn't been by this time such a sick, guttering firebrand that even the enemies of the working classes knew they couldn't harm him further. It was a lonely and abstracted group which followed the funeral wagon and stood by the graveside. There was not even a cantor there, since Mr. Polonick had not believed in all that, though Hoda, remembering Uncle's prosperous funeral (oh, her cousins knew how to treat the old man once he was dead), felt that it might have been nice to hear at least a cantor's voice bidding Mr. Polonick farewell on such a lovely spring day. As it was, all she heard through the glum silence of the comrades was the muffled slurp of her own sobs, and the low murmur of Daddy's prayers, which she was sure Mr. Polonick wouldn't mind, even though he wouldn't agree with them. She tried not to cry too loudly because Mr. Polonick would have recoiled from a noisy mourning. "Weep for the living," he would have said rather snappishly, towards the end.

But I want to weep for you, Mr. Polonick. Still, it was hard to do anything right. Even from her grief she was distracted by the sudden whirr of prairie birds shooting upwards beyond the graveyard fence. Mr. Polonick might not have minded that interruption in concentration, old school-teacher that he was, but it was with the idea of perhaps achieving a more perfect moment of grief in this pleasant place that Hoda decided to let the comrades take Daddy home when they left, and stayed on a while in the graveyard by herself. Alone, she wandered from grave to grave, stopping at Mamma's, stopping at Uncle's. Standing there, trying to conjure up the dead, she remembered all kinds of things, old sorrows and old grievances, and old pleasures too, strands of her unravelled self inextricably intertwined in the strands of those dead selves, and the way she thought of them now, yearning them back into existence, it hardly seemed as if there was any difference between old pleasure and old sorrow, so perfect were the proportions of grief and pleasure in the embalming fluid of her nostalgia.

Not that she really believed that Mamma, or Uncle for that matter, or anyone else was present any more in the grave-yard. She wasn't foolish enough to think of them as presences and try to take comfort from the thought. No, if anything it was the overwhelming sense of their absence that the sweet-smelling spring morning and the whirr and tree-lee of birds, and the skew stones that pinned down the graves and were themselves being slowly sucked down, and the gentle, vital desolation of the graveyard brought acutely alive for her. It was easy, wandering among the gravestones, to weep, and realizing that here she was licensed to weep aloud, she wept louder, and finding herself alone and free she wailed and let herself go entirely and mourned and keened, and her voice mingled with the spring rustling and returned pleasantly to her ears and she was comforted and found pleasure in her mourning, so much so that when another funeral party arrived and she heard the cantor's voice echoing with melodious melancholy across the fields, and approaching, heard the harsh, discordant counterpoint of grief, she was moved by a feeling that this at least was something which she understood, and gave way to some generous, companionable impulse of grief and stood and wept with these people too.

Whose business was it? Sometimes people made nasty comments to her that they ought to be ashamed of making, especially at times like these, when to insult a mourner is to insult the dead. Since when did you need an invitation to go to a funeral? Since when was death such an exclusive affair? If, after Mr. Polonick's passing, she kept on going to funerals it was not the business of the living to complain. What did they know about how she felt? Even Limpy, who kidded her sometimes about what he called her morbid streak, what did he know about how she felt and the things she thought about? When he wanted her all dressed up and playing hotcha momma she was there with bells on for him, wasn't she? His business didn't suffer because of what she did in her own time. When it came to what everyone else thought was so important, like having the good taste to be able to get dressed up with such style that she knocked their eyes out, she had proved she could do that all right, hadn't she, just as long as she had the moolah for some under-the-counter stuff? All right, so let them leave her alone. What could they know about that feeling she had, of fatness growing around her soul, or what-ever you called that thing that watched and squirmed and seemed to be gasping for breath inside of her? All right, so maybe it was morbid, for all she knew. She didn't like being teased about it because she wasn't sure herself why she went, and sometimes was even a little ashamed because she enjoyed herself when she was there, especially when the other mourn-ers had left and she wandered about alone. Even in the winter, when the snow banked up so high it covered many of the gravestones, and the wind blew straight down from the north pole across the trough in the world in which she stood, and every breath made rime, she stayed on when she could have got lifts home, and afterwards had to tramp, half frozen, to the streetcar stop. Morbid? How could she explain to Limpy that what she sought and sometimes found out there was the feeling of her own aliveness, an in-spite-of-herself, accountable aliveness that the spangled dresses and the black market chocolate bars and the plaudits of her admirers and the knowl-edge that she was a woman of taste and sophistication and something of a success in the world at last had not, somehow, been able to make her feel.

Anyway, how the hell should she know why she did it? Because she wanted to, that was why, and she often thought how nice it would be to bring food, like sandwiches along sometimes, and find a nice place to sit, and just sit there and look and breathe and smell and eat and eat and eat. The fresh air did that to you. But she didn't bring food, not because she feared her mourning would be rendered less genuine because she got hungry after awhile and ate, nor because she was par-ticularly worried about what people would say if they knew she brought lunches along to their funerals, but because if she started making picnics of these visits she'd feel badly about not bringing Daddy along, and Daddy was at an age when she didn't want to remind him too often of the eternal fields, though they had meant so much in his life. So she waited till she got home to eat, and was usually so ravenous by that time that she simply gobbled whatever she could find because she was in a hurry to get off to work.

As for what people thought, let them think. As long as they let her alone what difference did it make to her if they thought she was crazy? What difference did it make even if she was crazy, as she had sometimes thought she must be? Here she was and she was like she was and it was not for them to bear it but for her. Anyway, what did people know? If there was one thing that Hoda had learned it was that if people didn't want to be pleased you couldn't please them, no matter how hard you tried, so you might just as well please yourself. Who would have expected some dame to come running up to you when you were standing there quietly, waiting for them to bring the coffin out of the house, and to start yelling at you, "You're here already? Who invited you? Whenever you die, she's there! You're not to come to my funeral, you hear? I forbid you to come to my funeral! Don't you dare show your face at my grave!"

It was embarrassing to be yelled at that way when you were just standing around quietly and reverently, like everyone else. Hoda's first impulse was to retort with sass, "All right, you don't want my company? Tell me when you're popping off and I won't come." But she didn't, of course, not at a time like this, and not to such a madwoman, rude though she might be. Hoda had respect. So she offered instead, placatingly, out of her embarrassment, "All right. You can come to mine if you like." You'd think the woman would quiet down at that, but no, instead of being a little ashamed of herself in the face of such good manners, and showing a little respect too, she went on yelling about the way Hoda was smiling at her; what right did she have to smile? and on and on about how she didn't want a woman like Hoda at her grave.

Hoda did her best, by smiling apologetically and shrugging her shoulders helplessly and rolling her eyes and making doleful little compassionate gestures, to indicate to the other mourners, who were beginning to mutter restively at this breach of the funereal tone, that she couldn't help it and that the other woman was obviously a little crazed with grief or something, but it was not the time for protestations and remonstrations, and finally, to silence her critic, Hoda allowed herself to be driven off a way, with the result that she didn't get a lift when the party moved off, and had to follow on foot till she reached a point where she could catch a streetcar.

That was why even if she had known more precisely the kind of thing that people said about her graveyard habits she wouldn't have given a damn; no, she would have gone on letting people think what they damn well pleased, which they did, of course, just as they had all along, adding to all the other anecdotes and myths and rumours that had from time to time circulated about the fallen woman, the story that she had even been seen emerging from the gentile cemetery which stood adjacent to the Hebrew field, a circumstance which encouraged the suspicion in some that she mourned the goyem too. That shouldn't surprise anyone; she had never been noted for discrimination in the distribution of her favours before, had she?

By the simple persistence of being, however, Hoda had earned for herself on the whole a large tolerance over the years, and people merely said after awhile, "Oh well, that Hoda," as if to say, "Oh well, what can you expect?" Every now and then it's true somebody felt the need to cut her down a little, because she appeared to be getting too much enjoyment out of life or out of death, and it seemed unfair, but usually, when her name was mentioned, it was because a funny or a scandalous story or rumour had come into circulation, which in turn reminded many a solid citizen of other such stories, some personally experienced, and by now invested with that special glamour of distance which makes an acceptable anecdote even of the once inadmissible truths of the past, and reveals the present somehow anaemic by contrast. If you told one story about Hoda someone was bound to try to top it. It was by this time her fate to have been part, even if only fragmentarily, of the past of such a great segment of the community that she was something of a vested memory, as much to those who would not admit to having had any personal contact as to those who boasted innumerable encounters, and every story, new or old, in which she distinguished herself by being somehow still unrepentantly out of pitch with the rest of humanity was as welcome as the fragile daily illusion that nothing is really changing.

But Hoda knew that things did change, that they had changed a good deal for her by the time the war was ended. One of the positive results of her partnership with Limpy was the fact that she no longer had to hustle and take on all comers. She, too, could afford the luxury of choice; in fact she could afford to give the smashed and pulpy old mattress a rest for as long as she liked. For a while, out of patriotism, and in order to show her contempt for the snobbery of rank, she continued to entertain the armed forces, but made a big display of her preference for the enlisted men over their officers. However, partly because she realized, eventually, that both officers and enlisted men were inclined, given the chance, to prefer the two young chippies to her own ampler and more seasoned charms, Hoda, a little ruefully, though not very, withdrew to a small circle of more mature admirers, with one or the other of whom she could now relax without even bothering, sometimes, to charge him for it afterwards.

In some ways the years had been very kind to her. As she explained to those who tried to compliment her, other women got disgustingly fat as they grew older, and never knew how to carry their weight properly, while she who had always been disgustingly fat had learned through the years to wear her weight with distinction. She took a none too secret delight in hearing people say things like, "Why Hoda, you haven't changed at all! Hoda, how do you do it? You look as young as ever!" But she didn't fool herself. "Still the same old fat slob!" she would counter, dusting a sequin and shimmying her hips. She knew. By the time the war had ended, in the increasingly solitary leisure of her nights, she had had time to take notice of the working of time in her. Finding herself in the season of the little blue veins she was sometimes afraid, but would not allow herself to remain for long intimidated.

So what? "Big deal, so I ain't what I used to be, thank God! So what else is new?" Not that she wouldn't have been equally ready to defend what she used to be, if challenged. Though she still wept, in secret, over the particulars of her life, she scorned to repudiate the configuration of her existence. "All right," she used to say, "so I'm not the Duchess of Windsor." She did not begrudge her former rival." "She's got good taste in clothes too," she admitted; "maybe a little on the quiet side, but she doesn't have so much territory to cover, so she doesn't have to use her imagination so much." She nurtured no illusions about the royal couple, and had indeed lost interest in them to the extent that she didn't even think about her old idol and his wife unless they thrust themselves on her attention by appearing in the newspapers or illustrated magazines. At such times she felt about him very much as she felt about herself when she remembered all that had once seemed possible. And yet perhaps it wasn't true the way his life looked to her. How could one tell? Perhaps it only appeared as though he wandered now from comfortable nowhere to comfortable nowhere else, in search of comfortable nothing any more. What difference did it make?

"Listen, I'll tell you," she used to say, during the latter period of her kibitzarnia days, when Limpy or some of the others got to talking about how they'd like to be in the beds at least, if not in the boots of royalty; "they got their troubles; I got mine. And you know something else? I wouldn't change places with her if you paid me." About that she was definite. Oh she wished them no ill, but for all that she had once been infatuated with His Royal Highness, and had followed his progress, and had been frankly disappointed, but didn't hold it against him; on the contrary, was willing to encourage them and offer them moral support with the best will in the world; still, they shed no light.

"I hope they're happy," she always added, punctiliously, after expressing the gravest doubts. She felt her words, however, to be a false piety even as she spoke them, because she didn't even know what they meant. What was this "happy" anyway? She doubted if she'd know how to recognize it if she ever got an attack of it. And if she did identify it, what then? From what you heard it was so delicate you'd have to spend the rest of your life pampering it. Cough or sneeze or fart the wrong way and you blew it right out the window. "I've gone to bed to nurse my happiness." Sure, since when could someone like Hoda afford to keep that kind of pet in bed with her? At least pleasure paid on the line as it came. What good was happiness to humans anyway, if it couldn't stand their company for long? Maybe it really was different for royalty, though, with the kind of training they got. They took very small bites and blew very small farts, and when the time came they could beckon happiness before all the world, and dare boast that they could keep it happy forever, too. Well, good luck to them. People like Hoda needed something tougher to help sustain her kind of life. Happiness was for ageing ex-princes, and maybe for anyone else who could afford to match the trade-in value of an old empire in so-so condition. She did not dare, she was too superstitious to come outright to the conclusion that she could do without happiness, though she had managed thus far somehow, for fear that its poor relation, the less sensitive and far more familiar, unhappiness would rush in to fill the void that her admission might create. But she did admit to herself that she found the themes both of royalty and of happiness a bore.

For herself, at least she knew when she was well off, and she knew the species of numbness or contentment that comes with knowing yourself to be well off at last. Even her obsessions now had coats of fat on them, so that they no longer screamed raw-edged along her nerves, and though she scanned eagerly the faces of the young men as they returned from the war, and some she questioned with particular warmth, she no longer suffered with the old acuteness the disappointment of her expectations. She even wondered now whether there would be any point in meeting her David again. She would like to know that he had survived the war, if indeed he had fought in it, and if she could help him she would of course like to do that too. But if, as she hoped, he had survived the war and didn't directly need any help, it might be just as well for him if she were not tempted by any meeting to reach out towards him once more. For with the passage of the years and the blurring of old emotions, prohibitions that had once seemed absolute had lost something of their negative force, and she allowed herself occasionally the self-indulgence of a fantasy in which she revealed the truth to a young man of the world on whom, at twenty-three, it could not possibly have the shattering effect it might have had on him at fifteen. At twenty-three, looking back, he might be able to understand that she had all along been trying to help him. That was why perhaps it would be best if she never had the opportunity to see him again, though she could not quite bring herself to wish it, because it was such an awful thing for a mother to wish about her own son. And yet, if she were never to see her son again she would not be tempted by this need to confess and seek his approval, which in some partly defined way she knew was also the desire to shift something of the burden of knowledge from her own shoulders to his. To wish strongly either way was potentially disturbing, so she allowed herself to drift along without consciously committing herself to any wish at all. She had never been so well off; she was making a nice living; she still had her daddy, thank God, though he was a little uncertain in his memory nowadays, and didn't even always tell his own stories accurately any more, but they were together, and they were beholden to no one.

Live and let live. Hoda no longer nursed futile dreams. She had learned to cherish her freedom. Just because she was nice to that immigrant didn't mean he had a visa to settle in her life.

"I need to get married like I need a hole in the head," she told Lazar the mocky the first time he proposed to her. True, it wasn't a reply to his proposal; she would not have answered so rudely had she been paying attention to what he was saying. It was late, the smudge end of night. She had been working since mid-afternoon; she was tired and would have preferred to go straight to sleep, but that would not have been nice, since the D.P. had played since early evening, and a rotten player he was too, and had dropped a heavy packet, and had waited for her, and had even helped her straighten things out a bit after everyone went home. She had tried before, once or twice, to steer him to the young chippies, with whom she had guaranteed him a good time, and even promised if he didn't have one she'd make it up to him herself afterwards. But for some reason he was shy of the youngsters, maybe because of his scars, or maybe because they weren't members of our tribe and he wouldn't touch them after what their kind had done to him during the war. That wouldn't have surprised her, though not many deepees she'd run across felt that way. Mostly they just wanted to forget it. But she didn't. Hoda wasn't going to forget it and she wasn't going to let anyone else forget it either. Sons of bitches. The dumb government was bringing them into the country, too. Creeps. Creepy Germans, didn't even walk like people, strutting in a row down Main Street, cold blue eyes throwing chills. Fooey; she almost wished she were still in her hustling days, so she could tell them where to stick it; in a grinder, that's where. What bothered her was that she was afraid of them. It wasn't like getting sore and yelling it out with someone to and fro and that was that. They went on wanting to hurt you. They actually did awful things to people. They meant it for real. Someone ought to give them a taste of their own medicine. But who? To do that you had to be like them, and who wanted to be like that? Fooey to them. Fooey. You had to grow up to be a middle-aged woman practically to find out there really are bogeymen after all. That made it harder to be mean to someone who was a deepee, maybe from a concentration camp, and a good customer, who dropped a lot of dough at the tables. Like everybody said, these deepees did all right once they got over here, but Hoda didn't grudge them any prosperity, like some people did. They deserved a little luck, and a little fun too, even though you were dead beat and had thigh burn so bad you could hardly walk, and all you wanted to do was get home and drop in your cot and snore. What the hell, what right did she have to complain? What was she doing during the war while he was over these losing his wife and his family and everything?

Usually she understood him well enough, but it was so hard, when she was tired, to concentrate on what he was saying. She thought he was just asking her why she never got married, like guys did sometimes; not that they cared, really, just for conversation or curiosity or something. She had her answer pat. "I am married; I'm a part-time wife to the whole damn world!" she would reply, and steer them into something that was more like their own goddam business. The trouble was her Yiddish was getting a little rusty and she didn't understand Lazar's accent very well, especially when she wasn't paying much attention. She didn't want to seem to brush off his question, him being a mocky and all, so she didn't tell him that about being a part-time wife. She just laughed indulgently and threw out the comment, "I need to get married like I need a hole in the head," as if to imply, "I never wanted to, that's why."

Normally, she enjoyed it when Lazar walked her home, as he had been doing regularly of late. Tonight, however, she had actually hoped that he wouldn't wait around for her. It wasn't simply tiredness; that didn't prevent her from taking pleasure in the odorous Indian summer darkness, and in hanging onto the man's arm, and listening or not particularly listening to his low voice muttering the Yiddish words that he pronounced so oddly and she imitated so well to Daddy's amusement afterwards. It wasn't the fact that she had an early funeral tomorrow, either. That happened often enough, and would not normally have interfered with her enjoyment of the crisp balminess of the night and the crunch of leaves underfoot. How should she have known when she gave way this morning to the temptation to take a long walk like she used to, because it was such a lovely day, and had walked all the way back to town from the cemetery, that she would have to be alert to receive a proposal of marriage late in the night, even though her thigh burn was killing her? It would have been all right; she was used to thigh burn, but she didn't spend so much time off her feet nowadays as before. In fact she'd been on her feet almost without a break since she got to work that afternoon. All day she'd spent on her feet in the busy delicatessen, and half the night on her feet in the kib-itzarnia. Rub-rub kiss-kiss chafe-chafe rasp-rasp burn-burn glue-glue her thighs. Towards the end of the night's work it had got so bad, though she never let on because you have to keep the show on the road, that she had kept imagining the pleasure it would be to be able to waddle home alone, walking with her legs spread as far apart as she could, and the cool air fanning up her raw flesh deliciously. Oh well. At least maybe he wouldn't notice the odd way she leaned rather heavily against him occasionally, while trying, surreptitiously, to shake one leg loose of the other and fan it in the air. Perhaps, however, it was these extra little apparently affec-tionate pressures from her which stimulated him to make his proposal at this particular moment. At any rate, quiet man though he was, there was a streak of irritability in him, and he very quickly made it clear that he did not appreciate her facetious reply to his proposal of marriage.

What could she say? Now was not the time to talk about thigh burn, even in her own defence. Hoda apologized. She had misheard. She had misunderstood. It was his accent. Instinctively she seized the one factor which she could turn to playfully aggressive use in extricating herself from the embarrassment of giving him cause to accuse her of not knowing the proper spirit with which to reply to a proposal of marriage, particularly from a man like him, who had suffered enough to deserve being treated with the kind of respect he didn't often get from the slobs around the kibitzarnia. "How do you expect me to know what you're saying in Galician?" she wailed. "You call that Yiddish? I'd understand you better in Chinese or Scandihoovian!" She embroidered it extravagantly, hanging tightly onto his arm to emphasize the friendly nature of her teasing, and refraining from fanning her leg out.

He was not one to dwell on his grievance, but allowed himself to be quickly mollified, and returned, encouraged, to the question in hand. It was the reality of this question which Hoda had been trying to assimilate even as she coaxed him back into temper. Almost with panic she heard it reiterated, and found herself biting back the hysterical impulse to reply once more: "I need to get married like I need a hole in the head!"

"What do you need me for?" she blurted instead. "I mean," she added lamely, "you know what I am. I mean," she amended quickly, "I'm not ashamed of what I am, but I don't want anybody trying to tell me afterwards that he took me off the streets and made a mentch of me. I live my life and I know what I'm doing and I'm doing all right." Somehow, now it was Hoda who was upset and aggrieved, and Lazar doing his best to soothe her. She didn't know how she had got onto the subject but suddenly she found herself bawling him out for being such a rotten poker player. She didn't much like playing herself, but she had been around the sharks long enough to know that you couldn't be as indifferent and absent-minded about your game as this one was unless you didn't mind laying your hard-earned eggs in other people's pockets. Hadn't he lost enough in his lifetime?

But he had a one-track mind, and he somehow managed to bring everything she said back to his subject. Now it turned out he didn't even care for poker in the first place. He had come to the kibitzarnia originally because he was a stranger and alone, and he was not of an age to be drawn to dancehalls. It wasn't easy to find friends. In a place like Limpy's, as long as you were willing to spend a few dollars you could find temporary friends and company for an evening. What else did he have to do with his few dollars? Gradually, he had found one or two people from his own home district in the old country, had picked up an acquaintance here and there, but still he was drawn to Limpy's. If he still threw out his money now it was Hoda's fault. She was the only reason he came.

"My fault. My fault. Now everything's my fault. Everything's always my fault!" She couldn't help laughing a little, nervously, though she tried to put the usual vehemence into her voice, and now she fanned her leg out quite boldly, with an added little jerk. So what if he noticed? But he paid no attention, just gave her arm firm support for a man who was so thin and reedy. Well, he was a gentleman, that was obvious. "What do you mean, my fault?" She challenged him to spell it out. "What business is it of mine if you come or not?" But she continued quickly, lest he accept the challenge. "And anyway, even if you want to come, do you have to throw your money away?" If he didn't really like gambling why should he have had to go to such lengths just to find a little human company in the first place? After all he'd been through? Shame, while the rest of them had sat on their fat in this very selfsame kibitzarnia throughout the war, he had been living through whatever he had been living through. Actually, she didn't know exactly what he had lived through, only that he had lost his wife and children, and that he was relieved that first time when she was not visibly repelled by his scars. Hell, expect an old pro like herself to show what she felt about things like that, after what she'd seen in her lifetime? What could she feel, after all this time, except a spasm of pity, "Oh God, something else," when yet another revealed to her his private source of anguish and shame. Sometimes they were indeed horrible deformities of the human vessel, and only her overwhelming awareness of suffering and need had prevented her repulsion. But the strange thing was, so often they were such little things, such minor cracks and chips and variations in the human design on which her clients concentrated as much unhappiness as did the real possessors of the grossest deformities. In the minutest flaw men divined perfection withheld, and saw themselves cast down. At first Hoda had tried to point out to them that they weren't nearly as badly off as she was. Look how fat she was and she'd been that way all her life and she couldn't help it, and people laughing at her, and them being poor, and her mother dying, and her daddy being blind; but that was not what they wanted. They knew all that, and they didn't come to hear her troubles. So she had gradually learned never to draw attention while she was paying attention, never to demand comfort while she was giving comfort. And from the early pain of realization that nobody really wanted to know her, had grown her pride that nobody did know her, not really, not who she was, underneath, not nearly as well as she knew them, even though they talked about her and laughed at her and looked down on her. She wouldn't give them away, either. She didn't have to live off their weaknesses. If they wanted to do it to her, well okay, it had always been good publicity for her business, and she had even played up to it sometimes, on purpose, doing and saying things she knew they would use against her, that really had nothing to do with what she was like inside at all. There had been times when she had wanted desperately for some particular person to cross over her no man's land, to give her some sign that he would like to come closer, so that she could draw him to her heart. But it never led to anything in the end, though the guy was always glad to get it for free, and besides it was always bad for business when word got round she was playing favourites. Her old steadies resented it; well, they made cracks.

That's the way it had been, and by now, that's the way she liked it. Who did these refugees think they were, coming in and thinking they could take over wherever they felt like it? What kind of man was he anyway? He wouldn't have taken her for his first wife, she could bet on that. He probably figured that now he was all beaten and scarred up nobody else would have him. What made him think she was going to take everybody's chewed up leftovers? Maybe she'd been a whore all her life but it was a free country and in this country even whores could have standards, when it came to actually getting married.

"If you like, I'll quit gambling altogether," he offered.

What awful things she'd been thinking! It was like feeling he wasn't good enough for her just because he was a deepee and had suffered and lost everything. Where did she get off looking down on him? For all the sympathy she thought she had for everyone, did she even know, after all these months of friendship, what had happened to him, except in the vaguest way? "It's not what I like," she assured him firmly. "It's what's right. Why should you have to play if you don't like to play, just for the privilege of sitting with human beings once in a while?" On the other hand what kind of man was he if he didn't even confide in the woman he wanted to marry? What did she really know about him?

"I can't just come and sit," said Lazar. "It's a business. Limpy's got to make a living. You've got to make a living. If I came and just sat, after a while Limpy would say, 'What's this? A deepee shnorrer I don't need sitting around here, taking up a chair where a customer could be laying eggs.'"

A deepee shnorrer! How did he know? "If I want a friend of mine to just come and sit Limpy won't say a word against it, you can take it from me!" She was so irate she nearly woke up the block. A bird gave a startled peep from a nearby tree, and Hoda went on somewhat more softly. "If you want company you come up to the joint any time you feel like it, and I'll answer for it. Limpy and everyone else will treat you all right, like a real friend." It was simply appalling that someone had to go to such lengths to relieve his loneliness, that he had sat for night after night with people whom he thought would call him a deepee shnorrer. "And it's not up to Limpy to tell you where to lay your eggs either," she added firmly.

"I'll lay my eggs wherever you like," he assured her.

Hoda giggled involuntarily into the tart night air. She hadn't noticed before that he had such a good sense of humour.

"But if I come," he persisted, "and I don't play I won't be able to walk you home if somebody else happens to lose heavy or happens to ask you. And it's the only reason I'd come, so what's the use?"

"Don't worry," she replied, touched more than she dared acknowledge. "You can walk me home."

"But I don't want anyone else around when I walk you home," said Lazar.

The sly mocky! "There you are, you see? Are you trying to make a nice girl of me already?" she challenged with quick truculence.

He was silent. She glanced round at him with unexpected fear. He was walking with lowered head. "Anyway, who said anything about anyone else?" She tried to laugh out of a suddenly tight throat.

Lazar did not reply, but he did not reject the extra pressure that she put tentatively on his arm, and allowed himself to smile into the darkness.

He was a gentleman all right. He didn't just come and sit. He made himself useful. Sometimes he took over someone's hand briefly, and showed himself to be a better player in his caretaker role than when he had played simply and indifferently for himself. Sometimes he brought a bottle and treated the whole company, and sometimes he ordered sandwiches and drinks from the delicatessen for everyone there, at his own expense. Hoda had even, at times, to put a curb on his generosity. What the hell, why should he go and throw out his hard-earned cash for the benefit of every shnorrer who happened to come around? Oh they'd take all right; people would go on taking as long as you had an ounce of strength to go on giving. And if he was hanging around here just for her like he said, then she had some responsibility to make sure that nobody else took advantage of him. What was he after, anyway? Why did he have to keep hanging around? What did he want to keep on proposing for, when she kept on putting him off, night after night? Who did he think he was, Rudolph

Valentino? Get married. Get married. What did she know about getting married?

"That Galitzianer wants to marry me." She tried it out on Daddy one day, jokingly, just to hear the sound of it.

"When?" said Daddy, so quickly and eagerly that she was taken aback. "Have you decided when?"

"What do you mean, when?" she asked indignantly. "Do you even know who? The one with the Galitzianer accent you were talking to in the delicatessen." Danile was nodding eagerly to her words. "I didn't say I was going to marry him. I said he wants me to marry him. You want me to marry a Galitzianer?" She knew she was talking nonsense, talking loosely while she tried to recover from her astonishment that Daddy was so eager to have her marry, that at the first word, without knowing anything about the man he wanted to fix the date already. But she was mistaken, at least in part.

"Of course I know him," said Danile. "A fine man, an educated person, a man it's a pleasure to talk to. And what he's lived through, only our enemies should answer for. What that man has suffered!" Danile sighed heavily. "We should thank God for our rocks, and even our boulders are a blessing compared to the mountains that other men bear."

"You know him? How come you know him so well? How come you know about his mountains? How come you know what he's suffered?" She spoke not without a twinge of jealousy intermingled with her surprise. When she asked Lazar about his life during the war, he always put her off. The man wanted to marry her; surely she had a right to know something about him. He needn't worry about how she'd take it. She knew that over there people had had to do dreadful things in order to survive. "Another time." He always put her off. "Another time." All she got was proposals proposals till the very thought of walking home after work made her nervous. But Daddy knew. How come Daddy knew everything? What right did he have to go talking to her father behind her back? And Daddy to go on without even mentioning it, her own father; what right did Daddy have to help a stranger infiltrate her life? "Why didn't you tell me he talked to you about it?"

"I didn't want to interfere, Hodaleh,"said Danile gently. "If I said something you might think I was interfering. You know how angry you get sometimes. And you're right, after all; it is your life. That's what it means when we say that parents give their children life, isn't it? We give them life and we lead them a few steps along the way, and then they say to us, 'It's mine. You gave it to me. You can't control it any longer.' I learned to keep quiet a long time ago."

"Who said you'd be interfering?" said Hoda. "Since when don't I let you talk? Since when can't you tell me what you think? I'm still your daughter. It's your business too if I get married. You think I'd even think about getting married without talking it over with you? Didn't we always used to talk about when I would get married, and you would become a grandfather?" How long ago all those innocent plans had died. "Since when am I so hard to talk to? Since when do I get angry? Since when do I say you're interfering?" It was disturbing. It was all too disturbing. What right did Lazar have to come and stir up their peaceful lives? Danile sat still before the mounting crescendo of her questions, his eyes both vulnerable and impermeable, his face delicately immobile, his expression anxious and distant, the distance and anxiety somehow a function of what she was noticing for the first time, a new, a somehow incredible fragility. *Leave him alone,* she thought. What was the use of scolding him? All the same, what did he mean by it? How often in her whole life had she even raised her voice to her father? Was there anyone else she'd ever even cared about, so long and so constantly? " I didn't know I was so hard to get along with," she said with deliberately melancholy gentleness, knowing that he would have to reassure her, and wanting to be reassured.

"No, I never said hard to get along with," Danile hastened to respond. "If you were hard to get along with would I lie to him? Would I spend hours telling him just the opposite? What a sunny-natured little girl you were; how you were the smile in my heart, the sight in my eyes all through your childhood. Have I ever complained about you? Not even to myself, much less to anyone else. Remember how you used to trudge about all day to sell the baskets? So if you yelled a little bit sometimes, you think I minded? Didn't I know how bitter it was for you? I used to suggest, sometimes, that maybe all that company, and staying up so late at night, night after night, and some of them using coarse English words, not that they were bad youngsters, but still as a father I felt that maybe it wasn't good for you, wasn't good enough for you, not that I meant anything by it. But you used to yell at me then, Hodaleh, a little bit, sometimes, and go in your room, and I would hear you crying, and I would cry too. What could I do? If I drove them from the house maybe I would drive you with them. What was the use of upsetting you any more? You'd go your own way anyway and be even more unhappy. And what right did I have to complain? You were such a young child to be earning a living already; you didn't shirk from any kind of work; plucking chickens, climbing walls; if you wanted to enjoy yourself with your friends, how could I interfere? One thing that always used to upset your mother was to see young children staying out late at night without their parents even knowing where they were. So," Danile sighed, "you may have stayed up late and it may have been a little lively in the house, but at least most of the time you stayed near home. I explained it to him, how it was. He understands how hard things were in those days."

"What do you mean you explained? What did you have to explain to him? I don't owe him any explanations!" How uneasy Daddy's words made her. She was beginning to feel surrounded. Why was it that words never told you exactly what was being said? Why was it that sometimes all of a sudden you didn't want to know exactly what was being said? Why did your imagination always have to jump to imagine that maybe more was being said than the words were saying? Weren't the words themselves disturbing enough? It was a long time since Daddy had said things like this to her, if he had ever done so. It was a long time since they had talked this way at all. *I wouldn't marry you if you paid me!* That's what she'd snarl at Lazar if she had him here, the meddling mocky. She didn't remember any of that about having yelled at her father, or about him complaining about her friends and all that. Even if he had complained, she wouldn't have yelled at him, surely. She knew she'd been a loud-mouthed kid at times, but she didn't remember ever having yelled at Daddy. All she'd ever really thought about above everything else was how they could manage to stay together and she could manage to take care of him. Didn't he remember the great feud with Uncle? Maybe she had sometimes had yelling feelings in her voice; Daddy was very quick to catch feelings. It disturbed her to hear him say those things, though, hinting that all had not been the way she remembered, mentioning thoughts she didn't even know he'd had, implying the possibility of other perceptions, even, for some reason, appearing to be apologetic. Why should he be? Why wouldn't what you knew hold still? Even if Daddy's memory was faulty, if that was the way he was going to remember, what did it matter how things really were? And if his memory was not faulty, was hers? She had hardly as yet succeeded in holding her own memories to a formal pattern which would release a minimum of pain; how could she cope with new revelations from Daddy too? The minute you let yourself become too aware of another person's world you found yourself carrying that too, and if you appeared in that world, foreign to yourself and unattractive, how oppressively all the worlds weighed down on you. Oh what the hell, she'd only been a little kid then. Everybody yelled sometimes. Daddy didn't hold it against her. "You want me to get married, then?" she challenged.

"I want you to do what you want to do," said Danile.

"But you like him" she persisted. "Or is it just his story that you like?" She couldn't resist the little jeering thrust, and despised herself instantly for it.

But Danile seemed unaware of the sneer. "How can you like such a story? Ever since he told me, I've closed my eyes on it every night and opened them to it every morning. He has put pictures in my eyes and a stench in my nose, and cries in my ears that I cannot avoid, though I turn my head this way and that all day. Sometimes I have thought that the cruellest thing about being blind, is that you cannot close your eyes to what you see. Like it? If I could learn to bear it! And yet, I remind myself that he was plucked alive from all that dead flesh; out of all that pile of bodies he alone dragged himself free and crawled away from the charred pit. And when I remember the miracles of my own life I think how strange and wonderful it is that he should come to us." Danile was silent; his face reflected anew the old wonder.

"Pa!" she cried out, confronting him. "You want me to marry him, don't you?"

"No," said Danile. "I know some people think I'm a fool, and maybe I am, but I'm not such a fool as to try to tell you whom you should marry."

"But you want me to."

"I wasn't such a bargain either when they brought me to your mother."

She couldn't help it; she laughed. She laughed and laughed. Danile laughed too.

"Oh Papa!"

But that didn't mean that she intended to give in and marry the mocky. If they thought so they could forget it. If he wanted to hang around and bring her expensive presents and spend long hours with her dad even when she wasn't around, all right, she wasn't going to stop him. It was nice of him to keep her father company. He needn't think she didn't appreciate it. She went out of her way to invite him often to eat with them and to cook nice meals for him, just to show him she was grateful, and also because he was all alone in the world. It was only decent. Of course she didn't mind being courted; hell, what girl would? though he needn't imagine she hadn't been courted before. "I've been proposed to before," she made the occasion to let him know. She chose her words carefully. "The last time was not so long ago. I turned him down. Always turn them down when they get too serious." It was hard to gauge the effect of things like that on Lazar, though. He continued his proprietary hanging around, and naturally, since he was there, she gave him some thought, and since he kept on offering to marry her she gave a lot of thought to that, too, and to the kind of life he promised her. She was no gold-digger, but how could she help thinking about it? There it was, actually being offered to her, a husband, a home, a real life like everybody else had. All she had to do was nod her head and stretch out her hand.

Presto! And it would disappear. Well, no one need think that would surprise her. That hand she had stretched out, it was just getting ready to wave goodbye, that's all. Bye bye! As far as she was concerned, proposals notwithstanding, he was a free man, and she let him know she knew it. The same went for herself, though a subtle change in attitude toward her had taken place among her old friends and former customers lately. They had begun to act as though they thought she wasn't a free agent any more. True, she had had to turn them down a few times, because of her promise to Lazar that when he was there he would be the one to take her home. About that she was firm; she was a woman of her word. True also, he was always there. And then one night Limpy himself asked her, early on in the evening. God! She and Limpy hadn't romped on the mattress since she couldn't remember when. He swore his old lady was so jealous she weighed him when he left the house, and weighed him again when he came back in, to make sure he hadn't given any away. Not that he had that much to pass around any more! Only now his old lady was getting checked up in the hospital for a few days, and he figured he might never have the chance again.

Instead of taking him on gladly, as she naturally should have done for old time's sake, Hoda found herself making excuses, and wishing Lazar were already there to back her up in her explanation that she really did have a prior date. Limpy said he understood, though he didn't have to make such a big thing of how much he understood. Nor did he have to go and make a public joke of it, teasing her in front of the crowd. "Yeh, what's this, I notice you gone monogamous lately, Hoda?" She shouldn't have been, it was nobody's damn business anyway, but she was a little embarrassed, though she laughed it off. She didn't go on laughing, though, when hour after hour passed, and that night of all nights, for the first time in ages, her steady didn't turn up. She went on expecting him and expecting him, and still he didn't come. She could hardly hear what anybody was saying to her, her ears were straining so hard toward the door, and she kept giving herself excuses to slip outside and look up and down the street. She wasn't surprised. She wasn't surprised at all. This was it. She'd known it would happen all along. All that proposing. Sure, why not? Proposals are easy. Still, she found excuses to hang around the place when everybody had gone. She polished; she cleaned; she put away; a teapot slipped out of her hand and smashed, so she had to clean up the mess, didn't she? And once she was down there she might as well sponge out the floor. So what if the baby blue beaded satin dress got stained? It would have to get stained sometime. Nothing lasts forever; why should satin be any luckier?

By the time she let herself out of the kibitzarnia and set off for home she was in the foulest of tempers. Nor did the sight of Lazar, before she'd gone a block, hurrying along under the street lamps, do anything to modify her anger. If anything, the sight of its object fanned her to further fury, a fury the more frustrating because for once she didn't know how to express it, not until his first words of greeting, that is.

"You're late!" he made the mistake of calling out cheerfully, as he approached her.

That did it. Did she give it to him! And she couldn't have cared less if she had wakened the whole neighbourhood. She didn't give a good goddam who knew how she felt about being stood up and kept waiting and made a fool of in front of her old friends. Let dogs bark and windows go up and people poke their heads out. She would tell them something too if they started up with her, and the birds fussing up there, and the cats

462

flashing their startled green lights as they streaked across the street. Let them all know! He didn't have to explain! She didn't want him to explain! Standing her up was proof enough for her what she could expect from a big-talking mocky!

It was when she heard herself calling him a mocky, right out loud that way, that she began to cry. She didn't have to do that! That was a dirty thing to do! What right did she have to be yelling at him all over the street for anyway? He was here, wasn't he? She could have told him to go screw himself in a quiet, dignified way, couldn't she? And what was she crying for? He'd think she gave a damn! "I'm only crying because I called you names," she blubbered. "I'm sorry."

He murmured over her soothingly.

"But that's all I'm sorry about!" she growled. "It's not nice to call people names, even when they're sons of bitches." All of a sudden she was laughing. Then she was sniffing again. "At least you could have phoned to tell me you were going straight to my house. What do you mean keeping my father up so late anyway?" Then she was laughing again. "You're lucky I didn't bring Limpy home! He told me today I was going monogamous! You'll ruin my reputation." She couldn't help clowning it up a bit, now that she had had her little yell, and it was all just an accident how it had happened, with him being held up and then thinking it was too late to come to the kibitzarnia and going straight to her house, and then waiting and waiting and expecting her any minute, till long after she was normally through, and coming to see what had happened because he was worried. Worried! It was all very well for him to talk about being worried. Why did he keep on buttering up her father behind her back anyway? Lazar this, and Lazar that, it was all she heard from her old man nowadays, till she was sick of it!

"Why are you always talking to my father about me behind my back anyway?" Though the air had cleared somewhat she was not to be easily mollified.

"Because I want him to know that I think it's time you gave up the life you're leading and settled down," he snapped back now with unexpected asperity.

After a startled moment, she said, "You said that? What did he say?"

"He agreed," said Lazar quietly.

"What else did he say?"

"Nothing. What else is there to say?"

"Nothing," she repeated. "Nothing much. The life I'm leading. What do you know about the life I'm leading or the life I've led? What does he know, even? It makes me laugh, 'the life I'm leading!' Ha ha! Who's leading whom? A bear on a string, that's me. Give the string a jerk, smack my arse, I get up on my hind legs and dance a little, this way, that way, and show my big bare belly. And everybody looks and laughs. Only what's that got to do with being a bear? What do you want to talk about the life I'm leading for when you don't know a goddam thing about it?"

"I don't want to know anything about," said Lazar. "All I ask is that you do what I'm doing, forget the past and begin a new life together."

"That's easy to say," she said bitterly. "Sure, a new life. Who are you to be handing out new lives? You know what happened to the last guy went around offering new lives? They nailed him up!" Hoda laughed sourly. "And no wonder! Running down the local product. I don't want a new life! Why should I forget the past? I can't forget the past! I don't want to forget the past. It's me. Maybe you can just forget your past and everybody you cared for and cared for you, and how things were

464

and what happened and everything, but I can't. Maybe it's rotten and it's lousy but it's me, and I didn't want it should be rotten and lousy; I didn't want it should be the way it was; I didn't want it; I didn't want any of it but it's mine, and I've got to live with it and I've got to die with it, and you can't come along and make nothing of it, and tell me it's no good and I should forget it and bury it. Maybe I didn't want it and maybe I hate it but it's mine, and it's the only thing I've really got, inside of me, that's mine." She was weeping again now, quietly and bitterly, squeezing out that hot, scalding thing inside of her.

He was silent for a long time, silent while she wept, and he was right to be. What did he know? What did he know?

Finally he said, very quietly, "Should I have died then?"

"What do you mean?" she said, snuffling still over her private ache.

"Should I not have dragged myself out from under them? Should I not have crawled over them, clawing and grasping their jaws and their hair and their bullet-ridden flesh? Yes, my fingers sank into bloody holes, and I gripped and tore and pulled myself over them. Should I have remained with them in the pit until morning, when the others returned and poured the lye? Yes." Lazar laughed coldly. "They gave the lye to the whole of my life, wife, mother, children, village. I watched them the next morning from where I lay in the bushes, waiting for someone to notice my marks on the ground and track me down. I was lucky. They were too busy, and in a hurry to be through. And they hadn't brought the dogs back. Should I have died, Hodaleh? I often think so. What am I doing, alive? What can I do, alive? At first I didn't understand you people, and the names you gave us that I thought were in your foreign language; 'Maw-kee.' But finally I recognized the word; it was a word I knew very well, and I understood too why you called us 'Ma-kés,' curses, plagues, the cursed ones. Why had we clawed our way free to come and squat in imitation of life among you? You really want to cherish the past, Hodaleh? All right. Help me to bring my dead flowers to life from under a field of lye. But they are dead. And I left them. Yes, you were right in what you said before. That's what you can expect from a ma-kéh."

"But that's not what I meant. That's not what I was talking about! That's not what it means. It's not ma-kéh, it's mocky, mocky. It's just a name, a joke. I don't know what it means, maybe to mock, to make mock, to make fun of. It's not a nice expression. I didn't mean it."

"I don't mind," he said. "Make fun of the curses. If I were in your place I would do the same. When the time came I was just like everyone else. Flesh of my father, flesh of my sister, flesh of my whole world, I gripped them and I crawled over them and I can still feel the feel of them in my fingers and my elbows and my knees, and I have to remind myself, that's all that became of them, that's all my past amounts to, a horrid, jellied, fleshy consistency in the terrain over which I will crawl for the rest of my life. How can you remember what can never become the past? Help me, Hodaleh. I will not ask you to feel it or to share it. Just be with me."

He was crying! "I'm sorry, look, I'm sorry. Honest. I didn't know what you meant, honest. I didn't mean anything. I just meant about me, that's all, only not . . . I didn't understand, like . . . Let's forget it, like you say. We'll both just start with each other. I'll help you, honest I will, all I can. Look Lazar, it's so silly; two broken-down old crocks like us, rolling down the street in the middle of the night and leaking our insides out. I didn't mean that, about not forgetting the past, the way it sounded. All I meant was what happened, happened.

It's no use crying, I mean I won't cry if you won't cry. I didn't mean to blow off at you that way before, either. It's just the way the guys were teasing me at work, and you didn't even know about it, and you came waltzing along, so cheery beery beem. Listen, if we're supposed to be engaged, how come I haven't even got a ring? If you'd have slipped a ring on my finger I'd have probably said yes long ago! Then the guys would shut up, too."

It came out so easily she didn't have time to stop it. Well, so what? It was the least she could do after upsetting him that way. So she plunged right on. "At least I think we're supposed to be engaged, with all the proposals I've been getting, but so far a ring I haven't got. Proposals yes, but no little carats on the finger; sure, proposals are cheap." Why did he have to go and call her Hodaleh, just like Daddy did? It was her own fault. She had wanted to know what had happened to him and now she knew. Had she thought she would escape the responsibility of knowing?

"You'll have your ring," said Lazar quietly.

Now she had done it. Who gave a damn about his ring? Who needed his ring? He could have his watch back, too, for all she cared. They'd been doing all right, she and her daddy. What did she need the worry of another world in her life for? What did husbands do, anyway? They took care of things. Sure, how many husbands had she had crying into her boos about how they took care of everything.

"I changed my mind," she said. "I don't want a ring. We can't afford it if we're going to put a payment on a house, and I'd rather have a bedroom set first. For the master bedroom I want all white furniture with an antique gold effect." What was she babbling about? "If we can't afford the whole set all at once maybe we can get it on payments. Me and my ma we always had good credit. We always paid our debts, ask anyone. Or if not we can get it piece by piece, like I always used to do business." She laughed extravagantly at her own wit. Instant by instant her mood kept changing as she prattled on. One minute she was thinking, *so what does it matter, any of it? It's just a game, and I've picked up another hand to play.* What did it matter, win or lose? Almost simultaneously she wanted to send peal on peal of triumphant laughter trumpeting through the streets of the town. And then she was suddenly full of determination, and tenderness, and love? Is that what it was? Love? "I think I've got the makings of a good wife," she said. "You haven't even kissed me!" She nuzzled into him with elephantine coyness. What would it be like? Would she be able to please him? Would she be able to mediate between him and his dead? No wonder he had been so unsympathetic that time when she had finally confided to him how she felt about paying her last respects at people's funerals. "If you have to," he had said, so coldly. "But we will try to find pleasanter places to picnic in the time we have left." *I will help you, I will,* she vowed silently, fervently, and felt her spirit gathering itself up, her soul preparing to heave itself into the task.

Not until much later that night, it was really the next morning, and the first time in her entire career that she hadn't hustled her companion out before dawn – what the hell, they were engaged, weren't they? He might as well hang around so they could break it to Daddy together – did she feel it was safe enough to venture the question that had been at the back of her mind all night. "How did you get away from there in the end, the way you were wounded?"

"Oh well, I was wrong when I imagined that no one had noticed. One of the neighbouring peasants they had rounded up to pour the lye and cover the pit did notice the track I'd left. I didn't realize it at the time but he was very busy shuffling about while he worked, trying to cover up the traces. He came back later on that evening. I didn't know about it. When I woke up a few days later, they had me in the attic."

"And they looked after you? That was very fine of them!" she exclaimed. "There are some human beings!"

"Yes. He had it all figured out. He explained it to me. They're hard-headed, these peasants. He said that in the past he had often wished the devil would come and take all the Jews in the town. Well, the devil came along finally and did as he had been asked. But you had to be careful when you were dealing with the devil, especially if you were still a good Christian. So he was looking after me to prove that the devil couldn't do a perfect job, because only God is perfect, and he was of course on the side of God. The rest of the war he spent wishing the devil would do as good a job on the Germans as he had done on the Jews, as a man of God he himself would gladly do what he was doing for me if there happened to be a wounded German left over. You can't fathom these peasants sometimes, but he took risks. And his wife was good. At least, thank God, she never tried to explain herself."

"Was he trying to be funny? He knew that your whole life was in that pit," said Hoda. "Why couldn't he just shut up?"

"Perhaps that's why. You have to be very careful and impartial and hedge your position precisely when you're on God's side and still want to get some mileage out of the devil," Lazar explained dryly.

She had to laugh. That's what they were like. Crazy. All of them, the whole world. What more could you expect? What could you ever expect? Even themselves, what of them- selves, what were they to expect from one another? What did she expect from anyone at all any more? What would he

469

expect from her? That was the thing. Did he realize that this was all she was, this person? She took up a lot of space, and maybe he thought there was more to her than actually was there inside. Or did he care? Maybe he wouldn't even notice. She couldn't say that he had shown much interest in her inside so far. Look how he'd fallen asleep and left her to be entertained by the bubbles and wheezes and snorts of his breathing. Some company, when they'd only just got engaged, and she was lying there so bloody uncomfortable, half on the mattress, and half flowing over onto the floor, half asleep and yet unable to sleep, afraid to move though she itched and ached, lest she disturb him, and so tired she couldn't even think of what was worrying her. Whatever it was, it sure wasn't worrying him. Maybe he was too far gone to worry. She listened a moment, anxiously. He had managed to wedge himself with proprietary intimacy so that his breath fought its way noisily and ticklingly in snortings and whistlings and flubby purklings, in and out under the flop of her right breast. Could you be had up for manslaughter if a guy got asphyxiated under there? Silly. What could possibly come of this ridiculous idea of theirs of getting together? What could she possibly do for him? "Help me, Hodaleh!" He had said that. Sure. How? The answer came suddenly, brilliantly, on the back of the sleep bearing steed. *"I've got to remember this when I wake up,"* she thought joyously, and to make sure she would remember she repeated it to herself, the dazzling simplicity of it. You could solve any problem in your sleep. No wonder they always said to just sleep on it. If only a person could remember afterwards. She would remember, though. *"We'll get a wall-to-wall mattress,"* she would tell him first thing in the morning. He would be astonished at the brilliance of her solution. *"I'm glad I found you, Hodaleh,"* he would say humbly, *"I thought of it in my sleep,"* she would admit modestly. He would look at her with wonder. *"You have solved the problem of my life,"* he would say. *"Thank you for asking me,"* she would reply, and even in her sleep she could feel her eyes spilling over with grateful tears as she and small Danny stood watching the wreckers at work. She was astonished to see the inside of the orphanage for the first and last time as it was pulled apart, like a movie set. *"But I love here!"* she cried, weeping because Danile was dead and gone the gift of knowing, no matter what he didn't. *"Cherish your corpses!"* she cried out passionately to his name by her side. *"They give your life body."*

"Almost a real mother!" Lazar swam towards her. *"CONDOMS,"* she affirmed with energy. *"PRURIENCE,"* she held out her arms, a true bride. *"INCESTRY,"* she sobbed, as she reeled him in by his umbilicus. *"Sons!"* cried Danile. *"Lovers!"* she confessed, weeping extravagantly.

"Crackpot Hoda," she heard them laughing. *"Have respect,"* she cuffed the child who persisted at her side. Contrite, she tried to kiss him, grew frantic when she couldn't draw him near. "You're squashing me!" she wriggled madly to lift the cot off her back, and heard repeated, "You're squashing me, Hoda." Lazar struggled loose from her grip.

Hoda awoke, horribly embarrassed: "I'm sorry, I . . . never slept with anyone before." Hearing herself, she giggled, foolishly, but he was asleep again. Drifting off, she remembered miserably that she had dreamed her daddy dead, and dreamed a child with his name. *"I don't want you to die,"* she apologized to Daddy. *"He doesn't have to take your name."* Pregnant, she turned to Pipick firmly, *"I'm moving in."*

"Backwards," David explained eagerly to the class. *"She occupies her past; she inhabits her life."*

Hoda curtseyed deep, arose. With a magnanimous gesture she drew the magic circle around them, showing all she knew. Soon, she promised extravagantly, in the ardour of her vision, they would all be stirring the muddy waters in the brimming pot together.

AFTERWORD

BY MARGARET LAURENCE

Hoda, the protagonist of *Crackpot* – earthy, bawdy, wisecracking Hoda – is a prostitute. But Adele Wiseman's novel is no more a story simply about a whore than her first novel, *The Sacrifice,* in which the patriarchal Abraham finds himself killing a woman in an agonized parody of a sacrificial act, is a story about a murderer. *Crackpot,* like the earlier novel, takes us deeply into a whole complex world of personal and social relationships in which the tragic misunderstandings and distances between people are both pointed up and to a degree alleviated in a way that art can sometimes accomplish, by allowing us truly to see and feel the pain and the inter-connectedness of humankind, with our burden and necessity of ancestors and gods.

In a sense the novel's title expresses in one word the novel's themes, for, like all totally fitting and appropriate titles, it contains meanings and allusions which reverberate through the book. Crackpot is, at one level, Hoda herself, the idiomatic word referring to the neighbourhood's opinon of her, a view both humorous and cruel. By extension, it is also Hoda's father, Danile, whose wise innocence can be mistaken

473

by the clumsy-hearted for simple-mindedness. At another level, the title speaks of some of the underlying concepts and the life-view of the novel itself. The epigraph is this:

> He stored the Divine Light in a Vessel, but the Vessel, unable to contain the Holy Radiance, burst, and its shards, permeated with sparks of the Divine, scattered through the Universe.
>
> Ari: Kabbalistic legends of creation.

In an article in *Waves* (Vol. 3, No. 1), Kenneth Sherman pointed out that Ari was "Ashkenazi Reb Isaac, also known as Isaac Luria (1534–1572), a Jewish mystic born in Jerusalem who developed an extremely significant strain of Kabbalistic theosophy." Sherman went on to say, "In Luria's Kabbalistic work is his creation myth which is divided into three major experiences: *Tsimtsum* – the self-limitation or exile of God; *Shevirah* – the breaking of the vessels; *Tikkun* – harmonious correction and mending of the flaw." Without over-emphasizing the ways in which the novel reflects in structure and content this creation myth, it is fascinating to see how *Crackpot* draws upon and is nourished by ancestral creation myths and finally becomes in a contemporary sense its own legend of creation, growth, and reconciliation – the long journey through pain, a journey relieved by joy and accompanied by a survival humour, into a final sense of wholeness and completion. The novel seems to me to be a profoundly religious work, in the very broadest sense, ultimately a celebration of life and of the mystery that is at the heart of life.

Hoda learns the story of her beginnings when she is a child, just before the First World War, in the North Winnipeg hovel where she lives with her parents. Her gentle, unworldly father Danile gives her a birthright of pride and love which, told differently, could have been a horror story. In the Old Country, Russia, he and Hoda's mother, Rahel, were more or less forcibly married – in a graveyard, to ward off a plague. The villagers, following ancient superstition, sought among the Jewish community to find the most witless or crippled male and female whose union would magically appease the fates. Hoda's parents were not witless, but Rahel was hunch-backed and Danile was blind. In Danile's skilled and tender telling, the story becomes to the child Hoda a legend, a marvel, with her parents in heroic roles. It is only as the legend weaves its way through Hoda's life that she realized the true pain and courage of her parents. By this time she has known her own anguish, and is able to understand what an incredible gift her father has given her: out of demeanment, pride; out of the depths, hope. He had, both consciously and intuitively, handed on to her a heritage of strength and belonging.

The portrayal of Danile is done with such sureness of touch, such understanding, that this blind and frail man emerges as enormously wise and strong. In some ways he is a fool of God (and despite Saint Paul's well-known use of this term, it is far from being an exclusively Christian concept; it extends to many faiths and cultures), a person who is not understood in the slightest by most of the society in which he lives, for he is hearing the pulsing of a different drum, a man whose wisdom and spiritual power come from love, from contemplation, from faith, and yet whose naivete is also real and can be unwittingly damaging. One of Danile's literary antecedents seems to me to be Myshkin, in Dostoevsky's *The Idiot;* one of his contemporaries is Okolo, in *The Voice,* by the Nigerian novelist Gabriel Okara.

Rahel, Hoda's mother, doing domestic work in the houses of middle-class Jewish families, is also portrayed with great depth and complexity. Worrying constantly about her adored child, wanting to do not only well for Hoda but superbly well, Rahel constantly feeds Hoda scraps of food, partly, of course, to keep her quiet while Rahel is cleaning houses, and partly to express the love which, unlike Danile, she cannot express verbally. Rahel's death is one of the most moving parts of the novel. She knows she is leaving her child unprepared for life; she knows it in a way in which Danile does not. Her grief is not only grief for her own early death but the unbearable anguish of having to leave too soon.

By the time Hoda gets to school, she is already grossly over-weight. The other children make fun of her size, her poverty, her strange parents. The teachers are no better, not so much out of malice as out of sheer ignorance or – in the case of Miss Bolthomsup, a pathetic and unwittingly cruel WASP – because they are embarrassed and terrified by their often unruly charges.

Hoda is bewildered by the treatment she gets at school. She longs for affection and, romantically, for love, the real thing. What she finds is fumbling sex with the neighbourhood boys. Her sense of shame at her own appearance, her loud-mouthed bravado as a young teenager, her tenderness towards the boys, such as big dumb Morgan who initiates her into sex – these are shown with an intricate ambiguity. Hoda is trusting and naïve; Hoda is also learning that not everyone is to be trusted, and yet, because of Danile's early teaching, she does not easily give up that faith in human creatures. In fact, she never gives it up, even though she ultimately comes to see the fact of evil in the world. Life and society hurt her a great deal. She reacts with puzzlement, anger, pain, humour, and ultimately, with deter-mination to survive and to retain a faith in life itself.

After her mother's death, Hoda leaves school to look after her father. She takes on her role as prostitute almost without realizing it. When the boys come over, a whole group of them, she takes them into her makeshift bedroom one after another. Danile in his blindness believes (or needs to believe) that his clever daughter is helping them with schoolwork. Hoda believes (and needs to believe) that it is only the taking of money that saves her actions from blame – after all, she and her father need the few coins so badly, and, also, sex for pleasure *alone* is something she thinks is not permissible outside marriage. Her ideas of conception are unusual. Brought up in isolation, with no real friends, and by a mother who died too soon and who always told her severely never to discuss such things with anyone, Hoda has had to figure it all out by herself. When a woman is married, the man is finally able to shoot enough matching parts to make a complete baby. As long as she goes with different men, she will not conceive. Here we have almost a parody, and a very touching one, of the crackpot/creation theme – the parts ultimately and hopefully come together to make the whole.

When Hoda becomes pregnant, her notions about biology, and her own amply larded body, conceal her condition from herself. The birth is dark with terror for her. When she realizes what is happening, her main thought is to conceal the situation from her father. The scenes in which Hoda, unobserved, leaves the newborn child at the Jewish Orphanage, along with a garbled note which gives rise to wild speculations in the community concerning the child's royal origins (British, at that, for the Prince of Wales has visited Winnipeg an appropriate length of time before) are skilfully handled. The first could have slipped into melodrama and the second into slapstick. Adele Wiseman treads a very fine line here, as she does so often in this novel, and she does not take a false step. The tone is exactly right. We *feel* Hoda's panic, her urgency to get the child out of the house before Danile finds out, and later, her terrible sense of loss, and her attempts to submerge the memory. The community's response to what they mistakenly take to be the note's central message, namely that a lovely Jewish girl has slept with the Prince and produced this foundling, is both maddening and hilariously funny – the cynicism, the disapproval, the hope for "an enormous breakthrough in civil rights," the endless gossip and guesswork. This interweaving of the humorous and the bizarre with the frightening and the tragic is one of Adele Wiseman's greatest talents, for of course life presents all of us with similar simultaneous juxtapositions; but to catch and hold those tones, together, in writing, is something that only an accomplished artist can do.

The clue to the uproar at the orphanage, and a restatement of some of the novel's themes, are found in the note:

> In her note, Hoda had pieced together, out of the confused shards of her dream and desire and the longings of her shattered childhood, the following: TAKE GOOD CARE. A PRINCE IN DISGUISE CAN MAKE A PIECE OF PRINCE, TO SAVE THE JEWS. HE'S PAID FOR.

The themes of crackpot/creation can be seen here again – the vessel which, broken, still contains the sparks of the Divine and the potentiality of wholeness. In this disjointed note we can see many fragments: Hoda's shattering experiences of life; her dreams of love, and the prince in disguise; the "pieces" which would come together to make a child, a new life; perhaps the tales of a Prince of Peace, from her Christian teachers, combined with the sense of her own ancestry, gained from Danile, and hope in the coming of the Messiah, some final reconciliation of life's discordant aspects. Ironically, all Hoda herself means by "HE'S PAID FOR" is a reference to Danile's rich uncle, Nate, who has endowed the Jewish Orphanage but whose help to Danile and Hoda has been grudging and minimal, despite his emotional demands on them. Hoda feels that her child's keep in the orphanage has been, so to speak, pre-paid. The community, of course, does not see this simple fact, as they never connect the child with her. The reader, too, can see other possibilities of meaning. He has indeed been paid for, by Hoda, through her years of labour and her solitary birth-labour.

The boy is named, appropriately enough, David Ben Zion. His nickname is Pipick because his navel protrudes, as Hoda tied the cord herself, imperfectly. Hoda tries to refrain from wondering and thinking about the boy, and sometimes she succeeds. Sometimes, however, she experiences feelings alien to her, the desire to scream aloud and to run and keep on running, the breaking up and the cracking of the basic human earthen pot, the skull, the brain, the psyche. But she never breaks up totally, not ever.

At this point it should be said that this novel, among very many other things, is at one level a political novel, in the broadest sense. It portrays a whole community, North Winnipeg, with its influx of immigrants at various points in its history, spanning the years from World War I to the end of World War II. We are shown, through Hoda's eyes, the Winnipeg General Strike of 1919, the political groups and union organizers, the factories and sweatshops of that era, the poverty and despair of the Depression of the 30s. None of these historical events, however, is presented in any didactic way. They are seen through individual experiences. We feel it all as though it were happening right now, and to us.

The narrative is in the third person, but the voice is usually that of Hoda, and her idiom and changing modes of thought are caught exactly. The use of language throughout the book is extraordinarily interesting. Hoda's concepts when speaking with her father (in Yiddish, as we are meant to realize) and when speaking with her contemporaries (in English) are very different. We may speak what we are thinking, but the particular tongue in which we are speaking also determines and forms our thoughts. The lovely ambiguities, too, of the English language occur again and again. Danile, after the death of Rahel, is "wrapped in his darkness, rapping on his darkness, rapt and listening in his darkness for an explanation."

This is a sombre novel in very many ways, and yet it is full of a surging and irrepressible humour. Hoda's humour is to her a protection, an armour, but it is really felt and genuine, even though it sometimes has its darkly ironic side. There are marvellously funny scenes such as those in which Hoda turns up, brash and uninvited, at weddings, dancing with gusto despite her girth and nabbing a customer or two in the process.

Seldom does one find in a novel a character who is so alive and who is portrayed with such change and development as Hoda. As her understanding expands, she sees in retrospect what her early life was really like. She doesn't pity herself in the present, but she is able to feel pity for that child she once was, the child without a childhood. And over the years, the thoughts of her son haunt her. Under Hoda's jokey surface there is an area of darkness, the accumulation of years of bewildered pain and uncomprehended rejection.

Her final encounter with her son, who comes to her as a young man to a neighbourhood whore, is one of the most shattering scenes in contemporary fiction. If Hoda refuses the boy, he will either feel that he is unacceptable as a man, or he will have to be told who he is. Her choices are real, but they are narrow. What can she do to hurt him the least? This is Hoda's greatest act of love and greatest moment of suffering. Until now, she has had something of Danile's terrifying innocence, but not any more. She assumes here the dimensions of a truly tragic character, drawing into herself all the ancestral myths, all the strength and anguish of the centuries. She is even "denied that loss of responsibility in suffering, which is the gift of madness." Yet to the outside world, as she realizes, she will always be crackpot Hoda.

She still, however, has her life to complete. Lazar presents himself, the Lazarus who has risen, literally, from the grave itself, who has climbed over the dead of his family and his village in war-torn Europe, and has survived. His hurt and his need finally match with Hoda's, and the world may begin again.

In a wish-fulfilling or prophetic dream at the end of the novel, Hoda sees herself and her son and her people rising again, out of the holocaust that encompasses and is yet more than the Jewish holocaust – man's inhumanity to man finally overcome. The nightmare element, however, and the bitterness are present here, too. Hoda, about to marry Lazar, cries out in sleep, "CONDOMS PRURIENCE INCESTRY," an agonized comment on her own life as well as an ironically twisted version of Winnipeg's motto – *Commerce Prudence Industry.*

But at last, in the dream, there is wholeness:

> Hoda curtseyed deep, arose. With a magnanimous gesture she drew the magic circle around them, showing them all she knew. Soon, she promised extravagantly, in the ardour of her vision, they would all be stirring the muddy waters in the brimming pot together.

The shards, to continue to speak in the novel's metaphor, are many in this culmination, and they finally come together and fuse in a complete vision. The allusions occur on many levels. The Indian name *Winnipeg* means "muddy waters." In Hoda's experience, the community in which she grew up, with its mixture of immigrant peoples of different backgrounds and different degrees of wealth and poverty, was indeed a milieu of muddy waters. But she dares to hope, to look forward to the time when "they would all be stirring the muddy waters in the brimming pot together." In a wider sense, Hoda's dream embraces a whole area of world myth, in which the "magic circle" may be seen as the unending cycle of life and death, and the "brimming pot" as the fullness of creation in all its forms. Hoda herself finally becomes an archetypal figure, the earth mother, the Wise Woman of the tribes. Her son David, forever lost to her and yet never lost, says of her in the dream, "She occupies her past; she inhabits her life."

She does indeed. And as one of the greatest characters in our literature, she helps us more fully to occupy our own past and to inhabit our lives.

BY ADELE WISEMAN

BIOGRAPHY

Old Woman at Play (1978)

DRAMA

Testimonial Dinner (1974)

ESSAYS

Old Markets, New World [Drawings by Joe Rosenthal] (1964)
Memoirs of a Book Molesting Childhood and Other Essays (1987)

FICTION

The Sacrifice (1956)
Crackpot (1974)